PRINCESS of the BLOOD

A TAPESTRY OF LOVE AND WAR IN SIXTEENTH-CENTURY FRANCE

A Novel

by:

BRIGITTE GOLDSTEIN

Prologue

In the small hours of the 26th of August in the year of Our Lord 1572, the crouched figure of a woman hurried through the shrouding mist along the roadway leading south from the city of Paris. Casting an apprehensive look back from time to time, panting, gasping, she seemed goaded by an iron resolve to press on with her arduous journey. Neither her faltering step nor the weight of a bundle she held tightly concealed under her cloak impeded her flight. At the swelling din of hoofs pounding the pavement, she abruptly veered off the road and plunged with almost headlong down the slope of a shallow embankment that separated the adjoining fields from the highway. There, shielded from sight by the tall brush and wild grass, her body melted into the damp earth exuding the cool moisture of the summer night.

Barely daring to breathe, her lips moved in inaudible prayer. Prostrate, she hugged the ground as the horsemen thundered past. Raising her head but slightly, she made out what she had feared—sky-blue coats emblazoned with a white fleur-de-lys, the unmistakable emblem of the royal house of France.

Suddenly—her heart almost stopped—a detachment of soldiers started to fan out into the terrain on both sides of the road. Shouts! Clanking! Rattling!

"Search the bushes!"

"Don't let any get away!"

Cursing, coarse laughter accompanied the soldiers' scouring of the brush and fields with bayonets extended. Within arm's length of where the woman was huddling, the point of a bayonet poked the soil. She held her breath while her hand muffle the soft whimpers emanating from inside her cloak. After a seeming eternity, the soldiers were gone. They galloped down the highway—the clanking crescendo of iron hoofs fading with the settling dust.

Stunned silence. Then suddenly, the cries of a child pierced the stillness. The woman's hand had eased its pressure on the little mouth. Bathed in sweat and trembling, she lay sprawled on the ground, unable to move, her breathing staggered, her eyes imploring the child to cease its wailing. She knew they were not safe yet, the danger had passed only for the moment. More soldiers would come from the capital. They would sow their terror over the entire countryside. But for now the exertion had drained her energy and left her body leaden and numb. She needed to gather her strength and will to push on.

Her black velvet cloak had fallen open, revealing a woman of about forty years—although her pitiful condition may well have added several years to her actual age. Long black hair laced with a filigree of gray, sticky and unkempt, hung about her shoulders. It was difficult to discern her features. Her face was encrusted with dirt and sweat and what seemed to be dried blood smeared across her brow. Most arresting were her eyes. Vacuous, black disks staring into the brightening morning sky, numb and hollow; eyes that had witnessed unspeakable horror.

Her deplorable state contrasted sharply with her attire— embroidered silk on smooth velvet. Though torn and spattered with dirt, the exquisiteness of the workmanship was still recognizable. Fretting beside her was the child, an infant girl of maybe six months, who now started to crawl about on all fours. It was easy to see why the woman was so anxious to hide the child from view. Anyone encountering this child, with its rubicund face crowned by a thick tangle of flaxen curls, could not help but be enthralled by the glow, the irresistible spark that radiated from her bright blue eyes, giving an intimation of a special, if indefinable, presence.

As if to please the woman, the infant ceased crying and the child's natural curiosity took over. She scanned the surroundings, squealed and gurgled with joy at swarms of twittering, chirping larks ascending from a nearby hedge, soaring toward the warming rays of the sun that now had broken completely through the misty dawn, promising a splendid late summer day. The woman raised herself up with a start. The bright daylight would make it more likely that they would be discovered. Concern for her own safety was nothing beside her fear for the life and security of the child. It swept away the exhaustion that had immobilized her body after the close encounter with the soldiers and gave her heart to continue.

The numbness in her limbs dissipated as she resolved to move on. She surveyed the field, determining that she had best seek shelter in the forest abutting the other side of the fields. To stay close to the main road carried too great a risk. She knew the soldiers were ordered to track down mercilessly any of those marked for death who had escaped the carnage in the capital. No, it would be much safer to rest by day in the forest and continue the flight south under cover of night. Once she reached the city of La Rochelle, someone could surely be found there who would guide her and the child on the last leg of their journey home.

Renewed whimpering roused her from her thoughts. Her gaze came to rest on the child. Her dark, charcoal eyes, so starkly empty just a moment ago, suffused with doting admiration. Nobody would harm her precious darling as long as she lived. Tears of dread and joy streaked her smudged cheeks. She opened her arms and gathered her precious charge to her bosom.

The bells in the church tower of a nearby village church

summoned the faithful to morning worship. Human voices were heard from the road; the clanking of wheels grating against gravel stone signaled the beginning of the day's activity. This was the moment to act if she was ever to gain the forest undetected. She tucked the child deep inside her cloak and struggled to her feet. A momentary dizziness made her sway and stagger. Quickly she steadied herself and with firm strides she set out across a stubble-strewn, fallow field enclosed between acres bursting with sheaves of wheat awaiting the harvest. All the while she held the slumbering child firmly pressed against her heart, her lips breathing fervently: "My princess! My princess!"

Book
One

A TIME TO SLAY, A TIME TO DESTROY

Destruction followeth upon destruction
For the whole land is spoiled.

Jeremiah 4:20

*Religious strife between Catholics and Huguenots
ravaged the Kingdom of France in the second half
of the sixteenth century in a seemingly endless
succession of civil wars. Fanaticism and intractable
zeal on both sides dashed all hope for a peaceful
solution to the conflict.*

CHAPTER
1

The war came to Bonneval during Holy Week in the year of Our Lord 1588, at the time of what was known as the War of the Three Henries or the seventh civil war. Though the enemy armies did not meet in battle on the freshly ploughed fields fanning out in long, even strips from the edge of the village, the spring maneuvers of the army of the Catholic League were as devastating to the soil as if it had been ravaged in bloody combat.

Yet, if the villagers worried about a low crop yield and food shortage in the coming winter, it was not apparent then. The excitement caused by the arrival of the troops superseded, for the moment, their fear of famine—in ordinary times uppermost on the mind of those who eke out their subsistence from tilling the land. If pressed on this point, the good people of Bonneval would have given to understand that sacrifices had to be made for the cause of the Holy Apostolic Church in its fight against the canker of Protestant heresy that had festered on the body of the kingdom of France for all too long. Far was it from them to shrink from bearing their share of the cross in the sacred struggle.

The village of Bonneval, tucked among the gently rolling hills of the fertile, grain-growing region of the southern Ile de France far off the main arteries of commerce, had until then remained fairly unscathed by the bloody conflict that had rent apart the Kingdom of France for nearly three decades. The devout Catholics of this village had followed the course of the war as best they could from their remote vantage point. Any traveler who happened to stray into these parts would be greeted with a barrage of questions about how things were going. Or a villager's business might take him beyond the familiar confines, as happened a few times a year. He would then be sent off with stern admonishments not to be remiss in inquiring about the progress of the Apostolic cause. The inhabitants of this tranquil hamlet had been touched directly by the war only when one of their sons had gone to join the good fight. Few had returned to a hero's welcome; most lay buried in the soil of a far-off province of the kingdom.

Nowhere in the village did the news of the imminent arrival of the Catholic garrison arouse greater turmoil than at the local inn, a modest establishment, situated at the edge of the village near its northern approach. The rickety, thatch-roofed structure could easily have gone unnoticed, had the eye not been arrested by a splendid wooden shingle, suspended from a wrought-iron pole, on which was displayed a magnificent white horse and above it the inscription in gold-embossed letters: Auberge au Cheval Blanc.

"Sandrine! Sandrine! Where are you, you devil's brood?" The innkeeper's voice raged through the dingy, narrow hallways. "Just wait and see when I find you, you no-good wench! You'll . . . I'll. .!"

The domestics tended busily to their chores, keeping their heads lowered lest they had to bear the brunt of Thierry Legrand's ire. When Thierry got angry with Sandrine, one had better stay out of his way. Violent outbursts inevitably accompanied his frequent searches for the girl, who seemed to be able to devise ever new ways of evading him.

Thierry's rage against the girl had become particularly intense since that day, during the previous summer, when he had discovered her in a corner behind the sheds absorbed in reading a book. Reading a book! Neither Thierry nor his wife, nor anyone else in the household, and for that matter hardly anyone in the village, except the priest and the doctor, knew how to read and write. He was not aware that Sandrine should ever have been schooled in such matters as only the offspring of wealthy townspeople or the sons of aristocrats were afforded. The only way Thierry could conceive of the mystery of a girl, and a peasant at that, knowing how to read was—God have mercy!—for her to be in league with the devil.

The hired hands remembered too well Thierry's screams that accompanied the blows hailing down on the girl, who endured it all without a whimper. No amount of abuse would make her reveal how the book had gotten into her hands or how and where she had learned to read or who taught her. The spectacle of Thierry dragging the girl, almost literally by the hair, to the village priest did not go unnoticed in the village. Peasant women leaned out the window, shaking their heads, nodding their agreement that someday Thierry would regret having been so kind to this waif. Had they gotten wind of what the squabble was about this time, there would have been no telling what these superstitious, excitable souls might have done.

Fortunately for the girl, the priest was a more reasonable man, at least by comparison with his fanatical parishioners. He prided himself on being open-minded and of confronting life's vagaries with rational deliberation. As a young man, he had seen other parts of the world. He had once crossed the Pyrenees on a pilgrimage to Saint Jacques of Compostella. Back in the reign of King Charles IX, he had even gone to Paris to join in petitioning His Majesty to stamp out the practices of the Protestant Reformists who had then begun to decry the teachings of the Church and to challenge the very position of the Holy Father in Rome as God's representative on earth.

The priest only barely contained his surprise when he recognized in the book Thierry presented to him a French translation of the Old Testament, the kind he had heard was used in Huguenot assemblies. The possibility that one of his parishioners, and a young girl at that, could be infested with the devil's seed of heresy, cast this simple, well-meaning parish priest into an unprecedented crisis of conscience. But after some earnest soul-searching, he decided that a calm, cool-headed approach would be the best course. He abhorred violence and bloodshed and preferred to handle matters such as this in, what he considered a rational manner. He regarded it as his duty to do everything to save the errant soul and was certain that a quiet talk with the girl, alone in the confessional, would elicit the truth of the matter, he was certain of it. And as for the impetuous Thierry—God Almighty would surely understand and forgive the lie—he told him the book was a compendium of the lives of the sainted martyrs of the early Church.

The matter turned out to be more difficult than the priest had anticipated though. No amount of reasoning or coaxing, neither gentle pleas nor coercion, induced the girl to divulge her secret. Neither threats of withholding absolution from her nor vivid depiction of the hell fires of eternal damnation made her budge. Even then, he determined to keep this matter from his parishioners. Yet, her stubbornness gave him cause for grave thought, and the suspicion grew in his mind that maybe, just maybe, she was indeed in league with the forces of darkness. He would have to keep a close eye on this girl and when the time came for his annual visit to the bishopric in Chartres he would consult with his superiors.

Thierry was hardly appeased by the priest's explanation. He suspected that he was holding something back. For all he knew, Sandrine might have put a spell on this man of God. His suspicion was bolstered by the fact that the priest had kept the corpus delicti, preventing him from seeking advice elsewhere. He discarded the idea of stealing the book back and having his friend Etienne take it into town on the next market day to seek enlightenment from a book dealer. He had his reasons why he did not want to take Etienne into his confidence concerning this particular matter. He consoled himself with the thought that after all who was he to doubt a priest's word or to call a man of the cloth a liar? What if the book turned out to be what he said it was? Then he, Thierry, would become the butt of derision. The thought of the scorn and ridicule he would have to endure gripped his heart with an ice-cold hand and paralyzed his will to probe further.

But even if the priest spoke the truth, the puzzle remained— how did the girl learn to read? If the book was about the lives of saints, she was not likely to be in league with the devil. Was she perhaps one marked for sainthood? What if she was inhabited by the Holy Spirit? Had he not taught the Apostles and the Virgin Mary to speak in tongues? If he had it in his power to make people speak different languages, it would certainly be in his power to teach a peasant girl to read. No! Thierry shook his head. But then one never knew. And it was this uncertainty that enraged him most.

Doubts kept gnawing at Thierry's chest. After all, she was so different from everybody else. She was quiet and withdrawn, giving herself airs as if she was too good for the rustics among whom she had grown up. Nobody knew where she was born, who her real parents were. She was an infant when she came to live with the Legrands, brought to the village by an ailing old woman who soon was buried with her secret.

True, he had to admit, Sandrine worked harder than anybody around the house. She toiled from early morning till night, rose with the chickens before dawn, fed the barnyard animals, went to early Mass, helped in the kitchen, served the guests at the inn, scrubbed the floors, and prepared the guestrooms, and generally lent a hand wherever needed. On occasion, the Legrands would make a little extra by hiring her out for domestic chores to other households, especially to the local doctor and his wife, and never was a complaint heard from the girl's lips. But then she had this infuriating habit of hiding somewhere for hours, which fed Thierry's suspicions and anger.

Thierry's wife, the childless Berthe, shared none of her husband's misgivings about the girl, and in her unassuming way, she loved her like a daughter. She relied on Sandrine to take care of the lodgers who put up for the night, especially on the infrequent occasions—as now happened with the arrival of the troops—when there was a larger party of overnight guests to entertain. Berthe Legrand did not trouble herself with her husband's ruminations about the curious fascination the girl seemed to hold for the strangers who stopped at the inn, even before she had begun to blossom into young womanhood. So what if they treated her with a degree of deference and respect not customarily accorded members of the lower classes by those of higher station? Berthe thought it only right, for who was more beautiful than her Sandrine?

But she was unable to allay her husband's vexation about the riddle the girl posed, and she was too intimidated by his ill-temper to interfere. She was too meek to shield the girl from her husband's abuses, his constant spying on the girl, his frantic searches for books, his wild imaginings of what she was doing when she was alone. Even when Sandrine was a small child, Berthe did not dare take her side nor would she keep Thierry from confining the girl for long hours in the dark, damp cellar of the inn, as punishment for some alleged misdeed or transgression Berthe knew very well the girl did not commit.

On the morning of the day the garrison was to arrive, Sandrine had been so engrossed in her reading, she had remained unaware of the approaching storm until Thierry's angry screams were getting dangerously close to her hide-out in the hayloft. Irked by the disturbance, yet knowing better, she tore herself away from the ribald stories of Marguerite de Navarre and tucked the book inside the rafters. Only with the greatest unwillingness did she tear herself away from the glittering court of Nérac, in the sunny south of the kingdom, where Marguerite, the Queen of Navarre, held court long ago, surrounded by poets and philosophers, and she vowed to return this very afternoon.

Sandrine's imagination was still bustling with images of courtly love, of troubadours and ladies robed in satin and silk, of sumptuous feasts of roast meats and foul and delicate pastries, sweet wine and amorous intrigues as she was descending from the loft. A warm glow still flushed her face from the memory of Marguerite's account of ladies being courted by lovelorn suitors, in velvet and sweet fragrances, and their not infrequent yielding to the fervent entreaties.

"Ah, there you are! Good-for-nothing wench! What are you doing up there? You'd better not be reading again, devil's brood!"

Thierry's corpulent body heaved from exertion as he watched her sliding unhurriedly down the rickety ladder of which several rungs had broken off. Of course, the hayloft was a perfect place to hide! Why didn't he think of looking there before? But then again, how could he get up there without risking his neck?

The young girl skipped the last two rungs and jumped to the ground with the agility of a cat. Slowly she turned and met Thierry's bloodshot eyes with calm, defiant condescension. She was no more than sixteen or seventeen, clad in threadbare homespun, on her feet coarse knit socks but no shoes. A tangle of darkish blond tresses escaped from under her bonnet, falling to the small of her back. As she proudly stood before him, a good hand's breadth taller than he, she calmly explained to him, without flinching her bright blue eyes, something about stray chickens that needed to be chased from the loft. The chickens were all over the yard. It was impossible to tell whether some had been in the hayloft or not.

"Haven't you heard, a company of noble lords is due to arrive? They could be here any moment and you're fooling around with chickens! Officers of the Catholic League are here to stay the night. Get moving and fix up the lodgings!"

Sandrine nodded and, without a word, ambled around him and set out in direction of the inn.

Why did she have to leave him feeling foolish and powerless? Blind anger rose in him again. Seized by an impulse, he lunged forward and yanked her arm with such force he made her gasp.

"I was talking to you!" he screamed.

He was just given his grip another twist eliciting a renewed pained gasp from the girl when suddenly he felt a hand like a piece of lead on his shoulder. An unfamiliar voice, close to his ear, commanded: "Let go of the wench!"

The voice belonged to someone used to giving orders and to being obeyed. Like a dog whose master ordered him to drop his prey, Thierry released the girl's arm; bewildered he turned.

The man, who seemingly appeared out of nowhere, struck him with awe. The stranger, dust-covered, yet well dressed, was much younger than the sonority of his voice had made him believe. And quite obviously he was a noble man—the rapier girded on his hips was the unmistakable sign. To his horror, it occurred to Thierry that this must be one of the expected guests. He could have kicked himself for having neglected to pay closer attention to the sound of hoofs entering the courtyard of the inn. Why hadn't he been warned? Damned, this officer had to walk right into this domestic squabble. He cursed the day he had given in to his wife—instead of listening to the advice of his neighbors to abandon the girl somewhere, for, so they said, no good would come from harboring a stranger—and adopted the accursed wench. But all this was of no use now.

Adjusting his manners in the presence of a nobleman, Thierry bowed low, stammered his apologies, and added with deference: "Welcome, most noble Lord! Your presence in my humble establishment is a great honor for me and my family."

With a sweet-sour nod toward the girl, he answered the stranger's questioning look: "This is my daughter Sandrine, she will be at Your Lordship's service and will see to it that your stay under my humble roof will be to Your Lordship's complete satisfaction."

The young aristocrat just jerked his head and commanded him: "Go see that the horses are taken care of immediately!"

Thierry bowed repeatedly, cringing as under blows from a knout. He mumbled something about His Lordship's kindness and his pleasure and, still in a crooked position, he backed away.

Sandrine had observed the exchange with a mixture of amazement and disbelief—nothing like this had ever happened here before. Since she was not quite sure what she should do, she simply stood, her head tilted, and looked askance at her rescuer from below.

"Philippe, Count de Treffort-Salignac, captain in the army of the Duke de Guise, the most Catholic leader of the army of the Holy League," he announced with a slight, elegant tilt of his upper body.

Sandrine was at a loss on how to respond to this gallant introduction. For all she knew, he could be mocking her. Besides her elbow was still burning with pain and she had little desire to engage in artful conversation. If he expected her to kiss his hand in gratitude or fall on her knees, he would be disappointed. She had heard enough of the arrogance of his kind and the contempt in which they held the common people. One kind gesture would not change her view about the likes of him.

A few more moments passed in awkward silence during which he kept a curious gaze fixed on her. Finally, he added with a roguish grin: "And you are the innkeeper's daughter who will tend to my needs. Right?"

Sandrine thought his behavior altogether impertinent, but conscious of her position, she performed her curtsy and muttered: "I am at Your Lordship's service."

She had turned and started for the building when she heard him say: "Wait! Please don't go, yet!"

She turned, slowly lifting her face toward his.

The face she met was not at all that of the imperious soldier who had made his presence known with such commanding élan a short while before. Sandrine sized him up with hesitant curiosity. He was a young man of twenty-two or twenty-three, although it was hard to tell his exact age, the ruffled beard, rather than making him look more mature, gave him the appearance of a boy who had pasted some fuzz on his face. His bearing bespoke self-confidence and pride.

His attire though ruffled and dusty was still splendid to her eyes. The short cape of lustrous black velvet loosely draped over his shoulders was not meant to conceal the well-formed chest clothed in a scarlet red, smooth silk shirt topped by a perfectly cut doublet with slashed, long puffed sleeves, widely cut at the shoulders, and narrowing around the lower arms. Underneath the black velvet, ballooning shorts, leaving only a soupcon of the slender hips, a pair of tight black leggings displayed the sculpted, muscular calves. His neck was ringed with a simple, white, stiff narrow-fluted collar which forced his chin to remain slightly upward.

But what arrested her attention most were his eyes, eyes from which radiated an unexpected kindness, with not a glimmer of the arrogance she had first seen. She took a few steps closer and studied almost unabashedly the finely chiseled features, the long, curved nose, the broad soft mouth, the lower lip slightly drooping, framed by a mustache that extended downward and lost itself in the brush of the bearded chin. Suddenly she became aware of his gaze that had remained firmly fixed on her while her eyes had come to rest in his for she knew not how long. Her erstwhile curiosity suffused slowly into a sensation that engulfed her entire body with a pleasing sense of warmth as she had never felt before.

An intense shudder went through her, she felt her knees

softening. Then with an abrupt move, she turned and almost ran inside before another word was spoken.

Philippe, Count de Treffort-Salignac, scion of one of the most illustrious noble houses of France, the proud descendant of an ancient lineage, stood in the dirt of a barnyard in the village of Bonneval in the southern Ile de France, perplexed and humbled by a peasant girl, a mere child in rags.

From the moment he had witnessed the violent confrontation between the innkeeper and the girl, he had been struck by the girl's rare beauty that glowed despite her unkempt appearance like a raw jewel. But this was not all. There was something else about her that gave him pause, a quality, an aura surrounding her lithe figure that was less easily defined yet immediately apparent—a paradox of peasant docility and self-possession, almost defiant dignity.

Most striking was her height, which made her seem strangely out of place. Her erect carriage, her proud bearing, all contrasted with the gnarled, malformed figures of even young women one frequently encountered in the French countryside. The picture lingered in Philippe's mind. It left him pensive and stirred in him a strange disquietude. Peculiar legends of ancient lore, of knights and peasant girls which the people are so fond of recounting around the hearth on cold, dark winter nights invaded his thoughts.

For the rest of the day, the inn buzzed with activity. Everything was done to provide the illustrious guests with the best the house had to offer. Sandrine scrubbed floors and put the guest rooms in order. She laid out fresh linen and replaced the customary sacks of straw with feather bedding. She polished the pewter ware that was taken out only on special occasions. When she had a moment, she helped her mother in the kitchen with preparing the special meats she had fetched from the market.

The officers, meanwhile, sought out the services of the local bathhouse made available by the blacksmith who also doubled as a barber. Weeks in the field and saddle had afforded little opportunity for personal care, evidenced by the scruffy appearance of officers and men.

In the late afternoon, Philippe and his lieutenants, all restored to spit and polish and by now thoroughly famished as well, gathered at a corner table in what was called the "grand hall' of the Auberge au Cheval Blanc. Their discussion turned mostly on strategies and logistics over a meal as bounteous as was rarely served at the humble establishment.

But Philippe listened with only half an ear, if at all. He sat among his companions, distracted and distraught, little inclined to join as usual in the boisterous jesting. From the corner of his eyes, he watched Sandrine hauling heaping platters laden with boiled meats, legs of roast mutton, sausages, ham and poultry. He savored the offerings, not so much out of hunger but because he imagined that she had a hand in their preparation. Several times he called her over for a refill of the local brew.

While his companions talked of women and war, boasted of conquests and triumphs in both fields, Philippe's thoughts kept wandering back to the encounter in the barnyard. He was certain something extraordinary had happened—the brief moment when their eyes met, a moment of recognition as if fated long ago by a divine hand. He was sure that she too had felt it.

He noted with satisfaction that Sandrine had tidied herself up since the morning. Her hair was tied back, a fresh, starched bonnet crowned her head but was still too skimpy to contain the mass of curls. Her waist was wrapped in a huge apron, accentuating her nubile figure. She served the gentlemen with the subservience expected of her station. Before this day, it had never occurred to Philippe to question the justness of the order of society: the superior status of a few, the inferior status of the many. This was the way of the world, and it had never crossed his mind that things might be or should be different. He had always enjoyed the privileges of the aristocrat especially when it came to amorous pursuit. Peasant girls had been fair game. Here he suddenly felt some vague dismay, an indefinable discomfort about the difference of their stations, especially since she kept her eyes averted and never once permitted them to meet his.

His thoughts were interrupted by Thierry, who, anxious to show the captain his more convivial side, waddled over to the gentlemen's table heaving two full jugs of wine. Still huffing from the exertion of ascending the cellar steps with the load, he called out: "Here my good Lords, please do me the honor and partake of the finest wine my cellar has to offer. Any man fighting the pestilent religion deserves the very best and is always welcome at my humble place."

"Thank you, my good man," Philippe replied with good humor, "rest assured this festering disease will soon be cut out once and for all. You can count on the Catholic League to do its part. The preeminence of the Holy Church in the Kingdom of France will be restored before long."

Philippe's response encouraged Thierry to probe further. Who knows, he might get some first-hand information concerning the rumor that King Henri was softening in his position toward the Huguenots and was willing to compromise. To possess such information would give his standing among the villagers a tremendous, badly needed lift.

"And what about His Majesty the King? Will he agree?"

"Rest assured, the Duke de Guise will know to persuade His Majesty. Henri Valois will not abandon the Catholic cause,"

Philippe declared louder than necessary since the innkeeper was standing right next to him.

"Oh yes!" The officers nearly fell over with laughter. "The Duke can be very persuasive."

Uncertain whether he should join in the merriment, Thierry, still intimidated, contented himself with renewed pleas that the noble lords may honor him and make themselves at home in his humble abode.

"Sandrine! More wine for our illustrious guests!" Thierry was elated that the gentlemen, and in particular the captain, had been so gracious to confide in him—this is how he later related the exchange among the villagers, not without adding a few flourishes and embellishments that made him appear in more glorious light.

"How long do Your Lordships expect to honor us with your presence?" he was emboldened to ask.

Philippe responded again in a louder voice than was necessary to be heard by the innkeeper: "My troops are encamped outside the village and we shall be recruiting any able-bodied young men willing to join the good fight for the Duke de Guise and the Holy Church. As soon as we receive orders from the Duke, we shall march on Paris."

With a turn of the head toward where Sandrine was standing, he added: "The exact date is still uncertain, several days, could be several weeks. Meanwhile, we are pleased to accept your kind hospitality, my good man."

Sandrine poured the wine, her eyes steadily cast downward, avoiding Philippe's unabashed stare that was piercing her soul. Could he see how mortified she was at what she had just heard? Not enough that a vast gulf separated them—he, the aristocrat, and she, a common peasant—but he was also a fanatic. She knew very little about the Huguenots, but what she had heard about their teachings seemed not all that ill-conceived to her, especially since Doctor Morel and his wife seemed to think so.

She attended daily Mass, but she instinctively hated the army of the Catholic League—the stories of violence and devastation the troops were wreaking across the Kingdom of France, its leaders' determination to foil any reconciliation between Catholics and Protestants. She had overheard many discussions at the inn about the League, travelers passing through delighted the local villagers with stories of the great Catholic victories. Nobody seemed to care much about the price innocent folk had to pay for such triumphs.

Maybe she despised and abhorred all fanaticism and intolerance because she had suffered for so long from the mean-spirited bigotry and ignorance of the peasants of Bonneval. She knew that expressing a desire for peace with the Religionists was dangerous and it was better to keep one's thoughts well guarded. To hear the man to whom she had been drawn as to no other human being before speak like the worst fanatic mortified her soul.

As night began to fall on the village of Bonneval, the bells in the church tower rang out the end of another day of toil. After vespers, the inn began to fill with local folk, regulars, and curiosity seekers, as well as the common soldiers who were encamped outside the village. The recruiters started to mingle with the crowd, laying out their bait for able-bodied young men with the promise of great monetary and spiritual rewards.

The lure of adventure and fortune was great, but doubts were raised.

"What about the King?" they asked. "Would it mean we have to fight against His Majesty the King?"

The answer came back quickly as if it had been anticipated: "But we are fighting for the King! We are all fighting for France, a Catholic France!"

A cautious young peasant, one Mathieu, warned his fellows of the consequences if they jumped into this without careful consideration.

"If you join the League army you will have to fight against the army of the anointed King of France. You know the King wants to end the war, he wants to bring peace to the kingdom, the League only wants to continue the war at all cost. Think of that!"

Mathieu, proud of his courage in face of the awing presence of the soldiers and the noble lords, glanced at Sandrine who was observing the scene. Imperceptively, she gave a nod.

But he was no match for the recruiters, who were accustomed to the peasants' uneasiness about anything that smacked of disloyalty to the crown. They knew how deeply ingrained the French peasants' reverence was for their King, but this young man was more independent-minded than most and it might take some extra doing to disperse his qualms.

"But what if the King, God forbid, were a tyrant and he disregarded the wishes of the people?" Gaspard, the most eloquent among the recruiters, harangued the wavering crowd from the top of a table.

"What if the King lacks the resolve to fight the heresy? What if he even favors the heretics? How would you feel about that? Would you want to see Huguenot scum hold places of honor at the royal court? Would you want them to hold their devil's worship wherever they please? Do you want them to grow and multiply like boils on the body of France?"

"No, of course not," the shouts came back.

"But what if the King, good Henri Valois, who is, as everybody knows, under the thumb of his mother, the Florentine witch, what if this King is too weak to oppose the Huguenot plague and keep it from spreading?" Gaspard had gone farther than usual, but their glowing faces showed him that he had these rustics in the palm of his hand.

"Let's crush the Protestant vermin! If our King doesn't do it, then we shall serve those who will! Long live the Duke de Guise, the champion of the Apostolic cause!"

Mathieu's warning was trounced out by boisterous shouts of approval. Gaspard climbed from the table, sweat drenching his reddened cheeks, but satisfied with himself. His effort had paid off. He was a master of working a crowd into a frenzy, but he also knew that now was the time for some reassurances: "But, never fear!"

He motioned with his arms as if he were calming a tumultuous sea. "Good Henri, the Duke de Guise, will go to Paris, and believe me, he will gain the King's support, and the Queen Mother's as well. The war will end soon in triumph over our enemies and peace will be restored in the entire Kingdom."

Philippe and the officers watched the scene from across the room, bemused as usual by Gaspard's oratory antics. He may be simplifying a complex tangle of politics and theology, but that was exactly what these rustics needed. Thanks to Gaspard, scores of recruits would enlist the next day. Philippe would be ready to join the Guise army with a contingent of at least five hundred men.

While the soldiers stirred up the crowd, Sandrine hardly got a moment's rest from hauling pitchers of beer and cider to quench the parched throats; she rushed hither and thither with brimming vessels and empty ones, dodging errant hands, and ignoring suggestive remarks. The pain in her elbow became more intense, but there was no time to rest.

The scene with Gaspard had sickened her to the stomach and she felt a great desire to be alone. She was very proud of

Mathieu, her one true friend among the peasants and faithful companion of her childhood, but she was hardly surprised that these country bumpkins would sooner be duped by a smooth talker like this Gaspard than listen to reason.

As she descended the stairs to the cellar to fetch another jug of Thierry's best wine for the noble lords, Sandrine thought of the League captain who had aroused in her such unsettling, confusing feelings. But why should she give this aristocrat another thought? Then she thought of this place to which she did not belong. She had never been made to feel welcome by the villagers. But then, who was she? Where did she come from? What ill-starred fate had placed her among this superstitious rabble?

A ray of hope had appeared this morning. A nobleman had shown her the kindness and warmth she had hungered for all her life. The encounter had inspired in her a dream that he had come to deliver her from her misery, a foolish dream that she might find romance and happiness in some faraway place like Marguerite's court in sunny Languedoc.

What a vain, cruel dream! By what delusion had she dared to hope this League captain would be the deliverer she had yearned for? Forget about your dreams, poor peasant girl, he is a fanatic, a bigot like the rest of them! Nothing but an arrogant aristocrat!

As she made her way through the maze and clutter of shelves, barrels, and tools, she no longer held back the bitter tears. The single candle she held up barely illuminated the darkness. But Sandrine found her way. She knew every nook of this murky underground realm. She was at home here. When she was a child, this vast dank cavern had been her favorite hiding place. She would withdraw here to be alone. Here she would create a world of fantasy all of her own, for her alone to inhabit whenever she wanted to escape from the world above.

When she had first made the acquaintance of this cellar, she had been frightened out of her wits of the dark. That was when Thierry locked her in here to punish her for some purported offense she usually did not remember committing.

But in time, this subterranean kingdom of thick, saltpeter-sweating walls, barrels of beer and wine exuding a pungent smell of fermentation, of rodents scurrying in the dank shadows, became her private domain, an impregnable fortress that sheltered her from the enemies lurking above ground. Sometimes, she was a warrior battling alien invaders, other times, she was a princess locked in the dungeon, waiting to be rescued by a handsome prince. Only reluctantly had she given up this sanctum for the hayloft when her voracious habit of reading necessitated a brighter hideout.

Few were the moments granted her for tranquil play, sometimes in the company of her friend Mathieu. But there were far more moments, even hours, she spent in aching pain. She would have been able to take Thierry's violent assaults, she told herself. Yes, his beatings frequently left her bruised, once she even had a broken rib, but the taunts of the villagers were the most unbearable and caused her to lie awake on endless nights, wondering, yearning for something she knew not what, a deliverer maybe, and often longing for the day when she would take her revenge. The anguish of the memory of the helpless child unable to comprehend why she was branded an outsider, an intruder, an undesirable, overwhelmed her. Abruptly, she jumped up from the small footstool on which she was resting, kicking it over. She threw up her hands and furiously began to batter the dank, grimy wall with her bare fists. Her anger built into the elemental rage by stamping her feet, banging her fists, emitting savage shrieks, decrying an unjust fate.

She only became aware of another presence in the darkness when she felt her wrists clasped by a firm grip, forcing her to cease the pounding. Unable to resist, she sank panting to the dirt floor. The indistinct, yet familiar figure of a man knelt next to her. She felt his lips on her bloodied knuckles as if he wanted to kiss away the pain. Thus gently, yet firmly, constrained, her body slackened and the fury that possessed her dissipated.

She lifted her eyes, straining to make out his face through the veil of her tears by the dim flicker of the candle. All she saw were his eyes resting on her, the same gaze suffused with the same warmth and tenderness that had stirred her so deeply that morning in the barnyard. Maybe she had misjudged him up there in the tavern, where he was sitting among his peers, maybe she had been wrong after all to be so quick to distrust. Again, she felt the presence of that inexplicable something she had felt when they stood opposite each other that morning, the bond that seemed to tie them together inextricably, was still there. She did not resist when he put his arms around her and held her quietly for a long time.

CHAPTER

2

The last days of April brought renewed winter chills to the southern Ile de France. Intermittent hail and sleet threatened the glorious burst of spring flowering that had greeted the Feast of the Resurrection. But the tillers of the soil were only too well acquainted with the tricks April can play, and woe to crops planted prematurely if crushed by a sudden winter kill.

The Easter holy days had put a halt to the ploughing and tilling to prepare the soil for planting, but the chores around house and yard at the inn never ceased. Sandrine went about her daily course, rising at five, as always first feeding the barnyard animals, and then to early Mass. The entire day, from morning to even tide, was ruled by the familiar peals of the church bells, announcing the time to rise, the time to pray, the time to work, and the time to rest. Twice every day, the entire village assembled at the parish church for early Mass and Vespers. Anybody who would miss the summons more than twice in a row would set off a wave of rumors and speculation.

Sandrine never forgot the peasants' obsession with heresy. The slightest irregular behavior could trigger the most irrational response and entail the direst consequences for the one who had somehow aroused their suspicions. She had felt their ill-will herself too often not to heed the lesson of an incident that had occurred in the village long ago, a tale that was still being repeated with ominous mien by the superstitious folk to that very day.

It was in the reign of good King Henri II, father of the present king, when a young woman of Bonneval, the daughter of devout parents, refused to attend Mass from a certain day on and no amount of begging or cajoling could make her set foot inside the church. Soon rumors began to pass from mouth to mouth, whispers went from ear to ear. She was a witch, they said, and some even said she was a bride of Beelzebub himself. Since nothing like this had ever happened in the village before, not within living memory at least, the council of elders debated long how the matter should be approached.

When finally a delegation of villagers was dispatched to the parents' house to interrogate her directly, the girl was nowhere to be found. She had disappeared without a trace and to this very day, nobody knew what had become of her. To the villagers, the most plausible explanation was that she had gone off to the Witches' Sabbath. One neighbor swore he saw a black goat flying through the sky with a naked girl riding on its back on the selfsame day the girl disappeared. A search of the girl's chamber brought to light a cache of certain powders and ointments, the kind the devil was said to give his helpers for placing evil spells on unsuspecting neighbors. Almost two generations had passed since then, but the belief remained among the good people of Bonneval that anybody who shunned Holy Mass and the Holy Sacraments must be in league with the devil.

Absence from church services, for this reason alone, was rare. Only Doctor Morel and his wife could afford to be absent on weekdays—they lived at the far edge of the village and the doctor, assisted by his wife, a midwife, had to care for patients from several villages around. On Sundays, one of them would appear at Mass if only to dispel rumors, which were voiced from time to time, that they were secret followers of the new religion. But since their ministrations were indispensable to the villagers, nobody dared accuse them openly and they enjoyed some immunity.

Everybody else in the close-knit community, where no private sphere was too sacred for the piercing eyes, was a target for the rumor makers.

Sandrine had learned as a child to evade them, always to be on her guard. The why of the cold stares, peering squints, the scorn shown whenever she appeared was hard for the child to understand. She heard them call her the stranger or the foreigner, or the foundling and even gypsy. Rarely did they call her by her name.

Sandrine had learned instinctively to deceive. She attended Mass conscientiously, not to give cause for suspicion. Besides she truly liked the time in church for she could retreat into herself and communicate with the divine being in her own very personal way. Or, as she often did, her imagination could take flight and transport her into a far-off realm.

Since the League troops had come to the village, the small church was packed with worshippers. The soldiers were no doubt pious Catholics and attended Mass as their faith required them to do, but who would deny them the opportunity for ogling the local girls? Everybody, from the priest to the beadle, was surprised, however, to see the League officers attend Mass regularly in the modest structure. Speculation was rife about what this breach with established custom might mean. It would have been more fitting for the young noblemen to attend Mass in the private chapel at castle Bonneval, located at several miles distance from the village.

"But these are times of war, nothing is as it should be," they said.

What the villagers did not suspect was that the captain had ordered the officers explicitly to remain close to the troops and that he had politely declined an invitation from the castle to lodge there. Had they known this, eyebrows would certainly have been raised. It was not lost on them that the handsome young captain, who was seated in the pew of honor near the altar, had his eyes almost constantly fixed on the miserable foundling from the inn during Mass. Never mind that she sat withdrawn in the back of the women's section, and never looked up, her glowing face, burning red from the captain's unabashed gaze, would sooner be construed as a certain sign of guilt than of modesty and shame.

Sandrine was somewhat at a loss about what to do. The captain's attention flattered and mortified her. She had carefully avoided being alone with him after that first night in the cellar. Gossip, rumor, suspicion can destroy a life in a small village. She was afraid that the thought that plagued her at night wrote guilt all over her face. She had to keep her distance—she had to stay in control, she could not let herself be drawn into something that could only lead to her perdition.

Philippe's strange conduct did not go unnoticed either.

Relieved as they were not to have to perform the social rituals at the chateau, the officers still were puzzled why he had declined the hospitality of the local baron. Philippe seemed unusually tight-lipped and unapproachable; lost in thought most of the time. When questioned he answered with irritation and even uncharacteristic abrasiveness.

The second in command, Robert, Count de la Croix, his comrade in arms and inseparable friend since childhood, he too felt spurned. Like Philippe, Robert was the scion of a noble family of ancient stock. Together they had been trained for war from an early age, had learned the art of combat on horseback, in the tradition of their medieval forebears, and both excelled in physical prowess and swordsmanship. They had been nourished on knightly ideals of personal valor, honor, and absolute fealty to their overlord. The blood of their ancestors, the crusaders, was still alive in them. They too were imbued with a lust for battle in defense of what they deemed a great cause. But unlike their more rough-edged forebears, they were educated to some refinements like the study of the Greek and Latin classics and the art of courtly behavior. Maître Mollat, their tutor, had little patience with lapses of memory when the ten-year-olds recited the precepts of proper behavior in courtly society as laid down by Baldassare Castiglione. The lashes the master dealt out for the slightest mistake were more severe than those for mistakes made in reciting the writings of the ancients Cicero or Aristotle.

When the two noblemen turned eighteen, they were commissioned as officers in the army of what was called the Catholic League of the Holy Union. This band of radical Catholics had been specially formed as a force to combat the spread of Protestantism. Philippe's fathers, the Duke d'Evreux, and Robert's father, the Duke de Beaumesnil, had both distinguished themselves in the fight against heresy. Both looked to their sons to continue the good fight.

The young men's enthusiasm for the Catholic cause was matched by an equal passion for conquests among the fair sex. After five years on the front lines of battle, these irresistible rabble-rousers had gained a reputation as lovers that was as formidable as their fame as swordsmen. Their trail of victories was as glorious on the fields of battle as in boudoirs and neither shunned a lusty roll in the hay. Between bouts, their exploits in every field were recounted in great detail and often with grand embellishments over an abundance of food and drink for which they displayed an equally robust appetite.

From the day they had taken up quarter at the inn with the pretentious sign Auberge au Cheval Blanc in this remote village, Robert had been disturbed by the change he observed in his friend. Philippe was aloof and unsociable to a degree that was too much out of character not to give him thought. What could have robbed Philippe of his natural exuberance and joviality? Not only was he moody, but it also seemed that an almost unbreachable wall had arisen between them. Robert knew his friend too well to dismiss this behavior as a passing whim. What worried him most was that even during military strategy planning, an art in which Philippe excelled, he observed in him a vague absent-mindedness and sometimes outright disinterest.

Somehow, Robert had the feeling the girl at the inn had something to do with all this. Philippe had been a fool for love before, but never had he seen him in such a somber, brooding frame of mind. Philippe's volatile moods did not make it easy for Robert to find a suitable moment to broach the subject. At last, early one morning, they were alone on an elevation on the outskirts of the village, from where they observed a company of lancers practicing their advance in a field below. Robert seized the moment for a heart-to-heart talk.

Sizing up his friend, Robert exclaimed: "What a sight! You must agree, this is a truly formidable striking force. You will see, these French peasants can beat back any German or Swiss mercenaries the Huguenots put into the field—or even the King's troops if it should become necessary."

"The League employs foreign mercenaries too," Philippe responded with a dour, contrary tone.

He abruptly turned and walked toward the other side of the hill, wrapping himself deeper into his long, wide cloak. But Robert stuck tenaciously to his heels.

"You seem to defend the other side all of a sudden," Robert quickened his step and when he caught up with him, he blocked his friend's path. Philippe shrugged his shoulders and tried to circumvent the human obstacle in his way.

"What is the matter with you?" Robert exploded. "Ever since we have come to this godforsaken place, your behavior has been, to say the least, peculiar."

"What do you want?" Philippe's irascible tone told Robert that he was not inclined to listen to reason.

"You know exactly what I want," Robert insisted, almost shouting into the wind. "I don't have to spell it out. But if you insist, I shall. First, your peers were not consulted when you decided to take up quarters in this ramshackle village inn, evading the hospitality of the local baron whose castle would certainly provide more fitting accommodation. Then, we are forced to mingle with the peasants at Mass when the proper thing to do would be to attend Mass in town or the castle chapel."

"Lieutenant! We have a war to fight and your comfort is of minor concern, of very minor concern," Philippe interrupted him sharply. "You know as well as I do, how important it is for our mission to stay close to the troops, the very peasants of whom you were so proud just a moment ago, but whose company is not good enough for Mass, which is the very thing we are fighting for, the integrity of the Holy Mass!"

Robert was not accustomed to being spoken to in this manner. Never had Philippe addressed him this way, not even in times of their most virulent disagreements. Yet, he swallowed his pride for the moment.

The peasant girl at the inn came back to his mind. Philippe, who had conquered many a peasant lass, had never excluded him from his confidence. Could it be that his advances had been rebuffed? This has happened on occasion before, rarely, but it did happen, but then there was always another soul willing to yield to the Count's desires. If he wanted this particular one so badly, what kept him from ordering her into his bed? A nobleman's prerogative, it was called.

Philippe's sore state of mind cautioned Robert not to bring up the girl directly. He decided on the lighthearted approach: "Ah, I'm on to your scheme! You want to keep the competition away from the local baronesses—if there are any, we don't know since you never let us get close enough to find out. Maybe you prefer to make your conquests unhindered. But since when do you shun competition?"

"How can you talk such nonsense?" Philippe pushed him aside and with a few big strides began to descend toward the field where the troops were holding their war games.

Robert fired his parting shot: "Or, maybe you could use some help with a certain peasant girl?"

Philippe halted his step, his entire body was reeling as if a dagger had been plunged into his back. Robert knew he had struck home. A sudden vengeful desire seized him not to let this opportunity pass without twisting the blade.

"She is just a peasant girl, Philippe, a wench like all the

others!" he shouted mercilessly. "I've seen the way she looks at you. The glances she steals at you with those pious, cast-down eyes. You could have an easy time with her. She is ready to be plucked like a ripe fruit. Take my word for it."

"Get this through your scull, Lieutenant, she is not like any other. And if you don't have sense enough to see that for yourself, I shall tell you. Not only is she not like any other peasant girl, she is not like any woman in the world!" Philippe was staggering toward his tormentor like a wounded animal. The intensity of his friend's fury made Robert withdraw. After several moments of silence, he said sheepishly:

"But can't we at least talk about it? We are friends, aren't we?"

"Of course, we are friends. I don't know what possessed me to speak to you in this manner. Please forgive me."

Philippe put his arm around Robert's shoulders. The two men walked a few paces, each steeped in deep thoughts. They stopped near a boulder erected like a prehistoric altar on the hillside. The village of Bonneval, nestled in the valley below, gleamed in the brilliant haze of the sunrise and the lush green spring foliage.

Philippe searched for words. How could he make his friend understand what had been happening this past week if he did not understand it? He was himself still unable to fathom the mysterious obsession that was tearing his innards. Would Robert understand the passion that raged through his mind and body? How could he make him see that everything else had become unimportant, even ludicrous? Could he hope to make him understand that even the war, their cause, had become secondary? Could he tell his companion of so many frivolous, high-spirited adventures, amorous and martial, that their friendship had become secondary to him as well? No, he couldn't tell him any of this.

"She is different, I tell you," was all he was able to say. He shrugged. "I. . .I can't describe it, can't put my finger on it. Even you must admit that she is more beautiful than any woman we have ever encountered. But that's not even it. . .no."

He started pacing back and forth, raising his hands several times but then letting them drop in resignation. Turning back, he stopped in front of Robert. He fixed his gaze on some far distant point as if straining to find the solution to an impenetrable mystery written on the horizon.

"We have spoken only once, but I felt immediately that here was no ordinary peasant girl. There is something about her mere words cannot express. You must have noticed it too, this . . . indefinable quality about her, this . . . self-assurance, equanimity one could even say . . . most uncommon among peasants. She is a total paradox, mysterious and vulnerable— yes, that's what I think she is!" Philippe exclaimed warming to the idea.

"You know of whom she makes me think?" he continued with sudden eloquence and good cheer. "She makes me think of Jeanne d'Arc, the peasant maiden from Lorraine who fought back the British invaders during the reign of Charles VII. You know, I have been thinking, the French peasantry has from time to time produced remarkable women of great valor, innate wisdom, and great beauty especially in times of trouble—in times when France has been beset by enemies from within and from without—not unlike our own time. Could it not be that this Sandrine is destined to end this war and save France as did the Maiden at Orleans?"

"Jeanne d'Arc, the Maiden of Orleans! You are turning into a damn fool!" Robert exclaimed incredulously.

Robert hadn't paid much attention to the girl although his

male instinct had registered a pretty, attractive young female. That much he conceded, pretty she certainly was, but a new Jeanne d'Arc? Robert could only shake his head in wonderment. Could these silly remarks have come from the Philippe he had known all his life? He must be losing his marbles.

Yet, something about his friend's melancholy seriousness warned him not to make light of what to him was sheer folly.

"I wish this war would go away!" Philippe's declaration was as emphatic as unexpected.

Seeing that Robert no longer seemed bent on ridiculing him, he grasped his friend's hand, barely able to control the tremor in his voice, he spoke as if he was unburdening himself in the confessional: "I wish the Duke would go away. Oh, I know ours is a noble and righteous struggle. But what bloodshed, what waste of human lives, what destruction! Do you think the devastation this war has caused can ever be justified or made good? For the Duke de Guise, all this is just a means toward power. You know that, don't you?"

Philippe jumped to his feet and resumed his pacing with greater vigor. Then after a brief reflection, his hands dropped again to his side in exasperation: "Oh, Robert, I am just not sure anymore! I am not sure about anything. Do you think our Lord Jesus Christ wants us to cause so much pain and suffering for the sake of his Church?"

"Think of the orphans, the widows, Robert!" he shouted when no response came.

"No!" Robert screamed horrified. "You speak like the devil incarnate. What you are saying is pure heresy! I hope no one is overhearing us."

"No!" he repeated. "You cannot think this way! Never! The cause of the League of the Holy Union does not permit doubts, it is greater, more important than the lives or concerns of individuals. Sacrifices have to be made for a greater end. If we show only the slightest mercy for heretics, France will never be at peace. You must think of France and of our Holy Church—nothing else counts."

"I wish I had your certitude, Robert!" Philippe saw an unbridgeable gulf opening up between them, leaving them stranded on opposite sides. It was clear that for his good he had to hide his thoughts and feelings from Robert from then on.

"You are right," he continued in a conciliatory tone. "How foolish of me to let a peasant wench twist my mind like that!" He grasped Robert's arm and baring his pearly-white teeth, he burst into laughter.

"She is a beautiful wench," Robert conceded. "I certainly hope you will bed her before we have to move out of here," he added with a slap on Philippe's shoulder. At this moment, Robert was called away by the sergeant of his battalion.

Philippe was relieved to be rid of the numbskull friend. He needed to be alone with his thoughts. Yet, he was overcome with a sense of loss and regret, the loss of a friend, of his youth. Robert's simple view of the world was unable to distinguish between questioning assumptions and outright heresy, just as he could not understand the difference between lust and love. Simpleton that he was, he could no longer be trusted.

Ten days had passed since the troops commanded by Count Philippe de Treffort-Salignac had come to the village of Bonneval. Time was pressing, the call for the march on Paris was expected daily now. But Philippe was no closer to the longed-for quiet tryst with the object of his passion.

The political news was disturbing enough. Since it had become apparent that Henri III, the last of the Valois kings, was not likely to produce an heir to the throne, Catholic France shuddered in horror at the prospect of a heretic king. By rights of succession, the crown would fall to Henri Bourbon, the King of Navarre, a prince of the blood who also happened to be the leader of the Huguenot army. So abhorrent was the thought of a heretic king among the populace, particularly among the boisterous Parisians, that many favored the as-yet-unstated and far-fetched claims of the Duke de Guise to the throne. The Duke hoped to bolster his chances of becoming heir apparent through a grand gesture, a triumphant entry into the city of Paris that would impress the King with his popularity among the urban masses.

"As Paris goes, so goes France" was a proven political dictum that was not lost on any of the contenders. The question before the Duke was whether it was more advantageous to lead the League army into the city, an act of open rebellion against the King, or to limit his entourage to a small retinue of trusted supporters and to appear before the King a humble petitioner seeking reconciliation. The latter role was not well suited to the Duke's temperament and may have been the reason for the long delay.

Philippe, who had been chomping at the bits for action before coming to Bonneval, had counted on a stay in the village of three or four days before they would set out on the march on Paris. Now, he welcomed the unexplained delay, which he could not help but feel was a godsend.

Yet, so far Sandrine had given him no opportunity to be alone with her. Even when they found themselves face to face for a moment, she never slipped in her role of the subservient peasant. It irked him that she made him feel the social gulf that separated them, at a time when he would rather not think about the obstacles standing in the way of their love.

Yes, he said to himself, this is what it must be—love. It came to him like a revelation when she served him one evening at supper, as usual without permitting her eyes to meet his—he was in love with Sandrine. Why else would he reject any notion of simply ordering her to come to his chamber at night? Why else did his longing for her drive him to distraction?

The thought of invoking seigniorial prerogative was distasteful to him. He wanted her to want him, to love him with the same passion he felt for her. Maybe it was all insane, but the scene of their first encounter played endlessly before his mind's eye in every detail, every word spoken and unspoken, every look exchanged. Something had happened then between them—something extraordinary, he knew it in his heart, and he felt justified in his certitude that she had felt it too.

If doubts nevertheless crept into his thoughts, it was because he could not know that Sandrine had long learned to hide her feelings under a cloak of quiet reserve. He did not know the storm of emotions he, the stranger, had aroused in her and how fervently she beseeched God to make it subside. The longer his stay at the inn lasted, the more overwhelming became her desire to throw herself at his mercy, to abandon herself to his embrace. What did it matter that he was a nobleman? What did it matter that sooner or later he would leave to fight an onerous war?

In quieter moments, she just shook her head in disbelief. That she should have become so entangled in a web of passion and longing that she was ready to discard the beliefs that had sustained her in the misery of her daily existence. Did all this no longer matter to her? The answer she finally had to give herself was yes, a resounding yes, it did not matter one bit. None of the differences between them, the hopelessness, mattered enough to change her feelings for him.

Yet, she did not dare make a move or lend encouragement to his pursuit. How could she be sure he loved her too? True, he took a special interest in her, and she could feel his eyes pleading with her whenever their paths crossed—in the hall of the inn, even at church. Noblemen are known to prey on young women of the people. It's a sport for them, like the hunt, without regard for the devastation it causes.

The few noblemen who had stayed at the inn before had aroused her disgust. Their arrogance and condescension, their boisterous, loud-mouthed behavior as if the whole world existed only for their pleasure and whim gained them nothing but utter disdain from her. Their ill manners seemed a prerogative that was part of the order of the world—a fixed order with the aristocracy indulging themselves at the top and the masses chafing at the bottom. The Count's behavior certainly did not fit that pattern. Maybe it was part of the strategy of a sly fox and, therefore, even more dangerous. Sandrine wavered between hopes for the troops to depart so she would be relieved of the qualms tearing at her, and a burning desire for time to stand still so that he would never, never leave.

Sandrine withdrew further into her inner world and became more aloof than ever. All she could do was seek refuge inside the protective shell of her dream world.

She eagerly accepted tasks that would take her away from the inn and the village—collecting firewood or retrieving stray animals in the woods and fields. These outings gave her a welcome opportunity to spend an afternoon undisturbed with her reading, or sometimes she would call on the Morels at the outskirts of the village.

Because the search for lost livestock often took her a considerable distance from the village, she was absent from Vespers several times. Her absence was duly noted by Philippe who never missed Vespers since it allowed him to observe her quietly. When she failed to be there a third time, he decided to question Thierry.

He approached Thierry the next afternoon inquiring why Sandrine had not been at Vespers for the last three days. Thierry, still intimidated by the Count, was immediately convinced that the captain must be an agent of the Pope, sent to sniff out secret heretics. Where Sandrine was concerned, he was not sure himself what to think. But if she was a heretic, who would believe that he, her foster father, had nothing to do with it?

"Your Lordship, please think nothing of it, she just went out into the fields to look for a stray goat." Thierry's voice was shaking and beads of sweat formed on his forehead. He bowed repeatedly as he spoke.

"These animals can be very stubborn and sometimes refuse to come home," he added with nervous laughter. Then, remembering that a way of identifying heretics was whether they went to Mass or not—a true heretic would never go to Mass—he added quickly: "My daughter is a very good girl, a devout girl, she goes to Mass every morning."

"Shouldn't you send somebody to help her, after all, she is very young?" Philippe cut short the man's babbling.

"Oh, she is a strong girl. She is young, that's true, but she is strong and at home in these woods—she knows the terrain like nobody else," Thierry tried to reassure him, wondering why this aristocrat should care if a peasant girl was overburdened with work. As if these nobles hadn't always enjoyed themselves on the backs of the moaning peasants for as long as he could remember, and probably since the beginning of time.

Philippe noticed Thierry's puzzlement but decided to take advantage of his prerogative of not having to bother with explanations to a person of the innkeeper's station. He simply mumbled something about sending some of his men to help the girl search for the goat and asked for directions where she might be found. Having at last obtained the desired information,

Philippe mounted his horse and made sure Thierry saw him starting in the direction of the troop encampment. As soon as he was out of the innkeeper's sight, he turned and sped toward the forest.

The dull thump of hoofs on the soft earth startled Sandrine out of her reveries. Quickly she hid her book inside her smock and sought cover in a half-empty hay shack by the side of the path leading through the field. The cracks in the sides of the wooden shed afforded her a full view of the field. She strained her eyes to make out the approaching horseman, who had to be one of the soldiers. The villagers were not in the habit of riding on horseback.

A tremor of apprehensive delight seized her as the outline of the captain came into view. He kept his horse tightly reined in and moved very slowly along the path, his eyes attentively scanning the surroundings. He was searching for something or someone. She was quite certain that she was the object of his search.

What was she to do? If she remained quiet, he was not likely to detect her. She knew every inch of these fields and the nearby woods, she could easily slip away unseen once he had passed.

But why should she run away? Here was finally the opportunity to be alone with him, a chance she had been praying for—an encounter away from the stares and sneers of the prying peasants.

He was now parallel with the spot where she was hiding, passing slowly without stopping. In another moment, he would be out of sight and maybe out of her life forever. With the agility of a cat, Sandrine dashed out and jumped into the path calling after him.

She was still panting from the short sprint, when he, majestically enthroned on his horse, turned and trotted back toward her and dismounted. No words were spoken, no excuses made why they should chance to meet in this out-of-the-way place. Conventional artifices that govern the interaction between members of different classes and sexes were suspended. The irresistible magnetic force, both had felt from the first, was drawing them inexorably toward a fate determined long ago.

For a brief second, he paused, arrested by the picture of the woman rushing toward him along the path framed by hawthorn hedges in full bloom. She was clad in the same simple peasant smock of drab, worn wool, a rough linen cloak of similar color draped her shoulders, providing scant protection against the late afternoon breeze. The shabbiness of her attire accentuated rather than effaced the appeal of her figure. Her hair was tucked away under a bonnet, so that the features of her face stood out more prominently, the graceful elongation of her slender nose and the prominence of her cheek bones, the full-rounded sensuous lips, and sparkling eyes which seemed to Philippe of an incredibly intense blue. He was certain that nature had never achieved a more sublime creature.

Seeing him hesitate, Sandrine wavered for a moment, unsure of why he was holding back. But her doubts quickly vanished before the caressing velvet of his hazel eyes with the roguish twinkle, the kindest and most beautiful eyes that ever looked upon her, eyes that had haunted her from the first. His head was uncovered, exposing a crop of neatly trimmed fox brown hair. His collar was casually open. The lack of fashionable adornments gave him the appearance of a penitent, an impression that was accentuated by his black velvet costume in the somber Spanish style.

Coming face to face, their eyes became deeply submerged in each other, neither spoke, neither turned away. With a simple movement, he gathered her trembling body into his arms and held her firmly pressed against him. Unable or unwilling to resist she abandoned herself to his tender embrace.

As he slowly loosened her bonnet, a cascade of honey-blond curls tousled over her shoulders. He noted that she had washed her hair, and it was shiny and soft to the touch. Playfully he arranged it about her shoulders, and then pulling the strands together toward her back, he touched his mouth to hers, gently, grazing her lips with his furtively several times, then drawing closer, their lips fused in a long, sensuous kiss.

Sandrine let it all happen passively at first. Then suddenly, she flung her arms vehemently around his neck, her lips attached to his with impetuous fervor as someone drowning might hold on to a raft for dear life. For a moment Philippe was taken aback, almost frightened by the passion unleashed. This was not like the usual seductions—none of his well-rehearsed repertoire of charm and persuasion was needed here. She was his before he ever touched her, yet he was hers just the same. No conquest, only a man and a woman, fulfilling an ineluctable destiny to become one, body and soul.

A warm spring rain began to fall and Sandrine pulled him by the hand inside the shelter. She bent down and tried to push away the book that had fallen to the ground.

"What are you reading?" Philippe inquired as he sat on the straw covering the dirt floor, pulling her down beside him. Clutching the book, she quickly shoved it under the straw.

"Why nothing," was all she could say, annoyed that attention had been drawn to this silly book just then.

"Come on, I saw you hiding the book. Don't you trust me? I want to know everything about you," he said.

"I want to trust you, but how can I be sure?" She stared at the ground, avoiding his eyes. "There haven't been many people I could trust. After a while, you learn to distrust everybody."

He edged closer toward her and gently lifted her face to his, forcing her eyes to meet his. Softly caressing, he whispered: "Don't you know I am not them? Do you remember, the morning we first met? Right then I knew that a special bond was being spun between us. I know you felt it too! It was fate that brought us together and I shall never betray you, Sandrine!"

He had called her by her name for the first time. It sounded familiar and natural. Suddenly, she realized the peculiarity of the situation of having quite naturally fallen into intimate closeness with this stranger. By all counts, she hardly knew him at all, and yet, from the first, she believed to recognize in him a kindred soul as if they had known and loved each other in another world.

"Your Lordship has been very kind—kinder than anybody has ever been to me—but I am a peasant and I know my place."

"Would you call me Philippe? Your Lordship sounds very stuffy."

"Is your name Philippe?" she called out in a sudden burst of bright gurgling laughter, tickled that he should have such an ordinary French name. He had never seen her laugh before. My God, how beautiful she was when she laughed. He swore to himself that he would make her laugh with happiness always.

"When this war is over, I shall take you away from here. I promise."

"Hush," she placed her hand over his mouth, "no promises. Who knows when this war will end. Let's not talk about the war or the future. I want to think only of this moment. I want to burn it into my memory so it will last forever."

It seemed to Philippe that he had never been so happy in his life as on this evening. Sandrine rested peacefully curled up against him, trusting like a lamb. His thoughts wandered over the events of the two weeks since he had come to this secluded village. He tried to recall everything he had learned about her. Their intimacy was complete, yet she was still a mystery. Why disturb it? he said to himself. But his curiosity got the better of him. A thousand times, he had puzzled over what it was that made her so different from any woman he had known. A peasant girl who knew how to read and reason, possessed of knowledge far beyond what was usual for her station and age?

"Will you now show me the book you were reading?"

"How do I know you won't denounce me to the priest?" she tried to sound playful.

"You just have to trust me." There was this word again—she wanted to trust him with all her heart, but she still found it difficult. Slowly, still hesitant, she pulled out a well-read volume. His eyebrows rose with unconcealed astonishment that turned to disapproval, as he read the author's name: Marguerite de Navarre.

"You are reading the book of a heretic?" the accusation burst from his lips without reflection.

Sandrine's face turned ashen. She felt as if she had just been slapped with a force worse than Thierry's blows.

"She was not a heretic, she was brilliant, a kind woman, everybody around her loved her. And besides, she was open-minded and hated falseness and superstition. I should have known that you would not understand." Her whole body trembled with anger and disappointment.

"But what about her daughter, Jeanne d'Albret? That heretic of heretics! And her grandson, Henri de Navarre? He and his Huguenots are destroying the Kingdom of France, these heretics who brought us this war!"

A long, painful silence descended between them like an opaque curtain.

"Don't you think there must be a reason why so many people

follow the Religion?" she said at last. "Maybe it is that they are tired of the greed and immoral behavior of the priests? Maybe people feel they want to talk to God themselves and not have the Church decide what is right or wrong for them? What has the Church ever done for the poor except oppress and gouge them?"

"Well, you are right about one thing," he replied, taken with her impassive eloquence. "The clergy of the Church have not always behaved in a proper manner, but does that justify the burning of churches, desecrating the images of the saints, and, I have witnessed myself, even of the Holy Host? You haven't been out in the world to see what is going on."

He did not realize that he could not have said anything more stinging and was unprepared for the venomous outpouring of disdain.

"Ah, that's it. His Lordship thinks he is dealing with an ignorant, little peasant. How should she know or understand anything about the grand affairs of the world? She had better keep quiet and be trampled on like all peasants. Maybe some of the young men are good enough to be used for cannon fodder, stupid enough too to believe the talk of that Gaspard, but they'd better not dare question the wisdom of the princes! I should have known! I should have known! His Lordship is no better than all the rest!"

"Sandrine, please! You are being unfair."

"Unfair? How can I be unfair? His Lordship holds all the power in the world to make me do whatever he pleases? Everything is fine and wonderful, as long as the peasant remains quiet. It's the same thing with this war. Of course, it was the people you call heretics who have caused this war. There would be no war if they had kept quiet. Why would the Church make war against those who bear their cross in silence?"

"Sandrine, I order . . . I beg you to stop this tirade. You are making assumptions about things you know nothing about."

"And what is it, I don't know?"

" You condemn me without the faintest knowledge of how I feel, what my thoughts are."

A sense of shame overcame her for having attacked him for something he could help as little as she. Neither one of them was alive when this war began.

"Please forgive me," she said softly. "I don't know what came over me."

"I don't like the war any better than you do. But from the time I learned to walk, I had it impressed on me that I was to fight the heretics. My father would never tolerate questions about the righteousness of this fight. My whole upbringing, my training, everything was geared toward preparing me for this one purpose in life. It was my father's wish and I cannot deny that no one dedicated himself with greater enthusiasm to the cause than I. Now after five years of fighting this war, a war that nobody seems to know how to end, I can no longer justify to myself all the wasted lives, all the destruction. Oh, I still believe firmly in our Holy Church, but sometimes when the screams of the dying pierce my ears, I think why not let people worship God in any way it pleases them, as long as they leave others in peace!"

Sandrine moved closer. She was shivering and sought the warmth of his body, nestling against him.

"I could never disclose my thoughts and doubts about the justness of our cause to my father. He would never understand that one can have doubts and still be a good Catholic."

"Are you afraid of your father? Of what he might do if you went to him and confessed your doubts?"

"Afraid? I don't know if I am afraid of him. It just has never occurred to me to oppose his wishes. My duty as a son would not permit me to rebel against his authority. Besides, I have sworn an oath to the army of the Holy League and the Duke de Guise."

"I see the meaning of your words—noblemen are prisoners too, they too are not free," she said pensively. "But what about your inner convictions? Do they have to be set aside?"

"If family honor requires it, yes," he said unequivocally. "Individual desires are secondary to duty."

"Henri de Navarre is in the same position, I guess," she said simply.

"Like every man, he does what he must do. But since it is his ambition to be King of France, I have no choice but to oppose him. Even if the Duke de Guise is a less amiable man, I must support his claim. A Huguenot king would be a disaster for the kingdom."

"Be that as it may, Marguerite de Navarre's book has nothing to do with all this. This book is about love, and the obstacles people seek to overcome to be united with their lovers."

"I must admit, I have not read Marguerite's writings, maybe it was unfair of me to prejudge her because of the things I have heard about the kings and queens of Navarre all my life. Maybe you can teach me."

Philippe was astonished to hear himself speak this way. How strange! What irony! He, who had always been the one to know all the answers and the questions, was asking a peasant girl, still half a child, to instruct him in the writings of a renowned queen and sister of a King of France.

"Please, take the book. I don't need it anymore. I know it practically by heart. Take it, it will remind you of this night." Before he could thank her, he felt her body pressing against his, her lips covering his face with passionate kisses that made him forget once again the affairs of the world.

The rain outside intensified. A warm spring gale blew the dampness inside where it settled like dew on the two human beings, intertwined in perfect union—again time and place had vanished from their consciousness.

The bell in the church tower sounded the hour of midnight when the rider with the girl in the saddle behind him entered the yard of the inn. There was still a light in the tavern and Sandrine made out Thierry serving a few late guests from behind the counter.

"Where the devil have you been? I have been looking all over for you!" Robert came running up to Philippe. "The Duke's messenger is here. Looks like we're finally moving out."

Sandrine slid off the horse, without looking back, without a word, she hurried across the yard and disappeared.

"You idiot! Do you have to blurt out military orders so the whole village can hear them?" Philippe burst forth.

"You are being very unreasonable Philippe," Robert warned. "Everybody around here knows you went after her this afternoon. Of course, you were only exercising your prerogatives as a noble lord. Her father is worried that the marriage might be called off."

Philippe dismounted with a bounce and seized his friend by the neck: "What are you talking about? What marriage?"

"Let go, you're choking me. You haven't been yourself lately." Robert slowly straightened his collar, thoroughly enjoying the painful suspense in which he held his friend, stretching it until Philippe's glowering look induced him to explain.

"Well you know, these peasants make deals with each other, not unlike our people, like your father and the Montreuils." Philippe's glowering became more menacing and he seemed ready to cut the bastard's throat for bringing up the matter of his betrothal to Louise de Montreuil just then.

"Well," Robert obliged, "Thierry has promised his daughter, Sandrine, to the richest peasant in the village. He owes him a tidy sum. If the deal falls through, all his hopes for a better life will be gone. And you may just have ruined her chances of becoming the richest woman in this miserable village."

"I don't give a damn about Thierry and his hopes. I doubt he asked the girl if she wants that peasant."

Philippe was still flushed with the memory of this wondrous night. He had been looking forward to a few hours of quiet reflection, yes, and even soul searching. He felt his entire life changed. Now this intrusion by that lout, Robert, burned in his heart like a double-edged sword. The possibility that Sandrine could be married off had not occurred to him. He would have to speak with her tomorrow to make plans for her escape from this accursed place.

At this moment, the Duke's messenger approached the two officers and asked for a confidential conference with His Lordship, the Count de Treffort-Salignac.

CHAPTER 3

On the 9th of May in the year of Our Lord 1588, the Duke de Guise made a triumphant entry into the city of Paris. A jubilant throng hailed the savior of the Catholic cause, chants of Hosanna followed the small retinue on horseback as it trotted unhurried through the narrow passages of the Rue Saint-Denis, the Rue Saint-Honoré, into the very heart of the city. Riding in close formation behind the Duke, Philippe nodded at the joyous multitude, leaning down, from time to time, to press the hands reaching for him.

"Long live the Duke de Guise!"

"Long live Henri de Guise, the pillar of the Church!"

The swelling chorus numbed Philippe's ears and he hardly comprehended its meaning.

It was a perfect spring day. The clear blue sky was as untroubled as the mood of the people. Yet, Philippe felt singularly unaffected by the wave of enthusiasm that engulfed the ducal entourage. His mind was in a daze, his thoughts far away. The time when he moved with ease and pride among the powerful who turned the wheels of history had become a faint memory from another existence.

If doubts had ever intruded on his mind before then, they had been quickly stilled. Now they haunted him with relentless fury—doubts about the cause, doubts about the righteousness of the war, even doubts about the entire order of things as it existed in the Kingdom France.

Yet, he continued on his path, a deeply ingrained sense of duty goading him on. Reneging on the oath he had taken to defend the Holy Apostolic Church against her enemies was unthinkable; breaking his oath of loyalty to the Catholic League of Holy Union and Henri, the Duke de Guise, self-appointed champion of the Catholic cause, was impossible.

A listless spirit dulled his senses and blocked out the clamoring frenzy through which he passed as through a gauntlet. The whole spectacle unfolded before his blurred vision as before the eyes of a deaf person who perceives the world in silent dreamlike images. One desire, and one desire alone, burned in his soul—Sandrine, her embrace, worth more than all the gold and silver of Spain and the Americas!

Yet, he was soon to be awakened to the hard reality of the world. His attention would soon be commanded by an intense political drama unfolding on the stage of the city. This was to be the Duke de Guise's most glorious week, his great moment in history, and a triumph for the cause of the Catholic League and that of the Holy Church for which Philippe was to be a torchbearer. What was about to transpire in the days ahead raised the hope of thousands that France could still be spared the prospect of a heretic king.

Even though the Duke posed as a peacemaker, Philippe was not duped by his show of good intentions. He knew better—he knew that the self-appointed champion of the Catholic cause was bent on using his popularity with the Parisians to his good advantage. He may have left the bulk of his army encamped at a distance from the city, but he could not and would not dispel rumors that he coveted the crown.

Henri de Guise's bold gamble was to put King Henri III, who was without an heir, on notice that Henri Bourbon, King of Navarre, the leader of the Huguenots, was an intolerable candidate for the French throne. And were he ten times a direct descendant of the saintly King Louis IX, he had forfeited his right to the succession when he placed himself at the head of the army of the heretics. Guise was the people's choice, and the King had better take note.

As soon as the horsemen reached the Hotel de Guise in the center of the town, where they alighted, the Duke rushed off to call on first the Queen Mother, Catherine de Medici, and then the King in the Louvre. Such gestures of goodwill did little to erase the mutual suspicions in which the parties held each other. Nor did they deflate the dense atmosphere that stifled the city's air like the stench rising from the sewage gathered in the streets on a hot summer day.

The restlessness of the populace intensified as contingent upon contingent of royal troops, among them Swiss and German mercenaries, poured into the city and took up positions in the main squares. Speculation about the purpose of the garrison abounded; rumors cut their customarily wide swath through the city's quarters; fears, fanned by rumors, were voiced that the King planned to punish the Parisians by giving the soldiers free rein in the city. What this would mean was clear to everybody.

The citizens' gloomy mood was matched by determined defiance. Soon chains were drawn across the narrow streets to block the passage of horses. By midweek, Paris had become an armed camp. Royal soldiers were stationed in every quarter. The soldiers lounged idly about in the open squares. Incidents of provocation between soldiers and citizens became more frequent. Mounted soldiers launched sporadic skirmishes into the side streets, easily surmounting the chains. How could the citizens, armed with rocks and pitchforks, hope to prevail against mounted troops with firearms and bayonets?

On Thursday afternoon all hell broke loose in the city. A massive charge was launched against the populace. The King had not been taken in by the smooth-talking Guise.

The soldiers stationed in the Place de Grève spread out into the side streets with bayonets drawn. The same action took place simultaneously in other parts of the city. By nightfall, all would be over. The city would be subdued. But little did these soldiers count on the determination that inspires the hearts of those who feel betrayed. Time and again, the intruders were forced to retreat before showers of boiling water, the contents of chamber pots, of which there seemed an endless supply, and in some places before sheets of seething tar being tossed from the windows. The horsemen ran up against mountains of beds, commodes, tables, chairs, sundry household items—the Parisians seemed to have stripped their houses of all furnishings—and thus caught became helpless targets for ceaseless bombardments with eggs, tomatoes, and other, frequently evil-smelling, victuals. Every object that came to hand, the crafty Parisians turned into a missile.

On Friday, the 13th of May, reinforcements for the royal troops arrived. But it turned out to be the King's most unlucky day. The people had made good use of the cover of night and had bolstered the barricades. Every street, every alleyway in the capital had been turned into an impregnable fortress. By Friday afternoon, the royal troops withdrew from the city and the King with them. The news was shouted from one end of the city to the other: King Henri III, Henri Valois as the people called him, had left his city, slipped through the Louvre Gate like a thief in the night.

What the people, delirious with victory, did not know was that their King, upon reaching the heights of Saint Cloud, raised his fist and cursed his perfidious city. He swore never to enter its walls again except by breach.

For the moment, not a single cloud darkened the horizon. The people had carried the day. The Days of the Barricades were to live in the memory of those who were there as the triumph of the will of the people against oppression, not as the day the people humiliated their anointed King. The bells of the church of Saint Séverin, in the heart of the quarter of the "little" people of Paris, rang out jubilantly for three days without end.

However, the real power in the city rested in the hands of the Catholic League. The Duke de Guise was master of the hour. Stories were told of Guise men seen fighting shoulder to shoulder with the populace in every part of the city. Such an occasion called for a celebration and the Duke knew how to reward his friends and followers.

The sumptuous banquet held that night at the Hotel de Guise did honor to a man of the Duke's wealth and station. The best vintage flowed freely and the guests stuffed themselves to their heart's content with mounts of specially prepared delicacies of meats and luscious pastries.

Henri de Guise looked around the banquet table that evening, studying the demeanor of his supporters. There may be a handful here, he thought, whom I can trust. His gaze fell on the Duke d'Evreux, who was seated to the far right. Yes, here was a man, of calm dignity, who never wavered in his devotion to the Catholic cause or to the House of Guise, a great French nobleman who had dedicated his life to honor and duty. Lately, he was showing signs of being tired and withdrawn, the old fighting spirit, if not his devotion, seems to be lessening with age.

But if the Duke d'Evreux was getting too old to fight, he could look with pride to his offspring, one of the great swordsman of France, who, the Duke was certain, would not hesitate to put his life on the line for him. Yes, Henri de Guise, a man who had learned to mistrust everybody in the course of a life of intrigue and squabbles, on that night he was certain that of all the young warriors, no one was more dependable, more trustworthy than the Count de Treffort-Salignac.

"Philippe de Treffort!" the Duke called out to the young captain, who seemed more mindful of the tankard of wine in front of him than of the Parisian wenches courting his attention. "Tell us about the barricades! How did the Parisians come to build those formidable defenses?"

"The Parisians are an ingenious people, My Lord. Real fighters for what they believe in," Philippe replied.

"Come on, Philippe. No false modesty! I was told certain gentlemen were recognized in the crowd before and during the fighting. The gossipmongers of Paris say they were Guise men. How about that!" The Duke burst into uproarious laughter. "You should have disguised yourselves better, gentlemen!"

"We helped them along, made a few suggestions how to make the most of their positions, how to use the narrow streets to their advantage, nothing more—everything else was the work of the people. Why don't you ask the Count de la Croix?"

Robert was more than willing to share the limelight and claim at least part of the credit for the startling victory. He jumped on the table, and amidst laughter and prodding from his peers, he recounted how the League officers advised the commune of Paris in fortifying the city streets.

"Tell them, Robert! It was the King himself who provoked the situation when he sent in his garrison!" shouted the revelers, their faces aglow from the wine.

"You all remember what happened when the shopkeepers and artisans closed their shops to protest the presence of the garrison in the city? Why should the citizens put up with mercenaries at every square and street corner? Paris was turned into an armed camp. And what did the King do? He sent in that lackey of a governor, de Villequier, with orders to open the shops by force of arms! Well, he didn't reckon with the people of Paris! They won't buckle under to anybody, least of all under threat of force."

"Henri Valois never did understand his people—too busy cavorting with you know who!" Robert continued his railleries. "Or he would have known how obstinate his people can be. If pushed, they will put up one hell of a fight." Robert reeled with laughter.

"To top it all off. . .to top it all off he had the citizens' houses searched for weapons. At that moment he had a rebellion on his hands."

"By Thursday every quarter in the city was barricaded with piles of anything the people could lay their hands on—the Rue Saint-Denis was blocked with huge casks filled with sand and stones. Then the louvers of the windows were pulled down to hide the arquebusiers from sight. You all know what happened then."

The memory of the spectacular events of the past days

heightened the elation of the guests and rounds upon rounds of toasts were proposed to the good health of the Duke, to the Holy Father, and even to that archenemy of the French royal house, the King of Spain.

One bold soul shouted: "Long live Henri de Guise, the rightful King of France." But he was quickly hushed by the Duke himself. The King may be out of town, but spies were sure to be everywhere.

Philippe observed all this in silence. Had the whole world gone mad? Or was it he who had lost his mind? During the past few days, he had steeped himself in activity. Only action brought relief from the melancholy that shrouded his senses. He had traveled from quarter to quarter in Paris, organizing the people into a fighting force. This was his métier. He felt in his element when he assisted the merchants of the Rue Saint-Denis in smuggling cuirasses and other weaponry into their houses, setting up positions, devising strategies.

On the day of the barricades, he fought alongside the merchants near the cemetery of the Innocents—a five-hour battle against five detachments of Swiss and royal guards. The old fighting spirit had once again gained the better of him. With the prowess, quick-wit that had gained him fame, he had overwhelmed his opponents. Only one thing was different, this time—victory did not produce the rush of elation he had lived for in the past.

"Philippe, tell us how the people of Rue Neuve de Notre Dame whipped the soldiers who were molesting their women! Philippe, you were there, tell us about it!"

Philippe waved his hand and shook his head, and leaned deeper over the goblet in front of him.

"What is the matter with you? Don't you know how to have fun anymore?" Robert's cherubic face glowed purple with anger.

He lowered his head like a bull and approached Philippe's table with a wild glare.

"Ah, I know what is wrong with the good Count!" he hissed. "The gentleman is in love. The company of his comrades is no longer good enough for him."

Philippe turned away. But Robert's voice rose and for everybody to hear, he screamed: "Isn't that so Philippe? You would rather spend your time chasing peasant wenches than make merry with your friends? Wouldn't you? Of course, you would. And I think it is time that everybody knew how a queen of the barnyard has turned your head."

Philippe would have preferred to ignore the drunkard's provocation, but the last words struck too close to his heart. He rose slowly and moved toward his accuser. Robert took a few steps backward, alarmed by the wild fire in his friend's eyes. But he did not get far enough. In a single move, Philippe seized him, and lifting him with both hands by the collar, he flung him clear across the hall where the wastrel crashed against the wall, bringing down the host's priceless tapestries with him.

Under cover of the turmoil, Philippe stole away. He would talk to Robert in the morning when he had sobered and he would then straighten everything out between them. Afterward, he would call on the Duke and apologize for losing his temper and offer compensation for the damage to his tapestries. For the moment, he had no greater desire than to be alone.

Outside in the street, he eagerly breathed in the fragrant May air. On this wondrous night, all of Paris —children, the old and even the infirm not excluded—packed the streets illuminated by hundreds of bonfires. The barricades had been cleared away to make room for dancing and the endless to and fro of processions of worshipers chanting and carrying burning torches behind raised crosses and statues of the saints.

On the Pont Saint-Michel, Philippe halted his steps. Pensively he gazed at the pale rays of the moon bouncing on the gently rocking waves of the river. This bridge had been the first passageway wrested from the royal troops. As he pondered the events of the past five days, he should have felt elated. He should have felt pride about having accomplished a seemingly impossible feat. More than any other of the Duke's men, it had been he who devised the barricades. Without the help of a trained army, he had, in a brilliant stroke, turned a mutinous populace into a striking force that inflicted a humiliating defeat on the foremost power in France. Yet he was unable to summon up any sense of joy. His father had often said that the cause ultimately justified the means to victory over the enemy. But this victory was not one over the reformers, the heretics, the vermin that deserved to be crushed. Philippe shuddered. This was a victory over the anointed King of France.

His eyes fastened on his reflection in the water gazing back at him—a silvery corpse floating, swaying gently with the waves. How often had this river run red with the blood of those slain in the name of the Lord Jesus Christ and his Holy Church?

How often had he heard the accounts of the great massacre on the feast of Saint Bartholomew's in the year 1572—thousands of Huguenots killed in a single day? His childhood had been filled with stories of how the bodies tossed into it had caused the river to wash over its banks. When he was very young he once asked his father in front of company why such a terrible event was celebrated as a great day in Christendom. After a stern reprimand, he was sent to bed without supper. Not understanding what he had done wrong, but convinced that he must have given grave offense, he never asked such a question again. After all even the Holy Father is said to have congratulated the Queen Mother and assured her of precious rewards in heaven.

A sudden chill seized him. He pulled his cloak tighter around his shoulders and moved on. Aimlessly, he roamed the familiar streets. At the Rue Neuve de Notre Dame, where earlier that afternoon students and monks had joined the residents in one of the most ferocious battles, a joyous crowd greeted him and someone called out: "There goes the Count de Treffort-Salignac!" The next thing he knew, he was swept up in a wave of humanity. He did not dare refuse the jug of wine urged on him. Sweet pastries filled his mouth with a flavor so enticing as only Parisian women knew to create.

For a moment, he gave himself over to the warmth of the crowd. He savored the feeling of being one with the great, collective soul of the people. The picture of Sandrine appeared before him. She was a daughter of the people, or was she? Again, he was struck by how different she was from this fickle, impetuous rabble.

The urge to be alone again with his thoughts, with his memories and his longing for the woman he loved overwhelmed him. He quickly ducked out of the clutches of the singing and dancing throng. From then on he avoided crowded places where he might be recognized. He had to keep moving to keep from going mad.

In the small hours of the day, he finally returned to the Hotel d'Evreux, the family's town residence. He entered the vestibule longing for nothing but a forgetful rest.

To his surprise, he was met by François, his father's manservant. His Lordship was in the library and wished to see his son at once. Philippe was in no mood to face his father while he was in this state of physical fatigue and mental anguish. But he knew the Duke had been up all night awaiting his return. Filial duty did not permit him to disobey the call and he entered the library forthwith.

Philippe's relationship with his father had always been warm and cordial, though not without a vague sense of fear on the son's part what his father would do if he ever disobeyed his wishes. Since his coming of age, the relationship had grown into one of mutual respect and admiration. Maybe it was because of the long state of war in the kingdom that rebellion against paternal authority had never divided them. Duty, loyalty to the Church, to France, to family, these were the virtues that had been incessantly hammered into Philippe's head, virtues put to the test in the protracted religious and political crisis.

"Sire, you should not have deprived yourself of a well-deserved rest." Philippe greeted his father with a warm embrace. "I hope you did not worry yourself about me. I was just out walking. As soon as I get some rest, I shall call on Robert and then on Duke Henri and make my apologies to both."

"Oh, I am not worried about that." The Duke d'Evreux motioned his son to take a seat. "I am sure you will straighten things out with Robert—if he remembers anything that happened. And the Duke, well he is quite beholden to you and I don't think any real damage was done to his tapestries. People shouldn't flaunt their wealth with fancy decorations," he added. The d'Evreux residence betrayed a starker taste than most aristocratic dwellings. The walls at the Hotel d'Evreux were bare save for the fine oak wood paneling that lined all twenty-five rooms of the mansion. Illustrious forebears, going back centuries, looked on from the walls, some with a roguish smile, others with a stern frown.

"Frankly, what did worry me was your sudden disappearance. I did not know what to make of it. It seemed so unlike you just to walk away. And when I did not find you here, I became concerned. Of course, I understand if you had a secret rendezvous. But something tells me that this is not it. You have been very pale and withdrawn of late."

"You shouldn't have worried. I just needed to be alone for a while. I wanted to be near the people—I don't think anybody in Paris slept last night." Philippe did not see much purpose in this conversation. He felt tired and strained and annoyed at his father's insistence on being informed about what he had been doing as if he was a child.

"I was concerned because you hardly seemed yourself last night," the Duke repeated. "After such a resounding victory, I would have expected you to be elated, to join in the celebration. This day belonged to you more than anybody, my son. But you seemed melancholy, almost morose. Is there something you would like to talk about?"

"Yes, it was quite a victory. But a victory achieved at what cost?" Philippe burst forth. "The odium of having humiliated a King of France shall cleave to all of us like the boils of the plague. A Pyrrhic victory, nobody should rejoice in."

"But my son, you have taken an oath of fealty to the Duke de Guise, who is, after all, the champion of the Catholic Church! You would not think of breaking a solemn oath?"

"Of course, I would not think of it." Philippe barely hid his vexation at his father's schoolmasterly tone. "But what about the oath the Duke has sworn? Isn't the King his overlord? Isn't the King overlord of us all? To fight heresy is one thing, but rebellion against the legitimate ruler of France—that is quite a different matter."

Philippe's voice had been rising. His father signaled him to keep it low, lest they be overheard.

"Henri III and the Queen Mother have fought faithfully for the Apostolic faith," Philippe continued. "Is it a crime that after so many years of bloodshed, they should seek some way to bring peace to the kingdom before it is completely bled dry? Do you realize that there has never been peace in the kingdom in my entire lifetime?"

"We all want peace. But not a peace achieved at the expense of the Holy Church. Surely you must realize that the King's willingness to compromise emboldens the heretics and prolongs the war. Just look whom the King favors as his successor since he can no longer hope to produce an heir to the throne. Henri Bourbon stands to inherit the throne! France shall never know peace if the day comes when the crown rests on the head of this scoundrel. We must do everything to advance the Duke de Guise's claim—he can claim descent from the sainted Louis IX just as Henri Bourbon. The heretic forfeited his right when he renounced his conversion to the Catholic faith."

"You know very well that the Bourbon line is the more direct one," Philippe presumed to lecture his father. "And wasn't that conversion foisted on him in the wake of the great massacre? You told me so yourself."

He was standing by the window with his back to his father. He did not see the old man's face turn ashen at the mention of that fateful event. The sudden shrillness in the Duke's voice made Philippe turn toward him with a start.

"It had to be done! Don't think I derive any joy from the memory of that day! All those corpses littering the streets, and even the palace. But it had to be done. It was the only way to save the kingdom from coming completely under Protestant influence—that fox Coligny knew how to get the King's ear, even wanted him to get involved in some foreign adventure that would have provoked a war with Spain. It was not pleasant, believe me, but it had to be done—and the kingdom was saved."

The old man became so agitated, Philippe feared for his well-being. More soothingly he said: "I wasn't questioning whether it was right or wrong. I only meant to say that by law the King of Navarre will be the rightful King of France if Henri Valois should die without an heir."

"By lineage, yes," the Duke conceded, "but the people of France will never tolerate a heretic on the throne. Never!"

Seeing the futility of the argument, Philippe fell silent. Then he said softly: "I am so tired, tired of the war, tired of the suffering and misery of the people. You must understand this. There must be a way of bringing this whole mess to an end and I don't believe wiping them out one by one by military force is the answer. They seem to have God on their side as much as we do."

Oh, blasphemy! The Duke d'Evreux looked at his son in utter disbelief. Was this his son talking? Abruptly he moved closer, studying Philippe's face as if he wanted to assure himself that this was indeed his son and not an impostor. What was it that Robert had said at the banquet? He had paid only scant attention to the drunken babble. But now it seemed to him that maybe wine did reveal hidden truths.

"What did Robert mean when he said your friends' company was no longer good enough for you? And what was that about a peasant girl?"

"So now you even put stock in the pronouncements of a drunkard!" Philippe protested, his tone almost belligerent. Only once before had he raised his voice against his father's overweening control over his affairs. That was when he was told that he was betrothed to Louise de Montreuil and was to marry her when the time was right. He had given in then, but he was not sure that he would this time.

"You have to ask the Count himself what he meant. Right now, sire, with your permission, I would like to retire. I need some sleep before I pay my respect to the Duke."

"I think we both need our rest." The father placed his arm about the son's shoulder. Philippe felt its weight like a crushing burden.

CHAPTER

4

The Duke de Guise's face lit up, pleased to see Philippe enter the stateroom. He immediately turned away from the delegation of city officials, who had come early in the morning to plan the reorganization of the governance of the city, now under his control.

Philippe was taken aback by the effusiveness of the Duke's greeting and his showering him with compliments as he presented him to the notables: "This, gentlemen, is the hero of the barricades! To him, more than to anyone else, we owe this glorious victory for the Holy League to this young man. Gentlemen, I present Philippe, the Count de Treffort-Salignac. He deserves our gratitude and respect."

Philippe's protestations that praise belonged to the people of

Paris were drowned out by the dignitaries' applause. One by one, they walked up to him, pressed his hand, mumbling something about the future of France, our holy faith, and dedicated young men like him.

Philippe had come to apologize to the Duke for his behavior the night before and had expected to be greeted with anger or at least dismay but not to a hero's welcome.

Noticing Philippe's discomfort, the Duke placed his arm affectionately around his shoulder and led him away toward the window: "Gentlemen! Will you excuse us for a moment?" he called out. He lowered his voice and placed his face in intimate proximity to Philippe's ear: "I have great plans for you, my dear Count. The Parlement of Paris is eating out of our hands. The entire city is behind us, from beggars to bourgeois merchants, shopkeepers, students, and the entire faculty at the Sorbonne."

When he saw Philippe pensively sucking his lips, the Duke thought for a moment and then hit his forehead with the palm of his hand: "Oh, how stupid of me, and how selfish! I did not inquire whether you are feeling better. I was sorry to see you seemed not well last night."

"I came to offer my apologies. I hope no irreparable damage was done to Your Lordship's precious furnishings," Philippe replied.

"Oh, don't you worry about that. If this is what's troubling you, you might as well forget it. After all, an occasion such as this calls for a celebration, and if things get a little out of hand that's the privilege of youth!"

The Duke pulled him further away into his private study. Once out of earshot of the notables, he divulged his plans in the diffuse manner of the grand schemer without attempting to explore the thoughts of the individual he is addressing.

"Now let's talk about business. I am a generous man and I

reward well those who serve me well. You, Count, have earned the highest honor. For a man of your caliber and talent any door, any office is open. All you have to do is ask. Let me know what is your pleasure and it is yours. If you desire, I shall make you governor of Paris."

And with a roguish grin and a friendly poke with the elbow, he added: "What do you think? You don't want the governorship? You need only ask or for anything else your heart desires. By the way, you have made a great impression on my dear sister, the Duchess de Montpensier. She asks you to grant her the honor of dining at her residence tonight. She is having a little get-together, an intimate soupé for a few specially selected friends. I don't mind telling you that careers and fortunes have been made in the duchess's boudoir. She is most anxious to meet the hero of the barricades."

Philippe's mind raced frantically for a plausible excuse that would extricate him from the social pressure he felt closing in on him. He remembered Madame de Montpensier very well. She seemed to be everywhere in the streets of Paris during the last few days—unmistakable with the slight limp in her gait. She sauntered among the people, exhorting them to resist the royal troops with apparent total disregard for any danger to her own life. A woman of much courage and devotion, but a religious fanatic, and heaven only knows what else! It was generally known that the Duke de Montpensier had left the city in the royal entourage. Something told Philippe he had better keep his distance.

"There is one wish if Your Lordship will be gracious enough to grant me," Philippe finally replied. "I would like to request a leave from my duties to take care of some private matters."

Though disappointed at the modesty of Philippe's request, the Duke tried to be understanding: "Of course, anything you wish. You mustn't keep the fortunate young lady waiting."

As a devotee of the pleasures of the flesh, the Duke was not one to keep a young man from pursuing his affairs of the heart. Something told him that he'd better not probe. The lady in question was likely to be a married woman of some prominence.

"Well, as you know, my dear Count, the battle of the League is not yet won—heresy has not been wiped out yet. Difficult times still lie ahead before it can be said that France is truly free from this pestilence, until Navarre and his viper brood are crushed. But for now, go with my blessing, enjoy whatever gives you pleasure. Maybe on your return, you will be more of a mind to accept a position of prominence. Meanwhile, I know I can depend on the Duke d'Evreux, your honorable father, whose devotion to the cause has been nothing but exemplary."

His eyes suddenly lost their focus and he seemed eager to end the exchange. Hastily he led Philippe back to the stateroom, where the officials were kept waiting, and dismissed him with a furtive gesture: "Go on now. I shall expect you back within four weeks. I shall express your regrets to the Duchess. She will be so disappointed, but she can still have you on your return."

A light, warm rain fell when Philippe reached the point where the road leading southwest from Paris entered the density of the forest of Rambouillet, a favorite royal hunting ground. He had been riding at top speed, thundering through the countryside as if chased by a horde of devils. His servant Bertrand struggled behind him. Only the overgrowth of the forest brush, intruding on the roadway, forced a break in the steady gallop.

The slowed pace had the unwelcome effect of permitting doubts about what he was doing to enter his mind. What if Sandrine did not return his love? Impossible! In his heart, he knew she loved him and was waiting for his return. But even if this was so, why did she not see him off when he left Bonneval?

Why did she hide from him after their enchanting evening together? Maybe somebody prevented her—that peasant brute Etienne might have claimed her as his and locked her up. The thought of Sandrine becoming the wife of this crude peasant, or of anybody else, made him dug the spurs deeper into the side of his horse, but the creature was too exhausted to respond and no amount of coaxing would make him move faster.

All right, let's assume she loves me and she is waiting for me, what then? Will she live with me as my mistress? No, I want her as my wife. I want her to be the Countess de Treffort and one day she will be the Duchess d'Evreux. The family will be a problem at first, particularly his father. I know mother would only want me to be happy—she would overcome her sense of propriety and love Sandrine as soon as she meets her. Catherine, my good sister Catherine, could certainly be persuaded to be an ally. So what if Sandrine has no dowry, no title? I have wealth enough, the income from all my estates is more than we will ever need.

Of course, there was also the matter of his betrothal to Louise de Montreuil—what a stupid custom to promise somebody in marriage practically at the time of birth, just for the sake of enlarging the patrimony. Louise was a sweet and pretty girl, the last time he saw her she was nine and he was eleven, and when he last heard of her she was spoken of as having a passionate affair with the Duke d'Aumale, a lecher notorious in all of France. She may well be reasonable and release him from the odious vow.

He did not think the moment well-chosen and did not take up the matter with his father before he left Paris. His father had been disturbed that he should absent himself from the city just when he had gained the Duke de Guise's favor. He saw this as a most opportune moment for his son to build a brilliant career and position of power. If he played his cards right, he had told him, he could become one of the most powerful men in the realm. To forego a chance like this for some amorous adventure was incomprehensible to the Duke d'Evreux, who had always put duty before pleasure.

The rain fell more constantly now, saturating the dense foliage. The deeper Philippe and his companion penetrated the forest, the more difficult became their advance through the thicket and muddy pathway. Philippe dismounted. Man and beast slithered back and forth as he held on to the reins of the obstreperous horse, pulling it with one hand and pushing back the protruding branches with the other.

Bertrand dragged the pack horse in a desperate struggle to keep up with his master. "My Lord, we had better seek shelter before nightfall or Your Lordship will catch a terrible cold in this miserable weather."

Philippe had hoped to traverse the Rambouillet forest without having to seek lodging. He had ventured deeply into territory controlled by royal troops and he had to avoid at all cost being recognized. Under the circumstances, however, they had little choice but to follow the flickering light in the distance, which no doubt came from an inn. After another hour of arduous progress, they reached the inn, drenched to the skin and spattered with mud. As Philippe had feared, the place was packed with royal guardsmen. He would do well not to identify himself as a nobleman. He decided to pass himself off as a traveling merchant whose merchandise had been stolen by a band of brigands. He quickly briefed Bertrand on what to say if they were questioned: They were on their way from Rouen to Chartres with a consignment of silk fabrics when they were held up by a band of robbers who spared their lives only after they handed over their entire shipment of merchandise.

He rehearsed the story several times with Bertrand, who was, however, so exhausted and famished that he paid scant attention to what his master was saying.

At the inn, they were told that the rooms were reserved for members of the nobility. The host pointed to a corner in the main hall where they could spread a pack of straw on the floor. Bertrand was peeved that his master should have to sleep on a sack of straw on a hard stone floor with no opportunity for a change of clothing.

Philippe, seeing his indignation, pulled him close and whispered in his ear: "It's all right for one night. If you cause a commotion I shall pull out your tongue and cut it off. I don't like the looks of that captain. So just lie low and don't attract attention."

It had not escaped Philippe's notice that the captain of the guard was following their every movement with a suspicious eye as they spread their outer garments out to dry by the fireplace.

His uneasiness heightened when he saw the officer making his way over. He looked around and finally asked: "Did you use that sword when the bandits attacked you?"

"Oh, no there were too many of them, I didn't even have time to draw the sword," Philippe replied, suddenly aware that he had made one decisive mistake.

"Merchants don't usually carry swords," the captain muttered. "Where did you say you were waylaid?"

"About five miles north of here—at the edge of the forest," Philippe barely contained his anger at being questioned like this.

"The King's guards have been combing this area thoroughly—one can never be too careful with all the enemy spies around. But I haven't heard any reports of highwaymen. I even doubt they would operate in this vicinity with all the troops around."

"Is Monsieur suggesting that I am lying?"

Against his better judgment, the aristocrat in Philippe rebelled against the man's arrogance.

"That is exactly what I am suggesting. I don't believe you were robbed. I don't even believe that you are a merchant. You certainly don't look or behave like a merchant."

"And what does a merchant look like?" Philippe did not wait for the answer. He was tired of the banter and he almost regretted having made up this story. Without another word, he simply turned away from the officer and bedded down on the sack of straw in the corner pulling the rough horse blanket over his head.

No sooner had he fallen into a deep sleep than he was rudely awakened by a barrage of kicks. Philippe jumped up in fury, instinctively reaching for his weapon when he came face to face with three more officers of the royal guard.

"You see, he doesn't even react to being kicked the way a good bourgeois would! A good bourgeois would take his kicks with greater humility and answer an officer's questions with appropriate deference."

One of the officers who had studied Philippe's face intently shouted: "I remember this fellow. I saw him in Paris on the barricades. He fought like a lion in the company of his bourgeois friends near the Cemetery of the Innocents. But he is no bourgeois. He is the Count de Treffort-Salignac! Gentlemen, what we have here is a Guise spy!"

"Wait a moment. You are mistaken." Philippe tried a more conciliatory tone. With a discerning eye, he calculated his chances of fighting his way out of this situation. He could easily overwhelm these effete ninnies. But he had to be realistic. There were too many troops in the forest and his chances of getting out of the closed-in terrain were slim.

"Well, then let's ask your friend here whether you weren't coming from Paris rather than Rouen," suggested one of the men, grabbing shivering and frightened Bertrand by the neck.

"Let him go! I demand to speak to your commanding officer!" Philippe decided to drop all pretense and play it straight. He would explain to whoever was in charge of the royal troops in this area the purpose of his journey, certain that he could count on any French aristocrat's understanding that a lady could not be kept waiting.

When Philippe had finished telling his story—he did not mention, of course, that the lady in question was not a lady by the standards of French society—the Duke de Montpensier, who had listened without taking his eyes off the prisoner, burst into laughter: "My dear Count, this is such a marvelously amusing story, His Majesty, the King will be most delighted to hear it from your mouth directly. He is always looking for diversions, ways to escape the boredom of the affairs of state. I know he would never forgive me, were I not to invite the fabulous Count de Treffort-Salignac to his court."

Philippe's protests went unheeded. The royal adviser insisted and seeing no alternative, Philippe went along.

After the precipitous flight from Paris, the royal court had moved from residence to residence, from Chartres to Rambouillet and back again, several times, before finally setting up more permanent quarters at the Palace of Fontainebleau. It was there that Philippe found himself as the King's permanent guest. He spent his days pacing the walled rose garden extending from his living quarters like a caged lion. He lacked none of the amenities a young nobleman was accustomed to. Yet, he was not free to come and go as he pleased and he was under the constant watchful eye of royal guards even while he was asleep. None of the ruses he had devised during the last four weeks to escape the royal house arrest had worked. He preferred keeping away from the pomp and profligacy of the nightly banquets staged at the court. But the King commanded and he had no choice but to attend and be seen in the royal company.

Almost every night, the King took him aside and taunted him with monetary rewards and position.

"All you have to do, my dear Count, is join my entourage, abjure any loyalty to the Duke, and no royal favor will be denied you."

The answer was always the same evasion.

"I am already Your Majesty's loyal servant, but what would my word be worth, were I to go back on a solemn oath."

Unbeknownst to Philippe, royal agents had already circulated rumors in Paris that the Count de Treffort-Salignac had joined the court party and was among the privileged few seen daily in the company of the King.

Outwardly, this was of course true. Henri III kept Philippe close to his side on all state occasions, at the royal levé, at the royal hunt. Gradually, the impression was created that His Majesty had found a new mignon. Even the old favorite côterie was stirred to jealousy.

Helpless to extricate himself from the web in which the King had ensnared him, Philippe's sullen mood deepened as he sat among the courtiers, some of whom began to question the King's taste since this gentleman's presence certainly contributed nothing to the amusement at the court. He seemed unimpressed by the lavishness of the dinners and the lasciviousness of the entertainment. He made no secret that he despised Henri and his depraved "princes of Sodom," as they were popularly called—those fawning sycophants who spent their days in petty squabbles if they were not groveling for the King's favors.

The whole spectacle made him want to vomit. What troubled

times, he thought, when men at the center of power parade in garish vestments laden with brocade and precious jewelry, their starched neck collars of a size to give the impression their heads had been severed from the rest of their bodies—delighting the wags to compare them to the likeness of the head of John the Baptist being presented on a platter.

Philippe's erstwhile qualms in the wake of the days on the barricades about having betrayed the rightful King of France dissipated before this King's scandalous deportment. All of France had for years heard rumors about the King's penchant for the bizarre and the outrageous; he had been accused of every unspeakable vice under the sun, including sodomy. Philippe had always been inclined to regard these rumors as politically motivated fabrications. But the endless carousing, the excesses, and orgies he witnessed at the court reminded him of the old saying that wherever there is smoke, there is fire.

How could such a ridiculous, squandering buffoon, who spent his days lolling about with his lap-poodles and flagrantly shameless "mignons" lay claim to the love and loyalty of his people? A fickle miscreant ruled by constantly changing whims, from lecherous to celibate, from blasphemous to deeply religious and penitent, from benevolent to tyrannical. Even his doting and domineering mother was said to be living in fear of his violent temper and penchant for intrigue. Could such a man bring peace to France? Could he be the healer of the wounds of the kingdom?

Philippe remembered a debate he once witnessed between two learned scholars. One sought to define certain circumstances under which a rightful king could be removed from the throne by his people. He had immediately sided with the opponent who propounded that the monarchy was sacrosanct, the right to succession inviolable. Now his experience at the court of

Henri III gave him second thoughts. Maybe under certain circumstances, the removal of a tyrant could be justified. The doctors of the Sorbonne had of late expounded this theory in treatise upon treatise. The idea of the people's right to rebel was certainly on the minds of many people. Henri Valois made it very difficult to refute this idea.

Would Henri de Guise make a better king? Philippe was not certain about that either. The Duke was an ambitious and arrogant man, certainly a dangerous man, but he was mentally more stable than the King, and he was no fop. As for Henri de Bourbon, the King of Navarre, the man who was by right of succession next in line to the throne, Philippe had fought too hard for the Catholic cause to embrace the idea of a heretic on the French throne.

As the days were getting longer and the roses burst into full bloom, Philippe had much time to ponder these and other questions concerning the political and military situation in France. But mostly his thoughts revolved around his beloved Sandrine.

His only solace was the small, leather-bound volume of writings by Marguerite de Navarre Sandrine had given him as a token. He had carried it with him like a sacred relic. He never tired of reading the stories of men and women who devised endless ways of satisfying their longing for their lovers. There was nothing political in these pages as he had first suspected. But not even in reading could he find peace, nothing could lessen his longing to be with his love nor his rage against the cruel fate that conspired to keep him from returning to her.

The days and weeks passed without a sign that the King might be willing to release him from captivity. The court resumed its restless peregrinations—like the Israelites in the desert commented some critical spirits—they wandered from place to place, from city to city, roundabout, but never entering, the promised land that was Paris. Then in mid-June, Henri Valois suddenly decided to enter the Leaguer city of Rouen in Normandy, the home province of the House of Treffort and d'Evreux.

Philippe was especially distressed by this move. As long as the court was near Chartres, he could still hope to escape at a propitious moment to Bonneval which lay only a few leagues to the south. While they stayed at Rouen, Henri tightened the watch around Philippe, but during public appearances, he made a show of lavishing his attention on the well-known League soldier.

The royal predilection for handsome young men of well-formed, muscular bodies was common knowledge and the ubiquitous presence of the strikingly handsome Count de Treffort-Salignac at the King's side did not fail to get tongues wagging from Rouen to Paris. Philippe, for his part, had no illusions about the King's duplicity, a false move and he might end with a dagger in his back, or more likely, poison in his food.

Philippe's attempts to get word to his father were foiled each time. His hopes that Henri was holding him for ransom were also dashed and, as time went on, it became clear that Henri would not release the architect of the barricades for anything—humiliation could only be met with humiliation.

Judging from the King's volatile character, Philippe came to suspect that he intended to use him somehow as a pawn in a scheme of vengeance against the Guise party and the citizens of Paris. But even Philippe in his political astuteness could never imagine the bizarre, almost perverse drama of politics that was about to unfold.

What Philippe did not know was that the Queen Mother, who had remained in the capital, had been tirelessly at work to forge yet another compromise between the Guise party and the monarchy. So it came as a great surprise to Philippe, and everybody else when in mid-July the King issued from Rouen what was called the Edict of Union—in essence, a declaration of peace between the monarchy and the Guise party. King Henri was said to have given into this pact, a capitulation to the Catholic League, out of fear of his mother's powers of divination.

Who would have thought that two months after he had humbled the sovereign King of France, the Duke de Guise would be received at the royal court and be made Lieutenant-General of France? The King even acceded to the Duke's demand to convene the Estates-General by September at the royal residence of Blois in the Loire Valley.

Philippe might have warned the Duke not to be blinded by his success. He might have told him that the treacherous King was only biding his time. He might have, at the risk of his life, sent a warning signal when the Duke with characteristically overweening self-confidence followed the invitation to the court. But Philippe was no longer with the royal party when the Estates-General convened.

The momentous events of history had overtaken Philippe and had made him dispensable to both sides in the conflict.

The King, tired of wooing the recalcitrant Count, took the advice of his court favorite, the Duke d'Epernon, a most dangerous and ambitious man who had harbored great misgivings about the King's infatuation with the League captain. When the royal court arrived at Blois, Philippe was arrested and thrown into the dungeons, where Henri Valois soon forgot about his existence.

The Duke de Guise, convinced of Philippe's betrayal, had no reason to concern himself with his whereabouts either. To him, the whole affair explained the Count's rather strange behavior in Paris. Even his father, the Duke d'Evreux, though deeply disturbed and for a long time unwilling to face what seemed the obvious conclusion, finally conceded that his son must have become a turncoat and had, for whatever reason, left the path of duty and honor for the profligate life at the royal court.

In October, the Estates-General gathered at Blois, an assembly supposedly made up of representatives from the three estates, clergy, nobility, and commoners, but in reality, dominated by the Guise party. Philippe had become a negligible factor in the game of power between the King and the Duke de Guise.

Chained to the thick, sweating stone wall, the cell too narrow for him to stretch his legs, Philippe's last glimmer of hope faded. His rage against this foul act of treachery had subsided. He no longer tore at the chains as he had done in a first vain attempt to loosen them. The shackles only cut deeper into his flesh, already rubbed raw to the bone. Numbness settled on his mind and body, even the well of his tears had dried up.

Twenty feet above him, a small gridded opening shed the only source of light, the only faint link to the outside world. The days were getting shorter and a glum frost settled on the dampness of the walls. The prisoner convulsed in a perpetual shiver until one day the guard brought him an extra horse blanket to wrap around his emaciated body.

He no longer had the strength to call out, to make his voice heard amidst the clanking of carriages and hoof beats above. Neither did he persist in clamoring for the attention of the owners of the boots who stomped over the grid, unaware of the human misery below.

Time had lost all meaning. All existence outside the dank walls had become a blurred memory. One day, light snow began to filter through the grid and the usually tight-lipped guard told him that it was only ten days to Christmas. But what did it matter to one buried alive without hope?

A few days later, the heavy door opened. Somebody seemed to be speaking to him soothingly, but he could not make out the face or grasp the meaning of what was said. Philippe was only vaguely aware of being wrapped in a fur coat and lifted up. What happened after that was blocked from his consciousness by a perpetual stupor, closer to death than life.

When Philippe regained consciousness, he found himself buried under a pile of thick, down comforters. His body was suffused with the warmth of the soft, lily-white feather bed and he inhaled eagerly the freshness of the sheets. He lifted his head above the pillows but immediately sank back with pain. Slowly he tried again and this time used his elbows to support himself. He saw the bed was in the middle of a huge room bathed in glaring sunlight. Outside the window, he recognized turrets capped with snow. Next to the window sat a woman engaged in embroidering. But, this was a familiar face and a familiar room! Was it all a dream? No. The woman was his mother and the room was his own at the Château d'Evreux.

"Merry Christmas, Philippe," the Duchess d'Evreux called out. Before he could answer, he was submerged under a shower of hugs and kisses. He was certain he must have died and gone to heaven, for his mother had never lavished such open affection on him.

The Duchess d'Evreux had kept a silent vigil at her son's side since he had been brought home. Praying fervently, she fearfully watched the struggle between life and death that raged within the martyred body but tenaciously resisted succumbing to the fever that threatened to consume him. Finally, as night gave way to dawn for the fifth time, life seemed to gain the upper hand, and death, at long last, lost its hold.

Although he was now resting comfortably, exhausted but comfortably, he was still too weak to even turn and greet his friend Robert whose familiar voice sounded from the adjacent room. He noticed though that he seemed to be engaged in animated, even agitated discussion with another familiar voice he recognized as his father's.

"Merry Christmas, Philippe!" The Duke d'Evreux declared with good cheer as they entered his room moments later. This was a rather abrupt change from the somber tone of the conversation with Robert.

"Thank God our prayers have been heard at last! You are looking so much better today my son. How are you feeling?"

"Just a bit stiff in the bones, Sire," Philippe replied. "But tell me what you two were just talking about. Sounded ominous."

"It is nothing that needs to be discussed right now," Robert replied exchanging a warm handshake and embrace with his friend. "The main thing is to get you back on your feet, and soon. The King's hospitality is not good for anybody's health."

"You didn't think I had sold out to the other side? Did you?"

"Not to the enemy. After all, the King of France is hardly the enemy. But you must try to forgive us. All appearances indicated that you had joined the court party and had forsaken the League," the Duke d'Evreux tried to choose his words carefully.

"The King of France is my enemy now!" Philippe's face turned purple with rage.

"We talk about it later, my son, when you have regained more of your strength."

"No!" Philippe insisted. "We must talk about this now. I could not rest if I thought you still doubted my loyalty."

"Do you remember the morning after the Guise victory in Paris? You had left the party early. The conversation we had then, the doubts you seemed to have, the opinions you expressed about kingship, all this seemed to add up; it seemed to confirm the impression Henri Valois was trying to create. As we now know, it was all deliberately concocted by His Majesty. Believe me, my son, I told myself a hundred times, no a thousand times, that this could not be, that this was not my son, that there must be some other explanation. Robert felt the same way. We were both at a total loss what to make of the whole affair. You must forgive us for doubting. The evidence seemed so irrefutable."

"Our suspicions were aroused when the Estates-General gathered at Blois and you were nowhere to be found. When he was questioned, the King claimed no knowledge of your whereabouts. But, at first, we had no proof of foul play," Robert added.

"It took almost three months to confirm a rumor whispered by anonymous tongues that you were imprisoned in the dungeon at Blois. Once we had proof, fortunately, our good French public servants are not immune to bribery. For a fee, the night guard looked the other way while we, shall we say, effected your release. God in his infinite mercy had kept you alive!"

"Then I owe my life to the two of you." Philippe raised his arms, he wanted to embrace his father and his friend, but a sudden weak spell made him fall back into the pillows.

"As fate would have it, we owe our lives to you as well," the Duke said gravely. "We wanted to keep the news from you until you had regained your strength, but I see it is difficult to keep anything from you, your mental alertness seems already fully restored."

Grasping his son's hand, his eyes fastened firmly on him, the Duke spoke in a grievous tone: "News just reached us from Blois—the Duke de Guise and his uncle, the Cardinal of

Lorraine, were murdered on Christmas Eve in their chambers at Blois. There can be no doubt, the King has finally taken his revenge. The Count de la Croix and I would surely have fallen victim to the assassins had our care for you not taken us away from Blois only days before this treacherous deed took place. What will become of France, only God knows!"

"Oh, that wretched bastard!" Philippe tried to raise himself, but the effort was too much. Hatred filled him, and his every being cried out for revenge against his tormentors, the King and the evil Duke d'Epernon. He could not find it in his heart to mourn the scheming Duke de Guise. But that he kept to himself.

"My son, you mustn't torture yourself. The most important thing right now is for you to recover your health. The League has a strong and determined leader in the Duke de Mayenne, with our help he will carry on the holy struggle."

"But you know, very well, he is a mere puppet of Spain. All of this only plays into the hands of that bigot Philip of Spain. As long as France remains in a state of weakness through this endless strife and bloodshed, Spain will remain the undisputed power in Christendom—even the defeat of her Armada won't change that. We cannot let Spain, the declared enemy of France, direct the affairs of the kingdom. I am afraid, there is only one way if peace is ever to be restored and that is accommodation with the Protestants."

"Philippe, you sound like a member of the Politiques. Would you rather make peace with the heretics than form an alliance with the most Catholic ruler of Spain?" Robert was appalled. "You must still by under a fever spell."

"Call me what you want. It doesn't matter. If wanting peace makes me a Politique, then maybe I am a Politique. I dislike the idea of a heretic king as much as you do, but somehow all this misery and suffering France has endured for thirty years must end!" Beads of sweat formed on his forehead and he fell back into a semiconscious state. As through the veil of a dream, he perceived his mother scolding the two men and chasing them out of the room. Then he plunged into a long, forgetful sleep.

His mother's love and care restored Philippe's strength and appetite with remarkable speed. Within a few days, he was able to walk around the room. The Duchess was so happy to see her son back on his feet, she did not inquire, or maybe she forgot, about the name he called out again and again in his delirium, a name that sounded like "Sandrine." If it puzzled her, she did not pry.

The one who knew the meaning of the name remained silent. Robert's heart filled with dark foreboding. How was he to relate to his friend an incident that had occurred a few weeks after the Estates-General had gathered at Blois, an incident he had since put out of his mind and recalled only now? How was he to know that Philippe was still infatuated with that peasant wench?

His misgivings about Philippe's infatuation with the girl aside, Robert still felt an abiding bond of friendship and a sense of duty to relate what he had heard from the peasant Mathieu of Bonneval, who had, a few months before, appeared at Blois with an urgent message for the Count de Treffort-Salignac. But even now the days passed and Robert did not seem to find the right moment.

Then, finally, one afternoon, Philippe was, at last, strong enough to leave the confines of his chamber, the friends took a walk through snow-covered fields. These fields had been the scene of many a snowball fight in winters past, in a far-off time of good fun and laughter and little care about the ways of the world—a state of innocence marked by absolute certainty about what was right and what was wrong, of camaraderie and shared confidences, a state recalled with fondness by both men, but most deeply mourned by Robert.

"Philippe," Robert began hesitantly. "There is something you should know—and I pray to God that all is not lost yet."

Philippe looked at him puzzled and at his urging to be more specific, Robert began to relate the bizarre tale.

Early one morning, it was mid-October, the Estates-General were in session at Blois, Robert was taking a ride through the countryside when he was approached by a young peasant, who by the account of his servant, had been loitering around his path for several days. Robert was about to have him chased away, taking him for a beggar or a petitioner when it occurred to him that he had seen this young man somewhere before. When asked his name, the peasant identified himself as Mathieu of Bonneval. At the mention of that village, Robert inquired what brought him here, so far away from home. The lad explained, he had heard the Duke de Guise and his entourage were at Blois and he had come with an urgent message for the Count de Treffort-Salignac. For one week, he had come every morning to the gate of the palace hoping to see the Count. He was just about to give up when he recognized His Lordship, the Count's friend.

Robert's curiosity was aroused. He asked him about his business, assuring him that he would take the message to said Count. Mathieu related that three weeks before the wedding between Etienne, Mathieu's father, and Sandrine had taken place. Very early the next morning, even before the crowing of the roosters, the villagers had been awakened by terrible screams. Mathieu had recognized his father's voice. He looked outside and saw Etienne running up and down the street, hollering and screaming: "The witch! The witch! She put a spell on me!"

The priest tried to calm Etienne and the mob of peasants who shouted: "Let's string her up! Right now!" Only the priest's intervention saved her from being torn to pieces. He announced to the bloodthirsty mob that he would bring the matter before the Archbishop of Chartres. Following this incident, the girl was taken to the town of Chartres where she was kept and interrogated by the inquisitorial authorities. Mathieu's only hope was to find the Count de Treffort-Salignac, who had shown her so much kindness, and that he could somehow intercede with the Archbishop.

Robert had sent the young peasant away with the promise to relate the story to the Count. But not knowing where Philippe was, he had with customary insouciance put this episode out of his mind. Only Philippe's feverish outcry of the girl's name brought the incident back to his mind. He wondered. Could she still be alive? How long could anybody withstand the tortuous interrogations of the Dominican friars?

CHAPTER
5

The pallid winter sun suffused only barely the huge rosette window of the grand Cathedral of Chartres. Inside, a flickering sea of candlelight cast long, ghostly shadows against the walls of the arched caverns. A procession of bowing, hooded monks shuffled along the expansive naves, intoning the ominous trope of a dirge. The lament swelled beyond the Royal Portal and resonated in the huge square filled with mourners—moaning muffled intermittently by a single, doleful knell from the church spire.

Only a few days before, cathedral and square had resounded with exalted hymns of joy. A festive multitude had extolled the glory of the birth of Christ, the Savior, and the bells had rung out exultantly. Then on New Year's Day, news had reached the town from Blois. The Duke de Guise, champion and hope of the Catholic cause, was dead, murdered by the henchmen of the King of France!

Sorrow and grief gripped this town of devout adherents of the Apostolic faith. Where only one day before singing and laughter had held sway, wailing seized the populace. Flagellants appeared without a call, roaming the streets, tearing their flesh with spiked whips, exhorting the people to repent and prepare for the world's end. Countless bereaved went about half-crazed, frantically beating their chests. Men and women were seen rolling on the ground, their mouths foaming, their bodies convulsing in violent contortions.

Neither the sounds of joy and nor those of sorrow of the world above penetrated the underground realm of darkness where Sandrine lay captive. Even if the din had reached her ear, it would have remained barred from her consciousness. Time and place had lost all meaning, the world existed only, if at all, as a faint memory. Her body, ravaged by torture, existed outside her unbending will to survive, a will nurtured and sustained by a tenacious belief that Philippe would come to rescue her from the ordeal.

Four times she had confessed, had admitted to heinous acts in cahoots with the devil, and four times she had retracted. Each confession brought reprieve, each retraction renewed torments.

With almost superhuman determination she had raised her threshold for pain to the utmost. But daily she felt her body, emaciated and burning with constant pain as if a thousand knives were impaled in her skin, reaching the limit of endurance.

She knew there was only one way to stop her Dominican questioners' seething irons, pricking needles, one way to save herself from being stripped and whipped and having her limbs wrung in a vise, her body stretched on a rack, and then on the dreaded ladder: she had to confess herself guilty of the crimes charged against her, then the inflictions would cease.

The entire protocol of the chain of events her confession would set in motion had been carefully explained by the friars: the tortures would stop as soon as she confesses and she would then be handed over to the secular authorities for trial. Her confession would be used as primary evidence against her, as proof that the charges of witchcraft were founded in truth, and then she would be convicted and condemned to be burnt at the stake. A vicious noose was inexorably pulled around her. Philippe and a miracle were her only hope.

Her faith in Philippe had given her the strength to hold out, to postpone the trial. The ruse of confessing and retracting had worked so far because her tormentors were bound by strict rules, a fact she had duly observed and used to her advantage.

The Christmas season brought a longer breathing spell. Torture was suspended until after the Feast of the Epiphany. The young nun who looked after Sandrine smuggled in a few extra morsels of cake and meat from the sumptuous feasts with which the Archbishopric celebrated the birth of the Lord Jesus Christ. Sandrine's wounds began to heal, the pain eased, at least enough to turn her mind toward other thoughts. For the first time since she had been tossed into this living hell, she began to reflect on her situation. Her mind wandered back over all that had happened since Philippe had entered her life and left again to fight a war.

How long ago it seemed now! And yet she remembered his love, the sweetness of his embrace as if it had been yesterday. Was she a fool to have placed so much faith in a man she hardly knew? Was it possible that he had betrayed her trust and love?

No! No! Everything within her refused to give in to such doubts. Philippe will return! He will rescue her from these devils in monk's garb. She was certain. All she had to do was hold out long enough! A thousand times she told herself, the moment she was to lose her trust in Philippe's love, she was doomed. She had lived this long, had survived the tortures longer than anyone. There must be a reason why God gave her the strength to persevere!

She could think of a million reasons why Philippe had not come back in time to prevent the dreaded wedding. He was a soldier and this terrible, endless war was keeping him away from her. She only hoped and prayed he was alive; if he was alive, her prayers will be heard.

What if he doubted her love for him? She did not come out to see him off on the day the League troops left Bonneval. He had no way of knowing that Thierry had locked her in the attic after their return to the inn that night. He could not know about the tears she shed alone in the darkness, the days and weeks of solitary longing.

All summer long she waited. In late May, the stunning news reached the village from Paris. The Parisians and the League had humiliated the King of France. She waited. Hours, days, and weeks, she waited. She watched the dirt road from the North turned from mud to dust. Weeks and months passed and a dark abyss of melancholy open before her, drawing her deeper and deeper inside. Even her books held little solace and she soon stopped reading. She passed through the monotone of her daily pursuits in a grim daze.

One day, the end of summer was approaching, Thierry informed her that she would be married to Etienne Grosjean as soon as the harvest was brought in. She turned to Berthe, her mother. She implored her not to permit this to happen. Berthe placed her arms around her to comfort her; she did not dare oppose her husband's scheme. As always she acquiesced.

The memory of the wedding made Sandrine wince in anguish, even in her prison cell.

"Philippe! Philippe! Why did you forsake me? Why did you leave me in the hands of these monstrous brutes? Why did you all forsake me?" she called out.

She knew Berthe wanted to save her from a fate she knew was to her worse than death, but did not know-how. And Mathieu, oh Mathieu, her one true friend—hard to believe he should be the son of that pig Etienne—but he too was powerless.

Slowly, the memory of the wedding day and the night of terror that followed, all those images, which she had banished from her consciousness, impressed themselves on her. A calm detachment came over her. She did not resist and just let it happen.

First was the church ceremony. She almost fainted, so stricken was she with panic. Thierry dragged her down the aisle of the parish church as if he were pulling a mule. The villagers' laughter echoed in her ears. She was only vaguely aware of their gloating. Then the vow of obedience to her new master, unto death, the brutal kiss planted on her lips by the triumphant groom. The cheering crowd, the lewd exhortations to the groom, almost three times her age. Contorted peasant faces, rustics wallowing joyfully in her misfortune, this is how she saw them!

The wedding feast. The most lavish affair seen in years in Bonneval. The whole village, everybody down to the lowest field hand, gorged itself on the treats. Staggering piles of every variety of boiled meats, roast foul, and sausages were devoured and washed down with enormous quantities of wine and beer. Many of the guests had never seen such riches. Sandrine sat ossified among the uncouth rustics. She should have felt gratified at seeing the largess of Etienne's cupboard shared with the poor, but all she felt was disgust and contempt and a paralyzing fright.

The general merriment was heightened by the musical accompaniment from a group of strolling fiddle and flute players who roused the guests to song and dance. Thierry led her to the dance floor, swung her around a few times, and then handed her over to Etienne who did not seem much in the mood for dancing. He was frothing at the mouth and his body gave off a repulsive, sweaty odor.

Coarse, uproarious laughter from the men of the village. Sandrine recognized their faces, they had baited her with obscenities all her life. The grotesqueness of their stuffed mouths, their faces red, aroused by the thought of the breaking in of the young bride. Etienne boasting of his savoir-faire, proclaimed for everybody to hear what a lucky wench she was to be the recipient of his expertise. It was at this moment, Sandrine recalled, that she made up her mind—never would he touch her, she would sooner kill him or herself.

Then came the night. The pain of remembering was almost unbearable. But try as she may, she could not expunge her memory, she could no longer keep the images locked up in the reliquary of oblivion. She collapsed on the bed of straw on the cold dirt floor of her prison cell trembling with tears. At last, she found herself. She felt calm and almost at peace with herself. Slowly the wedding night came into focus.

There she was, in her white wedding gown, hoisted on the shoulders of stocky peasants who hauled her to the festively decorated bridal chamber like a virgin being offered on a sacrificial altar to a heathen god. She was dropped in the middle of a huge, herb-strewn bed. A group of women began to undress her under suppressed laughter and then left her lying there, lifeless, clad only in a thin, white linen chemise.

Berthe was there, weeping quietly, trying to reassure her with hugs and kisses: "Everything will be all right. You'll be all right, you'll see."

Sandrine clung to her. Everything inside her cried out: You know I won't be all right! Why don't you save me? Oh, please, please save me!

In her misery, Sandrine felt pity for her. She wondered about Berthe's wedding night. Did she feel anguish? Did she too feel she was being sacrificed like a lamb? Or maybe she was in love with Thierry. Hard to believe. Maybe it was the lot of all women to be humiliated and violated in body and spirit on their wedding nights. Even if by some eternal, divine decree this were so, she would not relent. Come what may, she would always belong alone to the one through whom she had tasted the sweetness of true love.

It was long past midnight when the guests retreated from the bridal chamber. She lay stretched out on the bed, the way the women had left her. She listened to the heavy gasps, amplified by the stillness of the night, at the other end of the room. She saw the blurred stocky figure of the man, who was now her husband and master, moving toward the bed. He had slipped out of his Sunday best and stood stark naked before her. All she could see was a ruddy torso covered with tufts of bristly dark hair. A stench of alcohol and sweat filled the room. Now his swarthy face, a contorted, scornful grimace, hovered above her. He closed in on her, self-assured, with deliberate slowness, like a wolf certain of his prey.

"Now my dear, I'll teach you what it means to be an obedient wife." His chest heaved with short puffs of breath. He lowered himself on the bed. She quickly rolled out on the other side and sought refuge in the corner by the window, wrapping herself in the curtain.

"You won't touch me! Don't you dare get near me!" she shrieked, insane with fright.

"Don't you dare get near me!" he echoed, drawing out the words derisively. "And how are you going to stop me? Heah?"

He charged at her like a raging bull. The attacker ran into a barrage of kicks and punches. But he was the stronger. He managed to seize her with one hand around the waist, holding her tightly pressed against his body while he pulled back her head by the hair with the other. Her nails ploughed through his cheeks leaving deep furrows running with blood. He retreated, reeling with pain, only to renew the attack with the ferocity of a wounded animal. Her chemise was ripped off and her bruised body pinned to the floor by his heaving hunk of flesh, his fetid sweat drenched her skin, as he pried at her legs, forcing them apart.

Then suddenly, a pained groan followed by a menacing roar. The attacker recoiled. She saw him reaching for his trousers and shirt. He was still getting into them when he bolted out of the room as if chased by a hundred demons. She heard him hollering and screaming something about a spell and a witch.

Sandrine, though startled by this unexpected turn, moved quickly to get away. She wrapped the torn chemise and a blanket around her trembling body and lowered herself through the window. Etienne was rousing the entire village with terrible screams.

She found temporary refuge at the Morels' house. No questions were asked, she was taken in, put to bed, where she soon fell into a deep, exhausted sleep.

The next day, the parish priest arrived at the doctor's house. He was very agitated and advised the doctor and his wife that for the girl's safety as well as their own, she had better come with him to the church. The whole village was out looking for her, and God have mercy on her soul should she fall into the hands of this mob.

"Etienne says she is a witch. He says she cast a spell on him so he would be unable to exercise his nuptial rights. He has found a very eager audience in the villagers. Every mysterious happening and misfortune of the last ten years is being recalled and explained by the presence of the witch. Many of the villagers now say they suspected her all along."

Turning to Sandrine, he tried to reassure her: "My child you will be safe at the church, they won't dare violate the sanctity of God's house."

Over the protest of the Morels, Sandrine followed the priest's advice. Once inside the church, the priest immediately beset Sandrine with entreaties to unburden herself, to save her soul, and confess to her "crimes." She shook her head as stubbornly as she had done when he had questioned her about the Bible. Her refusal to confess brought back his old suspicions that she may very well be a bride of the devil. The situation was far beyond what this simple parish priest was capable of handling. He advised her that he would have to hand the matter over to the jurisdiction of the Archbishop of Chartres who, he trusted, had more persuasive ways of dealing with such cases. After a day of holding back the raging mob, the priest escorted her before dawn with the help of Mathieu to Chartres.

All this had happened in October. Now it was late December and she had still not admitted her guilt.

After the Feast of the Epiphany, the Dominican friars returned to their grim task. Saving her soul from damnation had become the torturers' supreme challenge. Never had they encountered such stubbornness. Never had anybody survived more than two weeks without begging for mercy; although some expired before they could do so. The torturers' minds could not conceive of normal humans resisting for so long. She had to be one of Satan's favorites or maybe even one of his offspring.

Sandrine was dragged back to the torture chamber and made to kneel. She was sprinkled with holy water to the sign of the cross. The friars circled her three times in solemn procession, a ritual that was to make them immune to the taunts of the devil. They intoned their usual Te Deum and then came to a halt in front of her.

"My dear child," began the chief interrogator, "God in his infinite wisdom already knows the crimes you have committed. But as a merciful God, he extends his grace and forgiveness unto those who confess and repent their sins. A confession made voluntarily is more meritorious in his eyes than one extorted by torture. All you have to do is answer my question. When and how did you become a minion of the devil and what crimes did you commit to promoting his evil designs against the faithful in Christ?"

Sandrine adamantly shook her head, her lips tightly pressed together. The friar continued his coaxing: "Think of the salvation of your immortal soul. You need not fear death. This earthly life is but very brief, a mere prelude to life eternal. Confess and repent and you will be assured a life of eternal bliss in the presence of our Lord, Jesus Christ and his mother, the blessed virgin, queen of heaven, and all the saints. Take heed lest you die without confession and absolution, yours will be a life of eternal damnation in the fires of hell."

"Sandrine Legrand!" A second friar proclaimed, his voice rising to a shrill pitch. "We know you are in league with the prince of darkness. How could you have withstood our pleading for so long unless you were sustained in your stubbornness by Satan himself? But there is still time! You can still redeem yourself. Recant, cast off the curse of evil that is holding your soul captive. You only have to answer the questions put to you, truthfully and with a contrite heart! Let us start again. When did you become Satan's handmaiden and what method did he use to induct you into his service?"

The new round of tortures was more excruciating than any she had previously experienced. She was placed in strappado, her hands bound behind her back with leather strips pulled so tight, her wrists ran with blood. She was then attached to a pulley and hoisted to the ceiling. While the inquisitor read the questions aloud, his assistants, muttering their prayers, slowly lowered her a few feet and then abruptly stopped the fall with a jerk, setting off a circuit of pain that radiated through every nerve in her body.

Even then, the spark of rebellion still glowed in her. She shook her head with great vigor to fend off the pain. But as the jerking became more frequent and more intense, Sandrine's will to resist gradually whittled away. She might have withstood the jerking a while longer, but as she moved in and out of a state of consciousness, she vaguely became aware of one of the friars calmly threading several heavy weights through an iron chain. At once, the meaning of this became clear to her: they were preparing for the next level of torture called squassation!

She knew what to expect since the sequence of the tortures and their effects had been described to her by Brother Guillaume, a kindly, elderly man who genuinely desired to spare her the ordeal. Not without pride, he had boasted: "In thirty years of service to the Holy Inquisition, I have never seen anybody withstand the pain of having every joint and limb dislocated when lowered on this pulley, the body stretched by the weights tied to the ankles, and then being pulled upward."

"We always get a confession and the names of accomplices," he had assured her. "Of course, we use this procedure reluctantly, and only as a last resort when all other methods of persuasion fail."

Thus faced with certain death one way or other, Sandrine became obsessed with one desire: she would go her last way erect and in dignity. She wanted the world to know what she had endured. A confession would assure her a public trial, a public record would be made of her suffering. If it was God's will that she should be consumed by the flames of bigotry, at least her death would stand as a testimonial to the world, and to Philippe, of the injustice done against her. Rather than suffer every one of her bones to be broken, rather than waste away without a trace like a dog in the gutter, she would stand trial in an open court and go to her death with her head held high in full view of the world.

The trial was set to begin on the 15th of January in the year of Our Lord 1589 before the magistrates of the town of Chartres. Sandrine signed a confession that made known that she had aided the devil to promote evil in this world and to subvert the coming of the Kingdom of Jesus Christ. She no longer had any will to protest the absurdity of the charges. As the time of the trial drew closer, the last ray of hope slowly extinguished in her. Languid indifference came to pervade her spirit. She even longed for death now, believing that her fate served some higher purpose, whatever it may be. Death was preferable to being the wife of Etienne, and certainly preferable to a life without the man whom she loved more than life itself.

Sandrine was moved to a more "comfortable" prison cell. A swarm of charitable sisters dressed her wounds with strict instructions from the archbishopric to take care of her every need. Nothing would be more embarrassing were she to die before the trial! Did they realize the paradox? Probably not. The sisters moved about her with the hushed respect accorded a person marked for death.

The Dominican friar who had shown so much fatherly

concern for the salvation of her soul also paid a visit. His shiny face glowed even more than usual with pride and elation. He spoke to her in a kindly manner: "My child, when you enter the gates to the heavenly realm of eternal bliss, after a brief stay in purgatory, of course, where you will mingle daily with the saints and martyrs of our holy faith, maybe you can find it in your heart to mention something of the good work the Dominican friars are doing down here as Christ's soldiers in the frontline of the battle against the Evil One for the preservation of God's Kingdom on earth."

With a sheepish smile, he added: "And maybe it wouldn't hurt to commend your Brother Guillaume for having saved your immortal soul from the eternal fires of hell."

Sandrine just nodded. Oddly, she felt pity for this good-hearted, pious man who genuinely believed that inflicting excruciating pain was a service to the greater glory of the God of love. You fool, she thought, you pitiful fool. She knew he would never understand that his actions were flying in the face of the teachings of Jesus Christ in whose name he thoughtlessly stripped fellow human beings of their dignity and reduced them to the condition of beasts. If there was a God of justice, he will hold him and all other tormentors of innocent people accountable. But Sandrine was not so certain of this anymore.

It was close to midnight and Thierry was about to close up his tavern. He was just waiting for the few lingering revelers to finish their mugs of beer. Among them was Etienne Grosjean, who had come to the inn that evening to announce, not without a triumphant smirk, he had it from good authority that Sandrine had at last confessed and that she would be tried within a week. Thierry cringed as he listened to the peasant's maundering predictions of what would happen to his depraved bride. His testimony at the trial would expose her evil doings to the whole world whereupon she would, no doubt, burn at the stake. Thierry, though dismayed by the turn the events had taken, silently suffered his boasting, not daring to speak up against the man who held several liens on his meager property.

A sudden noise outside distracted the men's attention to the door through which a troop of League soldiers burst shouting into the tavern. With a quick eye, Etienne assessed the situation and stole away through the backdoor. He had no desire for an encounter with the young nobleman, who was wringing Thierry's neck in the vestibule of the inn. He would find out later what brought the captain of the Holy League back to Bonneval. Maybe there was something to the village gossip after all that he was Sandrine's lover. A sense of ill foreboding seized him. Here was a development he had not counted on just when everything was going so well. But he was not about to get into a quarrel with an aristocrat. Let Thierry take the heat, he deserved it, that double-dealing bastard.

Philippe and Robert had been riding posthaste for three days accompanied by Sergeant Gaspard and a handful of trusted followers. Their progress was impeded by icy conditions which made the roadways impassible in many places. The royal patrols along the way forced them to take circuitous back roads. Though careful to avoid another trap, Philippe allowed little rest for either man or beast.

Upon entering the inn, Philippe seized Thierry by the throat and jostled the innkeeper's corpulent frame as if he was a chicken about to be slaughtered. His grip held him so tight, the victim was unable to answer the barrage of questions hurled at him: "Where is she? What have you done to her, you swine?"

"She is at Chartres," Thierry finally managed to croak, "in the care of His Holiness the Archbishop, I think."

Thierry was still not sure whether the two noblemen were

not agents of the Holy Father in Rome. As soon as Philippe loosened his grip, the innkeeper fell on his knees imploring their lordships not to let any harm come to him. He assured them that he and his wife had done their best to raise the girl an obedient servant of the Church.

"She isn't our real daughter, you know. We opened our home to the old woman who appeared in the village one day with the infant. Never knew where she had come from. We didn't ask questions, just gave her shelter and food. The old woman was so distraught, she never spoke much, just held the baby like a treasure trove. When the old woman died, we took in the child, cared for her like a daughter. Who would have thought she was a witch!"

"You never treated her like your own, like an outcast you treated her, that's what!" The angry voice of a woman came from the kitchen. There in the doorway stood Berthe, the silent, obedient innkeeper's wife, her usual expressionless demeanor spewing disdain at her husband.

"You worked her mercilessly, worse than an animal. She never gave us any trouble, she never complained, but the whole village was always after her, pursued her with their hatred. Heaven knows why! She never gave any cause except she was different, more beautiful, and smarter than any of those dumb peasants."

Thierry's jaw dropped, for once he was speechless. Never had he heard his wife speak like this and now in front of these noble lords. He had no idea she cared much about the girl. She had rarely put a word in for her, never interfered. What do I know about this woman who has been my wife for twenty-five years? he thought. Not much, he had to admit. The thought flashed through his mind that maybe she too was a witch. How was he to know who was and who was not?

His suspicion was reinforced momentarily when he saw a tearful Berthe running up to Philippe, throwing herself at the nobleman's feet and clutching his legs.

Her voice rang with the moanful despair of a mother about to lose her child: "Please, most noble Lord, please save my little girl. You are our only hope. She was waiting for you for so long. She never said a word, but I knew she was waiting for you when she stood by the window for hours, watching the road all summer long. If you only had come sooner! But now you have returned! God bless you! Maybe there is still time, maybe it is not too late yet!"

Philippe raised her gently to her feet assuring her he would do everything in his power to save her although he did not know how he would make good on his promise. Robert, meanwhile, extracted from Thierry the information that the trial was to begin within a week at the magistracy of Chartres. Not much time, but at least a few days to form a plan of action.

"My good man," Robert addressed the innkeeper in the imperious manner of the aristocrat, "we have had a long journey, we and our men are hungry and in need of rest. Bring us some food and drink and prepare to put us up for the night. Then we'll talk some more. Oh, by the way, don't try anything underhanded with that pig Etienne. Hurry up now, I am sure my comrades are as famished as I am."

Berthe hurried into the kitchen wiping her eyes with the corner of her apron. She had not felt this elated since the day Thierry had given in to her entreaties to adopt the foundling as their child. It had seemed to her then like a gift from heaven, the answer to the prayers of a woman stricken with a barren womb.

Instructing Gaspard to keep an eye on Thierry, Robert retired with Philippe to a corner to discuss the strategy for the rescue.

"As in any battle plan, we must retain the element of surprise." Robert enjoyed taking charge since his friend was much too agitated to make a level-headed assessment of the situation.

"I don't think anything will be gained by beating on this treacherous peasant. He must be kept at all cost from sounding the alarm. It may be well to win him over to our side."

Seeing Philippe's dispirited demeanor, Robert placed his arm around his friend's shoulder: "Come on, let's get some nourishment and then some rest, at dawn tomorrow morning we will enter the town and stake out the place. I think I have a plan that will work."

CHAPTER 6

The town of Chartres brimmed with excitement. A solemn festiveness reigned in its streets as in anticipation of a momentous occasion. The opening of the trial was attended with great pomp and pageantry. From the cathedral's gothic spire, extending heavenward into the leaden sky, the bells resounded majestically as the town notables, clad in long black robes, bearing miens of portentous importance, marched in solemn procession from the cathedral, where they attended morning Mass, across the square hemmed in by a restive throng of townspeople, curiosity seekers, pickpockets, and beggars. Town guardsmen in harness and helmets wielded their halberds at the crowd with shouts to clear the way for the notables. The procession passed from the open town square into the twisted Rue Sainte-Foy to the town hall where the court held its sessions.

In the courtroom, the spectators' gallery was packed hours before the opening of the proceedings. Peasants, from miles around, rubbed elbows with the townspeople, the merchants, artisans, and craftsmen, and even mingled freely with members of the nobility. Women of all classes cast off the customary decorum expected of their sex and aggressively vied for the best seats.

The entire village of Bonneval, even some of the old and infirm, had come to town. Basking in the attention they attracted, the good people of Bonneval invaded the marbled halls of the court house in the small hours of the day to claim their seats in the front rows. Etienne strode with measured steps of pompous self-importance ahead of the other witnesses to the witness dock.

So great was the excitement in the courtroom that an orderly entrance of the magistrates was only possible after repeated calls for order. Once the notables were seated on the bench, the chief magistrate declared the court in session and called for the accused to be brought before the judges. Silence settled over the audience, not a sound was heard as Sandrine, clad in rough sack cloth, her hair cropped short almost to the scalp, was led to the prisoner's bench.

In the back row of the gallery, Philippe, disguised in monk's garb, rose in his seat but was pushed back by the firm grip of his companion's hand. Is this how he had to see her again? The hollowness of her cheeks, the paleness of her complexion, her beauty more haunting than ever, made his heart ache. He wondered whether she was aware of what was going on. Her mouth was frozen into an enigmatic smile, her eyes dark and devoid of expression, she sat perfectly erect, with almost serene detachment, still projecting that aura of mystery that had first arrested his attention.

How he longed to hold her, to comfort her! If he could only reach out to her, feel what she was feeling. Was she at peace with herself? Was she reconciled to her fate? How could she be? She must be torn by anguish and despair! But no sign of inner turmoil rose to the surface from behind the shield of stiff composure. He would give his own life to save hers!

The trial lasted three days. Sandrine was charged with witchcraft, consorting with the devil, and promoting his evil schemes against the faithful in Christ, a crime equal to heresy and punishable by burning at the stake. Witnesses were called to support the accusations. Many of those called to testify described in great detail how they had always been suspicious of her especially given the fact that nobody knew where she had come from to the village of Bonneval, nobody knew who her parents were. She might very well be Satan incarnate. After all, wasn't it well known that he takes many different forms and chooses the bodies of humans, especially those of beautiful young women, to inhabit so he can sow his evil undetected?

The first witness called was Solange, a midwife of sorts, a coarse, big-boned woman who maneuvered her considerable frame to the witness stand by paddling her arm with bombastic movements. Weighty self-importance spoke from her darting eyes. This was the day she had been waiting for a long time, the chance to tear the intruder at long last from their midst. More than anybody, it had been she who had fueled the village cabal of hatred against the outsider.

Upon being sworn to tell the truth, she began her testimony with a few obsequious words of praise for the good magistrates. In the name of the entire village of Bonneval, she wanted to express her gratitude for the great service the gentlemen were about to render in rooting out the source of evil that had hung over their lives for so long. As she pronounced the source of evil, she turned full-face toward Sandrine, her wry mouth twisting and twitching.

Turning back to the judges with a sweet, ingratiating smile, she went on to recount how several years ago her infant son was found dead in his cradle. At the time, she was inconsolable and could not understand why the Almighty would afflict her with such grief. But later she remembered that she had seen the accused near her house only a short while before the infant died.

"Need I say more?" she shouted.

Flushed with a sense of victory, as if she had scored a point in a wrestling match, Solange turned, self-satisfied, to acknowledge the wild shouts of indignation from the gallery.

"But, there is more!" Solange's shrieking voice rose above the clamor. "There is much more!"

The chief magistrate called for order in the court and with a kindly tone turned to the witness: "Please continue my dear woman. But remember, you must confine yourself to the facts, this court only wants to hear about happenings that support the charges against the accused. Go on."

"A lot of things were going on," she continued, "that made no sense. Who could have seen what was going on then? Only later, much later things became clear. My sister-in-law, God rest her soul, died after three days of agonizing labor. Thank God, I was able to save the baby. Neither my bereaved brother nor anybody else in the family thought of it at the time, but, I ask you, would you say it was a coincidence that the accused had come to the house with a cake just at the onset of labor?"

"But my poor sister-in-law wasn't the only one. Whenever a woman's time came, the accused was at the door offering her gifts from the devil, a cake, or some other dish, prepared with who knows what. One year, not too long ago, ten women from our village were carried off with childbed fever. Ten women in one year! Could this all have been a coincidence? Wouldn't you agree, it could only have been the work of the devil and his handmaiden, the accused!"

Thick, gleaming pearls of sweat oozed from her forehead and rolled slowly down the deep creases between the wads of flab of her cheeks. She paused, catching her breath.

"And what would you make of this one?" she challenged the magistrates and spectators alike wiping her face with the back of her hand.

"How would you feel, as a mother, if your children, first one and then the others, one by one, were struck with little red blisters all over their little bodies. At night they glowed with a fever so hot no cold compresses could bring it down. Wouldn't it tear any mother's heart to hear them begging to stop the tiny things crawling all over their bodies, but you have to stand by helpless watching your little ones suffer?"

She became so agitated, the chief magistrate ordered a chair be brought to keep her from fainting.

"But," she roared menacingly after a brief pause and jumped back on her feet with surprising spryness, "I remember the evil eye passing by the window where I was sitting watching over my little ones, imploring God not to let them die. In his infinite goodness, he heard my prayers, but others were not so lucky. I have lost count of the children who were laid to rest in their graves that year."

Pandemonium had broken loose by then in the gallery, shouts of "Death to the witch!" and "Let's get her right now!" filled the courtroom. Philippe seethed with anger, ready to charge forward if the mob should try to break the barrier of the town guardsmen shielding the beloved girl. But Robert held him back, warning that any premature move could ruin their whole enterprise.

"How can people be so stupid? What superstitious garble! And not only the peasants, but learned men like the magistrates!" Philippe trembled with anger. "How wretched she must feel about all this. Look at her sitting there in the center of the storm, undisturbed, with that tranquil smile." Admiration spoke from his words, but then a sense of powerlessness, of being unable to save her from the raging mob, overwhelmed him.

"How will we ever get her out of here, Robert? These fanatics won't rest until they see her dead."

"We'll use our ingenuity," Robert tried to sound reassuring, holding back his doubts.

"We have handled more difficult situations than this before, haven't we? Their superstition and fanaticism will eventually be to our advantage. But, we must have patience and wait for the right moment. We shall strike when nobody suspects it. Gaspard and our men are on their guard outside."

Order was finally restored in the courtroom. More witnesses were called. One by one they testified to the depravity of the accused. Litanies of calamities that had befallen the village during the past ten or fifteen years were recited. There were incidents of crop failures, heavy rains washing out harvests, and long droughts parching the soil, lightning striking beasts in the fields or setting fire to storage barns, farm animals, especially horses, running amok, cows refusing to give milk. Children and animals were born with deformities, especially common were children born with a clubfoot, a sure sign of the devil's handiwork.

So many were the misfortunes of the village of Bonneval, the testimony had to be continued the next day. As inexplicable as the occurrences were, every one of the witnesses followed Solange's lead and insisted they remembered seeing the accused, none of them called her by name, somewhere near the scenes of disasters.

As if all this wasn't enough evidence, the star witness, her chief accuser, was yet to come. Excitement had been building among the crowd in the courtroom and in the square outside in anticipation of the testimony of Etienne Grosjean, bridegroom of the accused, who had brought the evil nature of his bride to light. The news chanters had already made him a hero of their ballads.

As Etienne lumbered through the crowd to the court house on the morning he was to testify, bystanders reached out to shake his hand or touch his clothing. A man of such courage must be the recipient of special grace.

"Do you swear by God, the Almighty, to tell this court the truth and nothing but the truth about how you came to suspect the accused, Sandrine Legrand, to be a practitioner of witchcraft?" The chief magistrate instructed the witness.

Etienne swore to do as he was told. He tried to project an air of dignity, aware that it was the crowd's prurient interest that lent his testimony an air of the sensational. The presiding magistrate asked him to state his name and the purpose of his appearance before this court.

"I am Etienne Grosjean of Bonneval," he began, his tone slow and measured as of someone reading aloud from a written statement, but who was not comfortable with the written word.

"I want to thank the honorable lords presiding over this court for the opportunity to make known the evil nature of the accused of which I personally suffered great pain and misery."

"On the last day of September of this year past," he continued after a brief pause during which he wiped what was either tears or sweat from his eyes. "The summer's harvest had been brought in—our fears of a crop failure this year because of the heavy rains early in summer, fortunately, proved unfounded, I am happy to say, the harvest was more bountiful than usual and therefore it took a little longer to gather it all. It was then that I, with the purest intentions of making this wretch my wife, entered into the state of holy matrimony with the accused, Sandrine Legrand, at the Church of Saint André of Bonneval. Our good Father Girard, the parish priest of Bonneval, who later brought the evil doings of this woman to the attention of His Holiness, the Archbishop, joined us together as man and wife."

The presiding magistrate reminded him to restrict himself to the facts as they relate to the matter under investigation. "Please, go on," he prodded him, "but you must get to the point."

"Well, apparently her oath to honor and obey her lord and master did not mean anything to her—as one might expect of the devil's brood—but I was, of course, unaware of this when I took her, unsuspecting as I was, into my house. Not that I could not have chosen any woman young or old. You might imagine what a great shock it was for me to find myself thus duped by a witch on my wedding night."

He paused and let his eyes wander along the row of magistrates on the podium. Then he turned toward the audience, carefully gauging the level of suspense his tale was creating. He coughed and cleared his throat, savoring the sweet taste of holding the packed courtroom in the palm of his hand.

"Go on my good man! When did you first suspect that the accused was a witch?" The chief magistrate prodded him again, this time with some impatience. Cat calls were heard from the gallery, an air of restlessness began to fill the courtroom.

But Etienne remained oblivious of the shifting mood around him. He resumed his testimony, still with a deliberately slow, dramatic tone. He related how the accused resisted his attempts to exercise his rights as her husband and master. When he finally had subdued her, he said, and was about to pluck the fruit that was rightfully his, he suddenly felt his lust shrinking, quite inexplicably at first, this had never happened before, but then he realized he had been placed under a spell. It became clear to him then that she was a witch and that he had been cheated and duped by Thierry Legrand, who had raised this devil's brood.

A heavy curtain of silence fell over the courtroom when Etienne Grosjean was finished. Uncomprehending what was happening, he turned toward the gallery, looking for approval, but met only empty stares from a hundred expressionless eyes—no outburst of indignation, no demands for immediate retribution, just embarrassed silence.

Earlier, the spectators, especially the women, had been moved to tears, had been outraged by stories of women dying in childbirth, of sick and deformed children, even crop failures and demented animals had aroused their ire. Wild shrieks for revenge had been heard in the courtroom. Now, these same women sat silent, their faces darkened. Deep inside, each felt the shame of Etienne Grosjean's affront against all women. No pity for the pitiless lecher.

Etienne left the witness stand like a dog doused with water. He had lost ground for reasons beyond his understanding. His testimony was, nevertheless, duly entered in the court records as evidence of guilt against the accused witch Sandrine Legrand.

Philippe had kept his eyes fixed on Sandrine during Etienne's testimony. Not once did the frozen smile leave her face. Did the memory of the events which Etienne related before the court hurt her inside? Why did she not cry out in protest? Was she as impervious to the insults of this crude rustic as she seemed?

He blamed himself for having abandoned her to all this pain and humiliation. If only he had been there in time, the whole tragedy would never have occurred, everything would have been different. But no amount of self-recrimination and regret could change the situation now. He had to save her life, at all cost, and were it at the cost of his own life.

The court reconvened in the early afternoon for the final session. Order was called in the court. The chief magistrate turned to the accused:

"Sandrine Legrand, do you make this confession of guilt of your own free will and without coercion but from a true desire to save your immortal soul from eternal damnation by beseeching our Lord and Savior Jesus Christ for forgiveness for the sins you have committed in your earthly existence? If this is so please state so before this court."

"I confess of my own free will and without coercion to being guilty of the charges brought against me."

Sandrine's voice was barely audible, it was hollow, devoid of all emotion, and without inflection. It had none of the sonority Philippe remembered so well. She continued her brief statement as if she were reciting a passage committed to memory in a language she did not understand:

"I beg forgiveness of this court, of the Holy Church, and all those to whom I have brought harm. I abjure the devil and his evil doings and commend my soul to the care of God, the Father, the Son, and the Holy Spirit. I beseech the Holy Virgin, Mother of God and Queen of Heaven to beg her Holy Son, the Lord of justice and peace, for mercy and forgiveness. May it be God's will to forgive my sins and save my soul from eternal damnation. My fate is in his hands and the hands of those appointed to carry out His will here on earth."

She remained seated while the court clerk began to read

from a scroll, purported to contain her confession. The public pronouncement of the bizarre items enumerated in this confession triggered a general hysteria in the courtroom and grotesque forms of behavior that turned the trial into a scene of mass madness.

The presiding magistrate made little effort to curb the frenzy. Men and women chanted and danced, making the sign of the cross with frantic repetition. Friars, appearing out of nowhere, wandered up and down the aisles, sprinkling holy water over the heads of the crowd, others swung vessels of burning incense back and forth to the accompaniment of Latin incantations.

One friar placed himself near the balustrade that separated the visitors' gallery from the tribunal, holding aloft a huge wooden cross in front of the clerk who was reading the confession as if to shield the flock from the evil influence that was presumed to emanate from the words.

The women in the front row gripped their rosaries in panic and horror and mumbled feverish Ave Marias and Pater Nosters.

Only the court clerk seemed undaunted. Rising with dignity to the momentous task entrusted to him, he mounted a chair, and thus looming above the commotion, he strained his voice to the utmost to make himself heard. He repeated the reading of the confession three times as was required by law:

"I, Sandrine Legrand of the village of Bonneval, hereby confess to being guilty of the maleficia brought up against me.

I confess, of my own will and without coercion, to having carried out harmful and malicious acts at the direction of the forces of evil, Satan and his minions.

I confess to having been the bride of the Evil One, the Devil himself who endowed me with power to do evil.

I confess to having attended the witches' sabbath numerous times, riding on the back of a devil, and to having committed lascivious carnality at said sabbath and other despicable and unnatural carnal acts with said and other devils.

I confess to acts of intercourse with the Archdemon himself who gained control over my will by injecting my body numerous times with his ice-cold semen.

I confess to having conspired with the Devil to bring evil to this world and to establish the Kingdom of Darkness on earth.

I confess to having been a willing tool in all these evil schemes.

I confess to the crime of ligature against my lawful husband, depriving him of the ability to exercise his conjugal rights.

I beg forgiveness of God Almighty and all those to whom I brought pain and suffering through these and all other evil deeds I perpetrated against them.

I recognize with gratitude the efforts of the confessors of the Holy Order of Dominicus to save my soul from certain eternal damnation and the benevolence of the magistrates of the city of Chartres and their kind intercession on my behalf with our Lord, Jesus Christ, his Holy Mother, and the Saints in heaven to grant me forgiveness and admit my soul to the heavenly realm upon leaving my earthly shell. May they be granted their just rewards in the heavenly Kingdom to come. Amen."

The magistrates who acted as judges deliberated but briefly. Guilty as charged was a foregone conclusion. The presiding magistrate then pronounced the accused guilty of witchcraft and of consorting with the Devil. Her soul was to be duly dispatched to meet the Divine Judge. She would be accorded the mercy of being hung by the neck before her bodily shell would be burnt at the stake and her ashes strewn to the wind.

Sandrine was allowed one last statement. Under wild shouts of approval from the crowd, she congratulated the judges on having outwitted Satan and his accomplices and thanked them for having saved her soul from eternal damnation. She was then led away by a passel of monks.

"What have they done to her that she takes all this with such calm? This whole thing is preposterous!" Philippe was stunned and enraged. So incredible was everything to him that he expected to wake up any moment from a bizarre dream.

"These were her own words, she was convicted by her own words," Robert reminded him.

"Do you realize what they must have done to her to get her to sign such a confession? You have heard of the tortures they put people through to make them confess! Who wouldn't confess to the most absurd behavior under such circumstances?" Philippe's anger grew when he saw the doubt in Robert's eyes.

"Don't say it," he warned him. "I won't permit you to say it. The whole thing is absurd, do you hear? Absurd!"

"But she confessed," Robert ventured with a faint heart. The trial had made a profound impression on him and he was utterly confused and torn between loyalty to his friend and obedience to the dictates of the law and the teachings of the Church.

"Would she face death under the odium of such an enormous lie, if indeed it is a lie?"

"But it is all a lie! What choice does she have but to admit she committed these absurdities?" Philippe clutched his friend's hands imploringly: "You cannot let me down now, please don't let me down. In the name of everything we have gone through together, you cannot forsake me. My life will not be worth living if she dies!"

Robert rose abruptly, he could not bear to see the tears in his friend's eyes. For a moment he hesitated, then he shrugged. What the hell, this was a challenge.

"Let's get to work! There's much to be done between now and tomorrow morning."

The night before the witch-burning was to live in the memory of those who were present in the town of Chartres for a long time. Joy mingled with fear and awe among the multitude roaming the streets. Undaunted by the brisk January air, huge crowds packed the streets and public places. Nobody seemed inclined to be alone that night. Rejoicing in the triumph over the forces of evil, alternated with gloom and anguish evoked by the imminence of death in their midst.

Revelers formed a huge circle around the gigantic wood pyre that was being set up in the cathedral square, stepping to mirthful rhythms that soon dissolved into a frenzied danse macabre. Hundreds of people swelled the endless torchlight processions led by Dominican friars and as the night progressed, even the friars' chants of Jubilate Exultate gave way to a somber Dies Irae.

A fine, steady snow began to fall after midnight, robing the town in virginal white. Philippe and Robert checked with their men, posted at strategic points around the town. Gaspard gave the signal that everything was ready, as they passed under the northwestern city gate. The gate would be open the next day. Mathieu, who had joined the band at Bonneval, guarded the horses.

The two friends trudged through the slush of melting snow, each one lost in thought. Philippe's thoughts went back to that other restless night, in May, now a lifetime away, after the days on the barricades, when the people of Paris celebrated their victory over their King. How fickle the masses are, he thought. How sentimental, and yet capable of such cruelty. Again it struck him how different Sandrine was from the people among whom she grew up.

Ear-piercing shrieks in an alleyway a few paces away disturbed his thoughts. The two friends followed the murderous screams and passed through the alley into a narrow square. A ghastly sight presented itself. The shrieks came from a pig tied and suspended between two poles, blood dripped from a hundred open wounds while five or six young men attacked the helpless creature with sticks and knives, egging each other on with raucous shouts.

This game of animal sacrifice was not new to the two noblemen. They had seen it in many parts of the kingdom during the carnival season, but not this early in the year. Asked about the meaning of this rite, the young men obligingly explained, they wanted to prevent the evil spirit from reentering the town after the girl's death had purified the air. They wanted to sacrifice an ox, which would be more effective because of its bigger size, but could not find one quickly enough, so the pig had to do.

How can one blame these primitive, animistic minds for their brutality and superstition? This was the only way they knew to defend themselves against the vagaries of a miserable existence. The two friends turned away, their hearts filled with disgust and pity.

The snowfall became denser, streaming from the heavens like angel's hair. The friends sought shelter inside the cathedral. A sense of comfort and security embraced them as they merged with the crowd of worshippers assembled by the warming glow of the deep hues of red and blue of the majestic stained glass windows refracting the light of a thousand candles. Nuns cloaked in long, black robes, led a prayer vigil commending the soul of the girl who was soon to depart this world to the care of the Holy Mother.

As had been their custom on the eve of a battle, the two knights knelt in front of the altar and prayed for forgiveness of their sins, inveighing God's blessing and protection for their undertaking the next morning. Philippe prayed more fervently than ever in his life, beseeching God to save the life of the innocent young woman who had fallen victim to the false beliefs of a misguided world. His forehead rested against his tightly entwined hands as if he were wrestling with the divine being like Jacob on another night of uncertainty and apprehension.

Calm finally settled over the town. By dawn, the snow had erased all traces of the nocturnal excesses of chanting and dancing in the streets as the town was draped in virginal purity. The church bells began to ring out, summoning the faithful to early morning Mass. The priests in every church in town and the Archbishop himself in the grand cathedral reminded their flock to pray for the soul of the young woman and to commend her to the Holy Father in heaven.

By eight o'clock, still in semi-darkness, a shivering human mass was out lining the streets, five, and in some places six, rows deep. Thierry and Berthe Legrand stood at the corner where the Rue des Cloîtres Notre Dame widened into the cathedral square. Thierry's arm was wrapped around his wife's shoulder as much to shield her from the frost as to console her. He had become a different man since that night a week ago when his wife had opened her heart to the young nobleman, who seemed to have such a strange interest in Sandrine. Suddenly he became aware that she had feelings, concerns, and sorrows beyond the confines of the kitchen at the inn. The anguish of losing their only child had brought them closer than they had ever been in twenty-five years of marriage.

"There she comes!" A hushed whisper ran through the crowd as the ox-drawn cart carrying the condemned maiden came into view. The screeching of the wheels on the pavement was countered by the hollow funereal din from the tower.

At first, Etienne and Berthe Legrand could not make out

their daughter's face; their view was obstructed by a huge cross carried by a monk ahead of the procession. Then the cart with its miserable cargo slowly moved closer. A flood of tears streamed down Berthe's cheeks as she gazed, still incredulous, at the human figure standing erect and immobile like a statue on the platform of the rickety cart. The flowing, lily-white gown that draped her emaciated body hardly seemed enough protection against the cold, but she seemed as oblivious of the elements as she was of the crowd. Her hands stretched out in front of her, she held a thick candle that resisted the efforts of the priest, riding next to her in the cart, to stay lit. The picture of an innocent martyr, so young and so beautiful, Berthe thought. Her only crime was the hatred she aroused for being more beautiful than any of the peasants of Bonneval. For this, she now had to pay with her life. Was there no justice in this world?

Suddenly, she heard Thierry say: "Isn't it too early in the year for carnival games? Young people nowadays have no respect. They play their pranks anytime they feel like it."

A group of about five masked young men in dunces caps jumped into the street, right in front of the monk with the cross they engaged in a game of fool's chase. The procession came to a halt. What happened next, happened with such lightning speed, the onlookers hardly became aware of it until it was all over.

The town guards who brought up the rear of the cortège went to the front to see what was causing the delay. At this moment, two men on horseback, masked in the manner of brigands, broke through the crowd and approached the cart, before anybody could make a move, they had disappeared again. When the onlookers turned their attention back to the ox-cart, the condemned prisoner was no longer visible on the platform.

Only Berthe understood immediately what had happened.

"Oh it's him, it's him!" She fell around Thierry's neck like a young girl in love. The outburst lasted only a moment, then realizing all that could still go wrong, the two knelt on the rough cobblestones and prayed for the safety of their child.

Eyewitness accounts differed so greatly, they may as well have been describing different incidents. One woman insisted she saw the girl in the white robe levitate and ascend to heaven. Others swore they saw her being carried off by a huge bird, and still others wanted to have recognized a band of angels. Another swore the condemned rode off on a broom flanked by a horde of flying devils.

The most likely, but least believed version, had it that one of the riders, who emerged from the crowd, knocked down the priest on the cart, seized the doomed girl, and handed her to his companion. Both then turned and charged through the mass of people who were forced to seek cover to avoid being trampled. When the bandits, or whoever they were, reached the northwestern ramparts, they thundered through the wide-open gate and were swallowed up in the open countryside by a cloud of dust, the gate closing behind them.

In the commotion of the appearance of the two brigands on horseback, nobody paid any attention to the five dunces who disappeared into the crowd. At the southern gate, Mathieu held the horses ready. Gaspard bolted the northwestern gate, stalling an immediate pursuit by the town's guardsmen. Then he continued south where he joined his companions.

The fugitives with the girl meanwhile pressed on with their flight in a northwesterly direction. They did not come to rest until late at night when they entered the Carmelite convent of Sainte Hélène in Normandy.

CHAPTER 7

Catherine de Treffort lay prostrate at the steps of the altar in the cloister chapel—weeping softly, the tranquility of her mind shattered. The serene calm that streamed from the dim, ruby glare of the eternal lamp belied the turmoil of the Abbess's soul. She remained motionless until dawn broke through the narrow windows framed with compressed Romanesque arches. Hiding her melancholy from the world behind a stern façade, she rose to begin the daily routine of guiding the convent's affairs.

For two months, the same scene had been enacted night after night in the dark shadows of the chapel vault. For two months, the Abbess had been stealing away from her cell to seek refuge in prayer and meditation from the furies that tormented her body and soul. But for two months her most fervent prayers to be relieved of the anguish that had become her lot, from the maddening desires that consumed her body, had remained unanswered.

Disquiet had invaded her cloistered existence on a cold January night when her brother Philippe and his friend, Robert, Count de la Croix, had appeared at the gate of the convent of Sainte Hélène. In their company was a peasant girl, in terrible condition and near death. How could she have refused them entry and shelter? No, she had gladly extended the convent's hospitality and medical care for the girl. Three days later, Robert had continued on his journey homeward, leaving behind Philippe cleaving to the girl's bedside.

Philippe would have remained there day and night, had the abbess not invoked strict order regulations that male visitors had to be quartered overnight in the guest house outside the inner gate. The girl's life had hung in the balance for several weeks. So critical and uncertain was her condition that she called a priest to dispense the Holy Sacrament of Extreme Unction.

The fifteen Carmelite sisters at the convent took turns in keeping a prayer vigil outside the infirmary door. The order's infirmatress, Sister Claire, applied her art of herbal dressings to the wounds on the girl's arms and legs—cuts and bruises so hideous as if she had been mauled by a wild animal. Whether it was Sister Claire's herbal magic or the prayers were heard, slowly, ever so slowly, the girl's wounds began to heal. The fever subsided and the martyred body regenerated.

Catherine remembered her discomfort at her brother's profuse outpouring of gratitude—kneeling before her and kissing the seams of her gown under tears with an ardor that frightened her. Startled by such a display of emotion, she had cautioned him that the greatest difficulty still lay ahead.

Although the girl's physical condition had become stable, she still had not given any sign of awareness of the world around her. Loving care was needed to lift her from the lingering state of shock, maybe a miracle, she sensed only Philippe could bring about.

Her sense of Christian charity did not permit her to ask questions at first. It did not matter who the girl was and how she had gotten into such a battered condition, her first concern was to save a human life. But she was sure, and so was Sister Claire whose counsel she sought, that only the most severe and prolonged infliction of torture could have caused the gashing wounds and red scars. Her suspicions were aroused when news reached the convent of a condemned witch who had been snatched from the flames of the stake at Chartres—some eyewitnesses swore they saw her levitating toward the heavens and others were sure she had been abducted by a band of devils.

For days, the Abbess contemplated her dilemma. If this girl was indeed the convicted witch, how could she go against the dictates of the Church and harbor a heretic? But then, how could she refuse aid to a human being in such obvious distress? And what about her duty to her brother? It may be true that a nun's first order of obedience belongs to the Church, but her rational mind had never accepted as valid the Church doctrine that equated witchcraft with heresy, nor could she condone the practice of torture to extract confessions. She found this very difficult to reconcile with Christ's teachings of love and compassion. To bring clarity into the matter, she finally confronted her brother directly.

"My Lord," she addressed him more formally than usual, obviously anxious to distance herself emotionally from him. "I believe you might be interested to know that for the last few weeks the whole Kingdom of France, or at least so it seems, has been talking about nothing but the miraculous rescue of a witch at Chartres. The rescue took place just as she was led to the stake."

"Why are you telling me this, my dear sister? Why do you think I should concern myself with idle gossip? And why should you?"

He spoke softly. Maybe the lack of sleep had dulled his alertness, for he seemed not all alarmed by what she had said.

"I think you should know that the teaching of the Church is explicit on this point—witchcraft is a form of heresy."

"Do you believe in witchcraft?" he asked gently.

"The teaching of the Church is clear . . ."

"No, no!" He waved his arms vehemently. "I know what the Church says. What I want to know is what you think—whether you, Catherine de Treffort, my sister, whether you believe in witches. Do you?"

She looked at him in pained silence, searching for an answer. Finally, she had to admit: "No, no I don't believe in witches or witchcraft, nor do I believe in inflicting pain."

"Thank you, my most noble sister and friend!" He embraced her and thereafter the subject was never raised again. If the Church authorities were to hear about this, she would have to answer to charges of complicity in a crime. Strangely enough, she found it very difficult to feel guilty.

One day in early March, the Abbess entered the infirmary to check on the patient and chanced upon a scene of such rapturous joy, she withdrew quietly.

She was, of course, elated to see the girl had recovered. But the sight of Sandrine clinging to Philippe, holding his head and covering his entire face with passionate kisses and proclaiming: "Philippe, my dear Philippe! I was right, I knew you would come! You are my savior and I love you forever with all my heart!" was more than her tortured heart could bear.

Gratification at seeing the girl so full of life gave way to a sense of consternation at the intimacy that seemed to exist between the two. It was true, that more than once she had professed egalitarian leanings. Human life was of equal value to Christ the Savior. But something in her aristocratic upbringing asserted itself and revolted against such a transgression of the proper distinction between the orders of society.

This is how she explained her shock to herself. Deep inside, she knew that this was neither the only nor the real reason for her intense discomfort. She knew that what disturbed her was not so much that her brother was in love with this girl, her brother has had many passing fancies. No, it was the sight of a man and a woman in a sensual embrace that upset her inner balance and set her heart into turmoil as she had never experienced before.

Catherine quietly left the lovers to themselves, glad they had not noticed her presence. A rush of blood warmed her rounded cheek. Fortunately, they were partly covered by her veil. She hurried down the hallways, quickening her step when she felt unobserved. When she reached the solitude of her cell, she fell on her knees beside her cot, wringing her hands in desperate prayer. More fervently than ever she begged to be relieved from her obsession.

Prayer was still the most soothing balm on her soul. She soon regained enough of her composure to sit back and contemplate the strange sensations tugging at her. On reflection, she had to admit that she knew very little about her brother. Their lives had rarely touched though he was only two years older than she. They were reared in separate spheres, different parts of the same castle—he to be groomed to continue the family tradition of martial virtue, she to be groomed for the life of a lady of the manor. Her world was indoors, in the women's wing; her days were spent in docile, sedentary activities. Her brother's world, from early childhood, was outdoors, a world of physical activity.

When he was old enough to join the war, she had taken pride in stories of the League soldiers fighting for the Holy Church. She pictured her brother among the soldiers. He was to her the scion of an ancient noble family, a gallant swordsman, perhaps an amorous adventurer, but most of all he was a defender of the Apostolic faith—a picture that would fit any number of young noblemen in France—but she had no clear notion of what kind of person her brother was.

How could she have guessed that he, the noble Lord of Salignac, would risk his life to save a common peasant? He was a puzzle to her. The long days and weeks of anguish when he clung to the girl's bedside, the tears of joy at the first sign that she would live—this was not a man in lusty pursuit of a beautiful peasant, this was a man deeply in love.

Love! She wondered what it was like to be in love. Was it love that had possessed her ever since she had seen Robert de la Croix again? Was it the devil's snares? Was it love that fanned her maddening longing to be near him, to touch him, to be touched by him? Was it love that caused the most unfamiliar sensations to flow through her body, quicken the rush of blood at the mere thought of him, the mere mention of his name?

Robert had departed from the convent after he was assured that Philippe, who was near collapse, would get to rest for a while at the convent. As he told Catherine, Philippe had not yet fully recovered from the effects of his long captivity at Blois. Three days, they had spent close together, shared their concern for the one both loved. Three days, that marked the beginning of her obsession with Robert de la Croix.

The picture of his boyish good looks, the cherubic face, not even his scruffy beard could hide, the unkempt reddish-brown hair, his broad, muscular body was forever before her. She remembered every detail of every moment they spent together, every word that passed between them. She remembered his every gesture, no matter how trifling. Everything that happened between them during those three days was indelibly imprinted on her mind.

Robert did not say much about the girl, except that he was sure if she were to die, Philippe's life would be ended. He spoke more openly about Philippe's physical condition. One evening, during a quiet walk in the snow-covered cloister garden, he recounted her brother's capture by royal guards, the King's treacherous designs to make him out a traitor to the League, and the months of imprisonment in the dungeon at Blois. Robert had been surprised that she had not heard of her brother's ordeal.

She tried to explain that a nun maintains only scant contact with her family and the outside world once she has taken her vows. She remembered his glum look as he nodded his understanding. The conversation then returned to Philippe and the girl.

Robert's words kept echoing through her mind: "You see, my dear Sister Catherine, your brother was kept alive in his dungeon by his love for this peasant girl. I don't profess to understand this, but isn't it marvelous what miracles love can perform!"

"But, my dear Count, I am surprised you seem to think this whole thing to be more than just a passing fancy on my brother's part, surely it is not more than a fleeting infatuation," she interjected.

"I wish it were so," Robert replied. "But I have observed him closely. From the day he met her he became a different man, sometimes he seems like a stranger. No, Sister Catherine, whether we like it or not, this is no passing fancy—this woman is Philippe de Treffort's fate."

"But you must consider the girl's youth and station. Besides, Philippe is betrothed to Louise de Montreuil, as you well know."

Never will she forget the long, painful silence that descended between them like an opaque curtain, the wounded look in the watery blue eyes that held her suspended. She did not dare turn away.

Then, almost inaudibly, but clear as the sound of bells, he whispered: "Betrothals can be broken, as you well know, my dear Sister Catherine."

She was still searching for an answer when the tocsin sounded the closing of the cloister portal for the night. Their exchange ended and he dutifully retired to the guest quarters outside, leaving behind a gaping emptiness that threatened to swallow her.

It had never occurred to her that he should care much about the marriage arrangement that had been concocted between their fathers when he was seven and she was five. She never regarded him as her fiancé. He was her brother's friend, his companion in arms. She saw very little of either of them, sequestered as she was in the women's wing of the chateau. Occasionally, she would be taking some fresh air on the balcony with the ladies of her company, and she would catch a glimpse of Philippe and Robert practicing fighting on horseback or archery, or some other sport, in the yard below, and she might then point out Robert de la Croix as her future husband just to make her friends jealous.

Her education was to prepare her for the duties of a lady. She was instructed in needlework, especially embroidery, an occupation she thoroughly detested, but which took up much of the time of women of her station. She was also instructed in courtly manners, in singing and dancing, and how to make herself pleasant, yet unobtrusive, in the company of gentlemen. All of this interested her very little. With great eagerness, she engaged in reading and writing and she progressed far beyond the rudiments which were deemed sufficient for young ladies to follow the liturgy and prayers of the church service and to write letters and poetry. There was very little physical activity, and Catherine's governesses had their hands full taming her explosive temperament. In the end, they despaired of ever instilling in her the virtues of placid compliance and amiable subservience.

Her indomitable nature showed itself early when no manner of restriction could deter her from occasional outings on horseback in the course of which she would befriend the daughters of the peasants of the manor or dispense generous alms to the sick and the poor of the villages on her father's domain. In her defense, she would point out that dispensing alms was part of a lady's basic duties. The turning point in Catherine's life came when was ten. She accompanied her mother on a visit to a nearby convent one day to deliver clothing and food for the poor to the sisters. The company of the nuns was so pleasing to her, she stole away from her mother, entered the dormitory, and impulsively put on a veil she found there. She decided right then that she would enter the order and insisted on staying. Her mother's entreaties to leave with her met with stubborn resistance. Only after the Duke d'Evreux arrived at the convent in the company of armed guards was her resoluteness broken, for the moment.

Although she gave in that time, she startled her parents with the announcement that she had entered into a mystical marriage with the Lord, Jesus Christ, and that she would serve him through a life of poverty and prayer and service to the less fortunate of his creatures. The Duke was furious and to keep her from further contact with the nunnery, he confined her to the women's wing. For the next five years, she was a prisoner in her father's house.

If he thought he could break her will, he had miscalculated. On reaching fifteen, she declared that she would from now on consecrate herself to the life of a nun. He was so awed by her tenacity that he became convinced that it was truly God's will that inspired her and he permitted her to take the veil. Some delicate negotiations preceded to obtain release from her betrothal. Robert, who hardly knew the girl, certainly did not seem to mind having this bond dissolved.

After the requisite trial period, Catherine took the vows of poverty, obedience, and chastity. Due to her social standing and learning combined with great religious fervor and devotion to the communal life, she advanced quickly within the convent hierarchy. At the age of nineteen, she was elected the youngest Abbess in the Carmelite order. Rumors that her father's influence had something to do with it were quickly stilled by the excellence with which she performed her duties.

Catherine was a happy nun. She never regretted having renounced a world about which she knew very little. She found fulfillment within the secure confines of the cloister walls, her natural impetuosity was soon harnessed in the service of God. Her only aspiration was to undertake some day a pilgrimage to the Holy See in Rome, a wish that had to be postponed as long as war raged in the Kingdom of France.

Now her certitude, her serenity was broken, everything was suddenly in doubt. It seemed foolish for her to have believed the convent walls could shield her from the temptations of the temporal world. Was she guilty of overweening pride and God was punishing her? Would she ever again find that peace of mind, the absolute certainty that had inspired her when she took the veil? Was it fate that had brought her together with Robert de la Croix after so many years? Could it be that she had been too hasty in her youthful enthusiasm when she took the vows that barred her from all other options for her future even earlier than was required by the order? Questions, questions, questions battered her mind and she was at a total loss for answers.

A cold shiver ran down her spine. No, she would not permit herself to become entangled in a web of doubts and regrets. Robert de la Croix was only a temporary obsession. Surely, God was testing her and she will prove herself worthy of him. A sudden resolve entered her spirit. She would face the crisis head-on and be it the design of the devil to lead her astray or God's way of testing her fortitude, she would overcome it.

Her first order of business was to turn her attention and energy again toward guiding the affairs of the convent that had been slipping from her hands during the past two months. But before anything, she would have a private talk with her brother whose continued presence inside the cloistered sanctum was disruptive to the communal life of the sisters.

Later in the day, she requested her brother's presence in the refectory. She found it difficult to assume a stance of moral superiority since she no longer felt free of guilt and carnal desire, but as Abbess, it was her duty to guard the good of the community.

"I am very pleased to see Your Lordship looking so well," she began cautiously, hoping that the tremor in her voice was not detectable. "I have also been informed that the peasant girl has made remarkable strides toward recovery."

"Please, don't call her the peasant girl, her name is Sandrine, Sandrine Legrand." Philippe was unable to conceal his irritation at his sister's formality and particularly the condescension with which she spoke of Sandrine. He sensed this conference could only mean one thing, he was about to be banished from paradise. Not wanting to seem ungrateful for all she had done, he moderated his tone: "There is no need to address me thus formally. I am forever indebted to you and the venerable sisters of this convent, if I have offended you in any way, it was inadvertent and I beg your forgiveness."

His contriteness made Catherine uncomfortable. It would make telling him what she had to that much more difficult.

Still haltingly, she continued: "My dear brother, I was more than happy to extend a hand and provide shelter and care in your hour of desperate need. But now, this need no longer seems to exist and it is becoming difficult to justify your continued presence within this convent."

She began to pace back and forth in the Treffort manner of dealing with emotional strain.

"You must understand that as abbess of this convent I am responsible for maintaining order." She came to a halt in front of the crucifix and sent an entreating glance toward the man on the cross. "I cannot permit these cloisters to be used as a . . . a love nest. Can you understand this?"

"I understand very well." He bowed his head like a penitent sinner. He knew that his stay had to end eventually. He also understood that his presence put his sister in a delicate position.

"I have been guilty of indiscretion and beg your forgiveness." Philippe fell on his knees, his hands held out before him. "Maybe the saintliness and purity of your heart will help you understand a worldly man like your brother whose only excuse for his thoughtlessness is that he is in love."

"Please, don't call me saintly!" Catherine drew back in fright. "I am not sitting in judgment of you or your actions. I don't pretend to know whether a love such as yours is sinful or not. Only the Almighty can decide such a matter. But the life of the convent cannot be disrupted."

"Then, if I may indulge Your Ladyship just more time, beg for one more favor." Philippe rose, elated and encouraged by his sister's words. "If you will send for a priest, Sandrine and I shall be married tonight. We have no greater desire than to be bound together in Holy Matrimony forever."

Catherine's face turned ashen. Her hands reached behind her, searching for something to lean on. Philippe feared she might faint. When she finally recovered her voice, her tone was ice cold.

"You cannot be serious. Think of our family! You cannot expect such a, such a . . ."

"Common peasant to be accepted?" he finished her sentence with a derisive hiss. "Where is your sense of justice, Catherine? Doesn't the Lord, Jesus Christ, love all God's creatures equally?"

"This is not a point of theology!" Catherine's voice took on an unaccustomed shrillness. "You know very well that the question is one of duty and family loyalty—this is a matter of going against tradition, against a God-given order, and besides, whether you are going to break a sacred promise made to another noble family."

"Ah, so that's what worries you! Funny, I didn't think you of all people had the right to lecture anybody on the sacredness of betrothals!"

Catherine felt as if her heart had been wrested from her chest. But she did not retreat. With the fury of a wounded animal she lashed out at him: "If I broke a promise, it was to dedicate myself to a higher purpose, to the service of God. Never did I besmirch the honor of my family. My motivation was pure love for our Lord, Jesus Christ, not base carnal lust."

Philippe felt sorry that the argument had gotten out of hand. He had hurt her more deeply than he ever intended. He had hoped that Catherine of all people would understand his love for Sandrine and recognize the extraordinary qualities in this humble girl. Tears of shame streamed down his face and he again fell on his knees before his sister and sobbing he buried his face in the folds of her habit.

"You must love her very much." Catherine placed her hand gently on his head. She had never seen him weep.

"More than anything in this world! I could not bear to lose her again."

"I understand," she said. Never would he know how well she felt his pain. "But you must promise to speak with the Duke and Duchess and obtain a formal release from your vows with Louise before you get married."

This he gladly promised to do. Happy to have found an ally, he felt like lifting her and swinging her around, but he restrained his exuberance, unsure that such demonstrativeness would be welcome.

"I know you will love Sandrine when you get to know her better. I am certain the two of you will become friends."

"I love her already like a sister and I hope we shall have the opportunity to become more closely acquainted. Please, now you must go, I must tend to other matters."

He was about to take his leave but turned back once more.

"My dear Catherine, please permit me to indulge your generosity just this one more time. I am awaiting the arrival of Robert with news of the war. Please permit me to stay here until then. If it turns out that I have to rejoin the League army before everything is settled, promise you will take care of her. She has no place to go, she is all alone in the world. Within these cloister walls, she will be safe."

"In the name of the Lord, Our Savior, and His Holy Mother, I promise to guard her like a precious stone." She had quickly turned away, afraid he might perceive her palpitating heart. "When she is well enough, however, she will have to be transferred to the guest house. The rules do not permit lay persons to be housed within the convent's sanctum. You may, of course, stay for the time being, but I am counting on your discretion. You really must leave me now."

A sigh of relief escaped her lips when she finally heard the door close behind him.

Catherine leaned against the desk to keep from falling. She clutched her throat, gasping as if something was suffocating her. Robert would be back soon. Was this the reason she went back on her determination to send Philippe away now? Was this the reason she made herself an accessory to sin? The ground began to move under her. When she awoke she was stretched out on the floor in the refectory. How long she had been unconscious she could not tell, but, thank God, nobody seemed to have been looking for her, and her miserable state was not discovered.

CHAPTER 8

The opening and closing of the infirmary door roused Sandrine from a long, peaceful slumber. Without opening her eyes, she sensed Philippe's presence, his light step, the distinct scent of his body. Then she felt herself enclosed in his arms and she gently leaned against his chest.

Never had she known such bliss. The past weeks since she had returned from the darkness of the night that had enveloped her had been like a beautiful dream. From the moment she regained consciousness and beheld Philippe's beloved features, the horrors of the past became a distant memory of another, far-off existence. At first, she thought she had died and was in heaven. For where else could she awaken to the smiling, loving face with the warm, kind eyes, the image she had carried in her heart through the most execrable hours of her ordeal? But then she realized that it was neither a dream nor another world. Sister Claire's herbal potions did their part of healing her body. But Philippe's love healed her spirit.

Soon she was taking short walks in the cloister garden, supported on Philippe's arm for the energy still drained quickly from her. With the coming of spring and nature's rejuvenation, she too regenerated, and gradually, but steadily, her body filled with vigor and strength.

On Easter Sunday, amidst the rebirth, fields and meadows bloomed under a kindly resplendent sun, Sandrine undertook her first outing beyond the cloister. She attended Mass at the parish church in the company of the Carmelite sisters and since she was wearing the habit of a novice, she was hardly distinguishable from them. How her life had changed since the Easter season of only a year ago! It was then that Philippe had first entered her life. Like the Lord, Jesus Christ, she was martyred and reborn, resurrected from a dark crypt of suffering and humiliation.

Philippe was seated in the aristocrats' pew across the way. She returned his caressing glance, their eyes rested in each other heedless of the world. Gone was the time when she sat with her head lowered among the peasants, gone the shy, hunted outcast. Gone were the stares of instinctual distrust of everybody that had clouded her face. Love made her glow. Playful and almost carefree she moved among the nuns.

Philippe studied her face. It seemed to him that she was more beautiful than ever, a more mature beauty, but maybe for that reason even more captivating. The lily-white habit of a novice and the winged white bonnet that covered her cropped hair made her look angelic. He almost expected her to ascend into heaven at any moment.

Waiting impatiently for Mass to end and even before the last peal of the bell, Philippe left. He met her with two sturdy Percheron horse a short while later at the steps of the church.

"Commandeered from the convent's stable," he explained in response to her quizzical look.

He lifted her onto one of the horses, then mounted the other and off they rode into a Norman countryside ablaze in the colors of spring. Life brimmed all around. They made their way through the streets of the town in a steady trot, and then, once in the open field, they stirred the horses into a breathtaking gallop.

Sandrine drank in the sensation of unrestrained freedom. This is what she wanted—to be free, free from the shackles that had bound her all her life. She led the race over softly rolling, emerald hills dotted with rows upon rows of apple trees ready to burst into bloom. At last, they paused on top of a hill that afforded a splendid view of the river valley and the grand sweep of sparkling white chalk cliffs on the opposite bank. They dismounted and holding each other embraced, they gazed breathlessly with awe at the valley below while their bodies soaked up the warming rays of the brilliant spring sun.

This was Philippe's home territory. Only a few hours' ride away was the family's domain. This was the land of his childhood, the place where he had grown into manhood. The beauty of the land, its rich soil, the traditions of its people, its folklore and legends were all a part of him. A warm sense of peace and home filled him. With Sandrine nestling against him, life, the world, seemed perfect—the war was far removed, in another place from which they seemed to have escaped forever.

Holding her close, he pointed to a massive fortress, a citadel that rose majestically from a ragged promontory that forced the river into a sharp bend.

"There is Château Gaillard!" Philippe said with pride. "A fortress that goes back to the time of Richard the Lion-Hearted and King Philippe-Auguste. The inhabitants of the surrounding villages and towns still tell some fantastic stories about its history. Flights of fancy are often hard to distinguish from actual events."

Sandrine's curiosity was aroused. She had never seen such a grand structure and she insisted on learning more about it.

They settled on the ground and he began: "The fortress, although it is said to be impregnable, was once taken by storm, only a few years after it had been built by the English king whom they call the Lion-Hearted. At that time Normandy was a possession of the English crown—England had been conquered by the Normans, but be that as it may. . . The story that is still told around here—and there is no reason to doubt its truth—is of a great tragedy that occurred during the reign of Philippe-Auguste. The kings of France disputed the English crown's right to the province. The conflict caused much suffering for the inhabitants of Petit-Andelys, a small town north of the fortress, but it was a moment of great triumph for France."

"Now isn't that a familiar story—a great victory achieved at the expense of the common people!" Sandrine vented her indignation.

"If you want me to tell the story, you must be quiet and save your comments for later," he berated her. "Or I won't go on."

"Oh, please, please!" she begged, clapping her hands playfully in mock imitation of a small child bent on having its way. "I promise to listen carefully. I won't say another word."

"Very well then. As I said, the fortress was built by the English king, Richard the Lion-Hearted. Normandy was then a possession of the English crown, but the French kings were determined to make Normandy part of France. So Richard, fearing an attack by Philippe-Auguste, who was King of France then, built this formidable fortress, and as you can see he chose a perfect strategic spot.

After Richard died, his brother, King John, a greedy but not very clever man, made the fateful mistake of abducting the betrothed of a great French vassal. Philippe-Auguste lost no time in using this as an excuse to lay siege to the English bastion. This was in the year 1203. French troops occupied the town of Petit-Andelys. The inhabitants who did not know what to expect from the French soldiers sought refuge inside the château. But the beleaguered governor was unwilling to feed so many non-combatants and expelled them from inside the walls. About twelve hundred defenseless women and children, as well as some of the old and infirm, were caught in the crossfire of volleys of arrows from the French attackers and showers of stones hurled down by the English. Mercilessly embattled from both sides, the miserable band took shelter in a little valley—you can't see it from here—it was located exactly between the castle and the French lines."

Philippe paused and looked at Sandrine who had been following his tale intently, while the furrows of her brow were deepening.

"So what happened then?" she demanded impatiently.

"Do you want to hear it? It is too sad a story and I don't want to spoil our day."

"I do want to hear it. I promise nothing will spoil this day, but I do want to hear it."

"There was no shelter from the elements, no food, only grass. The people's misery was so great that half of them died of starvation and disease, others went insane." He paused again before continuing with a heavy sigh.

"To this day, the people in this area lower their voices when they speak of the despair of the survivors, who are said to have devoured a baby that was born to a pitiable woman just then. They might all have died had it not been for Philippe-Auguste, who chanced to encounter the wretched remnant huddled under the wall. He was moved to pity, so the saying goes, and had them guided through French lines to safety. Eventually, he stormed the fortress and wrested it from the English."

Sandrine had instinctively pulled away from him while he spoke the last words. She crossed her arms tightly in front of her as if she was overcome by a chill. Philippe got up and patted the horses, annoyed that she seemed to take this ancient tale so much to heart. He blamed himself for even bringing it up. But then she had promised that she would let nothing come between them and all it took was this silly centuries-old tale to put a chill between them.

"Sandrine, you promised!" he pleaded.

"I know. But I am stunned by this story. It may have happened long ago, but it could happen now. It's so typical how the common people always have to bear the brunt of suffering and injustice, especially in war. Through no fault of their own, they always get caught in the conflicts of the powerful. Look what is happening in France right now! War, nothing but war and destruction, for who knows what reason, what purpose! How can we find happiness if we care nothing about the cruelty and injustice in the world?"

"Who are you, Sandrine?" he wondered aloud.

"What do you mean? Don't you know?" She was bewildered by his question which did not seem to have anything to do with what she had just said.

"What I mean is that never have I heard a woman of any station, high or low, express such thoughtfulness. Most people look out for their happiness and leave the worries about the world's woes to someone else."

"Are you saying that because I am a woman, I should not concern myself with the affairs of this world? You think because I am a woman I should be thoughtless, selfish, shallow, uncaring? I haven't heard of many men, low born or high, who show much concern for the well-being of the people. From what I have heard, war is nothing but a chivalrous exercise, a struggle for power and wealth to you gentlemen of birth and rank! It is the women who suffer the loss of husbands and sons, the children who are orphaned and go hungry."

Sandrine's voice had risen furiously. She seemed to have gotten completely carried away by the flow of her argument, enamored with her haranguing as if she were exhorting a disgruntled crowd, seemingly unaware of the feelings her words aroused in Philippe.

She did not come to her senses until he finally grabbed her by the arms and shouted: "You are barking up the wrong tree! I am already convinced."

"You are hurting me!" she screamed. Quickly, he let go of her.

The picture of their first encounter suddenly appeared before him—an incensed Thierry twisting her arm. The thought that she was casting him in the role of this uncouth peasant was thoroughly distasteful to him. Yet, for the first time, he felt he understood why the innkeeper had lost his temper. Sandrine could be quite infuriating.

"So, you seem to think you know it all—all the questions and the answers as well. Don't you?" he lashed out. "You seem to think you know what battle is all about—all glamour and games—and the soldiers are nothing but insensitive clods, heedless of the devastation and suffering they cause. Have you ever tried to put yourself in the place of those who not only have to take part in the slaughter but who daily face the possibility of becoming the next corpse? Do you have any idea of how it feels to carry the stench of death in one's nostrils, day and night? Do you have any idea what it is like to be haunted by dreams of disemboweled bodies, agonizing screams of the wounded, the maimed, and the dying? Sure, after a while the senses become somewhat blunted, the horrors become commonplace, and even the stench of decaying flesh can fade. One can tell oneself a thousand times that all this is for a higher purpose, and maybe some succeed in duping themselves. Believe me, many of us will never be able to still the nagging doubts, doubts about whether so much suffering is God's will for the sake of his everlasting glory."

Philippe had turned his back to Sandrine, shouting, wrenching, unburdening his soul of years of unalleviated pain. Then there was silence between them.

Sandrine was too stunned to speak. How thoughtless she had been. What on earth had possessed her to hurt the one human being in the world who had given so much love to her? She moved toward him. Leaning her head against his back, she enfolded him in her arms.

"Please forgive me," she whispered. She wanted to console him for all the evil in the world as he had once comforted her in the cellar of the inn at Bonneval.

His anger began to melt. He nodded his head, remaining motionless in her embrace for a good, long while, savoring the warmth of her body that was seeping into his. Then he slowly turned toward her, without losing body contact, their lips met in a long, passionate kiss.

"I would never want you to be less caring than you are," he whispered while he gently removed her nun's bonnet. Her hair was still sparse, grown to about ear's length, giving her a boyish look.

"Of all the things I love about you, this is what I love best," he declared solemnly, "the compassion and pity you hold in your heart for those who suffer indignity and injustice. This makes you the special person you are."

"Look who is being silly now!" She laughed the gurgling laughter he loved so much. She pulled away from him and started to run down the sloping meadow toward the edge of the river. He hurried after her, pretending to have trouble keeping up with her, but when she slackened for a moment, he overtook her as she reached the plain near the river's edge and wrestled her to the ground.

"This is unfair! I can't run in this nun's habit!" she protested.

"Then let's get rid of this cumbersome garb!" He began pulling at the coarse-spun garment.

All the woes in the world melted away on this afternoon of unbound love. A kind nature looked on benevolently as the lovers drank deeply from the cup of oblivion, recapturing, again and again, the magic of being one in sublime embrace.

The afternoon merged with the early evening and a blood-red sun painted the chalk cliffs in a brilliant coral as it sank slowly into the river bed. The lovers, leaning against each other in entranced repose, feasted their eyes on the majestic spectacle.

How different was this Feast of the Resurrection from the one only a year ago! In her most vivid fantasies, Sandrine could not have imagined that she would be free, free from the shackles of village life, free from gossip and ill-will, free from fanaticism, superstition, and above all, free to love and be loved. Nobody would be awaiting their return, no evil rumors would attend their absence.

Their idyllic tryst was disturbed unceremoniously only by the almost simultaneous growling of their stomachs, reminding them that they both were ravenously hungry. Since it was already too late for the communal supper at the convent, they set out to seek the hospitality of an inn in the nearby village of Saint Martin le Beau.

A festive crowd of villagers was gathered at the Auberge au Coq d'Or, celebrating the Resurrection of Christ, the Savior, by consuming inordinate quantities of chitterlings and the Norman specialty of tripe braised in cider, passed with yeast cakes in the shape of the paschal lamb. All this was downed with huge amounts of apple cider and beer. Suddenly, the boisterous gathering fell silent, jaws dropped, and all eyes were fixed on the entrance to the inn.

The two strangers who had just then entered were a most unusual pair. The gentleman, elegant though somewhat ruffled, dressed all in black, a satin doublet with white open collar, velvet leggings, on his head an unadorned black velvet cap, was obviously a high-ranking nobleman. But what aroused the guests' curiosity most, was the young woman who leaned on his arm the way young lovers do. What made this sight so remarkable was that she was robed in the white habit of a Carmelite nun, but the cheerful, worldly glow in her eyes was not at all in keeping with the inward-turned, dignified manner one would expect of a religious.

The gentleman, who was greeted by the innkeeper with obligatory subservience, commanded the host to have someone look after the horses, and after a brief exchange, in the course of which the gentleman was observed to slip what looked like two gold crowns into the innkeeper's palm, the pair was escorted to an alcove adjacent to the main hall where a wooden partition shielded them from the curious stares of the onlookers.

Soon a steady stream of delicacies moved from the kitchen to the alcove. The innkeeper quickly scrounged together the best of what his cellar had to offer. For hors d'oeuvres, generous portions of foie gras followed with a steaming tureen of chicken vegetable potage and partridge pie. Several types of meat were already roasting on the spit over the fireplace since this was no ordinary Sunday. The pièce de résistance consisted of an assortment of meats and poultry—roast leg of lamb, chicken laced with truffles, wild turkey, and quails. Cream tarts and special Easter confectioneries made up the dessert.

Jugs filled with the innkeeper's choicest wine, the kind he usually kept under lock and key, accompanied the sumptuous meal. This must be indeed a most generous lord, for in the apple-growing region of Normandy the traditional drink was cider and apple brandy, wine was an expensive item since it had to be brought from more southerly parts of the Kingdom.

After the first excitement had worn off, the guests returned to their activities. Some were engrossed in rolling dice, others in a card or board game. From time to time a blithesome burst of laughter would remind the villagers of the presence of the strangers. The vivacious giggling soprano accompanied by a zestful baritone did not fail to raise eyebrows and cause exchanges of knowing glances, for only a man and a woman in love could express such harmonious joy.

As during a return a year earlier but in a different place and under different circumstances, the bell in the church tower announced the hour of midnight when the two riders entered the outer courtyard of the convent. After considerable time, their ringing was answered and the gate opened. The two entered arm in arm pulling the horses behind them. Sandrine, who was not used to heavy wine, bubbled over with intoxicated laughter. She also had never in her life eaten so much and felt she was splitting in the seams.

When they entered the inner courtyard, a figure stepped out

from the shadow of the wall. The Abbess's face glowed with ghostly sternness in the moonlight, but nothing betrayed the frustration of hours of nervous waiting for the pair's return.

"My dear child," she addressed Sandrine stiffly, "since you no longer require the care of the infirmatress, we have prepared a room for you in the guest house where you may make yourself at home for the remainder of your stay with us. We shall also have to get you more befitting clothes. Since I am responsible for the conduct of the sisters of this convent, you will understand that I cannot permit rumors to circulate that my nuns are cavorting around the countryside and feast at local taverns in the company of noblemen."

Turning to Philippe, she added not without a note of irony: "You see, my dear brother, news travels fast in these parts too."

Sandrine felt singularly unaffected by the rebuke. She was too exhausted and too intoxicated with wine and happiness to reply. All she longed for was sleep. Only briefly did the thought cross her mind that someone had been waiting after all and that someone had been spreading rumors about them. But nothing in this world could cloud her happiness on this day.

Not wanting to appear ungrateful to the Abbess, she kneeled to kiss her hand and asked her forgiveness if she had unwittingly given offense. Catherine motioned her to rise. She had taken quite a liking to the girl and admired her uninhibited, vivacious spirit. She acknowledged Sandrine's apology and added with a note of rebuke toward Philippe: "Of course, it is always up to the gentleman to take care not to compromise a lady's honor."

Before Philippe could protest and assure her that his love for Sandrine was in no way like the frivolous love games popular among the ladies and gentlemen at the courts, Catherine decreed they all must retire since the hour was very late, but she would like a word with her brother after morning Mass.

A short while later, Philippe crossed the corridor at the guest house, pushed open the door that had been left ajar, slipped inside, and quickly bolted the door from inside. His blood rushed warm through his body as he beheld Sandrine who was majestically perched on top of a stack of feather pillows in the huge wood-carved bed, the curtains drawn to the side. The whole picture reminded him of a queen's couchée. Today, he thought, she had passed the threshold into womanhood.

Still giggling with headiness from the wine, Sandrine began to fiddle with the buttons of his doublet, alas without much success. Frustrated in her endeavor, she finally gave up, threw her arms around his neck, and pulled him fully clothed as he was inside the feathery kingdom. But he wrestled himself free from her grip and insisted that he must undress. She watched between blinking eyes as he spread his clothes on the chair. Just a few minutes later, when he slipped back into the bed she had fallen into a deep, dreamless sleep.

In the weeks that followed, the guesthouse of the convent of Sainte Hélène's became the shelter of boundless, unrestrained lovemaking. Sandrine delighted in inventing new ways of increasing Philippe's pleasure while her own body learned to respond to his touch with sensuous abandon. The raptures of the nights ebbed only with the graying of dawn when oblivious slumber enveloped the lovers entwined in close embrace.

Time lost its meaning and the world ceased to exist. No plans were made for the future, no promises passed between them, no vows were exchanged. Love was freely given and freely received. The moment alone prevailed.

Catherine de Treffort knew she was making herself an accomplice in what the Church regarded as sin. But even though she might have to face episcopal censure, she could not bring herself to do what she should be doing and show her brother and the girl the door. Sensing the elemental force of love between them, she preferred that they made love in a sequestered place than take to the open countryside. The lovers lived withdrawn from the communal life of the sisters, who all seemed to have entered into a conspiracy of silence about the matter.

What disturbed the Abbess was that the two frequently missed the Matins and the Vespers, and only attended Mass on Sundays. But she did not want to press the point, since she felt the less they were seen together, the better it was for the peace of the community.

And who was she to preach morality and chastity? Had she not broken her vows in spirit, if not in actuality, many times during these past months? Was she not helpless to still the longing in her own heart? Maybe it was because she herself harbored an unfulfilled and unfulfillable carnal desire that she was so protective of the two lovers. At least these two, who had suffered so much pain to be together, should experience the love she would never know. Which ever way she turned, eternal damnation seemed to be her lot.

Sandrine recognized Mathieu immediately among the soldiers milling about in front of the convent gate as she was returning with Philippe from a late afternoon outing.

"Mathieu! Mathieu!" Sandrine called out, sliding off the horse. She ran toward the old friend, bubbling with excitement, her arms extended, ready to embrace him.

"What is the matter? Aren't you happy to see me?" she asked when he drew back with a formal, respectful bow. "Don't I get a hug?" she pouted like a disappointed child.

"My Lady, I don't think that would be fitting," he said bowing again with a nervous glance at Philippe who had followed behind.

"Have you gone mad? Where in the world did you learn to

talk like that? And you'd better not call me My Lady again or you'll get a box in the ear." Before he could fend her off, she placed a big smacking kiss on each of his glowing red cheeks.

Philippe had stayed back a few paces and watched the scene with an amused smile. The ease with which Sandrine fell into the speech patterns of the peasant patois delighted his heart. Poor Mathieu! He was happy to see her but was also deeply embarrassed by her unabashed familiarity in front of his comrades. He was finally saved when the attention of the soldiers turned to Gaspard who just then joined the group to greet his captain.

"Looks like we'll see some action soon, My Lord." Gaspard rubbed his hands together in eager anticipation. "His Lordship, Count de la Croix, is within conferring with Her Ladyship, the Abbess."

Philippe excused himself and disappeared inside. Sandrine locked one arm into Mathieu's and pulled him away from the soldiers.

"You must tell me how everything is going back home at Bonneval, and, especially, what you are doing here in the company of these soldiers."

"I can't tell you much about Bonneval. I never returned thereafter Their Lordships rescued you from under the noses of the fanatics. With you gone, I had no reason to go back to Bonneval—so I signed up with the League army." He watched her intently, apprehensive how she would take the news.

The memory of long debates by the pond behind the inn at Bonneval revived in his mind. She used to lecture him for hours on the evils of war, spoke about the injustice and suffering it brings to the common people—where she got her ideas, he never knew. He remembered her rebukes whenever he objected that war may not always be bad, that it depended on the cause one was fighting for. But even then he did not mind that she always had to be right—she was quicker to grasp a situation than he was—and just to be in her company, to be her confidant, was always reward enough for him. There was no other person in the world with whom he could talk, and he knew he was the only person in the village whom she trusted. His decision to join the army was his first act on his own. But, he had told himself, she could hardly object to soldiers or she would not be so enamored of the captain.

"I think you made a good decision," Sandrine reassured him with a patronizing slap on his back. "And I am so happy to see you, but what, tell me, brings you all here?"

"I don't know if I am at liberty to speak, but it seems the battle lines are drawn between the King's forces and the League. I heard them say that the Count de la Croix was sent by the Duke de Mayenne—he is the new League commander, his brother, the Duke de Guise, having been murdered—anyway, Count de la Croix seems to have orders for the captain, the Count de Treffort-Salignac."

Mathieu spoke haltingly, carefully watching the all too familiar furrow forming on Sandrine's forehead.

"This is what the soldiers have been saying. But there is a lot of idle talk among soldiers and the whole thing may not be true," he added quickly.

"Why shouldn't it be true? The war is still going on, isn't it? People are still hacking each other to pieces in the name of God, and it probably won't end until the entire kingdom lies in shreds."

Sandrine threw her head back with that haughty, superior wisdom that so often irritated people around her, and that could even anger those who loved her.

"Now even you have joined this band of murderers!" she

reproached him.

"I wish you wouldn't be so quick to judge people, Sandrine!" Mathieu cried. "I had no place to go. I could not possibly return to the village and face my father after all that had happened. I thought you of all people would understand. Gaspard and the Count de la Croix have been very good to me, and I won't be ungrateful."

Gaspard, who was just then strolling over to them, overheard part of the conversation. He placed his hand protectively on Mathieu's shoulder: "This young man is one of our best soldiers. You should have seen him in action at Chartres. Without his daring diversion of the militia, the rescue would surely not have come off so easily."

Sandrine's face glowed with shame. These were the men to whom she owed her life. Why did she let herself be carried away like this? Her fear of losing Philippe hardly justified this attack against an old and true friend.

"Please forgive me. I don't know what came over me. I owe my life to both of you; believe me, if it should ever be in my power, I shall make it up to you."

The two soldiers were greatly relieved to see Philippe and Robert emerged from the convent gate. A reward was not what either of them was seeking. What they had done, they considered a soldier's duty—and in the case of Mathieu, it was an act of brotherly love.

The two officers approached the group, but before Philippe could inform Sandrine of what was happening, the bell sounded the Vespers, enjoining everybody to hasten to the convent chapel.

Later that evening, while the company was seated with the sisters in the dining hall for supper, the Abbess made the announcement.

"My dear sisters, His Lordship, the Count de la Croix, is the bearer of grave news. It seems that difficult times are ahead for the League of Holy Union which is fighting for the cause of the Holy Church. I am told that his Majesty, King Henri, has done what we all have feared most, he has entered into an alliance with the heretic Henri de Navarre, and their combined forces are at this hour preparing to march on the city of Paris. The King seems bent on avenging himself against our good Parisians; even a pact with the devil is not too depraved for this man. Fortunately for the Church, we still have valiant defenders such as these two officers here. May God be with them and give them strength to triumph over the evil that has befallen our kingdom!"

She pointed proudly at Philippe and Robert, who could not help being somewhat uneasy about the Abbess's bellicose tone which was altogether out of keeping with her customarily subdued, dispassionate manner.

Before either was able to respond, the thumping noise of a falling chair drew the assembly's attention toward the lower end of the table. Sandrine had abruptly gotten up and without a word, she stormed out of the room. Philippe jumped to his feet, alarmed, and mumbling an apology, he ran after her.

As he opened the door to Sandrine's quarters in the guest house, he barely managed to dodge an object that came hurling at him from inside the darkened room. Straining his eyes to make out where she was, he pleaded softly: "Please be reasonable, Sandrine. I did not want you to hear about it this way."

"Whichever way does not matter. Just go to your bloody war. I don't care if you get killed." Her voice seemed to come from somewhere above the window.

"You are behaving like a child." He succeeded in lighting a lamp near the bed when he had to duck to avoid being hit by a flying stack of pewter plates.

"Don't you dare call me a child!" Sandrine screamed beside herself. She now became visible in the candlelight, perched on top of a display shelf, almost as if she was back at the hayloft, her refuge from an unjust and cruel world.

"Then please come down and let's talk like adults. Didn't you say yourself you understood that I had to go at some time?" He dropped into a fauteuil. "You know I shall be back. In the meantime, you have a place to stay here at the convent. Catherine promised that she will take care of you."

"You know I don't care about myself." The voice sounded calmer and came from right behind his ear. She had moved with such agility, he didn't even hear her coming down. "But was I wrong to assume that you no longer believe in the righteousness of this war or the League?"

"If you mean to say I want peace, the answer is yes. I want it as much as you or anybody. And if you mean I no longer believe peace can be attained by inflicting more pain and through the continued slaughter of human beings, however, misguided their views may be, you are right again," he replied, glad to see her taking a more reasonable stance. He never quite knew how to respond to her more volatile moods. At times she amazed him with an acuity and perceptiveness that seemed far beyond her age and, certainly beyond the world she came from, but then, he was equally baffled by the outbursts of an insensate child. Then again, she never failed to show remorse for her bad behavior, which made it impossible to be angry with her for long.

A wave of warmth rushed through him as he felt her kneeling beside him, her head resting in his lap.

"But would you want me to break a solemn oath, an oath of loyalty to the Apostolic Church and her precepts—the very precepts the Holy League is sworn to defend?" he continued.

He let his fingers run gently through her hair. "Maybe with all the knowledge and experience I have today, I would not take such an oath. I was raised with the notion that there are two kinds of people in this world—Catholics and heretics, and that the heretics must be destroyed like a disease before it spreads over the entire kingdom. It seemed a very simple matter then. It was them or us. This was my father's belief, and so it became mine. Now I know, this is a very simplistic view of the ways of the world. Still, other factors compel me to go—duty to my family is one, and . . ." He paused. She felt his body stiffen as he searched for the right words. His voice suddenly took on a dark tone: "And this will be my chance, a golden opportunity to avenge myself on the miscreant Henri Valois."

"I shall be here waiting for your return," Sandrine said, resigned. No matter what was in store for her, she knew she would find consolation in the life that was growing inside her. She would never be alone again and she would always have this token of their love. But she decided this was not the time to tell him.

The month of July was dominated by typical Norman weather. Only rarely did the sun break through the heavy rain clouds that opened almost daily, drenching the earth.

"The rain is good for the crops," the sisters would remind Sandrine, whose mood became gloomier the longer she was without word from Philippe.

Sandrine's life became embedded in the monastic routine, outwardly not very different from what her life had been at Bonneval. Between early Mass and evening Vespers, her days were spent helping with various chores at the convent. The only, but important, difference was the absence of any malice toward her. The nuns became her friends. They even treated her with the respect due to a lady, and many showed genuine affection for her.

The serenity of the cloister soothed Sandrine's soul. Inner calm replaced the anger against the world that once possessed her. Only at night, alone in her bed, she shed bitter tears of longing and desire for the one whose love had set her free. But as the weeks passed and she felt the life inside her stir with growing vigor, she took comfort in the thought that she was no longer alone and never would be again.

Sandrine was disappointed that the Abbess seemed not to respond to her gestures of friendship. She was not sure whether Catherine's aloofness came from a consciousness of status or her position in the convent hierarchy.

Then there were times when the Abbess became almost fiercely protective of her charge, like a mother of her child. When she became aware of Sandrine's condition, Catherine immediately forbade her to work in the fields and assigned her lighter chores around the kitchen. Mostly she urged her to rest and encouraged her to use the convent library.

Sandrine would have liked a more intimate relationship though. She wanted to know about Philippe's childhood, about his likes and dislikes, what kind of student he had been, she wanted to know everything about him. If she could discuss with Catherine some of the books she found in the library, ask her opinion, they might become closer. But Catherine gave her little opportunity to be alone with her.

The writings of Marguerite de Navarre were absent from the cloister library. That was hardly surprising. But Sandrine was most excited about the discovery of a book by a woman named Christine de Pizan. She felt an immediate kinship with her and she devoured her spirited defense of the dignity of womankind against the attacks on women's character that were so common in the popular literature. Also on the shelves were books that offended her sense of fairness, especially the ever-popular Romance of the Rose, which Christine had already denounced as a vicious slander of her sex. The more she read, the more probing became her mind, and Catherine was the only learned woman with whom she felt she could share her thoughts, whom she could ask the questions about the world that occupied her. But she did not know how to break through Catherine's reserved way.

What Sandrine did not know was that Catherine had many times been tempted to become more intimate with her, she too was lonely and longed for a kindred spirit. Sandrine would have been surprised had she learned that Catherine not only had great affection for her but that she envied and admired her. That she longed for Sandrine's spontaneity, her ability to give free expression to her emotions and desires, above all she envied her the unrestrained love she held for Philippe. How was Sandrine to know that she only avoided her because she was a constant reminder to the Abbess of a love she yearned for and would never be able to fulfill and that by keeping her distance, she hoped to hold on to her sanity?

Sandrine had no way of knowing what torrents of desire raged beneath the Abbess's staid exterior, that seemingly still water undisturbed by even a ripple. Robert's return had only fanned her passion. Like a precious gift, she cherished the memory of the long conversation that had ended in their confession of mutual love.

"Reverend Mother," she still heard him say, standing before her, straight, like a soldier standing at attention—no familiarity, not even the use of her name. He spoke simply, without artifice: "Since fate brought us together several months ago, Your Ladyship's image has been constantly in my mind and heart. I have become aware that my life can only have meaning in service to you—how and where I do not know, but I know my heart, my love, is yours forever."

How she had longed to touch him, throw herself at his feet, beg him to love her, liberate her from the demon that possessed her every waking hour of the day and night. All he had to do then was touch her and she would have been his forever. But she remained motionless, only a faint quiver in her voice betrayed the inner turmoil, the rush of blood, the pounding of her heart: "This veil will forever separate us. No earthly power can negate the vow I have taken. But of one thing I can assure you, you will always be close to my heart." She turned to hide the tears that filled her eyes.

The memory lingered, the memory of his gentle, soothing embrace, chaste, his arms around her, meant to bring solace to her heart. Their bodies did not touch, yet she breathed in his masculine aroma. Then his abrupt turning away, bidding adieu. His last words before leaving the room still rang in her ears: "It pains me to think that I should have caused you suffering. If it were in my power, I would want nothing more than to make you the happiest woman in the world. My thoughts and prayers will always be with you."

She called him back once more: "Please, don't blame yourself. Nothing you have done has caused me to suffer, only what I did to myself. Maybe fate is taking its revenge for my crossing the plans it had for us. I beg you to find it in your heart to forgive me for causing you pain."

With the passage of time, Catherine lifted herself out of the abyss of despair. Time heals all wounds, she told herself. But she was also certain that time would never erase her love for Robert de la Croix. What she hoped for was that her sinful lust would ebb with time and that she would learn to live with the emptiness left in her heart and the guilt for having betrayed both him and the Lord, Jesus Christ, to whom alone she had sworn to be faithful.

Then in the first week of August of the year 1589, a shockwave went through the Kingdom of France that paled all personal woes. The unloved King Henri III, last of the Valois kings and last of the sons of Catherine de Medici and King Henri II, succumbed to an assassin's dagger just as he was preparing to wreak his revenge on the city of Paris. Unmourned as he was, his death meant the realization of the worst fears of all good Catholics—the royal crown of France had fallen to a heretic. Henri de Bourbon, King of Navarre, leader of the Huguenots, had become Henri IV, King of France by the grace of God or, as some would have it, by design of the devil.

CHAPTER 9

"The tyrant is dead! The tyrant is dead!" Jubilation reigned in the streets of Paris. The people danced on the corpse of their anointed King. Priests and monks mingled their voices with the tumultuous chorus of joy: "God has heard the cries of his people! He has extinguished the accursed race of the Valois!"

How foolish, how misguided these people are! From the window of the Hotel d'Evreux, Philippe watched the sea of green scarves, the color of the House of Guise, being waved aloft by the multitude in mock mourning. How many times had he witnessed similar scenes of mass hysteria? Were they not always followed by greater pain and suffering, more cruelty and destruction?

His hatred of Henri Valois did not blind him to the disastrous consequences of his death. He had wanted his revenge on the miscreant king whose whim nearly destroyed his life and happiness. But did he want him dead? Maybe, but not this way. A hundred times he had rehearsed in his mind a meeting with the man who had callously caused him so much grief, but what he had imagined was a one-on-one, an equally matched duel.

Somehow he felt cheated now, cheated out of his revenge by the dagger of a cowardly little monk. Yet, he found no solace in the thought that a King of France had been disemboweled by an assassin. His fists tightened in frustration, powerless to undo the perfidious deed.

Just then, the clamor below turned to frenzy. Philippe craned his neck and strained his eyes. At some distance, two noblewomen in a slow-moving, open carriage waved and shouted to the crowd. The younger of the two leaned over the side of the carriage to press the outstretched hands. Only one woman in all of Paris would be greeted with such adulation.

"There goes Madame de Montpensier, the queen of the League!" Philippe summoned his fellow officers to view the spectacle. The gentlemen leaned out of the window straining to catch Madame's pronouncements to the adoring crowd.

The procession made its way slowly through the narrow city streets. Madame de Montpensier, her mother, Madame de Nemours, at her side, was decked out in plush green velvet, a matching cap with a long, green-tinted feather tilted to the side gave her a reckless, exuberant appearance. She now stood upright in the carriage like a victorious tribune, flushed with exhilaration, her voice hoarse from repeating over and over: "Happy tidings, my friends! Happy tidings! The tyrant is dead! Henri Valois is no more!"

"She is said to have embraced and kissed the messenger

who brought her the news this morning. Her only regret, it is said, was that the dying King did not become aware that she had a hand in the assassination plot. Hard to believe anybody should be filled with so much hatred—but this is what has been reported," Robert remarked.

"Does anybody know why she pursued Henri Valois with such relentless hatred?" Philippe wondered, then adding: "Not that I lack understanding for hating the degenerate, but her vendetta seems driven by a frightful passion."

"Rumors are many," replied Count de Brissac, "the most likely is slighted love. The two are said to have been lovers once, and Madame never forgave him his many infidelities, especially his rumored predilection for young boys. But nobody seems to know the exact reason for her fanatical invective against him."

"But what about Madame de Nemours?" asked the Chevalier de Rochambaud. "The whole town is talking about how, this very morning, she invaded a packed sanctuary at the Cordelier monastery. There she mounted the altar, and disregarding all etiquette of proper feminine comportment, harangued the crowd about the death of the tyrant in the vilest language ever heaped on the dead."

"Well, she may have been carried away, but this is not too hard to understand. A mother will never forgive the murderer of her son," explained de Brissac. "But let us not forget that these two ladies have been the heart and soul of the League in Paris for many years. Their rapport with the masses has kept the League spirit alive. We'd do well to be grateful for their unflagging dedication to the cause of the Holy Church. Madame de Montpensier was an inspiration to the Parisians when the Valois clique vacillated in the fight against the heretics."

"Gentlemen! Enough gossip!" admonished the Duke d'Evreux. "The Duchesses are doing a splendid service to the cause, but our main concern is the menace from the Huguenot army. Navarre was at the King's side in his last hour and seems to have persuaded the dying man to name him his successor. As if the crown was Henri Valois' to bequeath, he seems to have forgotten that kingship derives from the will of the sovereign people. And the people will never accept a heretic as their king! Gentlemen, our task is clear. Paris is still a beleaguered city and we cannot let the jewel of the realm fall into the hands of Henri de Navarre. The people will realize soon enough the time for rejoicing is premature. Indeed, as you are all aware, this may be the darkest hour in our long struggle against heresy— a heretic, heir to the crown of France! And if he received the blessing of the deceased king a thousand times over, we shall die a thousand deaths before we allow this vermin to occupy the throne of France. Gentlemen, it is up to us to save France from perdition. Now, more than ever our task stands clearly before us."

Cheers for France and the Catholic Church punctuated the Duke's call to arms. The gentlemen had gathered around the Duke, whose words set their hearts on fire. Their faces glowed in anticipation of action.

Only Philippe stood by silently. His father's single-minded cry for battle no longer stirred in him the enthusiasm of former times.

"How can we prevent the rightful successor to the throne from assuming his crown?" he interjected, enduring his father's stern gaze.

"He forfeited that right, my son, when he renounced the Church and embraced heresy!" Shouts of approval all around.

"The League will fight for the candidacy of the Cardinal de Bourbon. He may be Navarre's uncle, but he is a true prince of the Church. His right of succession supersedes whatever presumed right his renegade nephew may put forth."

Philippe threw his hands up in despair. "Have you all gone mad? A teetering old man with no heir! He may die any moment and Navarre will be his only legitimate successor anyway. Don't you realize, the cardinal's candidacy will at best postpone the inevitable? But it will certainly prolong the war."

"Would you have us abandon everything we fought for and leave the crown to the heretic? Since when are you afraid of fighting for your beliefs? Or, are you forgetting that you are a soldier of the Church and war is your métier?" The Duke trembled with anger. Never had he expected his son to engage in such breach of etiquette.

Even then, Philippe, as so often, shrank from risking an open rift with his father. With mollified tone, he suggested: "It seems to me, the best course would be to impress upon Navarre that France will not tolerate a Protestant king and that he must convert to the Catholic faith if he wishes to be king and bring unity to the country and an end this dreadful war."

"How can we put our trust in a man who has twice renounced the Apostolic faith?" Robert objected. "From all we have heard, this man is the devil himself."

"I have heard quite the contrary. Those who have had direct dealings with him are quite charmed and impressed with his gracious and magnanimous spirit."

"Gentlemen! May I remind you that it is our task to defend this city and not to make League policy," Count de Brissac interjected.

"Nothing is gained from such debates. As officers of the League, it is our duty to fight without questioning."

With his eyes firmly fixed on Philippe, he concluded: "Whatever the League Council decides, we are sworn to uphold and defend with our lives."

In the days that followed, League officers and men were

seen in all parts of the city helping the populace with erecting defenses against the expected onslaught of Navarre's forces. As in the days of the barricades, Philippe sought to forget politics and theology by steeping himself in the mechanics of a task at which he excelled. Would the barricades hold against a well-equipped, well-organized army ready to take the city by storm? It would be more difficult this time to persuade the citizenry of the imminence of attack by Navarre's army—if Navarre's forces should breach the walls, he would have to conquer the city quarter by quarter and street by street, maybe even house by house. Like children, the people were able to concentrate only on one thing at a time, and at the moment, they were still delirious with their victory over the royal house of France.

Not only the common people were misguided. Holy Masses were said in every church and parish for Jacques Clément, the Jacobin monk turned murderer of a king. Praise was heaped on him from the pulpits and he was hailed as one who sacrificed his life for the Apostolic faith. Could it be that the priests believed that this was the deed of a true saint and martyr? Philippe wondered.

But the madness didn't end here. Penning erudite apologias for regicide became the vogue among the learned men of the Sorbonne. No page of the ancient texts was left unturned to find written justification for the murder of a king. The capital was swamped with pamphlets expounding the ideas of one Jean Boucher, professor at the Sorbonne and author of a book that proposed that the Church, as well as the people, had the right to depose a king. He had justified the armed struggle of the people against Henri III on the ground that the power of the crown derived from the people. Only the Pope had unlimited power and could, therefore, release the people from their allegiance to a royal house.

Flyers proclaiming the sovereignty of the people littered the streets. And at every street corner, Boucher's students harangued the illiterate masses. Philippe and Robert busied themselves among the tanners of the Rue Santeuil, but the people turned a more receptive ear to diatribes and incitements than to the warning that they must build defenses.

"Look at this, isn't that interesting!" Robert remarked holding up a piece of paper from the debris floating in the gutter.

"What is it?" Philippe looked up disinterestedly from the map of the city he was studying.

"It's a pamphlet, unsigned, but clearly from a learned person, probably a master of the Sorbonne."

"Oh, this trash is all over the place," Philippe replied impatiently and turned away.

"No, listen to this," Robert insisted. "The Sovereign People are the foundation on which the king's power rests! The people make the king, not the king the people. The soul of the most modest among the people is no less than that of the grandest monarch! Only the Estates of the Realm can truly speak for the people!"

"Stop it already Robert!" Philippe cried. "I'm hearing enough of this wherever I go in Paris. Would you be so interested in the sovereignty of the people if France had a king who was doing your bidding?"

"My bidding?" Robert replied. "What do you mean by that?"

"Yes, your bidding, yours and the League's. All this talk of the people, and how power derives from the people, is just so much demagoguery. Yes, the people, especially the people of Paris, have fought bravely for the Church and even turned against their king, they deserve to be rewarded. But not with lies and self-serving notions. I wonder what would happen if the people turned against the League? Would they still be the source of all power then?"

"These are not the words of an officer sworn to defend the League and the Church," Robert replied.

"Robert, you think too much!" Philippe tried to make light. "We have work to do and shouldn't squander our time with idle talk. Navarre may attack any moment."

"You are a riddle, Philippe," Robert said in exasperation. "You seem to defend Navarre's right to the throne, and here you do your best to defend the city from the onslaught of his army!"

"Theory and practice are two separate things." Philippe knew this was not true, but he was trying to wriggle out of a situation. "Besides, we have both sworn an oath."

With that, the two friends turned their attention back to the task at hand.

Both felt that an unbridgeable chasm seemed to have opened between them, leaving them stranded on opposite shores. When did that weary look first appear in Robert's eyes? Philippe reproached himself with having been so preoccupied with his love and sorrows, he was unable to pinpoint when the change in his friend had first shown. Maybe if he had paid closer attention, he would not have been so startled when Robert hinted that he contemplated entering the priesthood when the war was over. So unexpected was this confession, Philippe was at a total loss how to respond. He burst into nervous laughter for which he still would have liked to kick himself. Never will he forget the expression of pain on Robert's face. He was sure this was the reason why Robert had since then avoided all private contact. Maybe he too mourned the loss of their friendship. Maybe he too felt a gaping void inside, a sense of being uprooted and alone, a stranger in a strange land.

Meanwhile, the business of war still kept them together. About the middle of August word came that the new King of

France—the Béarnais or Navarre, as the Leaguers insisted on calling the Bourbon king, Henri IV, when they did not refer to him as the heretic or renegade or worse—had withdrawn his troops from the area around the capital city and had moved into Normandy. Paris had been spared, the day of reckoning had been postponed, but nobody could predict for how long.

The two League officers halted their horses on a hillside overlooking the coastal plain of Arques. An impressive sight presented itself. A mass of men, weapons, horses poured in a seemingly endless stream into the plain and took up position at the confluence of the Béthune and Eaulne rivers. A bright-colored sea of banners flapped in the soft September breeze, cannons and swords gleamed in the sunlight. Moving closer, the two observers discerned column upon column of infantrymen, followed by more columns of horsemen and cannoneers, a veritable colossus lumbering through the Norman countryside in search of prey, callously flattening the earth underfoot.

"Just look at them! No army in the world could inflict defeat on such a magnificent fighting force!" Robert cried.

"Can't you see, they are taking up position right under the nose of the cannons embanked at the fortress of Arques," Philippe replied. "How can you let your enthusiasm cloud your military judgment? This mighty horde will turn into sitting ducks in this position."

"Your lack of enthusiasm is most blatant!" Robert replied scornfully. "Henri de Navarre seems to have had an easy time turning your head."

"Considering that he could have hung us as spies, his manner was most gracious and certainly superior to that of the masters we are serving."

"The devil comes in many guises and charm is known to be one of his most alluring qualities."

Philippe shrugged his shoulders.

"Let us not waste time with idle chatter," he suggested. "You will present the report to Mayenne of what we have learned on our expedition. I shall second what you say."

The two friends had been sent to scout out the strength of the royal forces when they were taken captive by royal guards in the forest around Arques. To their surprise, they found Henri de Navarre and his commanders encamped near the front line of their troops. Even more surprising, the new King of France accorded the League spies the courtesy of honored guests rather than treating them as prisoners.

Philippe could not help but be favorably impressed by the unpretentious, jovial comportment of the monarch who was seated with his men on the dirt floor of his tent. Together, they partook of a simple peasant meal to which the two League spies were invited.

"Gentlemen!" Henri addressed his captives. "Now that you had an opportunity to assess the strength of my army, what do you think my chances are against the Duke de Mayenne?"

"Frankly, Sire," Philippe replied, "in terms of numbers, the odds are overwhelmingly against Your Majesty."

"In terms of numbers, my dear Count, you are right," the King rejoined without letting this fact spoil his appetite. "You have something of a reputation as a military strategist Count. What would you do in my situation?"

Philippe became aware that Henri sensed his wavering and wanted to test his loyalty to the League. He determined to be more guarded, for this man was more astute than he had expected. But he should also know that the Count de Treffort-Salignac will never turn traitor.

"Sire, it hardly behooves me to give you military advice. I see you are surrounded by some of the finest strategists in France, and you are renowned for excellent judgment and courage on the battlefield."

"My dear Count, I did not ask you for evasive flattery. I want your honest opinion."

"In that case, Sire, I would abandon my position and avoid standing battle at all cost."

"Spoken like a true militarist!" Henri slapped Philippe on the back with such force he almost knocked him over. "But you are forgetting one factor, most military minds tend to leave out of consideration."

He paused and lifted his finger in a dramatic gesture. Then with a sudden change of demeanor, he planted himself fully erect, hands on his hips, in front of the League officers and proclaimed: "Go tell your master, we have the cause of justice on our side! And we shall prevail with God's help!"

The King's words echoed in Philippe's ears long after they had returned to the League camp. Was it God's will at work that kept the Duke de Mayenne from mounting a full-scale attack? Why else did he not press his advantage before reinforcements had a chance to reach the royal army? No doubt, as the odds stood then, the League army could roll over the royal fortifications and overwhelm the enemy by sheer force of numbers.

Yet, the Duke hesitated, content with a few skirmishes now and then to test the King's mettle. Most were quickly repelled. The days passed without orders to advance. Restlessness among the troops slowly grew into outright rebelliousness. Gaspard's daily reports to Philippe took on an ever more alarming tone.

"My Lord, if we don't move very soon, we'll have a mutiny on our hands. I'm afraid the rank and file will soon be so demoralized, mass desertion to the enemy side might take place. I've even heard some men proclaim that Henri de Navarre is the legitimate King of France and the League had no right to oppose him. The longer the troops are idle, the more likely it's that seditious talk like this will spread."

Philippe assured Gaspard that he was aware of the problem, but nobody could force the Duke's hand. He had sensed the growing sedition among the soldiers, but he remained silent and avoided the Duke de Mayenne's council, for did he not harbor what might be called "seditious" thoughts himself?

The encounter with Henri de Navarre had left a deep impression on him. Here was a man who was to all appearance a true king, a true leader. Simple and guileless in his dealings with subordinates, yet strong-willed and shrewd. He sensed in this man that rare combination of self-confident bravura and benevolence that was the mark of the true charismatic leader. Philippe could not help but feel that Henri de Navarre was a king not only by right of succession but by dint of personality as well.

Maybe other League officers were in a similar crisis of conscience. He recalled an encounter he had only a few nights before with young Charles de Chillon. He knew he had made himself an accessory to treason when he let the officer pass through the sentry, but the young man's argument in favor of deserting from the League army to join the royal forces was almost irrefutable.

The incident occurred when, as had happened for many nights previously, he was roused from a restless sleep around two o'clock in the morning. A nightmarish dream had left him bathed in a cold sweat. The rattling of heavy rainfall on the canvas of his tent made a peaceful slumber impossible. Left to twist and turn, his parched throat gripped by the invisible hand of a nameless terror, he rose and ventured outside into the rain-swept night. He breathed deeply the salty aroma carried over the plain by vigorous coastal breezes. Suddenly he was overcome with a wild desire to wash off all the tormenting thoughts, to cleanse his mind. Like someone gone mad, he opened his arms and offered up his body to the balming wind and rain.

Soaked and invigorated, he started to walk around the perimeter of the camp. All was quiet. If anybody was awake, the rain and mud probably kept him inside. He almost tripped over the sentry who sat hunched up by the side of the woods, his desire to rest disturbed by the seeping dampness. The man's misery aroused Philippe's pity and, disregarding army regulations, he sent him back to his quarters and took up sentry duty himself.

Leaning against the side of a tree, he gazed out on the plain enveloped in the darkness of a starless night. His thoughts wandered from Sandrine to Henri, the new King of France. Across the plain, on the hill, he made out the glimmer of lights where he knew the royal encampment was situated. His eyes strained to penetrate the darkness. Was it his imagination or was there a lone figure pacing on the footpath alongside the hill? Was it the King? What thoughts, what concerns might be keeping the King awake? Did he feel the tension from the imminence of battle or were his thoughts and prayers with the future of his kingdom? Will Henri de Navarre succeed where the Valois kings had failed, and bring peace to France at last?

A crackling noise nearby, then the neighing of a horse, attracted his attention. Carefully, he approached the spot from where the sounds came. In the dense underbrush of the woods, he made out the blurred figure of a knight on horseback in full armor. Horse and rider struggled to cut a path through the muddy terrain. Philippe instinctively drew his sword.

"Halt! Who goes there? Nobody passes through the sentry."

The rider did not answer but gave his horse the spurs with intense vigor. The heavy animal, weighed down by its armored rider, was no match for Philippe's fleeting foot. He overtook the horse, and in a swift move, wrestled the rider to the ground. A brief hand-to-hand struggle ensued. Philippe yanked off his opponent's helmet. Rather than an enemy spy, he uncovered Charles de Chillon, a young aristocrat who had only a short while before joined the ranks of League officers.

"I might have killed you!" The two men burst into laughter as they looked at each other, soaking wet and spattered with mud.

"I thought you were an enemy spy." Philippe extended his hand to help his opponent get on his feet. "If you want to go on a single skirmish, you should at least get a pass to get through the sentry."

"I am not going on a skirmish," the young man replied, pulling the reins to calm his horse.

"What! An amorous rendezvous in this weather and at this hour?" Philippe called out.

"No, it's not that either," Charles replied. After some hesitation, he added with a tone of defiance: "I am on my way to join the forces of His Majesty, the King of France."

"And who might that be? Right now, this position is much contested."

"I am speaking of Henri IV, the rightful King of France and Navarre."

"You had better lower your voice!" Philippe cautioned. He was appalled and, at the same time touched, by the youth's frankness. "You know around here such talk is considered treason. People have been killed on suspicion of treason and heresy alone."

"I am not afraid to die!" Charles de Chillon insisted. "As far as I am concerned, the League is a sham."

"Strong words from one so young and inexperienced!"

Philippe took an instinctive liking to this youth. The rain splattering the boy's clean, innocent face did nothing to cool his ardor. He saw in his eyes the gleam of pride and defiance of which he too was once capable.

"Eight months of service with the League is enough for me to know right from wrong. Wherever the League army goes, there is plunder and rape. The troops of the Duke d'Aumale even loot churches and monasteries. It is not uncommon for them to defile relics and sacred objects. I have seen it with my own eyes. Is that proper behavior for the presumed defenders of the Church?"

"But you are only speaking about a small troop among a huge army," Philippe protested what he knew to be true.

"That maybe so. But only a few months ago, when we took Villeneuve, the Leaguers behaved as if they were conquering a foreign territory. No shop was spared from pillage, anybody who got in the way was killed on the spot, and the guilty were never brought to justice. The women of the town became fair game. Who knows how many were ravaged and violated. Mayenne simply shrugs off reports of these outrages. I even heard of League soldiers who forced a parish priest, under threat of cutting his throat, to "baptize" cattle, sheep, and other farm animals. Such are the blasphemous excesses of the army of the Holy Apostolic Church!"

Philippe listened pensively. He knew only too well the truth of what the young man was saying. Since the Duke de Mayenne had taken command of the League after his brother, the Duke de Guise, was murdered, discipline in the League army had lapsed greatly. In many places, the soldiers had turned into roving bands of marauders.

"From all I have heard of the towns taken by Henri de Navarre's army, the exact opposite is true," Charles continued.

"Late in July, Navarre took the town of Pontoise. He sternly warned his men against pillaging private food stocks, and offenders were severely punished. The defeated soldiers in the town were even allowed to retain their swords. Wherever he goes, he treats people with kindness as long as they swear off further acts of opposition against him. Most of all, Henri of Navarre is a man of his word, and he is, no matter what the Leaguers say, the rightful King of France."

"But he is a heretic," Philippe rejoined meekly wondering why he listened to this talk so calmly when it would have been his duty to arrest this young man for sedition. Instead, he heard himself say: "A man should always have the courage of his convictions. Go forth and may God be with you!"

Philippe's eyes followed the youth as he lumbered through the deep furrows carved in the ground by the drenching rain until the darkness of the woods leading to Arques swallowed him up. An impulse seized him to call after him to wait, to join him on his journey, but he turned hurriedly back to the League camp.

He is a heretic, Philippe told himself a thousand times. Had it only been a matter of allegiance to the League, it might have been easy to break away. But his duty to his family, to his father who had dedicated his life, his fortune, to fighting heresy, he could not go against his father. To undermine his father's life's work would be too perfidious a deed even to contemplate.

Yes, he despised the political intrigues of the League leaders, despised their outrages. But wasn't his father different? He was neither motivated by material gain nor by a hunger for power. Never had he expressed anything but genuine abhorrence of heresy and a desire to preserve the traditional order in the kingdom. Under those circumstances, how could he, Philippe, ever hope to extricate himself from the web of filial obligations and conflicting loyalties?

How he longed to escape the world, its miseries and cruelties, and find oblivion in Sandrine's arms! Would he ever find the peace he desired? The fear of losing his beloved again and maybe forever never left him every waking hour and haunted him in his sleep. Was his recurrent dream an omen, a dark foreboding? He tried to ascribe his melancholy mood to the dragging inactivity—too much time to think. If at least Mayenne would make his move so he could shake off his obsessive thoughts in battle!

The days followed one another without word from Mayenne. The waiting became unbearable. By now, it had become less likely that the order to attack would come soon. The coastal region of Normandy was in the grip of the early autumn rainy season. The terrain was saturated with rain and the magnificent fighting force was mired in a field of mud.

More time to think, to dream, to agonize. Philippe had to talk to somebody to keep from going mad. But to whom could he unburden his soul? There was nobody near him he trusted.

In the back of his mind appeared the image of a woman, a fortune-teller among the camp followers. She had attached herself to him with such insistence when they first marched into this area, he had to order his men to remove her by force. If she tells fortunes, maybe she interprets dreams. But how find her among the huge herd of civilians who train after the combat troops with their goods and services? It may be difficult, but he had to try. If nothing else, the search for the fortune teller will provide a welcome distraction.

The camp followers had invaded the village of Martinglise by the hundreds—much to the dismay of the local inhabitants who were eager to reap the profits from the presence of the soldiers themselves. The entire village had been transformed into a huge carnival. Food and spirits vendors, carrying their wares on their backs, labored to keep up with the brisk demand for their products. At every street corner acrobats, jugglers, and pantomimes performed their acts to the accompaniment by roving bands of musicians. The lull before the storm of battle and the atmosphere of uncertainty were a boon to business of all sorts.

The village elders had petitioned the League commander to curb the activities of the herd of prostitutes who flagrantly plied their trade in the village square, a sight, they said, that corrupted the morals of the local youths. But they met with little sympathy from the Duke de Mayenne. The Duke's only comment was, so it was reported, that at least the soldiers did not have to rape the local women.

Philippe strolled along the main street. There were scores of fortune-tellers, but he had his mind set on the one who had accosted him so tenaciously. Somehow he felt that she had some special knowledge of his fate. If he only could remember her name. Zola! Yes, her name was Zola or Zora, or something like that. He was sure it started with a Z and was fairly short.

He continued between rows of caravans set up in a field at the edge of the village. His attention was attracted by a cobalt blue wagon from which the images of ghastly faces of supernatural creatures dancing in the round grimaced at him with eerie vividness. He was still undecided whether to approach this wagon and ask for the fortune teller named Zola or Zora, when he was pulled vigorously by the hand.

A raspy voice entreated: "Approach, My Lord! Approach! I can see you are a man of exquisite taste. Come inside, I have a fine virgin for you. You know there are not many virgins left around here. But you are in luck, I can still serve you with a fine, young virgin. And you need not worry, for you, I can make a special arrangement because I can see you are a man of quality—real gentlemen are rare. One gold crown will do and it includes wine and a meal. How about it?"

"No, no I am not interested!" he protested trying to disengage his arm from the gnarled hand that held on to him like a pair of pincers.

He turned to wriggle free and came face to face with the gap-toothed grin of a woman of indeterminable age, but who was surely far beyond her prime. A first glance she presented a repulsive caricature of womanhood—tangled, henna-red hair, hollow cheeks augmented by too much rouge, her bulging, voluptuous flesh straining the seams of her sparse black lace attire. Philippe studied this strange creature for a good while. Behind the grotesque mask, he perceived a spark of sympathetic warmth that encouraged him to solicit her help.

"Can you help me find a woman named Zola or Zora?"

"You mean Zoila?" she said, the corners of her mouth twitching with derision and obvious disappointment.

She squinted her already tiny eyes and probed his face thoroughly while nodding her head as if carefully weighing the evidence. "I see, you have a fancy for the more mature types! But why her? Why not try me, I could still teach you a trick or two." She made a coquettish half-turn with her bare shoulder and jerked her head toward the entrance of the wagon. "For you, there is no charge."

Philippe did not doubt that she was right, but this was not the purpose of his visit.

"Please forgive me, but this is not what I am looking for just now," he said gently, not wanting to rebuff her too brusquely. "This Zoila, she has information that is of utmost importance to me. Can you tell me where I can find her?"

Without answering, she moved slowly closer, her eyes firmly

fixed on him. Her gnarled fingers lifted his chin toward her with unabashed familiarity. He felt her eyes in his as if she was peering into the bottom of his soul.

Nodding her head she concluded seriously: "I can see, His Lordship is in love. I don't know what Zoila can do that I could not do a hundred times better, but since you insist, I will have one of my girls take you to her. I hope you will find what you are looking for, otherwise, my abode is always open. God be with you, My Lord!"

Philippe pulled aside the sheepskin canvas that covered the entrance to the darkened, makeshift hut extending from the caravan. A penetrating mixture of incense and sweet perfume wafted at him. He immediately recognized the woman seated on the floor behind a low table cluttered with paraphernalia used in the art of divination. She took no notice of him but persisted in the frozen posture she had assumed, her eyes closed in deep meditation.

His heart pulsated madly in his throat. Her pompous manner irritated him and he wondered what he was doing in this place. Did he expect this hag to unravel the riddle of his nightmare? A strange presentiment pulled him to step inside against his will and better judgment.

"Welcome to my humble abode, My Lord!" She rose to greet him as if she had been expecting him. He had to admit this diminutive woman who was certainly no longer young had withstood the ravages of time rather well. Her head, too large for the rest of her body, was crowned with a brightly colored scarf, tied in the manner of the gypsies. An inviting gesture beckoned the visitor to make himself comfortable on the pile of satin pillows arranged on the floor.

"Your Lordship took his time." She waved a stern forefinger at him and kneeled next to him. Without taking her eyes off him, she poured a cup of steaming tea and offered it to him with a plate of biscuits.

"His Lordship must fortify himself first," she insisted when he waved aside her offerings. "There is much time for talk. The battle will not take place before the day after tomorrow."

"How would you know when the battle will begin?" he said still irritated at her self-assured, condescending manner.

"Oh, I know the Duke's mind as well as I know your Lordship's." She gave off a hushed laugh as if they were partners in a conspiracy.

"You mean to say, the Duke seeks your advice on military matters? You must be joking!"

"On military and other matters," she assured him. "But, of course, I am not at liberty to divulge details."

"Then you are responsible for the delay of action. The whole army is on the brink of mutiny!"

"The omens have so far not been propitious for a victory. The day after tomorrow, when Jupiter and Mars face each other high in the sky, the time will be right. But you did not come to discuss military matters."

"I don't know wherefore I came here." Philippe shook his head. He started to pull himself up, but the woman's hand rested firmly on his thigh and his own will seemed to leave him. Her voice sounded sweet and enticing: "But you have not yet uncovered the meaning of your dream."

Startled, he sank back into the plush mount of satin. How could she know about his dream? He had not spoken to anyone about it. Suddenly, he felt light-headed, his vision blurred, he had trouble perceiving what she was doing.

"You must relax and finish your tea," he heard her say as from far away. A pleasant warmth rushed through him and drained all resistance. He wondered what she put into the tea, but before he could think further, a numbing, measureless void sucked him in.

"Damn, gypsy!" Philippe woke with a start. He had no idea how long he had been asleep. It could have been hours or just minutes. Tentatively, he opened his eyes. There she was, kneeling in the middle of the hut surrounded by flickering candles. Her body was upright and motionless. Her gaze was fixed on him making him feel intensely uncomfortable.

Why do these hags always have to stare? he thought. He was angered for having allowed this woman to gain control over him. Superstitious rubbish! Let the Duke believe in this hocus-pocus, he, Philippe, would not be taken in! She is a fortune teller and interprets dreams, so it is reasonable for her to assume that he came to find the meaning of a dream. It was as simple as that!

"Did Your Lordship have a good rest?"

"What is it to you, you old bat?" His surly manner did not seem to offend her. She edged closer and arranged herself on a pile of pillows in intimate proximity to him.

"Now, unburden yourself. Did you have the same dream just now when you were sleeping?"

"No, I was not dreaming at all. For the first time in weeks, I did not dream. Whatever it was you put in the tea, it erased the dream."

"Only temporarily. Do you remember your dream now?"

"Yes, of course, how could I forget? The same dream has been haunting my sleep every night for two months!"

"What is so frightening about it?"

"It always starts happy, with the happiest feeling imaginable. I am living with my beloved on a peaceful country estate, away from the world and its intrigues. We live only for each other surrounded by the laughter of our children. There are many children, I don't know exactly how many—a string of children as endless as our love. There could not be a more perfect world. Paradise must be like this." He paused.

"What happens to spoil paradise?"

"I don't know how to describe it. It's some terrible monster, a demon. I don't know if it is man or beast. It seems to change its form every time I try to get a good look. Anyway, this demon, or whatever it is, penetrates our world out of nowhere. It crushes everything underfoot and then . . ."

He paused again, unable to put into words the image of horror before his eyes.

"And then, what does it do?" she insisted patiently.

"It devours the children, one by one." Beads of sweat gleamed on his forehead, as he was writhing in anguish. "I try to stop him. I swing my sword through the air, with futile strokes, none can reach him. The dream always ends with the demon carrying off Sandrine. I hear her calling for help, but I am powerless, I cannot move. It's as if I am rooted to the ground. I see her disappearing into the night, her screams fade and then I wake up. This goes on night after night. I simply dread falling asleep!"

Philippe's head fell forward. He covered his face with his hands to hide his tears.

"This woman you love, she is a lady?" he heard her say.

"She is the future Countess de Treffort, and one day she will be the Duchess d'Evreux. Is that enough for you?"

"I mean what is her station now. Is she of noble birth?"

"What does it matter, to me she is the most elevated woman in the world."

"She is of low birth then. You will not be united with this woman."

"What do you mean?" He looked at her through a cloud of tears. She was laying out a deck of cards in front of her, studying them with serious intent.

"How would you know anyway?"

"The cards don't lie!" And after a pause spent in close examination of her cards: "I see a happy, fruitful bond between the House of Evreux and the Royal House of France."

"That's absolute rubbish! Which royal house are you talking about? Besides, I shall never be happy with anybody but Sandrine."

"But first, you must overcome the demon of your dreams," she continued without taking note of his objection. "Beware, he is near you, very close, but you will not recognize him readily."

"I have heard quite enough." Philippe struggled to his feet. "I see you are amusing yourself at my expense. Don't think I believe one word of your nonsense."

"Thank you for an entertaining afternoon. And this is for the tea." With a peal of nervous laughter, he threw two gold crowns on the table. "We shan't see each other again."

"May God bless you and keep you, My Lord," he heard her call after him as he stormed out into the twilight of dusk.

Something unusual must have happened. Gaspard accompanied by Mathieu met Philippe near the gate. Why are they waiting for his return at the entrance to the encampment? Could it be that the order for the attack had come after all?

"Hurry, My Lord!" Gaspard called out. Alarmed by the serious mien of the two soldiers, Philippe quickened his pace.

"Sire, it's the Count de la Croix, he has been wounded in a skirmish this morning. I'm afraid, he's not well."

"What skirmish?" Philippe inquired as they hurried toward the field hospital tent. "I gave no orders for a skirmish."

"Sire, it was the Count's plan, he wanted to show that the heretics' entrenchments are not impregnable and can be captured by a handful of men. And capture them we did, at first at least. In all the years, I have never seen His Lordship, the Count, fight like this. I don't mean to say that he was not always brave, but to see him this morning was an awesome sight. Like a lion, fearless he led the troop in hand-to-hand combat. It was as if he wanted to defy death as if he didn't care for his life."

Gaspard shook his head still trying to understand what went on in Robert's mind. "It just didn't make any sense from a military standpoint to take such risks."

The medical report was grave indeed: a severe head wound and a shattered right leg.

"His only chance is amputation of the leg below the knee. But even then there is no guarantee that he will live because of the deep cut to his skull," the doctor reported. "The patient will have to be transferred after the operation to a hospital in the nearest town still loyal to the League."

Philippe barely listened to the doctor's explanations. These men were under his command. Had he not been so preoccupied with personal concerns, this debacle would not have occurred.

"Were there other casualties?" he asked Gaspard. The answer was fortunately negative.

Mortified with guilt for having permitted this to happen, he clung to Robert's bedside, anxiously waiting for a sign of life from the body stretched out lifelessly before him. As he sat and waited, the implication of what the doctor had said slowly began to sink in. Even if Robert was to live, they would never again ride into battle together. It was hard to imagine Robert leading a sedentary life. He thrived on physical action. But he could get used to it, Philippe told himself. Had he not expressed the desire to follow a different vocation once the war was over? Oh, please, dear God, in your infinite mercy, please just let him live, he prayed.

An eternity seemed to pass. At long last, Robert opened his eyes. Philippe was encouraged for he recognized him immediately. Robert fervently grasped his friend's hand and tried to speak, but he was too weak, the words refused to pass over his lips. Philippe waited patiently.

After a few more vain attempts, Robert managed to speak, haltingly, his hoarse voice barely audible. As much as Philippe could make out, he implored him never to give up the fight for the Holy Church. Then with a sudden burst of energy, the infirm man pulled himself up to a half-sitting position, holding fast to Philippe's arm with glassy eyes.

"We must continue the struggle against heresy at all cost. And please tell Lady Catherine that I died defending the Apostolic faith and the Holy Father in Rome. Tell her we shall be united one day in a better world, but I want her to know that I loved her more than my life. She will understand."

The exertion pushed him back into unconsciousness. While he was still pondering the meaning of his friend's words, Philippe was told that he had to leave. The operation had to be performed immediately. Time was of the essence.

On the way back to the camp, Philippe tried to conjure up in his mind the women of Robert's recent amorous adventures. There may have been a Lady Catherine, but nobody by that name who had stood out from the rest came to mind. Philippe noted again with sadness how far apart they had grown, he had hardly been close enough to his friend in recent months to know who the lady of his heart might be. Could it be that, like his own love for Sandrine, Robert's love for this Lady Catherine was more serious than their past escapades? His heart warmed to the idea that Robert too had found true love.

He swore he would find this Lady Catherine no matter what. But before he could decide how he would go about it, his attention was drawn to more immediately pressing matters.

"Sire, His Lordship, the Duke de Mayenne requests your immediate presence in his council!" The Duke's messenger met him near his tent with orders to escort him forthwith.

Something really important must be afoot. Maybe the hag was right and the attack will finally take place. He put on his armored breastplate and helmet, girded his sword, and followed the messenger to the League headquarters.

The Duke de Mayenne greeted him in his customary scruffy manner. The two men thoroughly disliked each other. Philippe had little respect for the man's military judgment and despised the crudeness of his character. Besides he was almost convinced that he was in the pay of the King of Spain. The Duke's dislike for the brash young man was deepened by the suspicion that he may harbor heretic sympathies.

"Where the hell is the Count de la Croix?" the Duke bellowed when he saw Philippe entering alone.

"He was severely wounded in a skirmish this morning, and is at this hour under the care of the surgeon, My Lord."

"What skirmish? Who gave orders for a skirmish?"

"The Count acted on his own, Sire. He apparently wanted to show that the enemy's trenches could be taken by a handful of men."

"And did he take the trenches? As far as I can see the enemy is still holed up on that hill!"

"From the report I received, I gather that the attack was at first successful. Our men inflicted heavy casualties on the enemy but then ran afoul for lack of artillery support. That is when the Count de la Croix was severely wounded. His ardor and dedication to the cause made him neglect his own safety."

"Why that devil of a Count! Always in the forefront of the action. Where the hell were you when all this was going on?

Weren't these men under your command? I shall hold you responsible for what happened. But we'll get to that later. Right now, we have to turn our attention to the plans of attack for the day after tomorrow. Gentlemen, the day has finally come when the League army will smash the enemy forces and drive heresy from the Kingdom of France forever. With luck, we'll capture that dog Navarre, and we'll string him up right here. Does anyone know of any reason why we should not attack? Count Treffort you are the brilliant strategist, what is your opinion?"

"Oh, I think the time is very propitious, Sire," Philippe replied reassuringly. "Because on the day after tomorrow Jupiter and Mars will face each other high in the sky, I think the omens are clearly in favor of attack and victory."

The Duke looked at him, his jaw dropped in astonishment, his surprise turned quickly into obvious pleasure. "I think I might have underestimated you, dear Count. I am happy to see that you are familiar with the science of astrology—very important for a military leader. There may be a great future for you yet."

Philippe barely suppressed a burst of laughter. What a dupe this Duke was. But it didn't matter, at long last relief of this state of idleness was at hand. To have to think no more, dream no more, not having to agonize about right and wrong, about his father, or even about Robert.

"We are moving at dawn, day after tomorrow," he heard the Duke say. "Captain you will lead the advance. I expect you to rout the enemy from the trenches before the sun comes up. Then we'll bring in artillery and cavalry after you and clinch the victory."

Philippe led his men into action with the fury of a wild animal released from long captivity. A dense, gray fog hovered over the plain of Arques in the early morning hour of the 21st of September in the year 1589, drawing a solid, opaque curtain over the meadows and marshes. The first line of League foot soldiers slowly groped its way through the mire in silent, sightless procession.

Only Philippe seemed unperturbed by the poor visibility. He stormed up the side of the hill ahead of his men, and before long they captured the lower trenches, flushing out the enemy soldiers.

Theology and politics had little to do with the rage that pushed him forward. Ideologies had no meaning on this dismal morning in autumn, in the twenty-seventh year of civil war. He was driven by only one obsession, to reenact the skirmish of the previous day, to undo the injury inflicted, to make good for his friend Robert.

What power and determination a regretful heart can rally! In short order, Philippe's platoon rolled over the top of the fortification. The royal defense crumbled like a house of straw under the fury of the onslaught that drove the King's soldiers to higher ground. Up and up the slopes they went until they reached the escarpment a few feet below the royal camp.

"Gaspard, let the men take a rest and get a casualty count!" Philippe ordered his sergeant while he tried to patch a flesh wound on his upper arm. "Also dispatch a runner to the command post, we are advancing and need cavalry and artillery support now."

Gaspard came back with a report of eleven men wounded, most of them in serious enough condition to make them unfit for further combat. Fatalities were three so far.

"All right, let's move on," Philippe ordered. "We must reach the next line of defense before the fog lifts."

"Sire, the men are still too exhausted!" Gaspard protested.

"And what about the wounded?"

"Leave them behind, the medical units will be here soon enough," Philippe replied impatiently. With dogged determination, he began to scale the side of the trench, unimpeded by the slippery ground. He was the first to gain the high ground of the footpath. The rest of the battalion struggled after him under merciless exhortations from above.

And then the unexpected happened. Philippe's shouts dissipated in an ear-shattering explosion. The earth trembled beneath the hapless soldiers who clung like ants to the slope. The first blast was followed almost immediately by a second, and a third—a whole series of salvos in quick succession.

"Sacre bleu!" Philippe cried out looking back over the plain. In his zeal, he had not noticed the change in the weather. On the vast plain below the entire League army was exposed to his view, bathed in brilliant sunshine and within clear range of the three heavy cannons embanked in the tower of the castle of Arques.

"Why didn't they think of the guns?" Philippe slapped his forehead in frustration.

What a spectacle! Philippe's platoon, perched on a hillside captured in a spurious victory, sat by, as in the front seats at a theater, and observed a scene of total havoc being wreaked on the heavily armed Leaguers who were advancing on the plain directly into the line of fire while the guns pounded away.

"Like sitting ducks! Like sitting ducks!" The wind scattered Philippe's screams. "Why doesn't he order retreat? The whole army will be annihilated!"

By noon the League army was in flight. The advance troops still held the hillside. But what good was that now! Cut off from support, they were left to their fate. God was indeed on the side of the new King of France!

"My dear Count, what a pleasure it is to see you again so soon." From the mouth of anybody else, these words would have sounded affectatious or sarcastic, but there was nothing affected or underhanded about Henri Bourbon or the manner with which he addressed his prisoner. On the contrary, he seemed genuinely delighted to find the Count Treffort-Salignac in his camp once again.

"Lieutenant! Untie the Count's hands and feet immediately," the monarch ordered. "This is not how we treat our guests."

"With all respect, Your Majesty, this man is one of the most notorious Leaguers and a prisoner of war."

"He is a guest of the King of France and I shall not have it said that the King entertains his guests while they are kept in shackles," Henri corrected.

"I hope you will forgive me for not greeting you earlier." With a casual gesture, he invited the baffled Count to make himself comfortable in the royal tent.

"You must share this special drop of wine with me." Henri lifted a pitcher and filled two pewter chalices. "An excellent vintage, from the slopes of the Pyrenees. I had several barrels sent to me only recently. If you will forgive me, but I just cannot get used to the taste of apple cider. Beer, that's another matter. Even we wine-nurtured southerners find the local beer quite delectable."

"Well, as I was saying, I hope you will forgive me for keeping you here in chains for ten days," the King continued. "Unfortunately, I was detained myself with teaching my dear cousin Mayenne a lesson. He was desperately trying to reverse the bad fortune that befell him at Arques, which should have shown him once and for all whose side the Almighty is on. But my cousin is something of a thick-headed type. To undo my victory he tried to sneak into Dieppe so he could get behind my army. I am pleased to tell you his plan did not work. But I must admit, for several days we were in a stand-off until my reinforcements arrived—the good Queen of England, that splendid old girl, was gracious enough to contribute a few thousand troops to the cause of legitimacy. Only then did the Duke decide to count his losses and he withdrew the rump of his army from the field. It seems he does not like the odds of fighting against an almost equally matched force."

Henri punctuated his remarks with jovial laughter. His comportment was altogether relaxed as if he was engaged in conversation with an old and trusted comrade. Philippe listened attentively, uneasy about being cast in the role of confidante by the man who was still supposed to be his enemy.

"So what do you say, my dear Count?" Henri demanded to know with a good-natured slap on the prisoner's back—a gesture that seemed to be a habit when he wanted to express his deep satisfaction.

"Sire, I am not sure why I am being honored with Your Majesty's confidence. I am a prisoner of war, and it does not matter what I think."

"Oh, but it does matter to me, very much!" Henri retorted with mock indignation. "Do you remember what I told you the last time we met? Here in this very place? Do you still doubt that God is on my side?"

Henri placed his mouth close to Philippe's ear, shielding it with his hand as if he was letting him in on a deep secret, and whispered: "Well, what do you think now? Was I right? I don't mind telling you that I was a bit worried, after all, we had only three thousand men against your twenty thousand."

"Your Majesty has achieved a brilliant victory and should be congratulated," Philippe replied cautiously. "But the Kingdom of France is not yet in your Majesty's hands."

"Ah, I am pleased to hear you address me with Your Majesty! I see this as a step forward in our relationship."

"Your Majesty is the King of Navarre."

"Very clever, my dear Count, very clever!" Henri slapped his thighs with delight. Philippe's uneasiness increased, he simply was unable to determine what kind of game this Navarre was playing. Or whether he was altogether sincere? Then he was a man like none he had ever encountered.

"But you can tell your master or masters, that I am also the King of France and I have no intention ever to surrender this right which is mine by birth. They have to kill me first," he added in a more somber tone.

"May I suppose that I shall be granted leave?" Philippe asked.

"Are you that anxious to return to the likes of the Duke de Mayenne? If you will pardon me, he is my cousin, but he is also something of a scoundrel, the absolute scum of the earth! Hardly at all of the same caliber as you are yourself. No, no I do not need to flatter you. But I know a man for what he is when I see one."

"Sire, if I may speak frankly, politics is at this moment far from my mind and of very little concern compared to the anguish I hold for the well-being of a dear friend. I yearn to be at the bedside of the Count de la Croix who was grievously wounded in combat. At this moment, I don't even know whether he is still alive. I have been told that his leg will have to be amputated if he is to have a chance at all. Whatever the outcome, his military career will be ended. As Your Majesty will understand, he is in great need of solace and comfort only the presence of a friend can bring."

"I am deeply touched by your sincerity and devotion to a friend," Henri spoke seriously and deliberately while he replenished their cups with wine. "I see I was not wrong about you. I know you speak the truth because I had the opportunity to observe the Count de la Croix in action on the morning he was wounded. My soldiers had their hands full with him. He made such a racket yelling: 'Long live the Holy Church! Long live the Holy Church!' Quite a fanatic that young man! And you expect me to release you so you can bring comfort to such an enemy?"

"An enemy who can no longer do you harm, who is now no more than a human being in need."

"I am not sure that he can no longer do me harm even if he can no longer fight on the field of battle. He will most likely find other ways of stoking the cabal against me. But we shall know how to deal with that when the time comes, and who knows what tomorrow will bring. I had rather hoped that you would accompany me to Paris. But all right then, you may go and go in peace. I have more important affairs to tend to," Henri rose.

"Just remember one thing and mark my word. Twice you were lucky. If you should become my prisoner again, a third time, I shall not be as lenient."

With this he left the tent: "Lieutenant, get a horse for the Count de Treffort and have him and his men escorted out of the camp. He is free to go."

The news of the royal victory at Arques preceded Navarre's triumphal sweep through southeastern Normandy to Paris. The Leaguers did their best to belittle its importance, but the parish priests and mendicant friars in the towns magnified it by conjuring up lurid tales of pillage, murder, and rape before their credulous flock.

In reality, the rumors of a reign of terror invariably proved unfounded, and city after city in Normandy, once the stronghold of the League, opened its gates to the royal party. Word spread quickly that those who entered into a pact with the King were immediately granted generous concessions.

CHAPTER
10

"Sandrine has disappeared!" Catherine de Treffort announced with tears in her eyes. Philippe had immediately sought out his sister on returning home to the Chateau d'Evreux when he found the convent of Sainte Hélène's deserted. The people in the village told him that the nuns had left the nunnery for fear of the advancing royal army.

"We have searched for her everywhere. Nobody seems to remember seeing her leave. She is gone without a trace." She anxiously searched her brother's face.

"I had been hoping that somehow she had joined you," she added.

"But why, why would she leave without at least an

explanation? It just makes no sense!" Philippe felt the blood freeze in his veins. His knees were shaking and he had to seek the support of a chair by the fireplace to keep from collapsing under the weight of the naked terror that seized him. Biting his fist to muffle his sobs, he stared into the fire as if somehow he could wrest the answer from the dancing flames.

"We often spoke about you," Catherine said softly. "You were her life. But she was uncomfortable about coming here, she would have preferred to stay at Sainte Hélène's."

"What makes you think so?" Philippe asked.

"She told me so on the day we left the convent." Catherine sat in the chair next to her brother. "I saw no need to evacuate the convent, but our dear father, the Duke, believes that Henri de Navarre is the devil incarnate and his army a band of raping, pillaging marauders. He convinced the bishop that the nuns of Sainte Hélène were in imminent danger of falling into the hands of the heretic soldiers and should be allowed to take refuge here at the castle. With the specter of disaster hanging over us, I had the responsibility to assure the welfare of the sisters and, of course, also of Sandrine, as I had promised."

"The nuns had already boarded the carriages sent from Evreux when we noticed that Sandrine was not with the party. I then realized that I had not seen her all morning. I returned to the convent and found her in the library engrossed in a book, determined to stay. She declared that she was not afraid of the king. By this she meant Navarre."

Catherine paused. She rose and stoked the fire mumbling something about it being rather cold already for this time of the year. She decided this was not a fitting moment to share with her brother her suspicions that the girl may be a heretic or at least have heretic sympathies. Her knowledge of the Bible was certainly unusual, and so was her interest in the writings of

Marguerite de Navarre.

"I told her it was totally out of the question that she should stay alone at the cloister," Catherine continued. "I begged her to consider her condition, and besides I had made a solemn promise to you that I would look after her. She replied in a very calm and deliberate manner as if she had thought about this very carefully, that she was afraid of what might be in store for her at Chateau d'Evreux."

"I tried to assuage her worries, but when I took her hand to pull her toward the door, she put up fierce resistance. It was as if she had a premonition that something terrible would happen. But I had no time to linger, Navarre's army was within an hour of the convent. She begged me to understand her apprehension of the world outside. For the first time in her life, she had felt sheltered and safe since living within the cloister walls. From what I was able to understand, she was concerned she might become an embarrassment to both of us. Of course, I told her this was utter nonsense, and I was finally able to talk her into leaving the cloister. That was the last time we spoke alone. She disappeared three days after we arrived here."

Philippe looked at his sister in a daze. "What do you mean she did not want to become an embarrassment?"

"Well, she thought a pregnant nun would surely stand out in the crowd and people might talk. But I told her not to worry, I would protect her from any scorn."

"Pregnant? Do you mean to say she is with child?" Philippe jumped up and seized his sister's hands with such force, she winced in pain.

"Didn't you know she was expecting a child?" Catherine had assumed that Sandrine had told Philippe before he left. "She was so happy and proud. Her term cannot be more than eight weeks away."

"Then where is she?" he shouted. "We must find her! We must find her!" Philippe repeated the phrase over and over, more to himself than to his sister.

"There must be something we can do. Somebody around here must have seen her." He pounded a balled fist against his open palm in quick succession with such force, Catherine feared he was about to lose his mind.

"For God's sake, Philippe, you must calm yourself!"

At this moment, a servant asked permission to be admitted into the presence of his lordship and handed him a note. Philippe opened it distractedly, visibly irritated by the interruption.

"This must be a joke!" he mumbled. "The whole thing must be a prank or a bad dream. This cannot be real!"

"What does the note say?" Catherine demanded to know.

"It asks me to be at the well in the outer courtyard at eleven o'clock tonight. Somebody requested to meet me with information about the missing woman. What is this? A game? Maybe somebody abducted her! But why?"

"And who is it you are supposed to meet?"

"It does not say, the note is unsigned."

"It may be a hoax, but then again it may be a genuine lead. At any rate, I suggest we do not tell the Duke and Duchess anything about this matter."

"You are right. I have so much to thank you for, my dear sister."

"Believe me, I am as concerned as you are about the girl's well-being. I have come to love her as a sister in the time she was at the convent. You were so right, she is an extraordinary young woman, even though she is still almost a child. I am confident she will be found," she added the last words with more emphasis than conviction. Her heart was heavy with grave foreboding.

"What a rare and wonderful event to have the whole

family united for dinner!" The Duchess d'Evreux's doting eyes rested on her offspring. Catherine almost did not join them. But she finally gave in to her mother's entreaties to relax the monastic rules just this once and have dinner with her family. The sisters had sequestered themselves in an isolated part of the castle where they could observe the rules of the order as well as circumstances permitted. As was customary the Abbess took her meals with her nuns, only the food was brought up from the common kitchen.

The Duchess's elation at having her children at home did not blind her to the somber mood at the table. Neither one touched much of the delicacies she had specially ordered for the occasion. But she attributed Philippe's preoccupation to the bad turn the war had taken for the League. Of course, she would not be so bold as to ask questions. God forbid that she should pry in her son's affairs, just as she could never be accused of prying in her husband's affairs. She had always abided by the precept that a woman does not meddle with the world of men.

As for Catherine, she had never understood her daughter. Her only daughter had grown so distant from her since she had taken the veil. But then she had always been distant, even as a very small child, and was always of an independent spirit. So maybe it was only natural that she should have chosen the religious life. How else in this world, but as a nun, could a woman lead a fairly independent existence? A paradox perhaps, but true.

The heart of the mother still ached to think her daughter deprived of the joys of love and motherhood. But will she not also be spared the anguish and pain of endless days and weeks of waiting for the men to return from war, first the husband and then the sons, which was the lot of a wife and mother?

The Duchess looked up, alarmed by the sharpness of the

tone the dinner conversation between her husband and her son was taking. She had never heard Philippe speak like this to his father.

"Arques was only one battle. This does not mean the war against heresy is lost." The Duke shouted, his face red with anger. "You'll see, Mayenne will rally his forces—he is doing so right now in Picardie—and next time he will capture the renegade and put an end to this would-be king and the whole damned Religion once and for all."

"We have been saying the same thing for a long time. For years and years, I have heard it said, next time we'll finish them off, we'll end this war, and still, they prevail," Philippe countered with equal force. "Just consider the odds at the battle of Arques—a handful of royal troops against a massive League army. A splendid force of thousands of men and armor routed, thrown into total disarray. I saw it with my own eyes. Anybody who can win so decisively against such an overwhelming force can only do this with God on his side."

"I shall not tolerate such blasphemy in my house!" The veins in the Duke's temples swelled to the point of almost bursting. "Navarre may have the devil on his side, but never God Almighty."

"He seems to think otherwise," Philippe continued with merciless calm. His mother wondered what had happened to the obedient son they once knew. But her fright of what the Duke might do in face of being so deliberately provoked mingled with a secret satisfaction at finally seeing Philippe stand up against the tyrannical father.

"You had occasion to discuss this subject with Navarre himself?"

"Yes, I did, when I was taken prisoner due to the incompetence of that fabulous military genius Mayenne, who does not have enough brains to plan a battle. I am pleased to let you know that Henri showed himself a most gracious gentleman—and it may surprise you that he has neither horns nor a tail. He released me and my men after ten days."

"He released a captain of the enemy army? Under what conditions? To act as a spy?"

"No conditions! I resent the insinuation!" Philippe's voice bristled with anger. "I have done nothing to disgrace our family name. Navarre let me go so I could join a wounded friend whose condition gave me cause for grave concern."

"You expect me to believe that the devil has human feelings? And who is your wounded friend?"

"A man to whom I owe my life and more. You know him well. Robert de la Croix."

"Robert is wounded!" Stunned silence fell over the table. All eyes wandered in the direction whence came the hushed expression of anguish. Catherine had been following the exchange between her father and brother with avid interest, ready to intervene, if the bout should get out of hand. But the news of Robert jolted her out of her equilibrium.

"I hope the Count is recuperating well. The League needs devoted fighters like him," she added in a firmer voice, her eyes fixed on the plate before her lest those present should detect the blood rushing to her face.

The Duchess was the first to understand what was happening. Quickly she diverted the men's attention from Catherine and demanded to know whether this dear friend of the family was on his way to recovery.

"He is now under the care of his family, I am sure he will recover," Philippe began. "He fought like a lion leading a handful of men in a skirmish—a bit imprudent though."

"But," he added somberly, turning toward his sister, "I am

afraid he will no longer be able to serve the Church on the battlefield. His right leg had to be amputated below the knee to contain the spread of a gangrenous infection. We must thank God for having preserved his life."

Philippe's eyes rested on his sister while he spoke. Robert's words flashed through his mind: "Tell the Lady Catherine I died for the Holy Church and to the end, I loved her more than my life."

How could he have been so blind not to notice? This explained Robert's strange behavior. He knew his friend had fallen in love, a love, he thought, unrequited with no hope of fulfillment. But who might be the object of Robert's affection had not occurred to him. Now he saw very clearly that Robert's love was not unrequited at all, but it was returned with consuming, albeit hopeless, passion.

"Philippe! Philippe!" His mother's voice brought him back to the present. "I am sorry we did not know sooner about Robert. Oh, the shock you must have been in, my poor son!"

"I shall send a messenger in the morning to find out when it will be convenient to pay a call on our hero." With these words, the Duke rose from the table, the signal for everybody else to rise as well.

"My son, get some rest. A father and son should not have such heated arguments. Unfortunately, I shall be away at Rouen on business for a few days, but we'll find time to talk things over on my return. You must be very tired."

Philippe just nodded. He hoped for an opportunity to speak with his sister, but she had already retired to the part of the castle cordoned off for the nuns of Sainte Hélène's. He kissed his mother good night. For a moment, their eyes rested in each other in silent anguish. He knew, she too understood Catherine's pain.

At the appointed hour, Philippe hid in the shadow of the trees near the well in the outer courtyard. He breathed in deeply the cool, crisp air to still the palpitations of his heart. What if he was making a fool of himself and this anonymous person had no intention of keeping this nocturnal rendezvous. It could all be a trick by someone who wanted to amuse himself at his expense.

Fortunately, he did not have to wait long. In the moonlit night, he soon made out the cloaked figure of a man approaching the well. His back was bent, his heavy, laborious step indicated that he was a man of advanced age. Philippe could hear the man's short, heaving breathing as he plunked himself down at the edge of the well, taking a moment to recover from the exertion. Then he cautiously looked around in all directions.

"You may come out now, My Lord. We are alone," he said with a turn of his head toward where Philippe was hiding.

"François! You are perceptive for a man of your age," Philippe opened his arms to embrace his father's trusted manservant.

"These days one has to be vigilant at any age. That's the secret of survival and longevity. But let's not waste time with idle chatter."

François drew closer to Philippe and got straight to the point: "The woman you are looking for did not leave the castle voluntarily. She was escorted by the captain of the guard and left on the roadside to Rouen—on order of your father, the Duke."

"You mean to say my father banished her from the castle! But why?"

"That is all I know and I beg Your Lordship, please do not ask any further questions. For your good and the good of all of us, I beg of you, let the matter rest. I pray God may be with you, may he bless your soul, My Lord." He bent over the young nobleman's hand and covered it with emphatic kisses.

Before Philippe, stunned as much by the revelation as by the warning, had time to demand an explanation, the old man had disappeared.

That night Philippe was locked in a more desperate struggle with the demon than ever before. It was dawning when he sank into a dreamless sleep. When he awoke at noon, it seemed that the whole world had abandoned him. His sister and the nuns had returned to Sainte Hélène's. His father had embarked on his journey to Rouen and would not be back for several days. A welcome respite from the tension that was growing between them. No, François did not accompany him, he was told, the old man had returned to his native village a long time ago. Nobody had seen him around the castle in recent months. Only his mother's quiet, unassuming presence brought a measure of comfort to his dejected soul.

Book
Two

A TIME TO REND, A TIME TO SEW

CHAPTER 1

"Step right up, Ladies and Gentlemen! Step right up! Live the excitement, witness the fight of little David against the giant Goliath! The show is about to begin! Witness the duel between the midget and the giant! Relive one of the most decisive battles in the history of humankind!"

A burly, tall man, with a bushy mustache, twirled upwards at the ends, the flowing, brightly colored coat of itinerant actors draping his shoulders, ground out a tune on his hurdy-gurdy, all the while sizing up the gathering crowd.

Apprentices and journeymen milled about in the front of the makeshift stage under the Petit Pont. Mingling with the more prosperous elements of shopkeepers, artisans, and craftsmen were pickpockets, beggars, washerwomen, market criers, an army of "fallen" women—riffraff of every description from the bowels of Paris. Some looked over the crudely drawn posters depicting scenes from the play. Others demanded to know more about the production. The burly man responded with the eloquence of the seasoned huckster in a bit to beat out the competition just a short stroll away.

The city of Paris was a magnet for itinerant entertainers. Nowhere else could be found such a teeming mass of humanity hungry for distraction, some well-to-do, even wealthy, most destitute, living on the dole, a rough-and-ready audience not easily satisfied.

On any given day of the year, even during Lent, Parisians had their pick from among every imaginable form of entertainment. Acrobats and jugglers attracted crowds at every street corner in the lower-class quarters. Puppet shows and theater performances were commonplace. So were animal acts. Trained dogs and bears were ever popular. Strolling bands of musicians brought a note, if not of hope, at least of solace to the backyards of filthy, rat-infested tenements. Nor was this the only distraction available. It was said that the streets of Paris were lined with more prostitutes than the ancient city of Babylon.

The burly man at the hurdy-gurdy ended the tune with a rousing rally. He seemed satisfied with the size of the crowd that had assembled, just large enough for a good collection. He knew from experience that the suspense before the curtain is lifted should not be stretched too far.

"Let the show begin!" he bellowed toward the back of the stage. He had to repeat his call twice, each time with greater emphasis. Finally, the sheepskin canvas was pulled back to reveal a bare stage.

The hurdy-gurdy played a hushed variation of a tune

suggesting the grand entry of a king. A young boy of about fifteen or sixteen strode majestically onto the stage. He stumbled toward the audience, his view obstructed by an oversized broad-rimmed hat, decorated with a huge white plume. He gesticulated fiercely with a wooden sword and demanded to know: "Where are the Philistines? Show me the way to the Philistines! I am David, the rightful king of this land by the grace of God! Anybody who attempts to challenge my claim will be utterly destroyed. God will send down fire and brimstone on my enemies. Take my word for it, he told me so himself."

The audience cheered and roared with laughter. The boy raced around the stage swinging his sword through the air, emitting horrible cries that would scare even an imaginary army. Suddenly he came to a halt, his path was blocked by a man who towered above him. The music rose to an ominous pitch. Quiet suspense gripped the audience. The boy lifted his head slowly to face the man in a cuirass who unfolded a banner imprinted with a design of black fleurs-de-lys on a white background and stuck it in his helmet.

"It's the Duke de Mayenne!" Excited shouts from the crowd. "It's Mayenne and Navarre!"

"What can I do for you?" The tall man roared derisively.

"Well, maybe you can show me the way to Ivry! I am to meet there with a great warrior renowned in all the land for his brave exploits in battle. You might know him, his name is Goliath. Too bad he is a Philistine!"

The spectators' whistles and cheers at the mention of Ivry almost drowned out the actors' dialogue.

"And what is your business with this Goliath, the Philistine?" the tall man thundered.

"I am David, the king, and in all the earth there is only room for one true king. Goliath refuses to recognize this God-given fact. A mighty duel, trial by fire will decide the truth of the matter—it's Goliath or David. With the help of God, I'll crush the monster with my bare hands!"

"We can settle the score right here and now!" the tall man seized the slight lad by the throat and pressed his face against his. "I am Goliath, the Philistine, a warrior renowned in all the land. Let's see who will crush whom with bare hands."

The boy wriggled free. A chase ensued around the stage. The actors delighted the audience with shouts of insults and acrobatic stunts while the music from the hurdy-gurdy kept grinding on. Each time the tall man reached for the boy, the wight slipped through his hands with flips and turns. Finally, the pursuer weighed down by his heavy armor fell flat on his back and gave up the ghost.

The boy placed his foot on the man's chest, raised his sword, and proclaimed solemnly: "Thus will the Almighty deal with all those who challenge the rights of his appointed servants!"

Two young girls had started to move through the crowd during the chase scene shaking a collection box in front of the onlookers. They knew well that the trick of the trade was to approach the audience while they were still engrossed in the action.

Word of the play quickly spread among the Parisians. For the most part, there were wild cheers of approval, but there were also some boos of discontent. Within a week, David and Goliath had become the sensation of Paris.

More and more people came to the makeshift theater under the Petit Pont. Even members of the upper bourgeoisie braved the dangers of the Paris underworld to see for themselves. The audience became more boisterous, on occasion a brawl would break out between those who were amused and those who were offended.

"Mireya! Sandrine!" the burly man called out, "you'd better start collecting at the beginning of the show, our customers seem so engaged in the action, they may forget to pay!"

"Morin, I'd rather you left the collecting to me," replied an older, slightly florid woman who appeared from behind the curtain. "In this crowd, the girls might get hurt."

Morin walked over to the woman and squeezed her buttocks with a good-natured twinkle in his eyes: "You are the most beautiful woman in the world, Rosande, but youth has its advantages, and I think this crowd will respond more generously to our two young beauties. Besides you are needed back here."

She pushed him away before he could plant a kiss on her mouth, but he knew that she was only pretending to be insulted. In a family business, each member had a specific task to perform.

"Just look at the two," Morin pointed at Sandrine and Mireya moving through the aisles with their collection boxes. "Two total opposites, one fair and the other dark, both ravishing! Don't you feel that we now have two daughters, now that Sandrine has come into our life?"

"You know I think we are very lucky, she has brought so much joy. But I am afraid, Morin, I am afraid no good will come from this play—it is too dangerous to make light of politics and religion, especially in this city." And with a deep sigh, she added: "I wish you would just drop it. What was wrong with the other plays we had? They were good fun and offended nobody."

"Look at this crowd, Rosande. We have never played to such a crowd, and they keep coming. This is what the public wants. And we will, at last, make more than just enough to keep us fed."

"I just hope and pray, no harm will come to us," Rosande repeated. An infant's cries from inside the wagon drew her away.

Sandrine, too, felt uneasy about the attention the small group of itinerant actors attracted in the capital. Oh, certainly business had been very good this past week, better than it had ever been in the provinces. Their program contained a variety of other vignettes, most based on familiar biblical stories. What made these pieces so popular was that everybody took them as satires of the conflict between the League and the royalists, though no names were used. Sandrine wondered how long the Leaguers of Paris would tolerate being made the butt of derision. Although she delighted in singing and dancing the role of the Queen of Sheba in one skit, the sense of impending trouble never left her.

One evening, while Morin was playing the hurdy-gurdy before the start of the show, and the women were peeking through the curtain to see who was in the audience, a magnificent carriage, embossed in gold, pulled up in front of the theater. The splendidly attired woman who alighted attracted immediate attention. She was obviously a lady of great wealth, and neither the slight limp in her gait nor certain signs that she was approaching the middle of her years, tarnished her beauty and charm.

"Who is she?" Sandrine brimmed with curiosity.

"I don't know," Rosande replied. "But she seems no stranger to the Paris canaille. Look at the familiarity and even kindness with which she speaks to the people pressing around her. Let's ask Mireya. She is just coming in, maybe she heard something."

"She is the Duchess de Montpensier." Mireya bubbled over with excitement. "They call her the Queen of the Holy League. She is always riding around the streets of Paris in an open carriage and exhorts the people to keep up their support for the League and the Church. She hates Navarre and has been heard to swear he will never take Paris as long as she is alive."

"Her presence here tonight may then not bode well for us," Sandrine warned. "What if she takes offense?"

"Oh, Sandrine! You worry too much. Nobody takes our little vignettes seriously. We are not political, we entertain people. Besides if anybody is made fun of it's Navarre as much as Mayenne."

"That may be so, but I am not sure Sandrine isn't right to worry," Rosande interjected. "Here, time for the first act. Let me have the baby, Sandrine you are on. Go knock Madame off her feet! Show her you are every bit a queen as she is!"

During intermission, Sandrine solicited contributions from the audience. With a polite curtsy, she held up the box to the Duchess seated in the front row. For a brief moment, their eyes met. A spark of curiosity passed between them. Sandrine thought she saw a fleeting glimpse of recognition in the Duchess's eyes as if she took her for someone she knew. But then the spectacle diverted her attention. Madame ordered a servant to make a generous contribution and Sandrine continued to make her way through the rows of spectators.

Later that evening, the Duchess had left, Sandrine noticed several characters, she had not seen before, lingering near the stage. They peered with grim intensity at the crowd about to gather for the second performance. She linked up with Mireya who was working the other side.

"What do you make of those types over there?" she whispered. "Could they be from the police?"

"If so, they are probably looking for pickpockets or royal propagandists. If they were after us, why would they wait?" replied the ever-optimistic Mireya. "Or, they may be bodyguards for Madame de Montpensier."

"But she left some time ago, why would they stay around?"

The next morning, when Sandrine returned from the

market, Mireya greeted her with tears. The police had stormed their camp and had arrested the men of the troupe. Morin and his brothers, César and Gilles, had been taken to God knows where.

"Don't worry," Sandrine tried to calm the girl with more confidence in her voice than she felt inside. "I'll find out where they are and try to obtain their release."

She had no idea what to do, or how she would fulfill her promise. But Mireya immediately ceased crying.

"I shall take care of the baby while you are away, I promise." Mireya rocked the baby gently in her arms.

CHAPTER 2

Sandrine navigated her way around a wretched mass of humanity piled up in the corridors of the police prefecture—thieves, beggars, vagrants, prostitutes. Some had been arrested the night before while in pursuit of their livelihood, others were simply riffraff with no place to call their own who had been picked up for loitering in the streets after curfew. Many were women and street urchins, driven from the gutter by the hoary hand of March.

Sandrine had known misery in her life. Famine and disease were constant afflictions of the peasants. But never had she imagined the abject poverty of the city, the plight of thousands of people leading a doleful existence in crowded tenements or out in the open streets, infested with packs of stray dogs and rats; streets, narrow and sunless, running with human and animal excrement. All in the shadow of the splendid palaces and mansions of the aristocracy.

What a curious predicament she had gotten herself into, Sandrine thought. More than ever she hated the pretensions of the aristocracy, those who feasted on the broken backs of the moaning masses. Yet, she had come to Paris in hopes of finding an aristocrat, the man she loved more than life, the father of her child.

How self-serving she had been! She had encouraged her friends, without revealing her motive, to take their show to Paris in the secret hope that here, in the capital of the League, she might find Philippe.

The troupe was now already several weeks in the city and she did not even know where to begin the search. Every night she hoped and prayed that she might recognize him in the crowd gathering at the theater. But every night her hopes were disappointed. The chance that their paths would cross in this enormous city with its myriad quarters, an intricate maze of narrow streets and squares, arranged seemingly haphazardly and leading nowhere, were slim indeed.

But now a more immediate crisis required her attention. Somehow she felt responsible for this debacle. It was she who had suggested to Morin that here was an idea for a play when they heard the news of the second great rout of Mayenne's army on the 14th of March at Ivry. A true David and Goliath contest, she had called it.

She was still wandering along the corridors of the prefecture when she suddenly found her way blocked by a constable. "Do you have permission to enter this part of the building?"

"I don't know if I do or not." She was not very good at flirting with men but had noticed in the past few months that she seemed to elicit a certain response from the males of the species and if she asked nicely, she could get almost anything.

"Maybe you can help me," she said, smiling a sweet smile that promptly met its mark. "I am trying to find some dear friends who were arrested this morning. They are, of course, completely innocent and I would like to testify to that fact."

"Well, so many people are arrested every day, and they are all innocent."

"But my friends are innocent, and I can prove it."

"What is the charge?"

"I don't know, but it must be something silly, I am sure. They are actors, entertainers."

"Their names wouldn't happen to be Morin, César, and Gilles, three gypsies."

"Yes, that's them, actors and acrobats, honorable, law-abiding fellows."

"How did a beautiful girl like you get mixed up with such riff-raff? Your friends, if that's what they are, have been charged with sedition, defaming the Holy Church and a few other, equally grave, transgressions. For your good, take my advice and leave them to their fate. I would hate to see you end in prison too."

"But that cannot be. I know they are innocent and I'll say so to anybody."

"Maybe you should talk to Monsieur Hachette, the prosecutor. Up the stairs and to your left."

Sandrine thanked the man profusely and taking two steps at a time, she flew up the broad marble staircase.

Hervé Hachette was the quintessential, bourgeois bureaucrat, dressed in a black advocate's frock, his chin held up by a stiff white collar, his near-sighted eyes permanently frozen into a squint. He had the irritating habit of walking about with his hands folded behind his back, then coming to a sudden halt and rocking back and forth on the balls of his feet as if he were forever weighing pros and cons. He was a man of medium height and indeterminate age. The word that would describe him best was "drab." He was certainly not the type of man who excited the passion of women.

"Ah! Her Majesty, the Queen of Sheba! How nice of you to come. I was just about to send for you, Madame." Monsieur Hachette's mocking tone did not disguise his pleasure at seeing Sandrine.

"I demand to know why my friends were arrested!" Sandrine got straight to the point unaware of the presumptuousness of her demand.

"My dear child, must I point out to you that you are in no position to make demands? Your friends, as well as you, have been charged with sedition. You should know that meddling in politics is a dangerous game." He waved his forefinger at her like a schoolmaster scolding a pupil for bad behavior.

"We are actors. Our purpose is to entertain. Politics has nothing to do with our work."

"Well spoken! But the audience does not seem to see it that way. How do you account for your popularity? Because people are interested in old yarn like the story of David and Goliath? Come on, you cannot be that naive. The penalty is imprisonment for an indefinite period for all of you. The child in your company will have to be placed in an orphanage, of course."

He noticed with satisfaction the terror he had struck into her heart and was determined to press his advantage. "Of course, all this need not happen, if we can come to a, shall we say, certain agreement."

"What kind of agreement?" she inquired eagerly like

someone drowning would reach desperately for any straw being tendered. "I assure you, Sire, we are only humble, itinerant actors. If you wish we shall be on our way tomorrow."

"Well now, I couldn't let you do that, could I? The agreement I had mind was more in the form of . . . an arrangement," Monsieur Hachette said slowly drawing out every word. He moved closer toward her, certain that he had her at his mercy, and prepared for the final pounce. Gently he let his hand run through her hair. She drew back.

Maybe she was of a different sort, after all, he thought. And she may require a more subtle approach. Something told him that this girl was no ordinary gypsy. Judging from her appearance she was no gypsy at all. But neither did she fit the picture of the ordinary French peasant. Here was a mystery that beckoned to be solved.

"What is your name?" he assumed a more beguiling, fatherly tone. "Please have a seat, you must be tired." He pointed to a chair in front of his desk and placed himself behind it.

"Sandrine." She remained standing.

"Sandrine what? Where are you from?"

"From nowhere in particular. I told you we are itinerants, our home is the road," she replied.

"But your parents. Who are your parents?"

"My parents are dead."

"Were your parents also itinerant actors?"

"Yes."

"You know, for some reason, I don't believe you. I think you are lying and I shall find out why."

"Why should I be lying to you? You have me completely in your power; I don't think it would be wise for me to tell you lies."

"You are not only beautiful, you are also very clever. But,

I still don't believe you." He walked to the window, his hands folded behind his back. He stared out into the street, rocking gently back and forth first on the ball of one foot then the other as if he were weighing pros and cons. Somewhere, something does not make any sense here. His bloodhound instinct was aroused.

"Every day I am confronted with hundreds of people, hauled in from the streets of Paris for one reason or other," he finally said almost to himself. "There are thieves, beggars, washerwomen, prostitutes, drunks, actors, and acrobats, what have you, riffraff, the ugly dregs of the earth."

Suddenly he pivoted on his heels. "But has there ever been anybody like Sandrine? Should it be possible that the gutter would produce such beauty, such grace, such pride? When has there ever been a vagrant of such simple cunning?"

While he rambled on, he could see a nervous tenseness rising in her. He liked to create suspense.

"You are doing me too much honor, Sire. I assure you, you must believe me, I am just an ordinary woman of the people."

"Sandrine, Sandrine!" He repeated the name, sensuously, letting the sound roll over his tongue as if he was savoring an exquisite vintage. "Where have I heard that name before?"

"It is such a common name, you surely must have met many women named Sandrine."

"No, no," he insisted. "Something occurred not too long ago, something that had to do with a woman named Sandrine. It will come to me sooner or later."

"Surely, Sire, whatever it is that my name reminds you of, it would not have anything to do with me or this situation, which I beseech you to resolve in our favor."

"Probably not. All right, then. Let's get back to how the matter at hand can be resolved to everybody's satisfaction. As I see it, there are two ways. The first is very simple, you and your friends will be charged with sedition. Of course, you will have to be detained while you are waiting to be tried, which may not be before next spring. The courts are overloaded with cases, so there is no guarantee when or if a trial will take place."

He paused, his squinting eyes fixed on her face. As if he just remembered something, he turned abruptly and started to thumb through a pile of papers stacked on his desk.

Sandrine sank into the chair she had declined earlier. Should she be more ingratiating toward this repulsive, little man, who, it was clear to see, enjoyed the power he held over her? What if she pretended to go along with any arrangement he might propose? At the proper moment, what was to keep her from deceiving the miserable worm?

"What is the other way open?" Sandrine swallowed hard. "You mentioned two ways."

"Oh, yes!" he said with deliberate slowness. "There is an alternative." He placed two fingers on his mouth and gazed for a moment at the ceiling as if he had difficulty remembering. Then he tapped his forehead with the palm of his hand.

"Of course! But you will have to be a very, very good girl." He approached the chair in which she was seated and began circling it like a beast stalking its prey, then he came up from behind and placed his mouth close to her ear. Sandrine's back stiffened. A repellent odor exuded from his body and mouth, but she did not dare move.

"There is a house in the Rue Saint-Sauvieur," he explained in a low, conspiratorial tone. "You will lodge there with your child in comfort—servants, good food, beautiful clothes, all shall be provided."

"And what do I have to do in return for all this?" Sandrine whispered breathlessly.

"Not much. You just have to show some kindness to me from time to time, provide companionship."

"In other words, you want me to sell my body to you!" Sandrine jumped up as if she had been stung. She trembled with rage.

"My dear child, calm yourself! Surely, this sort of thing is nothing new to you?"

"I'd rather die a thousand deaths in the Asylum than let a detestable, slimy worm-like you touch me!"

"This is your last word on the matter?"

"Absolutely!"

"Very well, you shall have your wish." He called in two constables. "Take this woman to the women's house of detention. The charge is sedition and blasphemy."

Ear-shattering clatter! Sound of finality! The prison gate fell shut behind her. Its screeching echo reverberated in Sandrine's head as she was pushed into a dim, cavernous prison cell. A faint glimmer of daylight filtered through two narrow holes, carved into the thick, damp walls, and cast a spectral pall over the heaps of human refuse scattered about the dirt floor.

Sandrine strained her eyes to make out the dismal surroundings. There were at least a hundred inmates housed in this cell. A putrid stench of excrement and menstrual flow rose from the filth-encrusted creatures, hardly recognizable as women. Most languished in a dull stupor. If they talked at all it was only to themselves as if they existed inside invisible, isolated spheres. A horrible shock of recognition came over her: most of these women were utterly insane.

Slowly the realization of what had happened began to sink in. What if it was true that hardly anyone of the thousands of women, who are sucked into this hell every year, ever emerge again into the sunlight? How did she end up in this infernal pit?

Sobbing with anger and despair, she sank on the sack of straw to which she had been assigned.

Noël! the joy of my life, living token of my love, she moaned. What will happen to you? Will I ever see you again? That beast Hachette was liable to send him to an orphanage and her friends to prison. Why, oh why couldn't I control my disgust? Why didn't I just pretend to go along?

But it was too late now. Because of her stupid pride, she had lost her son. He was only four months old. How could he survive in an orphanage?

She had named him Noël because he was born on Christmas Day of the year 1589—a true gift from heaven.

The Oranto Brothers' acting troupe, with whom she had found a home a few weeks before, was on its way south from Rouen to the fair at Elbeuf. A dense snowstorm had made the road impassable, just at the time when Sandrine began to feel the first pangs of labor, forcing them to halt the caravan by the roadside.

The event turned into a true family affair. When she signaled that her time was drawing near, Morin lifted Sandrine on the kitchen table. Rosande, his wife, took charge, breathing along with her as if she felt each rise and ebb of her body. Mireya, their daughter, a girl only two years younger, held her hand. It was as if all three women experienced together the pain from the infant's struggle to get free. But it was a happy pain, a pain that faded with the first cry of the new life.

Noël was everybody's baby. Everybody in the close family circle doted on him from the day he was born. And what a beautiful child he was! To Sandrine, he looked exactly like Philippe.

If only Philippe could see him! But for the time being, it was probably better if he didn't even know where she was. She knew how mortified he would be when he would find her gone and she was sorry for the anguish it would cause him. Would he understand that she had no choice? Would it have made any sense to send a message telling him that she had been expelled from Chateau d'Evreux for reasons she was herself still unable to fathom? Philippe should not be put in a position where he had to choose between her and his father.

The memory of the encounter with the Duke was indelibly imprinted in her mind. As long as she lived, she would not forget the horror in the old man's eyes when he caught sight of her in the courtyard. What was it he saw? Did he know about her relationship with Philippe? She doubted it. Something told her that the Duke's horrified reaction had nothing to do with his son at all, that it came from something beyond anybody's ken.

One thing she knew instinctively from that moment on— the Duke d'Evreux was her enemy. Never would this man permit a union between his son and a nobody, she was certain. This man was a callous aristocrat, who had none of his son's compassion and kindness. Who but a heartless monster would order a woman, so obviously with child, to leave his domain, have her escorted under armed guard, and leave her stranded by the roadside in the middle of nowhere in driving rain?

For a long time, she had pondered the riddle of the Duke's behavior, tried to fathom his motive. Somehow it all made no sense. No human being was that uncharitable! Unless, unless there was something else, something not yet apparent to her. One day, she would find out, one day she had to find out if she was ever to find happiness with Philippe.

One day, she would return, but not before she found out who she was. Somewhere in this kingdom was buried the key to her identity and she swore to herself she would unearth it.

Only now, she got herself buried alive in this tomb and she may never have a chance to unveil the mystery.

Oh yes, the captain of the ducal guard handed her a pouch of gold crowns, compliments of the Duke—useless pieces of metal since there was no food or shelter to be had for miles, no town within reach of the spot where she was set down. She later gave the pouch to Morin without revealing its origin. She would not deign touch a hand-out from the Duke d'Evreux.

How lucky she had been! Lucky to have been adopted into this itinerant gypsy family. For the first time in her life, she experienced the warmth and security of a true family.

She surely would have died had Morin not stopped the caravan on that bleak, wet October day when she wandered, starved and disoriented, along the side of the road, weighed down by the heaviness of her body, her heart stricken with fear of losing the child.

The generosity of these strangers made everything well. When her son was born, her happiness was complete. Never in her life had she felt as deep a sense of fulfillment as when she nurtured her child.

Sometimes she worried that she did not miss Philippe as much as she should. Only at night, when her body was aflame with longing for his embrace, she knew that he was the only man she would ever love. At times she feared going mad with a desire to feel his body against hers, to touch her lips to his. The thought of another man, like that Hachette, touching her made her shudder with revulsion.

The Asylum! Everything she had heard whispered about this women's prison was true. But words could not capture the reality of this living hell. What mind had conceived this monument to human indifference and depravity? Thousands of women, if they can still be called that, reduced to ghostly shadows of human existence, buried alive! How long will it be before she too will become indistinguishable from this macabre horde of skeletons?

No! No! A thousand times no! She must get out of here! No use wasting time with self-pity nor pity for others. There must be a way out!

Yet, as time moved on, all hope and resolve slowly eroded. She soon lost count of the days and weeks. At first, she thought she could not survive another day, another hour without a word about her son, without assurance that he was well. Gradually, her spirit succumbed. There would be no miraculous rescue this time. Nobody even knew where she was. If Philippe were looking for her, he had no way of ever finding her. She thought of the time once before when she had given up hope and then he had appeared. But it wouldn't be like that this time.

This time was different. No public trial, not a trace. Not even her friends knew where she was, and heaven knows to what hole they had been condemned to rot.

"You will get used to it and after a while, you might even call this place home." The raspy voice came from the straw mattress next to hers. She had not paid much attention to her neighbors. All this time, she did not even know whether that rolled-up corpse next to her was dead or alive.

"Look on the bright side. You have food and a roof over your head, costs you nothing. Eah, where else can you get that? Free!"

"How long have you been in here?" Sandrine inquired.

The woman was probably not quite thirty, though her face was traversed with deep furrows, the legacy of a life of either great deprivation or of debauchery. Her body was in ruin with only faint traces of a once attractive woman who had known her share of admirers.

"It can get pretty lonely in here with no one to talk to. But what is there to do if you should get out of here?" the woman continued to unravel a life's philosophy formed in a world of neglect. "You can steal or beg, but there is much competition out there. Of course, as a pretty woman, you have another selling point, your body, with a body like yours you could make a career. But after a while, this too takes its toll, you start to sag, you get either too fat or too thin, then they don't want you anymore and you get tossed on the dung heap. I was a professional whore, the very best, mistress of a king!"

"You are putting me on. What king would bother with you?" Sandrine derided her although she welcomed the distraction from too much brooding.

"I am speaking about Arsène Rigoud, the king of beggars and thieves. He reigns over the court of miracles of Saint Honoré. There is no man more powerful in all of Paris. Even the police prefect and the provost of merchants listen to him. And I was his queen!"

"If he is so powerful, why are you in here?"

"I'm in here because he is so powerful. Understand? All he has to do is grease the palm of the police and let them know what he wants done, and it gets done." She raised herself up and moved closer to Sandrine.

"For years, I went about my business, peacefully. Never had any trouble with the police. Why should I? They were some of my best customers. Besides who would dare pick on the mistress of the king of Saint Honoré? We were royalty. I was no worse than those fine ladies who hanker after every handsome young man in town. And I am not ashamed to tell you that usually, these same young men preferred my professional services."

"Why then does this powerful man let you rot in this abominable pit?"

"As I said before, the human body is not made to last forever. Especially if you have whole armies rolling over you every day. It takes its toll. To make a long story short, about a year ago, I notice a new filly in Arsène Rigoud's stable, vying for my place, that bitch. Of course, I wasn't going to give up without a fight and Arsène Rigoud, a very sensitive man, he doesn't like fights. I'm really lucky he had me put in here, he could have broken every bone in my body. At least I'm alive."

Alive for what? You call this being alive? Sandrine was overcome with pity and disgust. But she would not succumb the way this woman did. Why, they even had her convinced that she alone was to blame and they were doing her a favor by locking her up!

Sandrine would not submit, she would take matters into her own hands and if it meant making a deal with the man who had flung her into this hole in the first place.

"Can you help me get out of here?" She had to try, maybe this woman had connections.

"What are you in for?"

"Sedition or some such nonsense. But I'm here because of a certain Monsieur Hachette. I refused to become his mistress."

"Ah! Monsieur Hachette!" The prostitute laughed a laconic laughter of recognition. "He was one of my steadiest. You were right not to become his mistress, the man is as dull as a doornail, no tingle. But in my profession you have to put up with a lot, you take the good with the bad."

She pulled out a comb and began untangling her hair as if she were getting ready for business.

"Your best chance is to get into the confidence of the governor of this prison. A kindly gentleman with a big heart, and he hates Hachette—he told me so himself. His name is I'm letting you in on some professional secrets here, but for a pretty face like yours, what the devil. You are much too young and too beautiful to waste away in here."

"But I have never even seen the governor. How do I get his attention?"

"You have to think of something, cause some kind of commotion. Good luck, little one." Sandrine was still pondering what she had just heard when she felt a big, smacking kiss planted on her cheeks.

"And when you get out," the prostitute added looking coyly down at her hands, "look up Arsène Rigoud at the court of miracles of Saint Honoré, everybody knows him there. Tell him his Mellisande sends regards. If you need help, he is the man to turn to. He will fall immediately for those blue eyes. Now no more idle chatter, you must get to work!"

That evening, when the attendants passed through, ladling out some thin slop called soup served with a piece of stale bread, Sandrine asked to be given a piece of paper and a pen.

"What the devil do you need that for? You know how to use it?" The attendants were hardly distinguishable from the prisoners, the same pallor, the same unwashed disorderliness. Later she learned that all attendants were prisoners, their special status was a sign they had survived this house of horrors longer than anybody. Not many reached this stage.

"I have to send an urgent message to Monsieur Hachette," Sandrine whispered cupping her hands over the attendant's ear as if she was letting her in on a state secret.

"Who the devil is Monsieur Hachette?" the attendant whispered back in a mocking tone.

"He's a very powerful man. Maybe, if you could just arrange to have the prison governor come and see me, I'm sure he knows who Monsieur Hachette is."

Without answering, the woman started playing forlornly

with the red silk scarf Sandrine wore around her neck. César had bought it for her at the fair in Rouen. The scarf meant a lot to her, nobody had ever made her a gift without expecting something in return. But César would probably not mind if his gift could get them all out of this mess.

"All right, you can have it," Sandrine arranged the scarf around the woman's neck. "How pretty you look! Now, please tell the governor, it's a matter of life and death and I must see him right away."

Several days went by. Sandrine saw neither the governor nor the attendant. When she questioned another attendant about her, she was told the one with the bright red scarf had asked to be transferred to another section. The malicious laugh of the attendant lingered as she pushed the food cart down the aisle, leaving Sandrine with eyes filled with tears of anger and frustration.

There must be some way to get somebody's attention! Did she survive the ordeal of the Holy Inquisition only to perish in this god-forsaken shit-hole? Her hand darted forward and seized the bread knife from the tray, her arm whipped around the attendant's neck pulling her back with her and retreated against the wall.

"Go tell the governor I'll cut this woman's throat if he doesn't get here immediately," she screamed at the other attendant.

"What makes you think he cares whether this hag lives or dies?" The attendant shrugged.

"Why don't you first find out from himself? What do you think he'll do if you leave your companion to die?" The tactic worked. Not even these ghost creatures were in any way unaffected by the threat of death.

"Very well done," Mellisande whispered. "You'll see, the governor is a reasonable man. Don't forget Arsène Rigoud, he can help you if you're ever in need. Just mention my name."

Another eternity passed. Sandrine tightened her grip around the woman's throat. If only her arm wouldn't weaken before the governor arrives. Most of the inmates sat in a catatonic stupor, unaffected by the drama unfolding near them. No chance of getting a prison riot going, Sandrine thought as she tried to decide what to do if this didn't work.

Fortunately, no other tactic was necessary. Things went better than she expected. A few hours later, after a tearful goodbye from Mellisande, she sat in the governor's office opposite a kindly, elderly gentleman who identified himself as Monsieur Perron, the prison governor.

"I try to respond to the needs and concerns of the inmates entrusted to my care," he said almost apologetically. "But as you can see, the large number of those incarcerated here makes it impossible for me to get to know all of them. Our staff is very small, a limited budget, you know."

"I beg your forgiveness for using such drastic methods to get your attention, Sir, but I must send an urgent message to Monsieur Hachette." If Sandrine did not feel contrite and amiable, she certainly made a very convincing pretense of it. Morin's school of acting paid off.

"If you are talking about Monsieur Hachette from the police prefecture, I am sorry to tell you that he has been sent to the Bastille, misuse of office, you know. I am afraid there is nothing I can do for you in this matter, my child."

"Misuse of office! But I am a victim of his misuse of office. He sent me to the Asylum and my child to the orphanage because I refused to become his mistress. Please, kind Sir, I beg you do not send me back to the prison cell. I must find my child, he will surely die at the orphanage."

Sandrine fell on her knees, her hands clasped together. A

flood of tears washed over her smudged cheeks.

"I cannot help you find the child you love so dearly," he said, gently lifting her from the floor. "But I can show you to a door in the prison wall to which only I have the key. But you must promise not to come to the attention of the authorities again. I shall destroy your dossier. No more political plays," he warned after perusing the dossier in front of him.

Sandrine was so overwhelmed with gratitude, she impulsively seized his hands and pressed them fervently against her lips, promising anything.

"Thank you, thank you, kindest Sir. I shall never forget your kindheartedness. May God bless you forever!"

"For your sake, I hope our paths will not cross again. Come, you must go now before anybody notices what is going on. May God be with you, my child."

CHAPTER 3

Sandrine did not have a chance to visit Arsène Rigoud, at least not immediately. Ominous quiet pervaded the city as she slipped through the small, iron gate in the prison wall in the early morning hours of she knew not what day. Only the distant sound of cannon salvos reverberated in the empty streets. She hurried along the Rue Saint-Antoine. Everywhere, tightly closed window shutters concealed any life inside. Even this early in the morning, the quarter usually bustled with activity. On this morning, the heart of the city lay deserted. Not until she crossed the Place de Grève did she encounter a human soul. In front of the Mayorie workers were dragging heavy objects into the open square and piled them up as if they were erecting a fortification. Barricades were also being erected near the Châtelet. Something truly extraordinary must be going on.

She reached the quay along the river. On the Grand Pont, League soldiers were setting up heavy artillery pieces. The Parvis de Notre-Dame was empty, but the half-open portal revealed a huge crowd of worshippers inside. Just then the hollow din from the tower announced the miracle of the Holy Eucharist. Sandrine knelt briefly and bowed her head, mechanically she made the sign of the cross, but she did not wait for the ringing to end. A numbing dread of what had become of her child and friends drove her forward.

Her heart raced feverishly as she descended the stairs to the quay beneath the Petit Pont. She saw it immediately, the familiar caravan, brightly colored, the harlequins with their broad almost grotesque grin, and the inscription "Oranto Brothers Theatrical Company." Her heart almost skipped a beat when she saw Morin setting up props on the makeshift stage.

Everything seemed the same as if nothing had happened. For a moment, she was not sure whether she was not waking from a bad dream. Did all she had gone through really happen, the arrests, Monsieur Hachette, the Asylum, Mellisande, the attendant who stole her scarf, and the kindly Monsieur Perron?

Sandrine collapsed in Morin's arms. César and Gilles took turns in comforting the girl they had given up for lost.

"Four weeks, we've been waiting for a sign, a word from you. We didn't know what to do, where to look," Morin said.

"When we came back from the police, Mireya told us you had gone to the prefecture to obtain our release. But nobody there knew anything about you."

"Has it been four weeks! If that swine, Hachette, ever crosses my path, he will have breathed his last!"

"You went to see Hachette? He sent us home the same day,

only with the warning to take the white plume from David's hat and no more alluding to the battle of Ivry."

"That slimy bastard! He had me thrown into the Asylum because I resisted his filthy advances. He told me you all would be imprisoned and Noël would be sent to the orphanage. Where is Noël? Is he all right?"

"My prayers have been answered! Thank the Lord and all the saints in heaven!" The screams of joy were unmistakably Rosande's who came rushing from the caravan. Behind her was Mireya, Noël nestled in her arms, exactly the way Sandrine had last seen the two.

Tears of joy streamed from her eyes as she held the tiny bundle in her arms. Her happiness became almost too much to bear when he rewarded her with a big cooing smile. Did he recognize the special warmth of her body? His head pushed forward, his tiny hands reached eagerly for her breasts. But all she could do was hold him closely, the long separation had dried the fount of nurture.

"Never, ever will I leave you again!" she promised, gently rocking him back and forth.

So absorbed were the friends with rejoicing in the reunion, they at first did not to take notice of the swelling boom of the cannonade.

"We'd better get inside." Morin herded the women inside the caravan. "The city may become a battlefield any moment."

"We must leave Paris as quickly as possible," Sandrine said urgently. "None of us is safe here from arbitrary arrest."

"I'm afraid it's too late for that," Morin said gravely. "Do you hear the artillery fire? Navarre's army has encircled the city. No one can get in or out. The city is under siege. The royal forces are expected to breach the gates any day, even any hour. But the Leaguers will not give up without a struggle."

"The bulk of the League army is said to be in Picardie," César added. "After the defeat at Ivry, Mayenne is not likely to come to the aid of the Parisians."

Sandrine's blood rushed to her cheeks at the mention of the League army. She realized that it was very unlikely she would find Philippe in Paris. Their stay in the city no longer served any purpose and now they were stuck for God knows how long.

Once again my fate is linked to the movements of Henri de Navarre, she thought, as it was when he swept down Normandy causing the nuns to evacuate the convent and move to Chateau d'Evreux. She felt an instinctive hatred toward this man who seemed to make it a habit of frustrating her plans. Not that she was concerned he might take the city—for all she cared, he was welcome to it, and may he reign as King of France forever as long as this accursed war was finally over.

"At least we are together," Sandrine heard Rosande say. Yes, she thought gently pressing the child to her heart, at least we are together.

"We have nothing to fear from the King," Gilles turned reassuringly toward Sandrine. "We are only humble theater folk. I'm sure he would be most amused if he saw our play about David and Goliath."

"Let Navarre take this city—the sooner, the better for us," César agreed.

"But the Parisians are not likely to surrender without a fight," Morin added. "Not with Madame de Montpensier and the clergy inciting them to resist."

"Even though, without the bulk of the League army or help from Spain, Paris cannot possibly hold out longer than a few days, a week or two at most. The food would run out," César opined, while Rosande placed a hearty breakfast of ham and eggs on the table and ordered everybody to sit down and eat.

"It can only be a matter of days before this crisis is resolved. Long live the King, Henri IV of France." The last sentence was added in a whisper. Sandrine seconded the thought with a heartfelt "Amen," while she devoured a double portion of the steaming hot meal, the most delicious, she thought, she had ever tasted.

Only a matter of days! A matter of days before Henri de Navarre would mount an attack, a matter of days before the city would be in the hands of the heretic pretender to the throne. Or so they thought.

The days turned into weeks, the weeks into months. Navarre tightened his stranglehold on the lifeline to the city. Supply ships sailing up the Seine River were intercepted, but he did not attempt to breach the walls. Like a gallant suitor, he wooed the city with tenacity but with forbearance. Patiently he waited for her to open the gates of her own will.

Whether he intended it or not, Navarre's courtship gradually squeezed the lifeblood out of the one he professed to love too much to violate. And yet the city, like a proud virgin, did not surrender. Within a few weeks, all animal life disappeared from the city streets. The stables were soon emptied of drawing animals, all ending in someone's pot. Even aristocrats moved about on foot for lack of suitable transportation. A vigorous trade in cats, dogs, and even rats flourished, but that too only for a short while—the stock of merchandise was soon depleted. The police were powerless to stop the plundering of food stocks at the markets of Les Halles and other shops and storehouses. But these too were soon empty. And still, the city did not surrender.

By the end of June, Paris had become a city of the dead and the dying. A foul stench rose from the decaying human corpses that piled up in the streets. Every day scores of people simply collapsed and expired. Not enough gravediggers were left to give them a decent burial, and not enough of those still alive cared.

The sight of people scraping blades of grass from the crevices of stones to still the pangs of hunger was common everywhere. And yet the city gates remained shut.

Sandrine looked at her crying baby. She had to do something to stop his crying that had started to grate on the nerves of the men. Hunger and idleness had set them against each other. The performances had long ceased to attract people. It was just as well. Even if they had taken in money, it was worthless, food was nowhere for sale. Their days were filled with almost constant bickering while they waited for something to happen.

Sandrine came to realize that, as things stood, she and the baby were only a burden to her friends, two more mouths to feed. True, there never was a word of complaint. Rosande stretched her remaining store of staples thinner every day, the portions she dished out became smaller and smaller, until finally, there was only one meal a day. But the portions were always equal.

When at first the food supply started to shrink and hope for an end to the siege faded, they heard of the vegetable patches outside the gate of Saint Antoine, reportedly impossible to reach—enemy soldiers had opened fire on several people who had ventured outside the ramparts.

They probably did not know how to move about unnoticed, Sandrine thought. She was willing to take the risk.

For several nights after curfew, she and Mireya stole through the gate of Saint Antoine and reached the other side of the ramparts undetected. They collected beets, string beans, and several kinds of turnips. On the second night, they were stopped by the gatekeeper, but he was easily made a partner with a cut of the loot. So it went for a fortnight. The trickiest part was the way back through the streets of Paris. With the vegetables bulging under their cloaks, Sandrine and Mireya meandered through side streets and courtyards, soundless and swift like cats on a prowl. At all cost, they had to evade the armed guards, who patrolled the city ostensibly to enforce the curfew, but who would surely not shrink from attacking anybody carrying food. Stories abounded about more than one person who was killed for a few edible scraps.

One night as they approached the gate, they heard the sound of gunfire. Dozens of people stampeded down the Rue Saint Antoine from the direction of the gate. On getting closer they learned that news of the vegetable gardens had leaked out. A raging mob of several hundred had attempted to break through the gate and when the gatekeeper tried to stop them he was torn to pieces.

Untold numbers were trampled to death. When the royal sentries on the other side saw the commotion, they opened fire. At least this is how the massacre was explained later.

The two women never made it to the gate. The throng running for cover from the royal fusillade pushed them back toward the center of the city. That night they returned empty-handed.

All Sandrine and her friends could do was hope that the government of Paris, run by a clique of ultra-radical Catholics, called the Sixteen, although they may well have been more, will soon come to its senses and surrender. But there was no sign of their giving in.

"The cellars of the magistrates are well stocked," César declared. "So why should they give in? And the hell, if people are dying by the thousands! Why should they care?"

"I saw the papal legate and the Spanish ambassador riding around near the Châtelet only yesterday, both rotund with puffy cheeks. They have the nerve to preach to the miserable citizens, who are barely holding on to life, to hold out against the heretic. We shall all find our reward in heaven, they say!"

Sandrine looked up in surprise, never before had she seen the usually reserved Gilles explode with such anger.

"Even worse," César added, "just the other day, the Spanish ambassador suggested that the people unearth the dead from their graves and grind down the bones to make flour for bread. Madame de Montpensier hailed the idea and got some desperate souls to dig up several bodies from the Cemetery of the Innocents."

"What a terrible notion! To disturb the peace of the dead and desecrate their final resting place! Is there no limit to the depth to which these people will stoop in the name of the Holy Church? I hope our Lord, Jesus Christ, will punish the guilty!" Rosande cried.

"Well, this is not the end of this outrage," César continued. "They baked some of this stuff into bread, which they called Madame de Montpensier's bread, though she declined to taste any of it herself. But those who ate of it were carried off to eternity within a few hours in a most horrible death."

"I hear Madame de Montpensier has a hard time holding on to her dogs. She keeps them locked up in her mansion for fear somebody will make mincemeat of them," Morin laughed trying, albeit unsuccessfully, to dissipate the air of horror César's story had created.

"There is no limit to human depravity," Sandrine concluded rising from the table. "What we have to do is beat them at their own game. There is still plenty of food in Paris, and I know where to find it."

CHAPTER
4

Sandrine was perched high in the crown of the chestnut tree that cast a long shadow over the square in front of the huge wrought-iron gate of the Abbey of Saint-Victor. Hidden by the thick foliage, she filled her stomach with chestnuts, doggedly she pried open the tough shells of the not yet ripened fruits with her teeth and fingernails. Further down, the tree had been picked clean as soon as the fruit began to show, but where she held out, there was still plenty—nobody climbed as high as Sandrine.

But the chestnuts stilled the pangs of hunger only temporarily. She kept her eyes trained on the entrance to the monastery. Patiently she waited for a propitious moment to slip inside for a raid on what she knew was a well-stocked larder.

For several weeks, she had paid her nocturnal visits to monasteries all over the city. The Brotherhood of Jesus, the Franciscans, the Benedictines, even the mendicant orders, all had become her targets. Everywhere she found cellars replete with slabs of salted meats, sausages, flour, and other cereals. The cloister gardens abounded with fruits and vegetables. Every night she brought home stores of goods to share with her friends and her child.

Was she a thief? Maybe. But if so, she was stealing from those who stole from the people. If God is a just God, he surely will not hold it against her. And just as surely will he punish the well-fed priests and monks, who exhort the people to make sacrifices they are unwilling to make. Sandrine's anger at the religious orders erased any reticence she might have had about committing the sin of coveting the possessions of others.

For weeks, her anger had been seething at the sight of columns of militant friars marching through the streets, day in and day out, inflaming an already frenzied populace. A curious sight they were indeed. Amidst death and decay, these strong, corpulent men, walked around with helmets covering their bare heads, harquebus and halberds slung over their shoulders, cuirasses tied over their hassocks, while they mixed the pious sounds of psalms and hymns with murderous shouts of "Death to the heretic Béarnais!" To steal from these violent gluttons surely was no sin at all, but a good deed.

Was it luck or the hand of Providence that had guided her so far? Sandrine liked to think that it was a little bit of both, aided by her ingenuity. She resisted Gilles' and César's pleas to let them accompany her. True, three can carry more than one, but three are also more easily detected. Alone she had a much better chance of fading from sight.

Several times, she had come close to being apprehended, but

each time she confounded her pursuers by vanishing as if into thin air. The skill, acquired while growing up in Bonneval, now served her well. But she was also careful, never reckless. She would never take the risk of returning to the same place twice. There were so many monasteries in Paris plus the residences of the papal legate and the Spanish ambassador, she and her friends might eat for the remainder of the siege.

Yes, she and her friends might survive, but her greatest concern was for her child. Nowhere was she able to find food suitable for an infant. Milk was unavailable. In all of Paris, not a single goat or cow had escaped the slaughter. Rosande prepared a pasty porridge from the barley Sandrine brought home. But while it stilled the infant's hunger, it caused a terrible upset of his delicate digestive system.

"Please, dear God don't let him die. Please don't take my child away from me!" Sandrine prayed fervently. "He is all I have. If I have displeased you, please punish me in some other way. Take my life, but preserve his!"

The armed monks posted at the gate of Saint-Victor readied for the early morning change of guard. It must be two o'clock, Sandrine guessed. These monks seemed to enjoy playing soldier. The bastards looked so round and chubby. With the taut skin of their clean-shaven faces, they looked almost cherubic. But what kind of men are they? Are their hearts made of stone? How can they turn a deaf ear to the anguished screams for bread which even now filled the warm summer night?

Without making a sound, Sandrine slid down the tree. She crossed the square and quickly melted into the shadow of the cloister wall. Damn it, there were no holes, no loose stones, the wall was too high and too smooth even for her to scale. She had to slip through the front entrance, somehow she had to get inside without being noticed by the monk-soldiers.

That night Sandrine's luck ran out. Had she become too self-confident? Why did she not withdraw when she could not find a breach in the wall? Did she think she had become so invincible that she could walk through the main gate without being seen?

She tried to wriggle free from the arm that was clamped around her chest from behind, but her enfeebled body was no match for the muscular arm that squeezed the air out of her.

"Well, what do we have here?" A second friar strolled over to where the first one had seized her. He held a burning torch under her face and closely studied her features.

"She looks familiar. Have we met before? Well, I guess not. Let's see now, what is a pretty girl doing out here in the middle of the night? You should be more careful," he said in a patronizing tone. "You never know who walks the streets of this city—scum of every sort, thieves, murderers, rapists." He stretched the last word with obvious relish, licking his lips.

"Brother, we'd better take her inside. We haven't had a girl for far too long."

Her screams for help went unheard in a night filled with unanswered screams. With a grunting sound of approval, the bigger of the two picked her up like a feather and carried her through the gate and behind the wall.

"You are fortunate you met two nice friars." The one who did all the talking pressed closely against her while the other still held her from behind. With deliberate slowness, he started to fondle her sore breasts. She felt his hot, quickening breath against her face, the rancid smell of sausage and wine made her gag. The image of Etienne, panting, holding her down, rose before her. Like lightning, her knee jerked up between the friar's legs. He reeled back moaning.

"Ah, you bitch!" He gasped for air, straightened himself, and started toward her again. Violent determination gleamed in his eyes as he ungirded his sword and placed it on a rock.

Sandrine watched his every move. He turned to his companion with a jerking motion of his head toward the gate, he enunciated his instructions with an exaggerated movement of his lips: "Let her go, Brother. I'll take care of her. Go guard the gate while I get even with this bitch. I'll let you know when it is your turn."

The friar nodded and made an unintelligible gurgling sound. The thought shot through Sandrine's head: he is deaf and mute. He could not be counted on to hear her screams.

Sandrine eyed the sword on the ground as the friar closed in on her. Again, she felt his heavy breath, he reached for her, tore her threadbare smock. She ducked through his arms. Before the baffled monk knew what was happening, he felt a sharp point in his back. He turned around. Two quick strokes across his cheeks, again he reeled back howling, his cheeks ran with blood.

"Don't bother calling your crony. You know he can't hear you." Sandrine felt in control. She would crush this miserable worm. "If you make one move you'll be done for." He stared at her, senseless with pain.

"I know who you are! I knew I had seen you before!" He forced the words over his blood-soaked lips. "The witch of Chartres! Yes, I saw you there at the trial. I would recognize that face anywhere."

An ice-cold shiver ran down her spine. The possibility of being recognized had not occurred to her, at least not among the masses of people in Paris. She was still stunned by this new situation and pondered what to do next when the friar suddenly got up and moved toward her. Before he reached her, the extended sword went straight through his chest.

The heavy thud of approaching steps tore Sandrine from her stupor. She stared at the blood-soaked corpse at her feet. Come what may, she had to be ready to kill the other one too, should she be unable to make her get-away.

The lumbering deaf-mute was no match for her agility. She ducked behind a bush, and while he bent down over his companion stretched out in a pool of blood, she slipped away.

She hurried alongside the massive cloister wall, hugging the shadows, and was soon swallowed up by the dark labyrinth that was the city of Paris.

CHAPTER
5

The last week of July smothered the long-suffering Parisians with sweltering heat. The stench of singed flesh, that had pervaded the city for months, intensified, biting the nostrils of those whose senses had not yet become completely blunted.

On the twenty-fourth of the month, the citizens awoke to artillery fire and cannonades so close, everybody was sure Navarre was finally storming the city. By noon, word went out, all the surrounding faubourgs were in the hands of the royalists. The city was presumed to fall in a matter of hours and the siege would at long last be lifted.

By nightfall, the city gates were still firmly locked. The monks who manned the guns on the ramparts had countered every royalist volley with an even fiercer volley, so it was reported until Navarre retreated and resumed the siege. The people were too enfeebled to even conceive of resisting the fanaticism of the churchmen. The crisis continued.

Sandrine, accompanied by Mireya, knelt in a back pew of the grand Cathedral of Notre Dame of Paris. She buried her face in her hands praying with greater fervor than she ever had in her life, imploring the Mother of God to preserve the life of her child.

However, she found her initial reluctance to enter the church justified when her meditation was disturbed by the bishop's militant sermon in praise of the brave monks. "Our good Maccabbeans," he called them, had saved the city from the heretics. It sickened her to hear such talk. Maccabeans was hardly a fitting term for these fanatical friars. The image of a cherubic moon face flashed before her. She could still feel the sensation of the sword traversing multiple layers of soft tissue of fat. Murderers, rapists! A canker on the body of the people! That's what they are!

Faint nausea seized her. Noël, treasure of my heart, flesh of my flesh, why should you have to die and these depraved worms are allowed to live? Her child's little body had become so thin, the skin draped loosely over the fragile bones, only his stomach ballooned. The voice from the pulpit declared that God looks most favorably upon those who suffer the death of martyrs for his faith.

Sandrine rose abruptly, she ran for the side door. Outside she leaned over the railing—a welter of disgust spewed forth uncontrollably from her sore innards.

"Sandrine! Sandrine! Are you all right?" Mireya ran after her friend.

"Yes, Mireya, I am all right." Sandrine straightened her

torso. "But I'd rather not go back in there. I don't think God is on our side. Let's go home."

Mireya had begged her to seek the help of the Virgin Mary to save the child whose life they watched seeping away. Only a miracle could save his life.

Sandrine had very little faith left in the healing power of the saints, who seemed to have forsaken the poor inhabitants of this city. Even Sainte Geneviève, the patron saint of Paris, turned a deaf ear to the pleas that rose daily from the parched lips of her martyred citizens. Only to oblige Mireya had she entered the cathedral. At her wit's end what to do, praying was all that was left and it could not hurt.

After Sandrine got so violently ill, Mireya agreed that they should return home. The two young women locked arms and, supporting each other turned into the Parvis of Notre Dame. As they started across the square, they caught sight of two well-dressed, though weary-looking women about to enter the cathedral. They were attended by a flock of servants. All were on foot. Sandrine recognized immediately the limp of Madame de Montpensier, but it was the other noblewoman, who stirred her curiosity.

"Who is the young woman with the beautiful blond hair?" Sandrine asked her companion. "She has such soulful eyes."

"She is Louise de Montreuil." Sandrine turned around. Before her stood an elderly gentleman. His manner and clothing were that of a well-to-do bourgeois, a prosperous merchant perhaps, although he seemed to have been more corpulent at one time. He apologized for intruding, but he had overheard their conversation and was glad to provide the information.

Without further prompting he continued: "She is regarded as one of the most beautiful women in France, of ancient aristocratic stock. Her father, the Count de Montreuil is a loyal

League supporter. She is betrothed to one of our great League heroes, the Count de Treffort-Salignac."

Sandrine felt her knees shaking, only Mireya's closeness kept her from collapsing. She struggled for a moment to regain her balance. This man seemed well informed and she might learn something of Philippe's whereabouts.

"If this Count is such a great hero, why isn't he here to save her and us," she inquired, imitating the cantankerous tone of the Paris canaille.

"I can't tell you where the Count is," the man answered politely. "He may be at the bedside of his friend, the Count de la Croix who was badly wounded at the battle of Arques—a great loss for the League. But the news has just reached us, the Duke de Mayenne is at Saint-Denis, just north of here, and as soon as the Duke of Parma arrives with his Spanish troops from Flanders, we shall show the heretics who is master in France."

Sandrine was fascinated. This man was a living almanac of League affairs. Maybe he had other useful information.

"Then this siege will be over very soon?" Sandrine inquired.

"Oh, yes! At most, it will be a matter of two or three weeks," he assured her confidently.

Two or three weeks! By that time we shall all be dead, she thought. The two noblewomen had reached the portal to the cathedral. Sandrine sent one last look after Louise de Montreuil when the woman suddenly turned toward her. Their eyes met briefly. She felt she should be jealous but instead was deeply touched by the warmth and sympathy in Louise de Montreuil's demeanor. A thought ran through Sandrine's mind. Then a sudden panic seized her that her child might be already dead.

Breathless, they reached the caravan. Thank God! The child was resting peacefully, though limp, in Rosande's arms.

Sandrine knew she had to do it. It may be a gamble, but it

was her child's only chance. She would make it through herself. She could scrounge for scraps of food here and there, and so could her friends. They all objected vigorously to the idea, but in the end, they had to admit unless plentiful food became available the next day or the day thereafter at the latest, the child would have less than a week to live.

Holding the little body wrapped in swaddling clothes tight to her heart, she kept close watch of the entranceway to the Hotel Montreuil. For most of the day, there had been very little activity. Even among the aristocracy, all social life had ebbed since the siege began. Quite obviously, Louise de Montreuil stayed alone in the house most of the time. She too was trapped in the city.

Around noon a package was delivered to the front entrance. Sandrine heard the man say something about compliments from His Majesty, the King of France. Was it possible that Henri de Navarre sent provisions to this noblewoman? His gallantry was well known, but she probably needed it less than others.

The infant in her arm began to fret. A wave of warmth and unbounded love filled the young mother.

"I shall come back for you, I promise," she whispered. The child nestled meekly in the nook of her arm. "I swear, if we make it through this, you and I shall never be separated again. The yellow butterfly will bring us back together."

It had not been hard to find a tattooer among the itinerant folk quartered under the Petit Pont. The man was a true artist and for just a shovel of flour, from Rosande's dwindling reserves, he copied onto the baby's upper left arm the exact likeness of the small yellow butterfly Sandrine bore on her upper left arm.

She had never paid much attention to the marking on her arm. Philippe had shown some curiosity. He had told her it was a not uncommon practice among the aristocracy to mark their children especially in times of great turmoil. But she had not thought much about it until now.

The afternoon dragged on. Only once did she see Louise behind the window. Sandrine wondered whether she was in love with Philippe.

The evening bells began to ring out calling the faithful to Vespers. Within a few minutes, Louise emerged from the house accompanied by two women. From their dress and deferential manner, it was clear that they were of socially inferior status, most likely a governess and a personal attendant. Flanked by two male servants, they walked toward the church of Sainte Magloire only a few paces away. Sandrine calculated the women would most likely return within an hour. The time had come for her to make her move.

Tears wetted the tiny face as Sandrine kissed the child gently goodbye. "I know she will take care of you. She is a good human being, I can see it in her eyes."

The street lay deserted in the still stifling heat of dusk. She mounted the flight of stairs to the entrance of the mansion and placed the baby on the top step. Only once did she turn back to make sure the note was securely attached to the bunting.

From her hiding place in the oak tree whose ancient branches overshadowed the mansion, Sandrine waited patiently for the women's return.

CHAPTER 6

The debâcle of Saint-Victor put an end to Sandrine's nocturnal raids. Even if she had wanted to, her friends would have prevented her from going out at night alone. So outraged were they when they heard what had happened, Gilles and César had to be constrained from going out and running a few of those knaves through with their blades. Rosande and Mireya did their best to comfort the trembling Sandrine whose nerves had left her completely as soon as she had reached the caravan.

"From now on, I'm in charge of provisions," Morin declared. "I have a source. The man drives a hard bargain, but I'm sure I can hawk some of our jewelry."

"But you said yourself that precious stones have become as

worthless as pieces of glass in Paris," César observed.

"Well that's true, money and jewels have lost their value with the scarcity of food. But this fellow is still sitting on ample supplies of cereal so he can afford to look to the time when this siege will be over. He has already amassed a fortune by profiteering from deals with the aristocracy. Rosande has a few pieces that should interest him. Of course, he doesn't like it to be generally known that he has a store of food, his life would be immediately forfeited. It took me some time to gain his confidence, but I think he's ready to do business with me."

"Where can he have gotten a supply to last until now? Have you seen what he has?" César was skeptical.

"My dear brother, for all I know it's stolen goods. But it's there, I assure you. Under the circumstances, I don't care where it came from."

"At least, let us go with you," Gilles said when Morin announced that he would meet with this "source" that night. "How are you going to carry the stuff without falling prey to the bands of hungry marauders who comb the streets at night. Three is better than one. I wish Sandrine had listened to us."

"Please, let them go with you!" Rosande urged her husband. "Gilles is right, it is dangerous to carry any amount of foodstuff around in the city."

"All right then, but you must wait for me at a distance from the house. This fellow is very suspicious. He will not admit me if he finds any reason to suspect treachery."

With Morin's source and Rosande's stretching of what was left of salted meats and sausages from the monastery stock, they subsisted from day to day, though a hollowness in the stomach of long-sustained hunger was ever-present.

By August, water had become the most precious commodity in Paris. The heat of summer beat down mercilessly on the city of death and the nights brought little relief from the swelter. A stagnant cloud of the stench of decay hung over the city, sapping the remnant of its citizenry of every vestige of energy and will to live.

"Is there no end to our suffering? Why is God inflicting such terrible punishment on us?" The moaning of the suffering masses rose to heaven but went unheard.

"God is only testing the steadfastness of his people! His rewards will be great for those who hold out against the lure of the devil!" the churchmen assured the despairing flock from the pulpits.

Sandrine decided she would not wait for her reward in heaven. She was obsessed with only one thought—she had to survive. One day she would reclaim her son and be reunited with Philippe. Her heart hardened to the sight of parched, shriveled bodies that collapsed before her eyes in the open street. Her senses had become so numb, the barrier of human bones she had to circumvent on her daily démarche to the Montreuil mansion aroused in her neither pity nor disgust. The only emotion left in her was a concern for her child's well-being. Every day she would observe the mansion from her hiding place in the oak tree that afforded an unobstructed view of Louise de Montreuil's sitting room. For hours she waited and watched for signs that her son was alive and recovering.

At last, she received proof that her gamble had paid off. She had been right about the spark of goodness she had perceived in Louise de Montreuil's eyes during that fleeting moment when their paths had crossed on the Parvis de Notre Dame. She could see the three women doting on the foundling, nursing him back to health. Their supplies may be meager and had to be rationed, but they were plentiful by comparison.

She noticed the same royal messenger, who had delivered

a package on the day she had waited with the child, return every third day with another package. At first, she had resented Navarre's generosity toward a noblewoman while the rest of Paris was starving to death. But now she could not help but wonder about the hand of Providence that seemed to guide the King who once again, however indirectly, touched her life. It may well be that her son lived because of the King's legendary magnanimity toward his enemies.

One day when she returned home, Gilles met her at the bottom of the steps of the Petit Pont and pulled her inside the caravan. Everybody gathered around. Rosande embraced her with a big hug.

"Thank God you are safe!" she exclaimed wiping the tears from her cheeks.

"What's the matter? What's there to be so concerned about?" Sandrine looked perplexed at the grave miens.

"Then you haven't heard the news?"

"No, what news? Noël is healthy and alive. I saw him through the window of the mansion just an hour ago. And you are all here. So what could be the matter?"

"It has nothing to do with Noël," said Morin. "But do sit down. There is a certain deaf-mute monk from Saint-Victor who has been combing the streets in search of the woman who, he gives to understand, murdered his companion. He has alerted the police and other friars in the city."

Sandrine felt her knees giving way, she gasped for air as if she had been kicked in the chest. Mireya rushed to her side and held her tightly embraced until the quivering of her body subsided. After a few minutes, Sandrine regained her composure.

"Wait a moment, the man cannot speak, therefore he cannot describe me. I just have to be careful not to cross his path."

"Oh, I wish this siege was over, so we can leave this accursed city!" Rosande exclaimed.

"I don't wish to alarm you Sandrine," Morin continued. "But the dead man did not die instantly. Rumor has it that he recognized the woman who assailed him and revealed her identity. He wrote some nonsense about a witch of Chartres on the gravel path where he expired."

Morin fell into a ponderous silence.

Then he remarked: "The deaf-mute is carrying a placard through the streets that says that the witch of Chartres was at large in the city, out to kill everybody. I have heard it said among some people in this neighborhood that the presence of the witch was probably the reason the city has been visited with all this suffering."

Morin had turned away from her while he was speaking so as not to appear as if he was accusing. The single, heart-renting scream made him whip around. Sandrine had fainted and was stretched out unconscious on the floor.

César lifted her up and placed her on a cot. Mireya wept softly. Nobody spoke a word, as if they were keeping a death vigil, they avoided each other's eyes in uncomprehending silence. What did they know about this young girl? They had never asked any questions. Everybody loved her like a member of the family. What dark secret was hidden behind this angelic face?

Sandrine revived and lifted herself on her elbows. She sent a furtive glance from one to the other. Five pairs of eyes rested on her, eager to be persuaded.

"I hope you will find it in your hearts to forgive me, and believe me I did not mean to deceive you when I left out part of the story of the friar's death," Sandrine began, at first haltingly, but soon she became animated, she wanted these good people to know the whole story. "Before the friar plunged into the sword I was holding—for this was the exact circumstance of his death, you must believe me—he recognized me as the accused in a witch trial at Chartres."

"But that is preposterous!" Rosande exclaim.

"No, Rosande, he was right, I was on trial for witchcraft at Chartres. I wanted to tell you, but I was afraid you would not believe me that I am not a witch."

Her tongue cleaved to the roof of her mouth and the words came over her lips with great pain. Rosande brought her a few drops of the rainwater she had collected on the rare occasions when the heavens had opened and drenched the parched city.

Sandrine's tongue loosened and she began to relate to her friends the circumstances under which she had been brought to trial for witchcraft. She told them about the village of Bonneval where she had been raised without knowing who she was, and the villagers who wanted to see her, the outsider and intruder, dead, and her miraculous rescue from the flames by the man she loves and who is the father of her child.

"Where is this man now and how did you happen to wander lost and in miserable condition along the road near Rouen?" Morin inquired.

"He's a soldier in the League army," she said simply.

"He must be an aristocrat then! But you hate the League and the aristocracy!" César exclaimed.

"I do, I hate the exploiters of the people, I hate the League and I hate this war and all its fanaticism, and all the misery it sows, the wasting of life! I know that he does not want this war to continue, only he's bound by an oath. He was away with his troops when his father chased me from his estate with nothing but a pouch of gold crowns."

"I still have the money for safekeeping. It is yours anytime you need it," Morin padded his belt. "You mean to say he's the son of the Duke d'Evreux? But why did his father chase you away?"

"This is the big mystery I hope to uncover one of these days. Somehow I feel he was frightened of me, even horrified, for reasons that are only known to him. His outburst against me, the very instant he laid eyes on me, is all the more puzzling since I am sure he's unaware that the woman he treated so unkindly was carrying his son's child. I am sure he did not know anything about our love. This is why I must find out who I am before I can return to Philippe."

"Oh, the terrible, terrible things you had to endure," Mireya hugged and kissed her.

"You will be safe with us," Gilles assured her.

"We won't let these fanatics touch a single hair of yours," César agreed.

"I think it's time that we all had something to eat." The ever-practical Rosande interrupted the protestations of goodwill. "It isn't much, but the barley gruel will sit like a rock in your stomachs for a while. To celebrate the occasion, we'll each have a little piece of meat as well."

After the meal, they all lingered around the table. It was as if nobody wanted to be first to break the circle. Sandrine turned to Morin. The brooding folds that had formed on his forehead since she had finished her story had not escaped her notice.

"You know I have to leave," she said, gently touching his arm. He nodded his head. The others protested, under no circumstances would they permit her to leave.

"I am eternally grateful to all of you for your trust and love, but that is why I must go. If I stay, your lives will be in danger. Once people are convinced that a witch is in their midst, they will never give up their search, because they believe if they remove the witch all their troubles will go away. You heard what Morin said, they are already saying that the witch must be the cause of their suffering. Here is a plausible explanation for everything that has happened in the last few months; this is something the superstitious mind can grasp. The hunt will be relentless. Anybody harboring a witch is liable to be killed by the mob. Alone, I can disappear, they will never find me, I assure you. The siege may be over in a week or two, I shall catch up with you somewhere south of here."

"Sandrine is right." Morin waved his arms to still the protests. "We cannot do much for her if the mob finds her here. We have a better chance if we separate and so does Sandrine."

"Here I want you to take at least this." He reached for his belt and pulled out a leather pouch. "It will be worth something again one day."

"No," she protested. "I shall never touch this money. I shall have none of it!"

"Don't be foolish. What are you going to live on? No time now for false pride!"

"Well, all right, I'll take half, you take half. You deserve at least some compensation for all the trouble I have caused you."

"What do you want me to say to that?" Morin counted out half the gold pieces, placed them in the pouch, and handed it to her.

With the promise that they would be together again soon, she bid her friends a tearful farewell. She turned abruptly, and without looking back, she disappeared into the warm, steamy August night.

CHAPTER

7

What none of them knew was that at the very moment Sandrine was bidding them farewell, an event took place in another part of town that closely affected their lives. About ten o'clock in the evening of the 10th of August 1590, the siege was in its fourth month, the gate to the Bastille opened and emitted Hervé Hachette to freedom. His release was conditioned on his making good on a claim that he would be able to find and identify the witch of Chartres.

For almost four months, Hervé Hachette, the disgraced former police prosecutor, had languished in solitary confinement in the forbidding fortress the people called the Bastille—although he was most likely better off there than his fellow citizens on the outside. He still received daily allotments of food and water, small amounts but enough to still the pangs of hunger. The long days and nights of idle brooding, powerless and alone, only intensified his desire for revenge against those responsible for his downfall—he was sure that Perron, the governor of the women's prison had denounced him.

Greater even than his desire for revenge, however, was his desire to come face to face with the woman who had jilted him, the actress from the gutter who had preferred prison to his love. Never before had a woman stirred in him such insane, single-minded obsession: he had to possess her or he wanted her dead.

Even after he had finally came to realize why this wench, Sandrine, seemed so familiar and that she was none other than the young woman who had been on trial for witchcraft at Chartres the previous year, his passion for her persisted; the thought that she was a witch even fanned the leaping flames of his lust.

He had seen the witch only from afar through a crowd of spectators, but there was no mistaking the distinctive, proud bearing of the figure who had stood erect in a white flowing robe in the cold winter breeze, unflinching like an angel, on the cart that was to take her to the stake. Swept up in the crowd, he too was unable to explain how she had suddenly vanished.

Of course, he was a rational man, learned in law, he did not believe in witchcraft. The knowledge of her past and the fact that he was the only one who could identify her, so he thought, gave him the power to subjugate her to his will.

Surprise gave way to delight when the news reached his cell that hundreds of mendicant friars were combing the city for the witch of Chartres who had presumably killed one of the monks. Hachette felt his opportunity had finally come.

After several attempts failed to gain the police prefect's ear,

Hachette got a note through to the Archbishop of Paris in which he made the startling claim that he knew where to find said witch, whose presence was the cause of all the misery the inhabitants of this city had to endure. After that, his release was only a matter of hours.

At dawn the next morning, Hachette, accompanied by armed police guards, came storming into the caravan of the Oranto Brothers' Theatrical Company.

"Where is the witch? Where is the witch?" Hachette raged through the small abode the gypsies called home, overturning every piece of furniture and equipment.

"All right, where is she?" He turned to Morin when it became obvious that she was not hiding anywhere. Although he shrunk to insignificance next to the bulky gypsy, the presence of the armed guards bolstered his sense of power.

"I think you owe us an explanation why you are disturbing the sleep of innocent people, destroy their property, and shout something absurd about a witch," Morin said calmly. "We don't know anything about a witch."

"I must warn you the punishment for harboring witches is death!" Hachette shrieked, the veins in his temples swelled with frustration. "You know exactly who I mean, that girl named Sandrine, your queen of Sheba. I should have kept you all locked up in prison then!"

"Oh! I know who he means! I swear we didn't know she was a witch," César said in a most innocent tone. "Believe me, if we had known, we would never have taken her in. We just felt sorry for her, she didn't seem to have a home. Anyway, she disappeared months ago, just around the time when we first had the honor of meeting Your Excellency."

Hachette looked up at him, unsure whether he was being made a fool or not. Was it possible that she did not return to this troupe after she got out of prison, God knows how?

"But what about the child? She had a child, wouldn't she have come back for the child?" he inquired.

"Not that slut," Rosande took her turn. "She had no feeling for the child." The corners of her mouth drooped derisively, and she described a suggestive gesture with her forefinger across her throat.

"And where is the child now?"

"Dead, died in this great famine, like so many children in Paris," Rosande held Mireya close to her, both wiping tears from their eyes. "The children are always the first to die. Just look around you, these streets used to be filled with children at play, some of them had to earn a livelihood at a tender age, such is the lot of paupers, but still, the children were everywhere. No more, the children are all gone. God rest their little souls! Grown-ups can always find some way, but what are the innocent, little children to do? If you have children, Your Excellency, I am sure you know what I mean."

"All right! All right already! Enough of this chatter!" Hachette's impatience burst forth. He could not quite rid himself of the feeling that he was being led around by the nose by this band of vagabonds.

"Let's concentrate on the purpose of this search. She's not here. Should I find out that you have deceived me, you will all burn at the stake or hang. For the moment, I'll let you go."

With a gesture of anger, he ordered the guards to untie their hands. These wretched actors were much more useful as bait for the big fish. Should she return, she will walk right into his trap.

On the way out, he kicked over a few life-size puppets leaning against the deserted stage. Then he turned around once more and shaking his forefinger menacingly, he shouted: "I shall find her, no matter what, and when I do, God have mercy on her soul!"

"She may be dead," Morin called after him. "The famine has taken the lives of so many people."

Hachette froze for a moment, that possibility had not occurred to him. What if he was right? She may very well be dead, people have been dying by the thousands. No! he felt it in the depth of his gut, she was alive. Somewhere in the labyrinth of this city, she was hiding. His bloodhound instinct would pick up her trail and sniff her out.

CHAPTER

8

Swift and unseen like a phantom in the night, Sandrine made her way through the backyards and alleyways, scaling walls and scurrying over rooftops—not even a cat was more agile. As long as she avoided the main streets where chanting friars held their endless processions, her chances of being discovered were slight. She entered deep into the heart of the city, now little more than a ghost town, a valley of bones and rotting flesh. In every neighborhood, people suffered from shortages, but it was the poorer quarters of the city that were hit hardest. From time to time she passed a moaning soul, but her presence stirred little interest.

She reached Les Halles where she meandered between sunless

alleys, a desolate landscape of empty stalls and storage buildings that once had been the city's bustling lifeline, its breadbasket. Not the faintest echo lingered of the shouts of food vendors, the cadences of market criers, hawking their wares, only eerie silence oppressed the aisles.

Here and there, a miserable heap of specters huddled in doorways of broken-down, wooden shacks. She stopped to ask for the court of miracles of Saint Honoré.

"You won't find any miracles there either," a human skeleton informed her. "What are you looking for?"

"I have a message for Arsène Rigoud, the king of beggars and thieves. I was told, everybody around here can lead me to him."

The skeleton pointed a gnarled bony finger toward the end of the alley.

"On the right down there, you'll see a big iron gate, that's the court."

"God bless you. I wish I had something to give you."

Sandrine pushed open the wrought-iron gate that had come partially unhinged and was flapping loosely. A jarring screech reverberated in the empty courtyard. What if Arsène Rigoud was dead? He was her only hope of finding a refuge from the witch hunters whose shouts even now echoed from the main streets and squares.

A desolate realm of ghostly shadows engulfed her. Was this the famed court of the king of thieves and beggars? *We were like royalty!* Mellisande's words echoed in her mind.

"What do you want here?" a gruff voice bellowed from inside the yard. An impressively tall man draped in rags moved from the shadows. At other times, he might have frightened her. But she had become accustomed to the sight of bearded, unkempt men with hollow, expressionless eyes and protruding cheekbones, images of a colorless ghost world. This one had a little more flesh on him than most, but the mere size of his frame, which at one time must have carried a mass of muscles and flesh, was still imposing.

"I have a message for Arsène Rigoud, the beggar king."

"A message from whom?"

"I can tell that only to the king himself!"

"Do you have anything to offer?"

"Maybe, but I'm dealing only with Rigoud directly." She knew she was taking a chance and had better not anger this hungry man. To give the impression that she possessed even the smallest amount of food could endanger her life. Even though he was haggard, he could still easily crush the life out of her and no one would ever know.

"I mean, do you have anything to eat?"

"Eat? Who eats in this town? I haven't had a bite in days," she lied.

"We don't need more empty mouths around here. Get lost!"

"I wouldn't be so hasty. I am sure Arsène Rigoud wants to hear my message. Why don't you go ask him? What if he gets angry at you for sending me away?"

"You are not only stubborn but also a cunning little vixen." He tried to laugh drawing in his breath heavily, but the rattling sound he made resembled more the bleating of a goat than human laughter. "I shall take you to him—we could use a little diversion around here. People don't only die from lack of food, some have given up the ghost from sheer boredom."

He led her down the stairs into the basement of a bleak, deserted tenement building.

"At one time, the huts around this court were not only filled with people, they were so crowded, whole families lived packed together in one room. Now, one person can have the run of an entire suite of rooms or more. What luxury, like the aristocracy!" They descended the stairs and in the course of their brief acquaintance if it could be called that, his manner had changed almost completely. He was hardly able to contain his flow of speech. It seemed that he was happy to have found at last a receptive human ear.

"At one time, there was a constant deafening noise of screams and laughter in this court, it was often unnerving, but now the quiet is enough to drive you out of your mind," he explained like a tour guide describing a deserted ruin of what once was a bustling center of human activity.

Sandrine just nodded.

"Here we are in the throne room of the king of beggars and thieves!" He pulled open a heavy wood-carved door and bid her enter.

A spacious, subterranean realm open before her eyes. The huge room was furnished with a mélange of fine rugs, chairs upholstered in velvet and brocade, and other pieces of handcrafted furniture, some adorned with fine wood-carvings, all of them, no doubt, once graced the parlors of aristocratic residences. Here they were carelessly stacked, the tops laden with a motley array of household objects and covered with a thick layer of dust. From the vaulted ceiling hang two huge wrought-iron chandeliers that held thick, low burning candles filtering a pallid light through veils of cobwebs onto the disorder below—a storehouse of thieves' contraband now become worthless.

"Well, here make yourself comfortable!" With a chivalrous gesture, he brushed the dust from one of the couches.

"Now, what's the message?"

"I told you already, the message is for Arsène Rigoud personally."

"Ah, what an obstinate little vixen you are! Don't you know

yet that I am the man you are looking for? I am Arsène Rigoud! Now, what is it you want? Out with it!"

"How do I know you are telling the truth?"

"Listen, I'm the only person here. If I'm not Arsène Rigoud then he is dead, so I might as well be Arsène Rigoud. What difference does it make?"

He's right, Sandrine thought. It does not matter whether he is the Arsène Rigoud or an impostor, this bizarre giant was the person with whom she had to deal.

"I need a place to stay for a while, and I was told that Arsène Rigoud was a generous man."

"Flattery won't get you anywhere. There are no more generous men left in Paris. Why should I burden myself with your presence? You don't even have any food to share."

"I can work for you," she suggested boldly.

"Work for me!" He laughed his bleating goat's laughter. "What, on earth, can you do?"

"I can do the type of work Mellisande did." It worked! He cocked his head to one side and looked at her with a long, probing stare. She had struck something in him, he must be the real Arsène after all.

"Mellisande! What do you know about Mellisande? Now here was a fine whore, probably the best!" he mused more to himself. "But those were different times, my dear child. She took in more in one day than the Queen of England takes in taxes. We were like royalty then! Now, in this wretched town of croaking carcasses, nobody even has a thought of buying the favors of a woman. It's a law of nature, when the stomach is empty, all other bodily urges cease."

He planted himself in front of her, still looking her over carefully.

"Your offer is very generous, thank you. Under different

circumstances, I should have been delighted to take you up on it. Only I have the feeling, then, you would not have made that offer."

"Well, if you have no use for me, then there is no point in my imposing on your time any longer. Thank you, anyway." Sandrine rose. Not knowing where to go from there, she walked hesitantly through the large wood-carved door.

She crossed the courtyard. The thug's call made her halt: "But you haven't told me what the message was. I presume it was from Mellisande. Is she alive?"

"Last time I saw her she was still alive. But she might as well have been dead, buried in that dismal hole you had her thrown into!" Her voice echoed accusingly in the empty courtyard.

"Believe me, it was for her good. I wanted her to be in a safe place."

"A living hell! You condemned her to a living hell! And she was even grateful for it!"

She continued to walk toward the wrought-iron gate. At once, she froze. One of the skeletons she had met before in the alley called out to Arsène with eager animation one would not have expected from such a hollow shell. "Arsène! Have you heard the news? The monks are swarming all over the city in search of a witch! They say it's she who causes all the troubles and hardships in the city these months."

Arsène crossed the courtyard, keeping his eyes fixed on Sandrine. She stood riveted to the spot.

"You fool, since when do you believe anything the priests say? You know they are just looking to blame someone so they can't be held responsible for the mess their fanatic spleen has caused."

"They say she already killed one friar. Monsieur Hachette from the police is personally leading the search. He's said to be able to identify her. Since nobody can leave town, she must be somewhere within the city walls."

"Witches have magic ways of coming and going. If she is a witch, she can just fly over the ramparts, you fool!" Arsène caught up with Sandrine.

"People believe anything nowadays," he said turning to her, his eyes firmly fixed on her face.

Sandrine's mind worked feverishly. Hachette was out looking for her! She had to get away, the look in Arsène's eyes bode no good. Abruptly, she roused herself from the stupefaction that had paralyzed. Panic-stricken, again she was the hunted animal, her bare feet hardly touched the rough cobblestones as she ran down the narrow alleyways, turning and turning in the unfamiliar, twisted maze without direction. A sharp sting between the ribs forced her to slow down. Approaching steps made her quickened her pace once again, but she was soon overtaken.

"You'd better go back with me." Arsène blocked her way. "Neither the police nor the monks will dare look for you at Arsène Rigoud's court."

She was struck by the well-meaning tone of his voice. Was it a trick, or did he want to help her?

"What makes you think the police is looking for me?" she said, stubbornly resisting the pull of his hand. What if he was trying to entrap her and then turn her over to Hachette? Why should she trust him? Mellisande's words came to her mind: "He is a generous man, he will help you if you should ever be in need."

"Quit arguing. You simply have to trust me. What alternative do you have?" He was right. What choice did she have? She followed him into a nearby underground tunnel that opened directly into the cluttered living quarters where they had just been before.

Word spread all over the city, the magistracy of Paris, at long last, was bearing down on the monasteries to share their reserves of comestibles with the suffering citizenry. Sandrine offered to go to a convent in the quarter of Les Halles where grain and salted meats were being distributed every day, but Arsène prevailed upon her not to be seen outside.

"I still have contacts, they will get the hand-outs," he said with a tone of finality. Every morning, he left his court and came back in the afternoon with enough to eat for both of them. Nothing to feast on, but enough to survive another day.

"Why are you doing this for me?" she asked him one evening while they were seated opposite each other among the clutter of looted furniture, between mouthfuls of a pasty barley gruel prepared with water drawn from a secret underground well.

"I am doing it for myself," he replied without stopping to shovel food into his mouth. "I like company. Many beggars and prostitutes who used to hang around this neighborhood left the city back in May when Navarre permitted a few thousand of the most wretched beggars to pass through the lines. Those of us who stayed tried to get by, but most are gone now. With my own bare hands, I buried one after another. Sometimes I wonder why God has spared me when everybody around has been carried off because they starved to death or some dreadful disease took them away. Who knows maybe God wanted me to survive to protect an innocent, young woman from the fanaticism of the friars."

There was that bleating again. That's the only annoying thing about him, Sandrine thought, inadvertently overcome with a feeling of warmth toward this strange man.

"How do you know I am innocent? I was convicted of witchcraft in a court of law. Doesn't that make you uneasy?"

"If it did, would I be sitting here with you? I know you are innocent because I know there are no witches. To hell with this whole witch craze thing and to hell with the whole lot of monks and priests who try to make the people believe that all problems can be solved by sending innocent people up in flames."

The longer he spoke, the more agitated he became. Sandrine was taken aback momentarily by the hatred that seared in his eyes, but her curiosity got the better of her.

"Have you ever witnessed a burning—I mean a person being burned at the stake?"

A dark shadow fell over his face and he lowered his brow before he began to speak, very slowly, almost solemnly.

"Many, many years ago, I was still a young lad, about ten years old—yes, I was present at a burning then—saw with these cursed eyes three innocent women devoured by the fire set superstitious fanatics."

She observed him patiently as he wretched to dredge up what was long buried but never completely forgotten.

"It all happened in a small village in Lorraine, the name doesn't matter, but it was near the city of Rheims. I remember it very well because it happened in the same year Charles IX was crowned there. That year, the village had an unusually large number of scrofula cases. The afflicted were taken to the coronation at Rheims. The newly anointed King touched his hand to the swellings, but nothing happened. Puzzled by the ineffectiveness of the King's healing hand, the villagers soon became convinced that there must be a witch who counteracted the royal powers. Before long, no reason why was ever given, fingers were pointed at the local midwife and her two daughters. Under torture, they confessed and that was the end. Nobody even knew or cared that the execution was witnessed by a child who lost all he loved in that brief moment when the thick smoke choked these women to death."

Sandrine had never seen such horrifying pain in a man's face. They looked at each other in stark silence.

"You need not tell me who these women were, but believe me nobody understands your pain and what they suffered better than I do," Sandrine finally said softly. She placed her hand reassuringly on his, but he pulled away.

"No need for pity! After so many years, the wounds have healed and the scars are invisible. Look here! Did I not make good here in Paris? I became a king, lived like royalty until this accursed siege destroyed everything."

Suddenly, he burst into laughter, bleating like a flock of goats. "You know, I have never told anybody this story. It would be better for you to forget it too. The main reason why I don't want to see you delivered up to those wolves is that I'm a great admirer of female beauty—even in this wretched condition you're in I can see that you are a beautiful wench—and I don't like to see such beauty willfully destroyed. Is that reason enough for you?"

"I'm very grateful to you, but you don't have to do all this for nothing. I can compensate you handsomely." She reached for her belt, then reached again. "You filthy, double-dealing thief, you stole my pouch!"

"Ah, you finally noticed! I've been wondering how long it would take you to realize it was gone. I took the pouch for safekeeping. For the moment at least, your gold crowns are worthless."

"How can I trust you if you rob me in my sleep?" she cried out indignant.

"You can't. And you should never trust anybody. The key to survival is eternal vigilance."

"You can keep the money for room and board."

One morning, Arsène was out meeting his contacts, as he called them. Sandrine was trying to put some order into the place when she was alerted by the sound of boots crushing the gravel in the courtyard as if a company of soldiers was marching over it. Male voices, muffled at first, then coming closer.

It was too early for Arsène to return, besides he never brought anybody to the court. What if he had betrayed her? He had told her never to trust anybody.

She peered through a crack in the closed shutter on the upper floor. At first, she could not make out anybody. They seemed to be off to the side. Then, her heart almost stopped, the group came into clear view below her. There he was, leading a squad of armed monks, her mortal enemy, Hervé Hachette. There was no doubt it was him—the short, almost square stature, the drab, black wool frock, the beardless face of the bourgeois advocate. He was talking with the skeleton man who had told Arsène about the witch hunt; both pointed at the building.

The group halted in front of the heavy wood door.

"Guard the yard, while I go inside," Hachette bellowed.

"Keep your eyes fixed on the door in case she should try to escape. With witches one cannot be too careful, fortunately, I have experience in handling such matter."

Still the bombastic, little bureaucrat, Sandrine thought. Just don't panic! He won't find her if she just didn't panic. The tunnel behind the hidden entrance! Hopefully, the skeleton didn't know about the secret passageway leading from Arsène's quarters out into the street.

She still heard Hachette cursing at the heavy door which resisted his attempts to gain entrance when she reached the throne room and slipped inside the hatch in the floor. Curled up and barely breathing, she pressed her ear against the door.

The hammering and banging persisted for some time—then

dead silence. Sandrine remained motionless. No matter how hard she strained her ears, no sound reached her.

An eternity seemed to have passed during which she dozed off she didn't know for how long. Then she heard her name being called. Arsène! A sigh of relief escaped from her lips. But wait! What if he is part of the search party? Impossible! She forced back her doubts and, cautiously, she crawled out of the hole in the floor.

"What are you doing down there? For a moment, I thought you had been foolish enough to leave!"

Without answering, she almost flew up to him and flung her arms around his neck, exclaiming ecstatically: "Oh, I'm so happy to see you!"

"Now, wait a second. What's going on?" He pried her arms from his neck and made her sit down. "Was somebody here? I noticed some tampering at the entrance door."

Sandrine nodded, her mind raced, she had to collect her thoughts and explain what had happened coherently.

"He knows where I am!" she finally burst forth. "Hachette was in the courtyard with a gang of friars. I saw them through the window. The man who told you about the witch hunt the other day pointed out this place to them. It seems they couldn't get through the door, but they will be back, I know they will be back! I cannot stay here, I must leave tonight."

"And where, may I ask, will you go? It's much more dangerous out in the street than in here." Arsène rose, he unlocked a cabinet and took out two pistols and two short-blade swords. He handed one of each to Sandrine.

"Here, do you know how to use these?"

"Not the pistols."

"You will learn then. By the way, I have good news. The army of the Duke of Parma is closing in on the outskirts of the city. One way or other, the siege will soon be over. Then we'll have to get you out of this town."

Before turning in that night, they barricaded the doors and windows. Arsène placed his mattress directly in front of the door, any intruders would have to deal with him first. The night was long and oppressive. From time to time, Sandrine sank into a yearned-for sleep but was roused by the faintest noise. By the lightness of his breathing, she could tell Arsène too lay awake, but they did not speak.

It was not until the night gave way to dawn that both finally drowned in a deep, restful slumber.

CHAPTER 9

The next morning the tocsins rang out jubilantly all over the city. Shouts of the news that the siege was over penetrated the court of miracles from the streets.

"Hallelujah! The siege is over! The heretic army has at long last withdrawn!"

In no time at all, the happy tidings spread among the citizenry, passing from mouth to mouth, from the ramparts to every corner and alleyway in the city.

But only a handful had enough strength left to join the churchmen in the celebration; the triumphal processions, the Te Deums were left to the friars. For many Parisians, the barges, laden with food supplies, that once again sailed up the Seine

River and docked on its banks several days after the blockade was lifted, came too late to save them from the still relentless scythe of the grim reaper.

While life in the city slowly revived, one man was dissatisfied with the turn of events. Why did the siege have to end now, when he was so close to his goal? Hachette sat brooding over his missed opportunity. Why didn't he just ram that blasted door? He knew she was in there, he sensed her presence, but he did not dare risk getting embroiled with Arsène Rigoud. He knew better than to take on the king of the underworld. That cunning little bitch, how did she gain the protection of such a man, of all people? The thought that the two might be lovers filled him with jealous rage.

But Hervé Hachette was not a man to give up easily. He paced up and down in his office at the police prefecture that had been temporarily restored to him, his hands folded behind his back. He halted in front of the window looking out on the river. He rocked back and forth on the ball of his foot with vigor, weighing pros and cons. If the friars had lost their interest in the hunt, all the better for him. He did not want to see her burn.

His blood rushed through his veins seething with the desire to subject the wench to his will. He would give anything to possess her. Foam collected around the edge of his mouth, so beguiled was he with lecherous thoughts.

Sandrine was practicing loading and firing the pistol when Arsène came back from an errand in the city.

"We have fresh provisions and good news!" he announced cheerfully. "Navarre retreated at the approach of the army of the Duke of Parma and he is now moving south."

"What is so good about that?" Sandrine said sullenly. "It only means the clergy will continue to rule the city."

"Seen from that standpoint, you are right, the news is not so good. But Paris will get some respite from the war. Isn't that all that matters now? To hell with politics, why should we care who is king or who should be king? When your stomach is empty and you face death, all this becomes pretty meaningless. But you are right, I'm sure Navarre will try again. He cannot be King of France without being King of Paris. Now for the really good news. Arrangements have been made with the sentry at the Louvre gate to let us pass through around midnight tonight."

Sandrine was irked about the impersonal speech he used whenever he was doing something for her.

"I shall accompany you as far as Saint Cloud," he added. "From there you will be on your own. I don't think I could breathe the air outside of Paris. My nostrils are too accustomed to the stench."

He was still laughing his bleating laughter when the frown on her face arrested his interest. "What is the matter now? Aren't you happy it's all over?"

She remained silent, staring at the food in front of her. She knew she should be elated, but her heart was heavy, anxious about the future. Where will she go from here?

"Listen, little one!" he said kindly. "You are free to go. Get out of this dreadful city!"

"Free to do what, to go where?" she finally burst forth. "What makes you think I want to leave this city? Why do I always have to part from the people who are kind and caring?"

"You'll leave because your life is in danger here. And, let's not get sentimental! I'll get word to your friends that you will link up with them at Monthéry. You'll see everything will work itself out."

"No, that would be dangerous. Hachette knows where they are and probably has the caravan under surveillance. I only hope that no harm has come to them."

"You needn't worry, I'll take care of Hachette. We have an old score to settle. He'll go straight back to the Bastille where he belongs."

Sandrine was unconvinced.

"Oh, by the way," Arsène continued. "I needed some money to bribe the guards at the gate, but there are eight crowns left, they will be useful on your journey."

He handed the pouch to her and after hesitating a moment, she snapped it from his hand and tied it to her waist.

"There's one other thing," she began, unsure whether to take him into her confidence about the matter that weighed most heavily on her. "I have to pay a visit to someone before I leave the city."

"I thought you knew nobody in the city besides your actor friends. It wouldn't be a secret lover?"

"It's somebody I know and don't know," she said seriously. "I have a child, I placed it in the care of a noblewoman because the infant was dying from lack of food."

"My lady you are something—new revelations every day about a checkered career! How did you get the lady to take the child? I won't even ask who the father is—probably some aristocrat who seduced you with his charm and then left you in the lurch."

"No, no," he waved away her protests. "This is an all too familiar tale, I've heard it many times. Why do you think young girls end up working for me?"

"You have no right to insult me like this!" Sandrine screamed at the top of her voice. "I can do without your help!"

She rose abruptly and tipped over the table pouring its contents into Arsène's lap.

"Where do you think you are going?" he called after her.

"To the Hotel Montreuil, if you must know!" Seething with fury, she stormed out.

The horse-drawn carriage readied to pull out of the driveway that swept in a semi-circle around the front entrance of the mansion at the very moment Sandrine entered the square. Keeping her distance to avoid being observed, she saw Louise de Montreuil leaning out of the carriage window, speaking to the driver with animated gestures.

A sigh of relief escaped from Sandrine's lips. Inside the carriage, one of the women was holding a child. Thank God, her precious love was alive!

During the last few weeks, while she had been confined to Arsène's court, the longing to see him, to hold him, had at times driven her almost to distraction. He is in good hands, she had tried to console herself. But she spent many a night suppressing bitter tears. Suddenly, a lump formed in her throat. Only now did she grasp the reality of the situation. What she was witnessing could only mean one thing, Louise de Montreuil was about to leave town with her child. She had to catch at least another glimpse of him. Impulsively, she started to run toward the departing carriage. But the coachman cracked his whip over the horses and with a jolt the carriage pulled away.

Sandrine stood bewildered in the middle of the square, tears blurred her vision, she breathed in the dust whirled up by the carriage as it disappeared into the twilight. We shall be together again, I promise, she whispered to herself.

Uncertain what to do, she turned and walked as in a void, without heed where she was going, her mind oblivious to her surroundings. The aristocrats who had been trapped in the city during the siege had all left for the country, and the streets of this part of the town lay deserted.

"I knew that gypsy was lying when she said the child was

dead. Only this is not where I would have looked. You are even smarter than I thought, my dear queen of Sheba!" Hachette's voice jolted her back to reality. Out of nowhere, he blocked her way. His mouth was contorted in a triumphant grin.

"The witch of Chartres! Queen of Sheba! Now even murderess of Saint-Victor! Very impressive credentials for one so young and beautiful."

Sandrine sent a furtive glance around. No friars were visible. Hachette was alone. Before she could decide what to do, he had moved behind her. With lightning swiftness, he clamped his arm around her waist and pricked her throat with the point of a knife. Holding still so as not to rub against him, she was seized by wrenching nausea. With a sudden jerk, she tried to pull away, but he was stronger than she had expected.

He pressed his face against her neck, a heavy, rancid breath blew at her. The image of Etienne's sweating rump hovering over a frightened half-naked bride merged before her with the chubby face of the friar. Etienne, the friar, Hachette, they all became one. A quick jerk with the knee was to mete out the same treatment the friar had received, but Hachette anticipated the move and softened the kick before it reached its mark. Her emaciated body rested in his grip as if squeezed in a vise.

"Now, listen to me and you had better follow my advice if you know what is good for you," he whispered, his voice hoarse and lecherous. "The monks of Saint-Victor would like nothing better than to send the witch, who killed one of their own, heavenward in a cloud of smoke. Wouldn't that be a pity? These fags have no appreciation of feminine beauty. But they'll never find you, my dear, if you do exactly as I tell you. The house in the Rue Saint-Sauvieur is still at your disposal if you submit to my will."

"How am I to submit to your will with a knife at my throat?"

"You promise not to resist?"

"What good would it do? Last time, I ended up in the Asylum. I'm not dumb, I learn from my mistakes."

Pleasantly surprised by her sudden reasonableness, which he took for a change of heart, he sheathed the knife.

"The house is just a few minutes from here. Nobody will dare lay a hand on you as long as you belong to me, I promise."

Sandrine walked in front of him in the direction he indicated. She was looking for a favorable moment to escape when she heard a croaking sound behind her. When she turned around, she saw Hachette sink to the ground like an empty flour sack.

"I told you it's dangerous to go out alone," Arsène scolded. Detached as in a dream, she watched the king of beggars and thieves pull his sword from Hachette's chest and wipe it clean on a kerchief.

"I told you I can take care of myself. Look at the mess you have created! What will you do with the body."

"That's a fine reception. He would have killed you or raped you or both if I hadn't chanced to be in the neighborhood. Not that I'm looking for gratitude. Well, you won't have to worry about him anymore."

"Yes, but unfortunately, the world is full of lecherous vermin like him and you can't kill them all!"

"I love your uplifting view of the world. Stop the jabbering already! Come on, we have more important things to do. We'll toss the body over the wall at the Cemetery of the Innocents. Nobody will notice him among the cadavers piled up there. Let's hurry, we must pass the Louvre gate at midnight."

Arsène Rigoud was a man of his word. Thanks to his deftness in buying the collusion of the guards, they passed through the Louvre Gate without a hitch. Hachette and even the deaf-mute monk had given a good description to the police of the woman they claimed was the witch responsible for the murder. But if the guards recognized or suspected her, they gave no hint.

Upon bidding Arsène farewell at Saint Cloud, Sandrine fell in line with the almost unbroken human chain that stretched south along the roadway in an exodus away from the capital. Secure in the anonymity of the crowd, she merged with the mass of downcast survivors fleeing the city for the open countryside.

"Henri Valois has wrought his revenge on the city that betrayed him after all."

Sandrine turned to see from where the remark came. A little, bony old man with bent back hobbled alongside her, struggling to keep in step. His mouth stretched in a broad, knowing grin, he winked at her as if he had some special knowledge of the ways of the world: "As always happens, the punishment fell on the just as well as on the unjust, and maybe even a little more on the innocent. Look around you, as far as you can see, among this huge human mass, not a single child, not one small child. The children never had a chance. A whole generation of Parisians wiped out—that's Henri Valois' terrible revenge even from beyond his grave!"

Sandrine just nodded. A sudden chill ran through her, she quickened her step. She was in no mood to hash over the events of the past months. She just wanted to out of this city. The man was too frail to keep up with her and she was not unhappy that he soon fell behind.

At Monthéry, she carved out a space for herself near the fountain in the middle of the market square, faceless in a faceless crowd of migrants, and awaited the arrival of her friends. At dusk, she wandered outside the town among the fields. A brook beckoned her to immerse herself. She let the whirls of clear spring water wash over her skin encrusted with layers of soot and filth. Even now, the foul city stench clung to her. As if to purge herself, to clear her breathing passages, she eagerly drew in the clear country air suffused with the wholesome fragrance of freshly cut wheat.

The familiar smell of harvest signaled the beginning of the change of seasons. She knew the heat of August was about to give way to the pleasantly cool nights of late summer. She had almost forgotten the feeling of unity with the cosmic expanse that comes from sleeping under the stars. Insatiably, she drank in the feeling of freedom, the sense of being one with the cosmic plan.

All the emotional turmoil of the past months drained from her and in its place settled a serene calm. She almost lost track of time and place as she studied the heavenly spheres in the clear, late-summer sky. Did the stars hold the key to the secret of her curious fate? Was her destiny determined by the constellations? However this may be, she told herself, from now on she must be the sole guide of her destiny. Never again would she leave her life up to chance.

Arsène was right, she must devote all her energy, her entire being, exclusively and relentlessly, to the search for the identity of her parents and the discovery of her self. His parting words echoed in her ears: "You must place this one goal above everything else and pursue it single-mindedly, and never give up, then you will succeed!"

The thought of Arsène caused a strange sensation to rush through her body. She was surprised at how much she missed him. Curious, how much she had come to rely on him! She had only known him for a few weeks, and yet felt lost without him.

Whether he felt the same way about her she would probably never know. Although he was no doubt fond of her, he did not allow what he considered expressions of sentimentality to pass between them. He was a man hardened by life, a life of crime, to be sure. And yet, there could be no more honorable and upright thief in all the world, she thought.

He had accompanied her to Saint Cloud—probably the first time in many years he had ventured beyond his natural habitat, the Paris underworld. Wasn't that indication enough of some special feeling for her? On the way, she told him the story of her childhood and the mystery of her origin. For some reason, she felt a need to make him part of her life, to share with him the secret of her life. He listened attentively and then heaped on her his good advice, like a father instructing a child upon leaving home. So intensely did she feel the loss when they finally bade each other farewell, the thought entered her mind that perhaps she was in love with him.

No! What she felt for Philippe was love! Her feelings for Arsène were very different, how could it be called by the same name? The attraction she felt for Philippe was intensely sensual. When she was with him, she could not get enough of stroking and kissing him and have him do the same to her. When she thought of Philippe, she yearned to be buried in his arms, lose herself in him, every part of her body ached to be joined to his.

There was nothing physical about her attachment to Arsène. They never touched. Of course, the long starvation had killed off any sexual desire, he had told her so. But even when he had regained some vigor, he stayed clear of close contact with her. The affection and gratitude she felt for him were one for a mentor, a father—for the man who made sure she had enough provisions, a warm blanket, and other necessities for the journey. The man who had told her that she had to unravel the riddle of her birth, but that she had to do it herself.

A sense of urgency pushed her on. Suddenly she had a feeling time was running out; time was a luxury she no longer had. She had to discover who she was, only then could she return to

Philippe and claim their son. An inner voice told her that she must begin her search where her life, as far as she remembered it, started—in the village of Bonneval.

CHAPTER 10

The brightly colored caravan of the Oranto Brothers' Theatrical Company rattled into the center square at Boisville, a village five leagues northeast of Bonneval. Not wanting to attract undue attention in an area of staunch League loyalists, Morin dropped the production of David and Goliath from the program. The company performed a less controversial staple of plays instead, mostly standards that were centered on domestic quarrels, henpecked husbands, and conniving women.

Sandrine was dismayed about this repertoire but said nothing. It amused the villagers and loosened their pockets. Besides, she was hardly in a position to be critical. Her friends had generously offered to take their show far off the main highway, down bumpy country roads where considerably less profit could be expected, just so she could pay a secret visit to Bonneval before deciding where to turn from there.

Régine Morel was startled by the knock at the door at such a late hour. It was not unusual for the doctor to receive calls in the middle of the night. But on that night, she was alone, just was about to retire. Her husband had been called away to attend to a dying patient in a neighboring village. He had left with specific instructions not to admit anybody. All sorts of riffraff were swarming over the area of late. Every day stories were told of robberies and how people weren't even safe in their beds at night.

Cautiously, she peered through the window. She did not remember hearing of gypsies in the area, but the woman who requested her attention, long black hair gathered in a brightly colored scarf tied in the manner of the gypsies, a black wool shawl draped around the shoulders, unmistakably belonged to that group of transients.

Only when she began to speak did Madame Morel recognize the girl they had not expected to see again. A cosmetic mask of rouge and black highlights, created by Rosande's artistic hands, and a wig had completely altered Sandrine's facial features, but her manner of speaking, her very distinct body movement so familiar to Régine Morel erased all doubts as to who this woman was.

Aware of the danger should she be recognized, the doctor's wife bade her enter quickly. Sandrine gladly followed the invitation to the doctor's house where she had so often found a haven. Her companion, Gilles, stationed himself outside ready to warn her of the approach of anybody.

A tense silence had accompanied them on their walk from Boisville to Bonneval, the place of so many anguished memories.

Fortunately, not a soul seemed to be awake as they grazed the outskirts of the village that lay peacefully nestled in the valley between the gently rolling hills of the southern Ile de France, illuminated only by the pale light of a harvest moon.

A few paces from their destination, Sandrine had halted her step, signaling Gilles to wait. From the tower of the parish church, the bell sounded the hour of midnight. Quietly, she counted the strokes. Another night, now a lifetime away, revived in her memory, a night when she was greeted by the sounding of midnight from the same belfry, then a harbinger of loss and sorrow after a fleeting moment of ecstatic love.

The proximity of Bonneval, the place where they first met and loved, suffused her body with longing for Philippe. She must not permit herself to be sucked in by a quagmire of emotions. Only her goal counted now, the goal to free herself from the shackles of ignorance. She had to be steadfast. She had a distinct feeling that the Morels could give her at least a hint of a trace to follow. She pushed all thoughts of Philippe from her mind and moved on.

The two women had hardly finished embracing each other, and Sandrine was still relating to the older woman, in as few words as possible, what had happened to her since that fateful wedding night when she arrived breathless and half-naked at the doctor's house and the subsequent trial at Chartres when their attention was drawn to rapping at the door. It was Gilles's warning of the approach of a rider. No cause for alarm, as it turned out. The good doctor Morel was returning home from his late-night house calls.

"Gabriel! We have a visitor!" His wife rushed to the door to meet him.

"Yeah, I saw the gypsy outside. I heard a group of itinerant theater folk was stationed at Boisville for several days. But haven't I asked you not to admit anybody so late at night when you are alone? With all the rootless dregs on the roads these days, a woman alone is a sure target for robbery and worse." He spoke in a hushed, but angry tone despite his wife's strange cheerfulness.

She pulled him by the hand into the living room, pointing to the young woman who rose to greet him, and called out: "Look who is here!"

"A gypsy woman, no doubt with a medical problem," he said still baffled by Régine's inexplicable behavior.

"It's Sandrine, our Sandrine!" she corrected him. "The gypsies are her friends, and, of course, she did not want to run the risk of being recognized in this area, therefore the disguise."

"All right, my dear, I believe you! But why don't you let her speak for herself?"

"My dear doctor, I cannot take off this disguise, but it is me, Sandrine." She fell on her knees before him and pressed her face against his hands.

"There's no need for that, my child," he said. "Sit down and let us know how we can help you. I'm sure you didn't risk your life coming here just to chat with us about old times."

"Gabriel, how can you be so indelicate?" Régine Morel pouted.

"Actually," Sandrine began, hesitating at first, but soon with the eloquence of one in desperate need. "That's exactly the purpose of my visit, to talk about certain events in the past. You have always been kind to me, all through my childhood when everybody else in this village made me so miserable, and I hope and pray you will extend your kindness to me just one more time. I must find out who I am, and I beg you to help me. Please try to relate to me everything you know, how I came to this village, who the lady was who left me with the innkeeper.

Even the smallest bit of information may be of use."

"We understand your desire to find out who you are." The doctor sat next to her. He took her hands in his. The wife meanwhile announced she was making some tea and disappeared into the kitchen.

"Unfortunately, we know very little and I cannot break a promise to a dying woman."

Sandrine pulled away. "You mean to say, you will not help me! Are the dead of greater importance than the living? If you are my friend, how can you be so cruel? My life depends on this information. How could you withhold from me anything you know that might help me for the sake of a promise made at a different time?"

"The woman's dying wish was that your identity should never become known for as long as you live. She was so certain that your life would be in danger were it known who you are. That's why back then we thought it best for you to blend into village life."

"Then why did you teach me to read and write?" Sandrine called out angrily. "You knew then that it was dangerous, you knew I would be suspect in the eyes of these peasants and still you taught me the love of books."

"Gabriel, I think it's high time we leveled with our charge!" Régine Morel emerged from the kitchen with a tray of tea and biscuits. She exchanged a stern glance with her husband.

"I'll take some of this to Sandrine's friend outside." Before leaving the room, she turned toward her husband: "Meanwhile, Gabriel, maybe you should begin at the beginning."

"The woman is right," he said to Sandrine. "Come, my child, I shall tell you everything we know, which isn't much, but it may give you some hint no matter how faint."

"I wish I could see your real face, but I guess it's better this way." He closed his eyes for a few seconds as if searching his memory for the exact moment when the story began some eighteen years ago.

"It must have been early October—the leaves had already changed their color and were beginning to fall. It was not long after the great massacre of the faithful brethren of the Reformed Church, on the eve of the Feast of Saint Bartholomew in the year 1572, a year none of us shall ever forget. One day, I was called to the sickbed of a woman lodger at the Auberge au Cheval Blanc. As soon as I laid eyes on the woman—a woman of about fifty, maybe more, maybe less, under the circumstances it was hard to tell—anyway, it was immediately clear to me that she was a member of the nobility, the minor nobility, but noble nonetheless. Her manner of speaking, her bearing, even while bedridden, all had an air of good breeding about it. It was also soon clear to me that I had very little power to save her life—she was dying not so much of any physical ailment, although she ran an alarmingly high fever. She was dying of a broken heart and spirit. Thierry informed me that the woman had arrived at the inn with an infant child a few weeks before. She seemed to be not without means for she paid him handsomely for the lodging."

He paused for a moment, pressing his eyes together.

Madame Morel came in from the outside. She walked to the windows and made sure the drapes were drawn tight.

"Your friend prefers to stand guard outside. He's very concerned about your well-being and has asked me to remind you that you must leave before daybreak. Please go on Gabriel, don't let me interrupt you."

"I attended her every morning for several days. Most remarkable about her was the way she doted on the little girl. She did not seem to care much about her own fate, but she was consumed with fear for the life of the child. Maybe it was because I was her physician that she eventually began to take me into her confidence. At times she was so agitated, she whispered, fearing that we might be overheard, with the urgency of someone who felt life slipping away and still had unfinished business to tend to, that the identity of the child must never be known."

"Please go on!" Sandrine urged him when he suddenly sank into a ponderous silence. "Did she say why she feared for the child's life?"

"No, she never did. But let me leave my conjectures for last." He rose and moved to a seat further away perhaps to escape Sandrine's boring glance.

"In a quieter moment, she confided that her name was Mathilde de Bécour. She had a family in a southern province of France, and she asked me to post a letter should she die. The letter's destination was Moissac in the province of Périgord. She never told me who the little girl was, only that she was left in her care by her parents and that she was an orphan. I tried to find out why and how she had come to Bonneval, but she became extremely agitated and was unable or unwilling to answer."

"There's something that might help you in your search!" He walked over to a commode in the corner, lifted the lid, and searched through its contents. At first, he seemed exasperated, unable to find what he was looking for. Almost furiously, he pushed aside the items stored in the chest. Finally, he took out an object and placed it on the table in front of Sandrine.

"I found this among her few belongings on the night when she expired, God rest her soul. I thought it best to hold it for safekeeping before Thierry would find it."

Sandrine examined the small case fashioned of fine inlaid olive wood with unconcealed disappointment. She had hoped the doctor had some concrete answers. Still unsure, she followed his urging to open it. Her attention was immediately drawn to the design of an emblem embedded in a red velvet lining, two yellow butterflies separated by a red band on a cobalt blue enameled background.

"This is an emblem fashioned for a noble family," Doctor Morel explained. "What is interesting about this one is not so much the red band which might indicate a link to the House of Bourbon, but the inscription. Here look closely."

"It is better to trust in the Lord than to trust in man," Sandrine read aloud. "It sounds like the Old Testament."

"That's exactly what it is. It is a quote from the Book of Psalms. But go on, finish reading."

"It is better to trust in the Lord than to trust in princes," Sandrine continued. "Our enemies compassed us about like bees, but the Lord extinguished them like a fire of thorns. Hark the rejoicing and triumph in the tent of the righteous!"

And further on: "The Lord is our light and salvation; for in times of trouble he shelters us in his sanctuary."

"Do you see?" the doctor exclaimed. "A Catholic noble family would have chosen a Latin inscription. Only a believer in the Religion would choose the Old Testament. Also, this particular quote encapsulates the Huguenot belief in the community of the faithful and the very personal relationship of the faithful with God."

"The Lord extinguished them like a fire of thorns," Sandrine murmured. "Well, so she was probably a Huguenot. I guess this information could be useful somehow."

"But you don't understand, my child. Yes, she was most likely a Huguenot, but more importantly, your parents, whoever they were, must have been Huguenots. Mathilde de Bécour came to the village a short time after the great massacre in Paris."

"Look," he entreated her when he saw a frown form on her

face. "The emblem belongs most likely to the noble household to which the woman was attached, a higher ranking family. Notice the butterflies, they are the same as the one you have on your arm. And what is most important, this kind of emblem must be registered somewhere in this kingdom, for no two families in the Kingdom of France are permitted to use the same design."

A revelation suddenly came over the young woman, her face drained of all color. She rose abruptly and retreated toward the door.

"You knew this all the time!" Her voice sounded strange and far away, then rose to a shrill pitch. "You knew and you left me helplessly delivered to the wolves in this village. They might have torn me to shreds, I almost died, and you did not lift a finger. To think that all these years, I thought you were my friends!"

She tried to open the bolted door, her eyes filled with tears of anger.

"Please, Sandrine let us explain!" Régine Morel placed her arms around the girl's shoulders and led her back into the room. "You have a right to be angry, but please consider our position. Doctor Morel and I are believers in Calvin's teachings, what is sometimes called the Religion, and you know what this means in this region. Even now, we still attend Mass so we won't arouse their suspicion. There are only a handful of Huguenot families in this area. We get together secretly every few weeks for prayer meetings, so far we have been lucky not to have been found out."

Régine Morel was a woman of strong convictions. She interpreted her childlessness as a directive from God to devote herself to the good of the community. In tandem with her husband, she never tired of caring for the sick, especially women in childbirth. They formed an almost inseparable husband-wife team, a bit eccentric as far as the peasants were concerned, but then they did much good and could be forgiven for not conforming in every way to village tastes and customs.

"Although we would have liked to adopt the child, that is you, even now I think it was a reasonable decision for us not to put her life in danger, as it surely would have been, were we found out in the community. You should have seen Berthe Legrand's joy when she received the little girl. We had every reason to assume you were in good hands. We thought it would be best for you to fit in with the rest of the villagers as the innkeeper's daughter."

Sandrine sat quietly weeping, rocking gently back and forth, her face buried in her hands.

"Why, then did you teach me to read and write?" She finally repeated. "I did not understand then, but I think I know now. Berthe hired me out to families in the village as household help from the time I was six years old. Only you never had me do any work but used the time I was at your house to teach me, to instill in me a love of learning. I guess I should be grateful to you, and really, I am. The knowledge you gave me has helped me get through much hardship, but at the time, in the village, it made no sense."

"It made sense to us," Doctor Morel assured her. "You were so bright, so different, even as a child. We could not let this talent go completely to waste. You learned so quickly and eagerly, never had enough. Somehow, I suppose, we always felt that we owed you this much, that you were born for greater things, than to live and die a peasant in Bonneval."

"Also, we always felt you were one of us," Madame Morel added. "That is why we taught you the Old Testament and the precepts of Calvin's teachings."

The knock on the door reminded them that day was about

to break. Sandrine thanked the couple profusely, begging their forgiveness for having lost her temper. Another knock on the door. The cry of the rooster pierced the graying dawn. She gathered the wooden case with the emblem and, her companion at her side, made her way back through the woods to Boisville.

CHAPTER 11

The setting sun shed its last iridescent vermilion autumnal light over fields and meadow. Its rays no longer had the strength to warm the air already permeated with the crisp, clean smell of the coming of winter. The hunting party of several dozen equestrians, crouching in their saddles to ward off the chill, trotted noisily into the cobblestone courtyard of Miremont Manor, ahead of few hundred beaters on foot, ahead of them, packs of hungry dogs. Bringing up the rear were the servants who transported the bloodied carcasses of the day's game—several deer, a boar, a good score of pheasants and partridges, hares and even a fox— all promised a grand evening feast to crown a day spent in an invigorating, relentless chase.

"A perfect ending to a perfect day!" The guests, still in their riding gear, mingled before dinner in the parlor, rubbed their hands in front of the fireplace, as they recalled the details of the day's events. The hunt was unanimously declared to have been a great success and cups of hot Calvados were raised to the health of the host.

"You are a perfect lord of the manor, Philippe! We hope your presence will bring some life to our region. The social season around here needs some enlivening. Winters are such a dour affair in these parts. We certainly hope to have you here at least for the season! The war needs its heroes, but even a hero needs to rest and enjoy the finer things in life!"

Since he had taken up residence at this most remote of his estates several months before, the Seigneur of Miremont had been avidly courted by the local barons. For the most part, Philippe had politely turned down their invitations, preferring a reclusive life of contemplation. Only on rare occasions had he called on his neighbors who had at first regarded his presence with a certain amount of suspicion. Speculation had been rife why a hero of the League would retire to this isolated frontier between Normandy and Brittany.

What they did not know was that he had come to Miremont to find solace, if not forgetfulness, in the simple pleasures of long horseback rides, in solitary walks through the pristine countryside of rounded hills crowned with dense forests—only here and there a few cultivated fields hugging the slopes—and of marshy meadows of the river valley which line its banks.

Miremont and its medieval manor house of fieldstone in the Breton style, a picturesque, steep slate roof framed by corner turrets were situated on a hilltop overlooking the Selune River. Philippe found its homeliness more conducive to thought and study than the gray granite fortress of Salignac in the north of

Normandy. Here he could spend hours by the window and let his eyes follow the flow of the gently meandering river to its estuary on the Emerald Coast—on a clear day he could see the colossal magnificence of the monastery of Saint Michel rising from the windswept sea.

Miremont revived in him an old dream, the longing to put down roots in a permanent abode away from the world of politics and war. A life of contemplation had always held a special appeal for him. Should he be overcome with a thirst for action, he could always indulge himself in the Norman landed gentry's passion for breeding and racing fine horses. But these were all pipe dreams now. Life without Sandrine had no meaning for him and the future was but a bleak, gaping hole of nothingness.

The rage against his powerlessness that had possessed him had subsided now and a languishing apathy had taken hold in a calm day-to-day existence. But his state of mind resembled more that of a sedated wild animal in captivity than that of a free man at peace with himself.

Among those around him, his brooding, melancholy disposition stirred whispers of concern, especially among the servants. But the person most alarmed was his mother, the Duchess d'Evreux, who, sensing that something terrible had happened to her only son, had been deeply disturbed by his retirement to Miremont.

Following her motherly instinct, the Duchess had decided to find out for herself why her son was hiding out in this provincial backwater. After several days at Miremont manor, she concluded that the best antidote to his melancholy would be marriage. Immediately upon her return to Evreux, or civilization as she liked to say, she would make arrangements with the Montreuils for the wedding with his betrothed, Louise de Montreuil.

It was also at his mother's prompting that he had invited the local barons for a day of hunting—a temporary measure against his appalling social isolation.

"My dear Count, what is your estimate of the League's ability to hold out against the heretics?" Philippe turned to the baron who asked the question and was about to give a polite, but evasive answer, when he noticed that the man's attention was absorbed in tenaciously extracting the last bit of meat from a drumstick that made an answer superfluous.

"Even if Mayenne gives up, the Duke de Mercoeur is organizing resistance from an impregnable position in Brittany," another baron picked up the topic. Philippe's reputation as a League soldier had reached even these remote parts and the country squires felt compelled to assure him of their support for the cause.

"We heard that Ivry was a rather disturbing affair."

"Yes, indeed it was a disturbing affair, to put it mildly. It was more like a rout." Philippe laughed nervously. "Ivry was quite a blow and maybe the death blow to the League. And before that Arques! It seems the League army has lost its élan, even its purpose."

"That is a very strange observation coming from a warrior of the reputation of the Count de Treffort-Salignac."

"I am a realist. It does no good to deny the obvious." Philippe felt beleaguered as more of the barons gathered around, eager to absorb his every word.

"But don't forget, Navarre has not taken Paris yet, and without Paris, he will not be king in France!"

"That's right! All is not decided yet. Remember the Duke de Parma forced him to retreat from the siege of the capital."

"But he was not beaten by the League army," Philippe interjected. "It was a foreign army, and a Spanish one at that.

How can we let our affairs be guided by Spain, the traditional archenemy of France? Think about it, gentlemen!"

"Do you think it better if the destiny of France were in the hands of the heretics? In such a case, the war will never end!"

"The Huguenots don't want to rule France, they just want an end to persecution and intolerance. Let's face it, Navarre is the rightful heir to the throne, whether we like it or not. Mark my word, gentlemen, in due course he will embrace the Catholic faith and bring peace to the kingdom. May God grant him strength and endurance to fulfill this task soon."

"Amen!" Shouts of approval were interspersed with expressions of grave misgivings.

"This does not sound like the view one would expect of the son of the venerable champion of the Catholic and Apostolic faith, the Duke d'Evreux!"

The accusation, hurled at him by a caller in the back of the room, made Philippe seethe with anger.

"I have fought long and hard for the Catholic Church and the Apostolic faith. I for one have proven myself in battle and I have earned the right to form my own opinions! The time for bloodshed has passed, the time has come for healing, for an end to the suffering of the people, an end to the devastation of the land. Peace had better come soon if France is to survive."

"Let's be done with politics, already! Gentlemen, let's enjoy the bounteous proceeds of our hunt!" The host exhorted his guests to make merry and ordered round upon round of heaping platters of roast venison and heavy sweet wine. The already heady assembly needed no further prompting.

True to the adage, a full stomach is the best peacemaker, the barons left the woes of the world to be solved by others and fastened their attention on the pleasures of gluttonous excess. As was the custom among Breton country squires, the feasting extended over several days. By then, most of the guests were in such an apoplectic state, they did not even notice that their host had quietly slipped away.

"Philippe, of course, I would not say anything in front of your guests, but I am astonished about the things I have heard from your mouth these last few days." The Duchess d'Evreux spoke softly but not without admonishment. Mother and son stood together on the balcony enjoying the panoramic view of the hill country and the river valley below, brushed with a spectrum of earthy tones of brown and yellow that exuded a nurturing, though deceptive, warmth.

A cool breeze, filled with the raunchy saltiness of the sea just twenty miles downriver, playfully tousled the plumes of the Duchess's velvet toque, a fashionable rimless cap under which was gathered her mass of bright auburn hair, now interspersed with fine silvery streaks.

How beautiful she is! The thought inadvertently passed through Philippe's mind. It occurred to him that he had never really looked at his mother before—he had never seen her as a woman. She had always been such a quiet, self-effacing presence who had little to do with his life. For the first time, he noticed the regularity of her fine facial features, no longer in their first flowering, but still most appealing. An unassuming dignity radiated from her elegant bearing. Like Sandrine, he thought. He now believed to discern a few similarities between the two women although the Duchess's youth was waning and her beauty was corseted in the fashion of the wealthy. It was not hard for Philippe to imagine Sandrine in his mother's magnificent taupe velvet gown, adorned with gold embroidery, the tight-fitting upper bodice outlining her soft, feminine forms, and extending in a v-shape below the waist, with the skirt tumbling in ample pleats so low as to sweep the ground, her arms enveloped in wide puffed sleeves and around her neck a ruff with stiffly starched flutes but open at the front to reveal a deep cleavage and ropes of pearls around the neck constraining her movements. Philippe tried to imagine his mother as a girl of seventeen. Was she once wild and tempestuous like Sandrine?

He knew very little about her. All he knew was that she came from an ancient aristocratic family in the province of Poitou where his father had told him, she stood to inherit several estates whenever the area would be wrested from Huguenot control. His father had so dominated his life that he had been cut off from any influence of his mother and her family. For the first time, the question flashed through his head why it was that they never had any contact with his mother's family. Nobody ever spoke about them, not even his mother.

A sudden urge seized him to ask questions he knew she would not deem appropriate for a son to ask. He wanted to know details about her childhood, how she came to marry the Duke d'Evreux? Had they been betrothed? Did she love him? Was she ever really in love with someone else?

Just then, the coachman announced the horses and carriage were ready for the journey. The Duchess's lady-in-waiting approached and draped a long, quilted cloak over her mistress' shoulders. It was just as well, Philippe resigned himself. She would have been shocked had he posed questions of an intimate nature.

"I shall send word when the wedding preparations are complete. Don't you think it would be wonderful to have the wedding on Christmas?" She leaned forward and breathed a kiss on each of his cheeks.

"Madame!" The urgency with which he called out made her pause. "Please forgive me, but I cannot marry Louise de Montreuil."

She looked at him stunned as if he had announced the demise of a close friend. Her reaction baffled him. How could she not have noticed that he was in love with someone else?

"I was rather hoping for your help in obtaining a dissolution of this betrothal. Please, Mother," he pleaded softly, taking her by the hand and leading her inside the privacy of his study.

"First Catherine, and now you!" The Duchess seemed unable to comprehend what was happening, but she still loosened the clasp of her cloak and was willing to hear him out.

"Louise seemed to be the best choice—good family, a devout Catholic, a sizeable dowry—there are no other heirs to the Montreuil title and lands, you know. And have you seen her recently? What a beauty, and such grace, the finest flower of the French nobility! You could not possibly not like her."

"It is not Louise de Montreuil. For all I know she may be the most wonderful person in the world, but I am in love with another woman! Please try to understand!"

"In love with another woman! You mean to say you cannot marry Louise because you are in love with somebody else?" The Duchess gave off a burst of nervous laughter. She found the meaning of her son's words difficult to understand or what one had to do with the other.

What a curious world we live in, she thought. She hadn't met the Duke until a few days before they were married. She was sixteen and he was ten years her senior. There never was any love between them, but she never failed in her duties as an obedient wife. Love! Oh yes, she had known love once, the pain had long been buried. A placid numbness had taken hold of her that never left her although she didn't think about it much anymore. The only active love she had left was for her children, and yet she had never been able to be close to them. The Duke's overbearing control over their offspring had relegated her to a marginal place in their lives.

The Duchess cast a probing glance over her son. For the first time, she did not see him through the lens of social conventions, and she permitted herself to acknowledge his unhappiness. His pain became hers as she watched him across the room, while he stared wistfully into the dancing flames in the fireplace.

"You know your father will be outraged," she said softly at first, then suddenly her speech became more animated, and rebelliousness seemed to creep in. "But maybe it is time to protest the inhuman notion of the preeminence of tradition, duty, family honor, raison d'état, noblesse oblige, or what have you, all the nonsense that requires a constant sacrifice of love and personal happiness."

Having had her say, she picked up her cloak and gloves and added in a conspiratorial tone: "I shall make your request known to the Duke when I return home. You can count on me, no matter what."

"Why are you doing this?"

"Because my son deserves to be happy." She gave his cheek a light coquettish slap with her gloves. He didn't remember seeing her so elated.

"Well, I hope you will obtain approval from the young woman's parents, and you will honor us soon by presenting the lady of your heart at Chateau d'Evreux."

To her astonishment, her words caused a renewed fit of dejection. Philippe began to pace up and down, wringing his hands, his mouth twitched as if he had been whipped.

"But what is the matter, my son?" The Duchess placed her hand on his arm, forcing him to halt.

"Mother, I have lost her, she is gone!" Tears gleamed in his eyes.

"You mean she is dead?"

"I don't know. She may very well be dead. I left her in Catherine's care at the convent when I received orders to return to the League army, the summer before last. Then the nuns were evacuated to Chateau d'Evreux and she disappeared from there without a trace."

"But why would she have left? She left no message with Catherine?"

"No, nothing. Only, I have heard she was escorted from the castle grounds by armed guards on orders of the Duke, but I have no proof. Did he ever mention anything to you?"

"No. But you know I don't enjoy his confidence. Did he know who she was, I mean, did he know of your relationship with the young woman? Maybe he felt she was getting in the way of your marriage to Louise."

"I have never spoken to him about Sandrine, nor has Catherine. For him, she was one of the nuns. She just disappeared and I don't know where to search for her."

"Could she have gone back to her parents?" The Duchess suggested cautiously since this possibility must have occurred to him.

"No, she has no parents. She is all alone in the world, she has only me."

A disdainful "Oh!" escaped from her lips. Quickly she caught herself though: "I am so sorry for all the unhappiness that has befallen you. I think it may be best if you spoke with your father frankly yourself."

"You know it is impossible to question him. I have spoken to the guards and was told they left her by the roadside in the rain near Rouen. Mother, she was carrying my child! How could she have survived all alone?"

The Duchess extended her arms in a helpless gesture as Philippe sank to his knees. He buried his face in his hands, sobbing uncontrollably. The mother knelt beside him and held him for the first time since he had been an infant. By the twilight of leaping flames in the fireplace, a miracle occurred, the miracle of bonding between mother and child, a bond that had been severed by the rites of the warrior class so many years ago.

The lady-in-waiting requested to be admitted and announced the hour was getting late for the start of the journey.

"We shall leave tomorrow morning then. Have Antoine unhitch the horses." The Duchess declared resolutely.

"Philippe!" she continued in the same resolute tone after the bewildered servant had left, "I think it is essential that you return to Evreux with me tomorrow. Nothing will be gained by burying yourself in this . . . this hole. You must never give up hope! The moment you lose hope, your life is spent."

November was the most dismal month of the year in the northern province of Normandy. Endless rains, whipped ashore by the gusts of a furious sea, drenched the countryside and buried the roads under a mass of mud. Philippe rode alongside the carriage that transported the Duchess d'Evreux and her entourage. Heedless of the wind and rain, he was obsessed with the thought of holding fast to the image of Sandrine, to prevent it from fading into a misty phantasmagoria.

Only the excited shouts from the attendants of the traveling party whose progress was impeded by an opaque curtain of constant rain and almost impassible roadways brought him back to reality. At this moment, the carriage had come to a halt, its wheels were spinning in the mud and resisted the horses' pull. The efforts of the coachmen assisted by Philippe and his retainers, Gaspard and Mathieu, brought no results until the ladies alighted from the carriage.

The scene was repeated every few miles, making the journey

a drudgery every step of the way. At night, the party put up at local inns wherever one could be found. Most of these accommodations were lacking in basic comfort and afforded the weary travelers little rest.

On the fifth day of the journey, the sun's rays finally parted the clouds and drew a triumphal ark of brilliant colors over the landscape dotted with villages and chateaux. The travelers breathed a sigh of relief when the lofty castle-keep of Chateau d'Evreux, situated on the high point of a wooded elevation, finally came into view.

When the carriages and riders crossed the moat and came to a halt in the courtyard, the Duchess d'Evreux, mindless of travel fatigue, her clothes and face caked with splashes of mud, demanded to be immediately announced to the Duke. Philippe would have liked to have some time to clean up and ponder how best to put his request to his father, but his mother, once she had made up her mind that her son had been wronged, was adamant to have this matter taken care of at once.

Undaunted by the presence of several of the most powerful barons of the region, among them the Count de Montreuil and Robert de la Croix, she did something she had never done before—she demanded her husband's immediate attention.

"Charles!" she declared after a perfunctory exchange of greetings, "Philippe and I have a family matter of utmost importance to discuss with you."

"My dear Beatrice, I am sure, whatever it is, it can wait until dinner time," the Duke retorted, perplexed, yet firm. "As you can see, I am detained in council."

With this, his wife ceased to exist for him and he turned to greet his son with obvious pleasure.

"My dear Philippe, you have just come in time. Come on in, the Count de Montreuil was about to propose a plan for the rallying of our forces and the final defeat of the heretic pretender."

He placed his arm around his son's shoulder who looked back at his mother as she reproachfully called out his name. With a helpless shrug of the shoulders and unable to resist the pull of his father's arm, he followed him to the table where the assembled lords poured over maps and battle plans.

"You have the backbone of a lizard! Crawling at his feet like that! How could you!" Never before had Philippe seen her so beside herself with anger. "I was ready to stand up for you! Put the tyrant in his place!"

"How responsive do you think he would have been if you had broken a private family matter to him in the presence of all the barons? The moment was not well chosen. I shall speak with him when we are alone."

"Don't think me ungrateful," he added apologetically. "From the bottom of my heart, I appreciate your concern, your support, and I am grateful that you jolted me out of the state of inaction into which I had fallen. Believe me, I shall take the next step, but you must let me go it alone. Assurance of your love is what I need now."

"That you have, my son, always. You are always in my prayers. May God be with you and protect you—you certainly need his help."

The exchange between mother and son was interrupted by an announcement that the Count de la Croix requested to be admitted to Philippe's quarters.

"How wonderful to see you looking so well, my dear Count!" The Duchess opened her arms to receive the longtime family friend who propelled himself forward with the aid of two crutches, but otherwise, he looked fine. His cherubic face had grown rounder and even shinier. The enforced physical inactivity had padded his once lean frame.

"What have you been doing with yourself?" Philippe embraced his friend warmly and bade him sit down. "I see you are still involved in the planning of military strategy."

"I only lost half a leg, not my brains, nor my desire to see this war come to a felicitous end for our Holy Church."

"I am sorry, I did not mean to offend you, only last time we spoke you intended to retire to a life of study and devotion."

"Oh, yes that is right. I have taken the lower vows of the Holy Order of the Carmelite Brothers. I am preparing for the final vows. Since I cannot serve the Church on the battlefield anymore, maybe this way I can still be useful."

The Duchess looked at the young aristocrat. Her daughter's anguished outcry echoed in her memory. Only once had she seen a stream of emotions break through Catherine's controlled facade. She remembered it very well, it was a year ago at that fateful family dinner that had given her such cause for elation and had ended in anger and gloom. It was then, when hearing of Robert's injury, that Catherine let show through her inner pain of an unattainable love for a brief moment.

"Have you thought about this carefully?" asked the Duchess. "Final vows are so . . . so permanent. I should think a man like you wants to marry, have heirs."

He sadly shook his head. "No, Madame, I am certain, family life is not for me. Since I have no hope to be joined to the woman I love, I prefer a life of celibacy and devotion in service to God and his Church."

The three looked at each other in silence, each filled with a heavy heart. The Duchess stood behind the chair where Robert was seated. She placed her hand on his shoulder, and almost inaudibly, she whispered her daughter's name.

"Yes, Madame." The answer was a simple statement of fact,

without sentimentality. "God's will be done."

He was resigned to his fate and at peace.

Suddenly the Duchess looked furiously from Robert to Philippe and shouted: "You are both such fools! Why don't you fall in love with women you can have?"

Then, smoothing her dress, she just as abruptly was transformed back into the dignified lady.

"Well, I have to tend to my duties. I hope to have the pleasure of seeing you both at dinner."

The two men waited for the door to shut behind her.

"Well, I guess the cat is out of the sack. How did she know?"

"She didn't, but she saw it in your eyes, and she saw it in Catherine's eyes a year ago. Robert, is there no way she may receive dispensation from her vow?"

"No! A vow is a vow, and a vow of chastity is forever. I don't want to create a false impression, the honor of Her Ladyship, the Abbess is above reproach. But we have agreed that our love can only be redeemed if I take the vows as well. Don't look so sad, the world is not coming to an end. Let's talk about you. I hear the wedding will be soon."

"I don't know what you are talking about! What wedding?"

"Yours with Louise de Montreuil, of course! You are lucky to be betrothed to such a beautiful, not to say wealthy, woman."

"Don't be ridiculous, I don't even know her." Philippe was annoyed that Robert should have forgotten about Sandrine.

"So maybe she is beautiful, but you know very well I cannot marry her. The reason for my coming here is to obtain a dissolution of the betrothal."

"Don't tell me that peasant wench still has you in her thrall?"

"You can be so unbearably arrogant, Robert! Yes, I am still in love with the peasant girl—her name is Sandrine—and nothing in this world will ever change that fact! Can you get this into your numb skull?"

Philippe walked to the window so he wouldn't have to look at the smirk on his friend's face. He was annoyed with himself for letting Robert provoke him. Why did he feel he had to justify his actions, his feelings? He owed an explanation to no one, neither Robert nor his father nor anyone else in this world!

"She is a crafty little thing that Sandrine of yours. Do you know that Louise is raising your child?" The bombshell exploded with the force of a thunderclap. For a moment it seemed that Philippe was intent on squeezing the life out of his friend. Only the appearance of a servant with a tray of the refreshments brought him to his senses.

Philippe quickly dismissed the servant and demanded to know the meaning of Robert's outrageous remark.

"Well, you spent so much time in the backwoods, you don't know what is going on in the world," Robert deigned to answer.

"Tell me, is she alive? Do you know where she is?"

"No, I don't know her whereabouts, but it seems that she was alive in Paris a few months ago, as late as July or August."

"She was in Paris during the siege?"

"As suggested by the evidence she left on the doorstep of the Hotel Montreuil, yes she was apparently in Paris then. And so was Louise, trapped by the barbarous heretic."

"Can we leave politics out of this for the moment and get to the point?"

"Your betrothed, Louise de Montreuil, was in Paris, the reason matters little. When the city was cut off from the outside world by Navarre's army, she found herself trapped inside the walls. You have heard of the terrible hardships the brave Parisians endured for the sake of their faith. She got by as best she could, spending many hours in prayer."

Probably with the Chevalier d'Aumale, Philippe thought,

his fists clenched behind his back, straining to keep his temper under control. If Robert would only stop sprinkling his remarks with unessential religiosities! But he did not think it wise to antagonize him further since he seemed to have information of vital importance concerning Sandrine.

"One day, either in late July or early August—the misery of the inhabitants had reached unbearable proportions—Louise discovered at her doorsteps an infant in such sickly condition she feared it may not survive. There was a note attached to the bunting addressed to her by name begging her to save the life of the child for the sake of the love of Count Philippe de Treffort-Salignac. Of course, it might just have been a trick devised by any mother concerned for the life of her child. But how many commoners can write? The note also said his name was Noël, no last name, but that he was born on Christmas Day of last year. That makes it about right, doesn't it?"

"Oh, it is good to know you are still keeping a calendar of my amorous engagements." Philippe laughed nervously. "Where is the child now? No trace of the mother I presume?"

"I am afraid not. The child is in the care of Louise at Bonneterre. He has recovered from the ill effects of malnutrition and, believe me, he is in the best of hands."

"But something is wrong here," Philippe said after some consideration. "Sandrine would never give up her child. Catherine tells me how happy she was to be with child."

Suddenly, he jumped up and he exclaimed: "Robert, Robert! Please, help me, I am going out of my mind!"

"Philippe, you have been out of your mind since the day you met this peasant. You have not been yourself since. Your only salvation is to rid yourself of this infatuation. You must come to grips with the fact that she has forsaken you. Be reasonable and marry Louise. You could not find a woman more beautiful, sensitive, cultured, and of impeccable pedigree and breeding."

"You cannot be serious, Robert. Everybody knows she has been carrying on with the Chevalier d'Aumale, a rabble-rouser and notorious fornicator of the first order."

"The Chevalier died in battle at Saint-Denis in defense of the Holy Church," Robert informed him gravely.

"All right! All this does not matter to me anyway. I simply cannot marry Louise and be she the most beautiful and most virtuous woman in the world! Nor can I marry any other woman. My love belongs to Sandrine and should she be dead, then I shall have to live out my life alone. I had hoped that you, at least, would understand this."

Robert lifted himself out of his chair and reached for his crutches. "I guess there is not much else to say," he said, "The Duke and Duchess expect us for dinner soon. Let's try to behave like well-bred gentlemen."

"You seem well informed in every way. So where may Louise be found at this moment?" He was told she was at Bonneterre, an estate in the northern part of Normandy near the border of Picardie, a good two day's ride away. He invited Robert to accompany him thither the next morning but was politely refused. With a shrug of the shoulders, Robert pointed out that a hard gallop over rough terrain, once a favorite activity, was unfortunately no longer possible for him.

CHAPTER 12

Bonneterre sparkled with the glaze of a thin layer of early snow. Only in a few spots on the hilltops had the rays of the pallid sun melted the frost and the rich, black earth of the region was exposed to Philippe's view as he entered Louise de Montreuil's domain on a clear November day. Nestled against the eastern slope of a rounded hill, the impressive brick manor house with a steep, partially snow-covered tile roof, smoke rising from two massive chimneys and seemingly leaning against a shield of dense trees on the western side, left no doubt about the wealth of its owner. This impression was further confirmed by a sweep over the boundless plain of the river valley, dotted with lakes and forests, to the north. No trace was left of the engagement of armies that had laid waste the rich soil on numerous occasions, testimony to the resilience of the land and its inhabitants.

Bonneterre was a good land in times of peace. It was also part of the rich patrimony of Louise de Montreuil, sole heiress to the Montreuil estates which extended from Normandy north deep into Picardie. A matrimonial alliance between the houses of Evreux and Montreuil would create a powerful, solidly Catholic force in the northwestern region of the kingdom. The two barons had hatched their plan, using their children in a scheme of power without not foreseeing, or unwilling to take into account, the intervention of fate, that unpredictable element governing human lives.

Philippe was pleasantly surprised by the cordiality with which he was received by the lady of Bonneterre. Even more surprised was he when he realized that he had found an ally in this, admittedly, beautiful and kindhearted woman. She too, he learned, was in love with another man, a scholar and a commoner, who had captured her heart with the beauty of poetry and philosophy. Truth be told, she more than welcomed the prospect of a dissolution of the marriage agreement that was as odious to her as it was to her betrothed.

Already in the first hour of their conversation, he warmed to her unpretentious charm to such a degree that he felt relieved to learn that her affections had not been wasted on the notorious Chevalier d'Aumale with whom gossip had linked her, but for whom she had only a passing fancy some years before. The immediate friendly rapport between them made it possible for both to speak frankly and without artifice. By dinner time, their friendship had deepened and like two conspirators they plotted how they would obtain the consent of their parents to dissolve the betrothal.

At one point, a woman, obviously a lady-in-waiting,

approached and whispered something in Louise's ear whereupon the baroness excused herself.

Philippe sat alone, savoring the warm glow of the candlelight and slurping more of the heavy, sweet wine in front of him than was his habit. He had left Evreux without bringing up the matter of the betrothal with his father. To soothe his mother's vexation, at what she regarded his lack of courage, he promised to act as soon as he had sought out his betrothed's advice. Deep inside, he was torn by feelings of guilt for not having told her the real reason why he was so anxious to travel to Bonneterre, but he feared if his mother found out his child was in the care of Louise, her meddling might multiply his problems even more.

A good half hour passed before Louise returned to the dining hall. Again they sat opposite each other in quiet council. Her fawn brown eyes rested on his face as if she was searching for an answer to a riddle that had occupied her for a long time. Philippe finally broke the silence. Maybe it was the alcohol that emboldened him.

"The child!" he said softly. "Please grant me the favor, I must see the child."

"Tomorrow," she said simply, apparently not at all surprised that he should know about the child nor that he should wish to see him. "He is asleep and I think we should both retire. I am sure you could use some rest after the long journey. Tomorrow you must tell me your story."

As soon as Philippe saw the boy he was certain he was his son. He turned to Mathieu for his opinion who confirmed that nobody but Sandrine could be the mother of this delicate child that was just attempting its first steps in a nursery filled with toys and was attended by two doting nannies, twin sisters from Picardie. The sky blue eyes and the soft, curly blond hair were unmistakable, Mathieu assured his master.

Philippe turned to Louise. He saw the amazement in her eyes at the apparent intimacy between master and servant.

"Mathieu knows Sandrine better than anybody. They are close friends since childhood," he explained.

"Was there any other communication from the mother beside the note?" he asked. "Please think, even the slightest hint . . ."

His voice broke off. She guided him away from the nursery to a niche by the window, leaving Mathieu to play with the child.

"For several weeks after the child was found at the doorstep of Hotel Montreuil," she began reaching back for a hazy memory, "the coachmen and other servants told me of a young woman, ragged and emaciated, as was almost everybody in Paris then, who was seen lingering about the square. I never actually saw her, but I was told that sometimes she sat for hours in the crown of the oak tree in a rather precarious position."

"That could only be Sandrine! Nobody climbs trees like Sandrine!" he exclaimed not hiding his pleasure at the thought. Louise looked at him, eyebrows raised. He apologized for interrupting and begged her to continue.

"This went on for about two or three weeks, then she was no longer seen for several weeks. She didn't appear again until the day we left Paris." Louise paused for a moment as if she had to search her memory for what happened.

"I saw her only in passing. The carriage was about to pull out of the driveway when I saw a woman running across the square. For a moment I was afraid she might get trampled by the horses. Whether she was the same woman who had been seen several weeks before I cannot tell. She may very well have perished in the famine. You cannot imagine the horror that filled the streets of the city, starving beggars everywhere, the entire town resembled a graveyard, and we did not have much left ourselves to give."

"She might still be in Paris!" Philippe said to himself. His thoughts trailed off and he listened only distractedly to what Louise was saying. How hope springs eternal! He needed no further proof that the woman Louise described was Sandrine.

That afternoon, they took a walk in the brisk air of the garden lined with barren rose bushes bending under the weight of caps of snow. Philippe carried the child swaddled in a blanket. This may be the last time he would hold his son. Louise adamantly refused to give up the child she had come to love as her own. The rapport between them had cooled slightly over Philippe's demand to have the child put in his custody.

"Strange," Philippe mumbled to himself, "his mother was a foundling too."

"She must be an extraordinary woman," Louise said softly, straining to recapture the earlier warmth between them. Philippe nodded. He was unwilling or unable to bridge the awkwardness that had arisen between them. Louise stiffened at what she saw as his ungratefulness and was now anxious to be rid of her visitor.

Philippe did little to make the last evening he spent at Bonneterre more pleasant. His behavior was nothing short of self-indulgent and rude. The next morning, even before sunrise, he ordered Gaspard and Mathieu to saddle up. The farewell was cordial, but brief. Louise assured him that she knew no greater pleasure than to persuade her father to burn the marriage agreement that tied them together.

That year, Christmas at Bonneterre was a very special celebration. The entire household rejoiced in Noël's first birthday. He in turn delighted his adoring admirers with his first firm steps down the corridor without falling flat on his face and stomach.

A letter arrived for Louise from Philippe with a long apology. It had been posted in Paris where he had gone, he said, in search of Sandrine. The letter softened her feelings toward Philippe but did not weaken her resolve never to give up the child. She hoped to have children of her own someday, but doubted that she would ever produce a legitimate heir since her father was not likely to agree to her marrying a, if not penniless, so at least completely untitled, poet and student of philosophy to whom she had sworn eternal love and fidelity.

Raphael Floris had come into her life three years before, at a time when the eighteen-year-old young woman sought to mend a broken heart by immersing herself in the study of ancient philosophy. She had come to realize that what she thought was love for the Chevalier d'Aumale, a married man and notorious philanderer, was but the desire of a young girl to be accepted into the then fashionable inner circle of the Guise clan. Although she was soon cured of her infatuation with the dashing soldier, her friendship with Catherine de Montpensier may be the reason why she was still being linked in gossip with the Chevalier.

Louise paid little attention to the gossipmongers. She regretted the death of the Chevalier mainly because he now no longer served as a decoy to distract the society vultures from her real love. She did not care whether noses were snubbed at the commoner, all she wanted was to live in peaceful bliss away from the world.

Raphael, an exotically attractive young man whose curly dark hair and fiery charcoal eyes betrayed his Iberian origin, had introduced her to the beauty of poetry and philosophy, and soon to the secrets and raptures of love. She had never a man who was able to put the most profound and most beautiful thoughts into words in as exquisite a manner as he did. Never had the touch of a man roused her to such ecstasy.

After the experience of having her virginity shattered by the Chevalier in a bout that left her feeling violated in body and spirit, a feeling that was only deepened during every subsequent encounter with him, she had come to harbor serious doubts that a woman could ever enjoy this kind of activity, and was ready to forgo it altogether. Raphael taught her otherwise.

Life without Raphael had become unthinkable. The months she was forced to spend away from him while she was trapped in Paris, had given her a taste of the utter desolateness in store for her were she ever to lose him. Never again, she swore to herself, would she permit them to be separated for so long.

At the time of Philippe's visit, he had been called away to Antwerp to the bedside of his ailing mother and Louise awaited his return with great trepidation. She knew his father, a wealthy merchant and manufacturer, would like his only son to enter the family business and settle down in the material comfort of bourgeois existence.

To the father's chagrin, Raphael had never shown much interest in textile manufacturing or the very profitable network of tanneries that were the basis of the family fortune through virtual control of the production of hides in the low countries. Everything the older Floris touched seemed to turn to gold. Almost inadvertently he had become the most successful book publisher in Flanders when he bought a print shop upon observing his son's voracious appetite for reading even at an early age, in the hope that Raphael might find that type of commercial enterprise more palatable than dealing in hides. Even in this, he was to be disappointed.

He soon resigned himself to the thought that his son was taking after his mother's family, Iberian Jews among whom intense discussions of literature and philosophy were a common past-time. Not that there wasn't a goodly number of Jews in the city who made their living in commerce, but his wife came from a family of learned rabbis. The family had been driven from Toledo in Spain by Queen Isabella a few generations before and had continued to produce men of great learning in their new home in Antwerp.

Rebecca Floris' family was not too happy when she married a Christian merchant and at first, they had severed all bonds with the renegade daughter. But when Raphael was born a reconciliation of sorts took place. When the boy was old enough to learn to read and write, his maternal grandfather, a rabbi, took over his education. He not only instructed him in Hebrew and the Scriptures but also in the classical languages and philosophy.

At the age of sixteen, Raphael left home. He first attended the university at Leyden, but his thirst for knowledge soon drove him to seek out famous lecturers at far-flung centers of learning. His career as a wandering scholar took him all over Europe, to Italy, Germany, France, as far as Cracow and Prague. Paris was one place where he spent little time since the dogmatic Catholic theology that dominated the curriculum at the Sorbonne was ill-suited to his probing, universalist mind.

By the age of twenty-five, he had drunk from more fountains of wisdom than most people in a lifetime, but he had not acquired any skills that gave him a means for support.

While on the road, he earned his keep as tutor to the offspring of the bourgeoisie or the aristocracy. In that capacity, he was first introduced to the young Baroness de Montreuil who, he was told, desired to be instructed in the accumulated wisdom of human knowledge. He expected to meet a pretentious, whimsical aristocrat, good for a few crowns but instead encountered a young woman who was as thoughtful as she was beautiful, and against his will and better judgment, he almost immediately fell in love.

Raphael knew that their life together at Bonneterre could not last forever. Louise was a very independent-minded and strong-willed woman, but even she would not be able to defy customs sanctified by centuries of tradition. No woman, especially one who stood to inherit vast landed possessions, could resist the pressure to marry, and not just anybody, but a nobleman of the realm. As long as she was officially betrothed to Philippe de Treffort, she was shielded against the inducements of other suitors. Once it would be known that the marriage contract was dissolved, the stampede would be hard to stem. By the same token, Raphael also knew that their love would never diminish.

So they lived for the moment, with intense devotion to each other, never speaking about that distant time when, not their love, but their relationship had to change. Raphael often had to suppress a feeling of guilt for listening quietly to her spinning of tales of their life together with their children and even grandchildren, but he did not have the heart to spoil her fantasies. She surely knew these were imaginings, and she held fast to them to still her secret trepidations about the future.

Philippe's visit brought home to her the reality of her situation, and when Raphael returned, he found her in a state of near panic. For days she was inconsolable. At night she was unable to find the rest she longed for and even the resourceful Raphael was at a loss what to do.

"I know I promised Philippe, but I have come to the conclusion that I cannot talk to my father about dissolving the betrothal," she said leaning against Raphael as against a pillar to keep from falling. "He will immediately find another marriage prospect, somebody less pleasant than Philippe, I am sure. I know these barons. Most of them are uncouth, two-fisted, and ignorant brutes. Even if my father found a prince, I wouldn't want him."

"You know," she dabbed her eyes with her handkerchief and looked at him half-crying and half-laughing, "at twenty-three I am almost an old maid."

"There is one way out," he said seriously. "I know it is a difficult decision for you, but why not renounce all this and move with me to Antwerp? You would want for nothing."

He felt her body stiffen in his arms as he continued. But for once he wanted to state his case and disperse any suspicions that he may be a fortune hunter.

"My father's assets are as great as yours, maybe even greater. Of course, he owns little real estate, his assets are in commercial stock. I shall build you the most magnificent mansion in all of Antwerp, and you will be the toast of the best bourgeois society."

Without a word, she slowly unlocked his arms from around her and moved away. With eyes lowered, she intently studied her folded hands as she pressed her palms together in a frantic rhythm. Finally, she lifted her face to him. The pain in her eyes made him regret he ever brought up the subject.

"If I had but to follow my heart, Raphael," she began haltingly, "I would not hesitate one moment, not even a fraction of a second, to leave all this to be your wife in Antwerp, and, believe me, whether you are rich or poor, or just getting by, matters little to me. But I have an obligation to my family as sole heir. It would mean my father's death if his possessions reverted to the crown, and now even more so since there is the likelihood that the crown will remain in the hands of the heretic—Henri de Navarre if you prefer. No need to look so disapprovingly, I know you don't agree on this point. For my father, he is still the heretic and that makes matters worse. The Montreuils have held title to these lands since the twelfth century, and some parts even longer. Who am I to forfeit their title and let it fall into who knows whose hands? You understand my position, don't you?"

"I am fully aware of the legal entanglements and understand your position very well," he said softly, gathering her back into his arms. "Let's not dwell on it any longer. What matters is our love. I am forever your humble servant under any condition fate dictates."

Philippe's letter with a package was delivered by messenger from Paris on the day after Christmas. The package contained a present for Noël, a plush stuffed bear toy of the kind peddled by itinerant merchants from Germany. In the evening, after Louise had, as usual, sung the child to sleep with a lullaby, the two lovers arranged themselves in front of the fireplace in her chamber. The thick walls of the house were no protection against the draft of icy winds sweeping the plain. Only when situated directly in front of the fireplace was it possible to get comfortable. Even then, one often froze in the back while roasting in the front.

Sharing their body heat inside a warm blanket kept them warm. Louise was especially fond of making love in this position, but that evening Raphael resisted her wooing. Something else seemed to be on his mind as he stared into the flickering flames.

"Will you tell me what's in the letter?" he finally asked.

"Oh! Is that what's bothering you? I didn't know this letter was so important. Of course, I shall let you know what's in the letter, I just don't see the hurry."

"All right, if you insist, I shall read the letter to you, right now. It is very long, but you will see right away that you have no cause for jealousy. Philippe has absolutely no interest in me. He is in Paris chasing after a girl who may not even exist."

She climbed out from under the pile of blankets, walked to her dresser, and returned with a thick bundle of papers covered on both sides with a densely compressed, irregular handwriting.

"Here, why don't you read it to me? I am curious myself what he has to say, I only just glanced at it."

They pulled close together. She held a candle to the letter and he began to read. His eyebrows rose with scorn after the first line—the style of the letter was too overwrought for his taste—but soon the lovers' compassion was stirred by the account of a human fate so bizarre, so tragic, their own woes paled by comparison.

Most venerable Baroness, my dearest friend:

On my way back to Evreux from Bonneterre, where I was the lucky recipient of your gracious hospitality, I was unable to think of anything but to deplore the fact that I had caused a cloud to hang over our friendship as a result of my self-centered and entirely inexcusable conduct. I pray you will find it in your heart to forgive my infraction and hope to be afforded the opportunity at another time to serve you in whatever manner Your Gracious Ladyship may see fit. I know how fortunate Noël is to be the beneficiary of your generosity and love. Nowhere could he have found better care than in your loving hands, and I know he will repay you with eternal gratitude and love just as I do.

As far as the matter of obtaining a dissolution of our betrothal is concerned, I am afraid the Duke d'Evreux is not as amenable as we both might wish. My stay at Evreux was very brief. I saw no purpose in prolonging it in face of the Duke's intransigence. For the moment, I deem it best for all our interests to let the matter rest where it is. As long as the war continues, the pressure for the conclusion of the marriage bond will not be too intense from any quarter, especially since the Duchess d'Evreux no longer insists on it and felicitously has come to the realization that one should not compel two people to enter the state of holy matrimony if both are otherwise committed.

I have come to Paris in the hope of finding at least a trace of my beloved Sandrine somewhere in this city. Whether I shall ever find her is, however, uncertain. The streets are filled with thousands of people existing without adequate food or shelter. Starvation is still rampant among the beggars who far outnumber potential donors of alms. Never before, have I observed the Parisians in such pitiable condition. My daily routine has been very simple. I have made it a habit of wandering the streets of the city from early morning until afternoon. After some rest, I usually go out again in the early evening before it gets too dark to recognize faces. I must have turned every corner in this city a hundred times, from the Louvre to Saint-Honoré and Saint-Antoine, the Ile de la Cité, and the neighborhoods on the left bank of the Seine of Saint-Marcel and Mont Sainte- Geneviève. I have even combed the student quarter around the Sorbonne several times. This method of finding a missing person may not be very efficient, but it is the only way I know how to go about it. Somehow I still hope that if I mention her name to enough people, someone among them may have heard of her or had contact with her.

Several areas have been cordoned off, no one from outside is allowed to enter because of an outbreak of the black plague. The possibility that she might be afflicted with this dread disease makes me shudder.

Going to the police is out of the question. It is true, she might have had some brush with the law, but I must tell you of something I learned a few weeks after I began my search that gladdens my heart that I did not turn to the police as at the same time it causes me the greatest anguish for her life.

My dear Louise, to show you in what esteem I hold our friendship, I want to be open with you, and I don't mind saying, take you into my confidence.

When I first arrived in the city, I was so intent on finding the woman I love, I paid no heed to the chanting of the friars who habitually wander through the city in endless processions. Until one day, I stepped aside to let a procession pass in a narrow alleyway, when I became aware of the words of the rhythmic incantations being repeated over and over. What these friars were shouting was 'Death to the witch of Chartres!'

On inquiry, I was informed that the friars' peregrinations in search of the witch had been going on since the siege, when a woman, who had been identified as the witch who had escaped the stake at Chartres, had killed a friar and was thought to have caused all the calamities the city has had to endure. You may have heard of this episode yourself while you were in Paris.

I do not doubt that the woman they are looking for is Sandrine. Of course, the accusation that she is a witch is preposterous, although, truth be told, she was condemned as such at Chartres almost two years ago. If she caused the death of a friar, I have no doubt she did it in self-defense. I was also told that a certain police prosecutor, who had claimed that he could identify the woman they were looking for, had disappeared under mysterious circumstances. The entire affair is simply ludicrous, but it causes me the greatest apprehension and anguish.

Just to think, all these months she must have been hiding from the bloodhounds somewhere in the bowels of this miserable city unless she managed to pass through the sentry unrecognized which is not likely. In any event, I shall continue my search. I cannot do otherwise, my life is meaningless without her.

Please permit me to write to you from time to time.

Your most humble and obedient servant, Philippe de Treffort.

In the years that followed, Louise received several more letters from Philippe, each a more desperate cry from a tormented soul, each filled with sinking hope, yet buttressed with determination to go on.

At one point he wrote: "Maybe it is God's will that I must spend the rest of my days traversing this city of which I know every stone, every building, even the thousands of faces I pass every day and to whom I have become a familiar sight. Then God's will be done!"

And then again a few months later: "The man, people observe on his daily rounds through the maze of streets and alleyways, has become but an empty shell set on his course by some ineluctable force; his heart, numb and unfeeling, is become but an oppressive weight, a dead stone, in his chest."

"Please stop reading! I can't take it anymore!" Louise shouted at Raphael. "For over two years now, he has been indulging in this exercise of self-pity. Not that I am unfeeling or unsympathetic, my heart bleeds for him, but how much longer can he carry on like this?"

"Orpheus!" Raphael nodded his head as if he had just found the answer to a riddle. "Yes, Orpheus searching the underworld for his beloved Eurydice. He has only two choices, continue the search or end his life."

"Please Raphael, isn't there something we can do? We can't just sit idly by as he slowly wastes away like a leper!"

"I don't know what we can do. A patient must be willing to accept treatment before a physician can apply his healing art. If it makes you feel better, I shall travel to Paris to find out what condition he is actually in. Sometimes the written word paints a much more alarming picture than the actual situation warrants."

What he found was, albeit, even more alarming than the letters had indicated. Raphael was waiting almost a whole day at the Hotel d'Evreux for Philippe's return. While passing the time at the library, he was struck by the somber mood among the household staff, their demeanor was such that one might be led to believe they tended a house of the dead. The major domus expressed his regrets for not being able to predict the time of his lordship's return since he kept a highly irregular schedule if it can be called a schedule.

Night had already fallen when a man, he had not seen before but who was pleasantly surprised to see him, greeted him warmly and apologized profusely for having kept him waiting. His whole bearing indicated that he was the master of the house, but Raphael was struck by the incongruity between the man's outward appearance and the social grace he exhibited toward him. If this was indeed the Count de Treffort-Salignac, he bore little resemblance to the description he had received of him. Raphael found it difficult to see this crusty, unkempt individual as a dashing young aristocrat, renowned for being a fastidiously impeccable dresser and hero of so many battles. His hair and beard had not been touched by a barber's shears in many months. Nor did he seem to be in the habit of lavishing much time on personal hygiene and was careless in his choice of clothing.

Is this what love can do to a man? Raphael thought. His poet's soul was moved to unspeakable pity, wrenched by the reddish dullness in the man's eyes in which the font of tears seemed to dried out long ago.

"The Baroness has asked me to express her grave concern for Your Lordship's well-being." Raphael addressed the gaunt figure.

"I hope the Baroness will grant me forgiveness for putting a strain on the friendship she has so graciously extended to me. You may also tell her that I am quite rational. It is true, at times my mind has been so obsessed with finding the woman I lost, I feel pushed to the edge of insanity. Then I ask myself what if I put an end to my life and Sandrine comes back, do I want to inflict her with such pain? You may tell the Baroness that I firmly believe, Providence will bring my beloved back to me someday. I must believe this to go on."

He spoke openly and without artifice taking it for granted that Raphael was privy to his letters and the various aspects of his unhappy love affair. He toasted his guest with a glass of claret, and then, abruptly, he changed the subject.

"Tell me about the boy? How is he? Must be quite big by now!"

"Yes, he is a nice boy," Raphael replied only too happy to talk about a subject so dear to both their hearts. "He is almost three and a half years old. Very strong and active. I think he looks a lot like you."

Both men were at a loss for what else to say. Raphael walked over to the wall of shelves stacked with books, the writings of the ancients, philosophers, and poets, as well as more contemporary writers.

"You have a very impressive collection."

"My grandfather began to collect the works and my father continued the tradition. But they are mainly decorative dust collectors. Now that I am no longer interested in fighting wars, maybe I shall find time to explore their contents."

"Sandrine loves to read," he added softly more to himself than to his visitor.

"Louise told me you are a man of great learning." Philippe tried to return to a conversational tone, but immediately an urgency gripped seemed to grip him as if he had little time left. "I beseech you, kind Sir, teach my son the beauty of literature, let him delve into all sorts of writings, teach him to perceive the beauty of the world so he may value the accumulated wisdom of the thinkers of all ages. When I was three years old, my father girded a sword around my waist—I was hardly able to walk with it because it was dragging on the ground. 'My son,' he told me, 'one day you will be a great warrior, you will exterminate the enemies of God, wipe out the heretics in the Kingdom of France and cover yourself with glory and bring honor to your family.' I don't want my son to fall into the trap of fanaticism cloaked in notions of duty and honor. Yes, teach him duty and honor, but also respect for others and most of all for himself."

Raphael placed his hand reassuringly on Philippe's shoulder. "I am deeply touched and honored by Your Lordship's request, I hope to prove worthy of the trust you place in me. But the hour is getting late and I must return to Bonneterre tomorrow, the Baroness is anxiously awaiting news of Your Lordship's state of health. I hope you will follow her invitation to visit Bonneterre as soon as you can get away from Paris."

"Most delicately put, my dear Raphael!" For the first time in a long time, Philippe felt almost light-hearted. He enjoyed the company of this self-confident, yet unpretentious bourgeois man of learning. Then, following a sudden recognition, he added: "I am a bad host. You must be starved. Let's see what the kitchen has to offer before we retire."

Philippe never visited Bonneterre that summer. As much as he yearned for the company of his friends and to see his son, he feared their happiness, and he feared the emotions seeing the child would evoke. He might have been able to overcome these fears, had it not been for the conviction, grown into an obsession, that Sandrine might be trying to find him just as he was absent. And so it was that he was riveted to the family residence in Paris.

Only rarely was he seen now on outings in the streets. He received no one and all invitations went unanswered. Even Madame de Montpensier, who on first hearing of his presence in the city had done her best to draw him into her social circle, had ceased her efforts. Locked inside the library, he perused the dusty tomes one by one with feverish intensity as if somewhere between their pages lay the answer to the secret of life.

Great excitement swept through the city at the news that King Henri IV attended Mass at the Cathedral of Saint-Denis, on the outskirts of Paris, on the 25th of July in the year of Our Lord 1593—an event Philippe had ardently prayed for several years before. Yet, even then the parish priests and friars persisted in spewing their poisonous invective against the King from their pulpits. Some did not even shy away from defiling the memory of the King's late mother, Jeanne d'Albret, the Queen of Navarre, and spread the vilest lies about alleged lewd excesses with Huguenot ministers.

Philippe could only sadly shake his head. What baseness! To what depth these professed servants of the Church had sunk! But he no longer had any will to protest. The affairs of the world no longer touched his soul.

In the old days, he would not have left unchallenged the Jesuits' pronouncements that anybody who welcomed Henri's abjuration of the Protestant faith and joined in shouting "Long live the King!" would be excommunicated. What kind of monsters were these Jesuits who preached to the people in the street that not even the Pope had the power to absolve the heretic? But Philippe simply did not care anymore. He did not care when a three-month truce was declared between Navarre and Mayenne at the end of August. The prospect of peace came too late for him; for him, there was no peace, only numb acquiescence in the inevitability of events.

In early December of 1593, the Duke d'Evreux, disregarding signs of his failing health, arrived in Paris to attend a League Council, called to oppose a proposed extension of the truce to the end of the year. Is this a dream or is it happening? Philippe said to himself as he sat listlessly among the Catholic nobles, listening to the exhortations by the Papal Legate and the ambassador of Spain never to accept peace with the heretic and were he to embrace the Catholic faith a thousand times. Then the Duke d'Evreux rose and enjoined the assembled conspirators to swear a solemn oath never to surrender the crown to the heretic.

Philippe felt intensely uneasy. He looked up at the man whose words held the assembled entranced. It was as if he saw him for the first time. Could this stranger be his father? he thought. Could he be of the same flesh and blood as this man? Suddenly his heart pounded madly in his throat, heavy sweat broke through his forehead. He fumbled to open his collar and gasped for air. The flickering torchlight lengthened the shadows in the closed room. Could it be that this stranger, his father or whoever this man was, face aglow with unrestrained hatred, vile invective spewing from his mouth, could this man be the demon of his dreams?

Book
Three

A TIME TO HEAL, A TIME TO MEND

The sons of them that afflicted thee
Shall come bending unto thee;
And all they that despised thee,
Shall bow down at the soles of thy feet.

Isaiah 60:14

*In January of the year of Our Lord 1594, the
Huguenot leader Henri de Bourbon and Navarre is
crowned King of France in the grand Cathedral of
Chartres. As Henri IV he seeks to end the protracted
civil war and bring peace and religious toleration to
the Kingdom of France.*

CHAPTER
1

"Your Ladyship must keep still for the fitting or the dress will never be ready on time! You'll either miss the coronation or you'll have to go in rags." Rosande was wringing her hands in exasperation. The object of her reprimand paid no heed to her words and continued to turn and sway in front of the mirror, dancing to a tune only she could hear. The thick folds of ruby red velvet, adorned with gold embroidery, rustled gently to the rhythm of her step while a crew of a half dozen seamstresses knelt on the floor around her struggling desperately to pin the hem in a straight, even line.

All who saw her agreed that Marguerite de Montauban looked

stunning, one might even say breathtaking, in her magnificent robe that was being specially tailored for her attendance of the coronation of the new King of France.

"But, I feel like dancing! Come on, Mireya, take my hand! Let's dance!" She pulled her friend up to the little pedestal and together they began to chant the first lines of a sweetly haunting gypsy melody.

"Do you know why I am so happy, Rosande?" Marguerite called out when they broke off laughing because neither one could remember how the song ended.

"I can think of several reasons. But whatever the cause of your elation, believe me, nobody gains greater joy from Your Ladyship's happiness than I do."

Rosande turned her attention to the seamstresses: "This should be enough, time to take it off. If it pleases Your Ladyship, raise your arms to avoid being pricked as we remove the gown."

"Careful! Slow and careful!" Rosande hovered over the disrobing, guiding every step. "All right! Now take the gown back to the workshop and finish the hemming. It looks ravishing."

When the seamstresses had left, the three women burst into laughter.

"Sandrine, you are an impossible lady!" Rosande gasped.

"I think she makes a perfect lady!" Mireya snuggled up to her friend. "The way she instructs the servants, kind but firm and dignified. I have it from good authority, the entire staff is completely smitten with the new mistress for she is not only kind but beautiful as well."

"That she is," Rosande agreed, suddenly getting serious. Her heart pounded as she regarded the woman in the white undergarment who was still dancing in the niche by the window, humming a cheerful tune. The orange light of the evening sun glistened in her honey-colored curls grazing her shoulders. How captivating is her smile and how infectious her seemingly carefree laughter? Yet, Rosande knew how heavy was her heart. At night, she often heard her sobbing. All the riches in the world could not still her longing for her child and the man she loved.

"Rosande! Rosande!" Sandrine's voice woke her from her reveries. "Have you packed your coffers yet? We must leave by Sunday. It's a long way to Chartres."

Rosande had dreaded this moment. She had delayed telling her, but now the moment had come when she could no longer avoid it.

"Sandrine! I didn't want to spoil the preparations for you. But we won't be going with you, we must join Morin and César as soon as possible. It is better not to delay what must be. We shall all miss you."

"I understand, you are going to abandon me!" Tears welled in Sandrine's eyes. "How can you do that right now when everything seems to be going so well? You are the only friends I have in this world."

"We are always your friends. But you don't need us anymore. Soon you will have many new friends. Your friendship will be sought by the most illustrious people in France. Just imagine, you will be at home in the highest circles, at the royal court! We are just itinerant actors, we wouldn't fit."

"But I do need you, especially now. I need your guidance, your support. Who will tell me how to comport myself in front of these illu-stri-ous people? I am frightened Rosande! Mireya please, talk to her, make her change her mind! Just go with me to the coronation. Morin will understand." She sank to her knees and clutched Rosande's skirt.

"Please, you mustn't do that!" Rosande enclosed her in her arms holding her tight against her ample breasts. Mireya, unsure of what to do, approached the two and stroked Sandrine's hair.

"Will I ever see you again?" Sandrine straightened herself and dabbed the tears from her eyes.

"Some day, I am sure. God willing!" Rosande said without great assurance. "It is said that time will heal all wounds. We still need some time. Right now you must forget about us, or at least, you mustn't worry. Mireya and I shall be fine, and so will Morin and the others. You must think of only one thing, Sandrine Legrand, the poor peasant girl from Bonneval, is no more."

Rosande took her by the hand and led her to face her image in the mirror.

"Look at yourself," Rosande made her stand in front of the full-length mirror. "This is who you are: Marguerite de France, Countess de Montauban, a princess of the blood, cousin of the King of France. You will know how to comport yourself when the time comes because it has been bred into your lineage. It flows in your blood."

Rosande's well-meaning words could not erase the apprehension that gripped her as she began her journey north on a dreary January day in the year of Our Lord 1594. The farewell almost broke everybody's heart. Even Gilles was unable to hold back the tears. They exchanged promises of being together again, but in their hearts, they all knew that their parting would be for good. A chapter had come to an end in each of their lives.

As her friends turned south toward Marseilles and for the New World to where Morin and César had gone before them, Sandrine, from then on Princess Marguerite and Countess de Montauban, was transported in a magnificently carved, gold overlaid carriage, restored to its original splendor after nearly twenty-three years of disuse, from the sunny southwest of the kingdom to the inclement clime of the wintry north she knew so well. The cortège of five coaches, loaded with coffers stuffed with a wardrobe fit for a queen, toiletries, and other necessities in preparation of a long absence from her new home, was attended by a swarm of foot servants and ladies-in-waiting and was flanked by a troop of armed guards on horseback to protect the travelers against the scourge of brigands that infested this region.

This is how her companions described the peasants who frequently waylaid wealthy travelers. Marguerite knew better—she knew the despair that drove the people to crime.

How strange! Why did people, like the Huguenot ministers and magistrates of Montauban, who accompanied her on her journey—for it was not proper or safe for a lady to travel alone—why did they feel called upon to advise her on matters they knew absolutely nothing about? What did they know about the peasants, the peasant mentality as they called it? In sanctimonious tone, they told her how one must guard against the laziness, the murderous impulses of the common people, who are, they say, not all that badly off.

A most curious fact to her was how these members of the bourgeoisie so readily defended the rights of the aristocracy against the peasants. Unbeknownst to her pious companions, she carried in her baggage a petition to the king entrusted to her by one Jacques Corbu, the leader of the peasant rebellion in the Périgord region. She had sworn that, at the first opportunity, she would make known to the King the plight and misery of his people. Nobody need tell her about the conditions or the mentality of the peasants. She had shared their lot for most of her life.

She felt nothing but disdain for her self-satisfied travel companion, and from the corner of her eyes, she looked over the rotund burghers debating what the King might do to calm the unrest among the peasants stirred up by the Croquants. Call them Croquants, call them whatever you want, she thought. What do you know about pangs of hunger that devour the innards of the people at night?

Whether from revulsion against these dour bourgeois gentlemen or the movements of the carriage rumbling over the rugged terrain, she was suddenly overcome by a feeling of nausea. She signaled the coachmen and the entire convoy came to a halt. Without explaining her reason and resisting offers of help, she disembarked from the carriage and plunged vigorously into the fields on the wind-swept plateau, undaunted by the constriction placed upon her by the unaccustomed clothing. She had only one desire, to escape from the stuffiness inside the carriage—at least for a few moments, she wanted to breathe free.

Almost out of breath from the exertion of lumbering through the soft earth of the fallow field, she settled down on a tree stump. Deeply she drew in the cool, crisp air. She had come to love this stark, rugged landscape of luminous yellow, the limestone crags, and breezy plateaus; she had spent many hours these past months getting acquainted with the country so different from the Ile de France and Normandy.

She had only given up her outings into the countryside because she could not rid herself of a sense of discomfort at the sight of peasants in the fields and villages halting their activities, the men respectfully removing their head covers, as the carriage carrying Marguerite de Montauban passed by. She wanted to call out to them: "I am still Sandrine, I know your anguish and your pain, your hopes and joys. I have ploughed and harvested, my back has been bent in pain like yours, I have sweated and toiled alongside you. I am one of you, one of the people of

France."

She swore never to forget what it meant to labor all day and still bed down hungry on a pallet of straw at night. Only two summers before, she had roamed the southern provinces of the kingdom with Rosande and Mireya. They had combed hemp here and harvested olives and grapes there. Everywhere the work was hard and the pay was pitiful.

How curious! Despite the hardship, the want, she felt free then. Only once before in her life did she have such a sense of boundless freedom. That time now seems so long ago, almost in another life, that spring of unrestrained love when she had conceived her child.

Maybe it was because she had tasted such unrestrained freedom and love that she felt doubly the constraints of tradition and decorum that now tightened around her. She sent a glance toward the roadway where several dozen people had been halted in their track simply by a move of her hand. But she derived no pleasure from this power. This was not what she understood by freedom.

Scorn overcame her at the fawning that surrounded her and only made her feel more intensely the shackles of privilege and wealth. Well, let them wait a while longer.

Her thoughts turned to Philippe. Doubts and questions raced through her mind. Will he appreciate all that she is going through for him? Was she doing this for him as she liked to make herself believe? Will he love Marguerite as much as he loved Sandrine? Will he miss the shy, abused girl, barefoot and in rags, he fell in love with? What if he will not accept the fact that this girl was gone forever? Will he understand that she was still the same person, that she was still the woman whose love for him will never diminish?

Carried on the wings of her reveries, she lost all sense of time and place. The lavender shrubs surrounding her permeated the air with a sweet smell that dulled her senses with a pleasantly sedative aroma.

The dull thump of horseshoes on the soft earth called her back to the present. The captain of the guard, respectfully reminded Madame that the nearest inn was a good two-hour ride away. It was advisable to start up if they were to reach this destination before nightfall. With his help, she mounted the horse as graciously as possible, given the encumbrance of her dress, and rode side-saddle behind him back to the waiting entourage.

For the remainder of the journey, she deported herself most pleasingly and even deigned to engage in light conversation with her companions from time to time. Slowly, Sandrine, the peasant girl from the village of Bonneval, began to grow into the skin of Marguerite de Montauban until the two fused into one. To the world, she presented a façade of dignified aloofness, her thoughts and feelings were locked deep inside.

The tremors of the carriage bouncing over the rocky terrain at high speed made it impossible to read. So for the most part, she pulled back the curtain to take in the spectacle of the changing landscape. The road made its gradual ascent to higher reaches, skirting the snow-covered peaks of the Massif Central visible in the far distance. Somewhere she had heard it said this was the land of the troubadours. If she let her imagination soar beyond the confines of time and place, she might just be able to hear the love songs of yore, which are said to haunt the air around the castle keeps guarding the hilltops, rising once again from the valleys to the top of the mountains.

She relished picturing herself as a maiden at the time when her ancestors went on Crusades to the Holy Land. Locked in a tower, her heart would melt to the sweet sound of a love song streaming with passionate ardor from the lips of a lovelorn troubadour. I have never heard Philippe sing, she thought. But then he would more likely have been a Crusader than a minstrel. What silly thoughts! She tried to tear herself away from her idle musings. This land only seems enchanted from inside a gilded carriage, she said to herself, reality was much more sobering.

Halfway between Perigueux and Limoges the carriage suddenly jolted to a halt. A flood of curses from the coachmen pricked the ears of the passengers. Marguerite leaned out of the window. The coachmen and the captain of the guard were engaged in animated discussion with two rustics who were blocking the road. She quickly assessed the situation. They had no weapons so it could not be a holdup. Try as she may though, she was unable to make any sense of the torrent of shouts and wild gesticulations.

Finally, the captain turned his horse and approached his mistress.

"Madame, it seems the road up ahead is impassible. An avalanche wiped out the roadway the night before. According to the locals, it will take at least three days for a crew to clear the road to make way for the carriages to pass through."

"Three days! Did you tell them we are in a hurry?"

"Yes, Madame, they promised they will do their best as long as it does not ice over, a few days will suffice to clear a passage. But with these peasants, one never knows for sure. Meanwhile, they will lead us to an inn where Madame will find rest and comfort."

"Offer them ten gold crowns if they can clear the way in two days."

"Isn't that exceeding generous, Madame?" Nervous laughter accompanied his reproachful tone.

"Captain, what is your name?"

"Jean de Bucheron, Madame!"

"Captain de Bucheron, I presume you are a career soldier?"

"Yes, Madame, fifteen years of service in the municipal guard of the town of Montauban."

"Have you ever cleared a road from an avalanche in freezing weather, or maybe worked in the fields with the sun beating down on your bent back?"

"No, Madame, these are tasks for common people."

"Until you have had the experience of common people, Captain, don't ever presume to lecture me again on what you consider to be exceeding generous."

She looked around. Satisfied to have made her point understood, she quickly resumed a more gracious attitude. She called to the coachmen and the peasants, her tone sweet and ingratiating: "Gentlemen, please guide us to where we may find shelter and provisions."

"Oh! and Captain!" she reached for a pouch and handed it to him. "You will take care of the compensation, won't you?"

The moment the carriage pulled into the yard at the Auberge au Lapin Rouge, Marguerite had a feeling of having been in this place before. Of course, most country inns in France resembled one another and as the adopted daughter of an innkeeper, any inn she entered would have something of the familiar about it. But this one seemed more specific.

A young man came out to greet them. He apologized profusely for the state of disorder the inn was in. He would see to it that this was corrected promptly. He was the innkeeper's son, his father, the innkeeper himself was detained by the avalanche—an unusual occurrence around here, he assured them—while attending the market at Thiviers. The rooms would presently be put in order to accommodate the illustrious guest. He would see to it that Her Ladyship would find everything to her liking.

Meanwhile, won't the company make itself comfortable in the big hall by the fire. His mother, the innkeeper's wife, would presently serve refreshments. And not to worry, there were plenty of provisions in store, nobody had to go hungry.

"Gentlemen, I think we are in perfectly good hands here," the Countess chirped and her companions could but agree. She turned toward the innkeeper's son with a mellifluous tone: "My good man! Isn't that what the noble lords call you, my good man? I would prefer to know your name so I can address you properly."

"My given name is Jean-Pierre, but everybody calls me Pierrot, Madame."

"Well, Pierrot did you say Thiviers is only a few leagues away?"

"Yes, Your Ladyship, just on the other side of the mountain."

"In that case, Pierrot, I would like you to show me the barn that is attached to this inn. Don't look so aghast! You do have a barn, don't you?"

"Why, yes, Madame. But I don't understand!" He looked for help to the gentlemen, but they only shrugged their shoulders and rolled their eyes heavenward. Female whims, probably. Quite temperamental, this Countess!

"Just lead the way!"

The motley group followed the young peasant and the lady who wrapped herself in a heavy blue velvet cape and braved an icy wind as they traipsed goose formation across the barnyard. The captain brought up the rear but stayed at a distance. One tongue lashing was enough in one day.

Inside the barn, the Countess went straight to the far corner. She seemed to know exactly what she was looking for and where to find it. She stopped in front of what looked like a broken-down wagon, covered with straw and cobwebs.

"Pierrot!" She waved at the young peasant over her shoulder without turning around. "Can you remove some of this dirt and debris so the inscription becomes visible?"

Pierrot obliged and set to work.

"Ah, there they are!" Everybody stared at the wagon to see what she was referring to.

There they were. Her eyes sparkled as she beheld the harlequins, their bodies twisted in acrobatic contortion, their beaming grimaces, forever unchanging, frozen in time. The colors had begun to fade and the paint was peeling, also the wood was chipped in places, but there it was, clear to see, the proud inscription: Oranto Brothers Theatrical Company.

The sight of the caravan made her blood rush and almost overwhelmed her with emotion as if she had chanced to meet an old friend. None of these strangers around her could know what this old wagon meant to her. They would never know about the momentous events this narrow space had witnessed— warm shelter for a downtrodden, outcast from a hostile world, and most of all, it was the birthplace of her child. What glorious memories were attached to this rotting jalopy!

"Pierrot, is there a good wheelwright in this village or nearby?"

"My father is skilled in that craft and he is teaching me as well. An innkeeper has a hard time making ends meet nowadays. It helps to have other skills, Madame."

"Don't I know it," she said softly under her breath, then louder for everybody to hear, she said: "Pierrot, I shall pay you fifty gold crowns. What I want you to do is fix the broken axle, I believe it is the front axle that is broken, clean the wagon, inside and out, paint it, but be careful not to paint over the harlequins, and when the weather permits, in the springtime, take the wagon south to Chateau Montauban in the Tarn valley.

Do you think fifty is enough?"

"Your Ladyship is most generous," Pierrot stuttered. "But my father told me the wagon was left about three years ago by a troop of actors, gypsies I think he said. They didn't have enough money for the repair, but they promised to come back when they had earned enough. What should we tell them if they return and the wagon is gone?"

"You needn't worry about that. The wagon will be returned to the rightful owners. Meanwhile, just do as I tell you. If you count this, I am sure you will find about fifty crowns."

With that, she handed him a small leather pouch. She turned abruptly and, without deferring to her companions, she made her way back to the inn. The dignitaries slowly trailed behind her in bewildered silence, their curiosity thoroughly aroused.

Later in the evening, after a hearty meal of succulent cassoulet, the company gathered in front of the fireplace. Wrapped in wool blankets, some passed the time with card and board games, while others sat quietly resting their gaze on the flickering flames.

Even when the fire was beginning to burn low, nobody moved to exchange the warmth of the glowing hearth for what they knew to be a cold bed. One of the notables suggested a round of storytelling to pass the time. The idea was greeted with enthusiasm by all. What better way to while away a long, cold winter night! The ministers and magistrates, and even the captain, all took turns. The imaginations were soon fired with tales of war and heroic deeds, of love and loss, or most often, of some injustice done.

Each one of the gentlemen had already narrated several stories when one of the ministers turned to Marguerite. She had listened quietly and had become engrossed in the ancient lore her companions recalled. Good always struggled against evil in these tales that had been passed from mouth to mouth, from generation to generation since time immemorial—at least nobody could recall when the chain of these tales began.

"If it pleases Her Ladyship, will you honor us with a story of her own?"

"I am afraid, I am not very good at telling stories although I love to listen," she said evasively.

"But, maybe Madame would be kind enough to relate the story of the painted wagon? I hope Madame will not deem it too presumptuous if we assume that she is no stranger to this inn, but has passed here before. Naturally, we are all curious," the minister insisted.

"Very well then, but I must warn you, you will not find this story as intriguing as some of those we have heard."

Marguerite slowly savored a sip of dry red wine and arranged herself closer by the fire which Pierrot, seeing that the company was not about to disband, stoked up with a few more logs. For a moment, she closed her eyes, folded her hands, and knitted her brow as if she were presiding over a séance and was straining to conjure up the images from the depth of her memory.

After a long pensive pause, she began to speak, haltingly at first, in a flat monotone, but soon her voice began to soar.

"The painted wagon you saw in the barn is the property of my good friends, the Orantos, itinerant actors and acrobats who roamed the kingdom, wandering from fair to fair to entertain the common people and bring joy to their dreary lives, even if only for a fleeting moment. These good Christian people— rarely have I seen people as filled with Christian charity and mercy as these gypsies—these people adopted me into their family as one of their own in my moment of greatest need when all hope for mercy and charity from a hostile world had left me."

She paused trying to suppress a sense of annoyance against herself for feeling compelled to justify her relationship with her gypsy friends to these stodgy members of the bourgeoisie. She regretted having given in to their entreaties to tell the story, but when she saw that rather than passing judgment on her friends, their faces were eager with suspense, she continued.

"In the early spring of the year of our Lord 1590, the Oranto Theatrical Company found itself in the city of Paris. The great victory of Henri de Navarre at Ivry had inspired the idea for a play that would depict the confrontation between the boy shepherd David and Goliath, the giant Philistine. Although no names were mentioned in the play, everybody who saw it took it to be a portrayal of the struggle between Henri de Navarre and the Duke de Mayenne.

We were quite unprepared for the overwhelming success of the performances if that's what it can be called, among the people of Paris. Even members of the Catholic aristocracy and the clergy came to the makeshift theater we had pitched in the poor quarter of the city under the Petit Pont. Nevertheless, as you might imagine, in a city such as Paris, where the clergy rules the government and the police, we were soon forced to close.

But this only as an aside. The siege began soon thereafter, and interest in theater waned even among the Parisians. We struggled through the terrible famine as best we could. You may recall the siege lasted from early May to the last week in August of that year. With the help of the good Lord, we survived, barely but we survived. When the gates opened again, we decided to leave that miserable place behind us. We turned south since I had reason to believe that it was there where I would find my true identity."

She was now in her element as an actress. The words flowed melodiously from her lips, and she carried her audience easily along on the journey.

"I had good reason to believe that the key to the secret of my birth was hidden in the town of Moissac. My ever-faithful friends offered to accompany me there, concerned as they were for my well-being and fearful lest some harm should befall me were I to go on the journey alone. As you know, there is always talk of bandits who infest the king's highways.

Our progress was slowed by the need to earn a livelihood, compelling us to linger wherever a local fair was held. Fortunately, it was autumn, a good time for fairs after the harvest. But the southern part of the kingdom always remained our goal.

Once we had left the Loire Valley behind us, we encountered ever smaller numbers of patrons. Limoges was a great disappointment. Some patrons, especially the towns' artisans and craftsmen, were attracted by the novelty of seeing women act on stage with men, but their number was not large enough to still Rosande's complaints of too little money to feed the family adequately.

To make matters worse, the condition of the roads deteriorated and it became harder each day to maneuver our creaky wagon over the rough surfaces. The need to find fresh horses added to our troubles.

I urged my friends to turn back north, to let me go on my way alone, but they would not hear of it."

While she paused, the captain filled her wine cup, a gesture she acknowledged with a diffuse, though gracious nod.

"So how did the wagon end up in the barn of this inn?"

"Oh, that part is very simple," she replied with a flippant gesture of the hand. "The men were so anxious that we should reach the milder climes before the start of winter, they drove the wagon at breakneck speed over almost impassible roads. It was the beginning of November and the rains had washed out most roadways. More than once, everybody had to pitch in to pull the wagon out of the mud. Then just south of Thiviers, not far from this inn, the wagon collapsed under the constant strain. The front axle broke, and we were stranded with very little money and a bleak outlook for the future.

No amount of cursing from Morin, the leader of the group, at his brothers helped the situation. The only thing to do was to leave the wagon at this inn where we had found temporary shelter—the innkeeper was kind enough to agree to store it in his barn—and to continue the journey on foot. Morin assured us that in the south of the kingdom seasonal labor was always in demand. If we all put the savings from our wages together, we would be able to reclaim the wagon the following year.

He was right about the demand for field hands in the south, but little did he know how scant were the wages. It was impossible to put anything aside. All we could do was live from hand to mouth. Finding work was always a matter of getting there first. Whenever word spread this orchard or that plantation was hiring, a scramble ensued among thousands of migrant workers. Not infrequently, we would hear of an opportunity and then find ourselves shut out once we arrived by a stream of itinerants ahead of us.

Some types of work were better suited for men, others for women. So not infrequently, the family separated for several months. The men found work cutting wood, and we women would comb hemp for a bowl of watery soup a day and a pile of straw to rest on at night. I shall never forget the summer, we worked near Lyons picking leaves for the silkworms to eat while our stomachs were empty most of the time."

She paused and fixed her eyes on the captain. Without a word, she leaned over and reached for the sleeve of his shirt to feel its luxurious softness. Still stroking it she exclaimed:

"Ah! my dear captain, I see you are wearing a beautiful silk shirt. Have you ever thought about the sweat, the bent backs, produced by picking mulberry leaves from sunrise to sunset so the silkworms can eat and produce the fiber for this soft shirt that caresses your skin with its sensuous touch? Of course, you haven't! Why should you? Please, don't let it bother you!" She raised both hands to ward off his protests.

"Let me continue. Better conditions and more reasonable wages were found in the olive fields in Provence. But the tediousness of the work, the exposure to the sun's merciless rays in a permanently bright sky, no relief all day except for a brief rest in the shade at noon—believe me, all this does not fail to depress the spirits of those who are strapped to the treadmill of survival.

Well, gentlemen, one might say I was lucky to have escaped from the life of the migrant worker, but we should never forget that the unfortunate masses of our people know no relief from a life of toil and receive very little reward for their sweat."

"But, Madame," the minister who usually did the talking began, "you have been placed into these conditions by a set of most unfortunate circumstances, not the least cause being the fanatical persecution of our co-religionists by the Papists. But you must consider the most exalted birthright that has now, through the infinite wisdom and mercy of Our Lord, been restored to you. It does not behoove us, however, to put in question the wisdom and justice of the divine plan that has divided human society into different classes of people. As Your Ladyship is aware, mysterious are the ways of the Lord. Even if we, in our human frailty cannot comprehend his wisdom, we cannot doubt the righteousness of his design to choose some for eternal salvation. In the same way, we cannot doubt the righteousness of a higher and lower status among people. Even if it is difficult for us to discern the justness of his ways, God always works for the common good."

"Reverend Sir, when I accepted the Huguenot faith, I understood the teachings of Jean Calvin to mean that it is wrong to submit to tyranny and injustice. Shouldn't these concepts be extended to an obligation on the part of the faithful to denounce social injustice and the exploitation of the poor masses by a privileged few?"

"Your Ladyship is right on this point, but we have to leave it to the Consistory to care for the poor in the community. It would be against divine law to try to erase the distinction among the classes. Only misguided radicals like the Anabaptists hold to the erroneous notion of egalitarianism."

Marguerite fell silent. She knew any further discussion was useless. Since she had received instruction in Calvinist teachings and had officially become a member of the Religion, it had become clear to her why there was no end to religious strife in the Kingdom of France. If she had hoped to find more rational thinking and less fanaticism, less self-righteousness among the Huguenot brethren, she was bitterly disappointed. Lack of genuine compassion, a spirit of intolerance, and a pursuit of self-interest were present in the same measure as among those of the Apostolic Faith.

Maybe she too was motivated by self-interest. Did she not adopt the Huguenot faith because she was advised that the heir to the House of Montauban could never be a Catholic? How ironic! How her fate almost paralleled that of Henri de Navarre! To gain his kingdom, he had embraced the Catholic faith, and she embraced the Calvinist faith to claim her patrimony. Once again, she was awed by the link that seemed to exist between her fate and that of a man she had never met. But now, at long last, their path was to cross—that was the purpose of this journey.

Was it irony or fate that she should be en route to the coronation of the same man whose nuptials her parents attended almost twenty-two years before, an event that had turned into, what has often been called, a blood wedding?

Her parents must have traveled the same road, had gazed at the same landscape, the same fields and trees, hills and mountains, the windmills and castles, on their way to meeting their fate. She shuddered to think that maybe they stopped at the same inns, this very inn here at the outskirts of Thiviers. Their hearts must have been filled with joy and hope in anticipation of the fulfillment of the promise of peace the wedding between the Huguenot King of Navarre and the sister of His Most Catholic Majesty, Charles IX, King of France, heralded. A cold shiver ran over her. She did not want to contemplate what might have been! The present held enough pain for one person to bear! Let the past be!

CHAPTER 2

Later that night, when she finally retired to the best room the inn had to offer, she could not find the restful sleep her body yearned for. The thought of her parents' tragic fate, the memories dredged up by telling the story of the painted wagon, all tormented her mind as she alternated between a state of half-consciousness and half-sleep.

The image of the bruised body of a young woman lying in a field intruded on her mind's eye and refused to let her go. No! She did not want to think about it, not now! But the image persisted, the battered face so dear to her, the black curls awash in blood and dirt. Why did she let herself be persuaded to tell the story? Why tear the scab off a wound that had finally begun to heal?

But she did not tell them Mireya's story. She had not taken her bourgeois companions into her confidence. Why should she? They were strangers to her? What she told them was only part of the story. How could she hope for their understanding, what it meant to be a woman under such conditions, the burden of insults and humiliation women and young girls had to bear? She did not relate to her companions the events of that terrible night that were indelibly burnt into her mind with the searing forge of outrage, the day Mireya, sweet, little Mireya was violated.

If only she had been more insistent, more trusting of her instincts! Maybe she could have spared her friend, who was like a sister, the pain. She had seen it coming, but she did not prevent it. Her face glowed with shame, her heart was torn with guilt, even now after all this time, when things had presumably been set right again.

She knew Mireya was never the same again. There was a lingering sadness in her eyes even when she laughed. It may have been her imagination, but from that time forward, she often felt Mireya's eyes fixed on her, silent, reproachful as if she wanted to say why did you not save me, why?

Sandrine had observed with growing uneasiness the longing glances that passed between Mireya and the foreman. She knew the type. From the day he hired them to pick the mulberry leaves, she had an intense dislike for the man that only intensified the more she saw of him. Her distrust was confirmed by the way he treated the army of women and children who worked under his tutelage in the fields. The derisive twitch of the corners of his mouth, the cruel satisfaction glowing in his eyes when he meted out punishment for the slightest infraction, the arrogance with which he relished the power he wielded over the hapless workers. No extra moments of rest, no extra water, no matter how much it was needed.

Sandrine watched him pass several times a day by the spot where Mireya was working, flicking his leather whip with an air of self-importance. While all the others were chided with harsh commands, Mireya was showered with compliments and praise. It was perhaps little wonder that she did not want to hear of Sandrine's misgivings about the man. Rosande just shrugged it all off with the remark that it could not hurt to be in good stead with the overseer. If only she could have spoken to the men. Morin would have understood her apprehensions. But they were far away working in the iron-ore mines of northern Spain.

Tears of shame filled her eyes even on that night at the inn near Thiviers, on her way to the coronation of the King of France, and to a new life. Mireya's voice filled with happiness rang in her ears. She practically flew into the one-room hut, where they were housed. With what elation did she announce the news! He had asked her to go with him to a dance on Saturday night over in the neighboring village!

Seeing her in such a state of bliss, Sandrine did not have the heart to warn her not to go. Rosande too shared her daughter's excitement. With hands that can create wonders, she sewed together a dress from a few pieces of an old curtain.

"A good marriage could help us all," she said.

Should she have tried to prevent her from following the invitation under the circumstances? She began to doubt whether her harsh judgment of the man was justified. She began to think that maybe she was too suspicious of people in positions of authority. Maybe she was wrong about this man altogether. Maybe he was just performing his duty.

It certainly was not hard to understand that a young man should take a fancy to Mireya. She stood out among the women working in the fields. Her raven black curls loosely held together with a colorful scarf tied in the manner of the gypsies, sparkling charcoal eyes gave her a singular, exotic charm. She had an acrobat's ease of movement, entirely comfortable with her lithe, petite body. Unlike so many young women whose skin was ravaged by smallpox, hers was smooth and silky, of the shade of olives. Growing up in the world of the theater had taught her early the importance of taking care of her appearance even when means were sparse. Like her mother, she somehow always managed to look well-groomed, no matter how strenuous the work.

Sandrine found her at the edge of the field behind the row of workers' shacks in the small hours of Sunday morning. She had been awake all night, her heart heavy with doubts and foreboding. She went outside for a walk hoping the fresh air would ease the pounding in her forehead. All was quiet. Like the quiet before a storm, she thought inadvertently. Immediately, she scolded herself for being such a fool.

"You will see," she said half-loud to herself, "nothing is going to happen. She will be perfectly all right."

The night was beautiful and clear. She inhaled deeply the soft summer breeze, saturated with the sweet fragrance of a thousand flowers mixed with the ever-present mulberries. Still unable to find peace of mind, she returned to the hut and sat in the entrance door, waiting. Finally, as the endless night gave way to dawn, she thought she heard a faint rasping sound. She rose, straining to determine the direction from where the sound came. Silence. She walked to the back of the hut, and now she heard a muffled call for help.

Stark horror froze the blood in her veins. She recognized Mireya lying face up in the field, her body and face disfigured with bruises, sullied with blood and dirt, her new dress shredded.

A soft indentation in the earth ran from the field to the back of the hut, a trail of blood along which Mireya had dragged herself until all strength had left her. Sandrine gathered her in her arms. A gush of blood issued from a deep cleft in her friend's stomach.

For days, Mireya remained suspended between life and death. Her eventual recovery was a miracle only a mother's love could bring about. Those who saw the martyred girl then, her body rent by horrible pain until she slipped into a state of unconsciousness, hardly dared to hope for her to make it through.

The foreman denied having anything to do with the assault on the girl. He claimed, she left the dance early in the company of someone else. There was no lack of witnesses who would testify to the truth of what he was saying. Sandrine knew he was lying, but she lacked proof. Mireya lay silent.

At summer's end, Mireya's body had healed enough for them to keep their arranged rendez-vous further south with Morin and his brothers. Morin immediately sensed that something terrible had happened to his child. He was not one to tolerate his daughter's silence. However, painful it may be for her to relive the outrage, without honor there was no life. Only by punishing the offender could the family's honor be restored.

Under tears, Mireya finally related how she had gone to the dance with the foreman after he had pursued her for weeks. At first, she had repulsed his advances, he being a man of position and she just a migrant field hand. But he told her he did not care who she was, he swore he was madly in love and could not live without her. He looked so sincere with that handsome smile.

Oh! Mireya, you dumb, blind little girl! Didn't you see the cruelty, the arrogance in his eyes? Yes, he was handsome, but everything about him breathed conceit and cruel contempt.

She went with him to the dance, but he did not want to stay very long—almost as if he didn't want to be seen with her. He said on such a beautiful night, they should go for a walk.

When they reached the fields, he pulled her toward him and covered her face with kisses so rough her nose started to bleed. She pushed him away, but he kept coming at her like an army on the attack. She tried to scream, but he pulled out a knife and threatened to cut her throat if she made a sound. He then had his will with her, brutally tearing her apart, thrusting into her with the ferocity of a wild animal. When he was done and she started to cry, he plunged the knife into her stomach. He left her for dead in the field. Poor, little Mireya! How is this wound ever to heal?

Why didn't they go to the authorities, Morin demanded to know. What can the word of a field hand, a gypsy at that, do against the testimony of a whole band of people who were ready to swear he was elsewhere that night?

She will never forget the terribleness in Morin's face when he straightened himself up. She knew there was nothing in this world that could dissuade him from doing what he had to do to avenge the crime.

"Gilles!" Morin's voice was rough and gravelly, ominous in its firmness, "you take care of the women! Take them to Toulouse and wait there for our return. César and I will join you in a week's time."

She never saw Morin and César again. The week went by without any news from them. A month passed when, one day, Gilles came rushing up to the women screaming something incomprehensible. She had never seen Gilles so beside himself.

"They did it! They did it!" He danced around, delirious with joy.

"Who did what?" she asked.

"Rosande! Mireya!" He called everybody together. "The story is making the rounds about a family of mulberry growers near Lyons—it must have been Morin and César, who else?"

"Gilles, you make no sense. Please calm yourself and start at the beginning." Rosande took him by the hand and forced him to sit down. "Here have a sip of water, that will cool you off."

"The migrant workers are spreading the story from town to town all over the south." He wiped his mouth with the back of his hand. "A few weeks ago, so the story goes, every single male member in the household of mulberry plantation owners near Lyons was found slain. They say it was like a visit from the Angel of Death."

"Do they know who did it?"

"No, the perpetrators vanished without a trace. Some people think it was a band of brigands, but nothing was taken. Only . . ."

"What? There is something you are holding back!" Rosande seemed to have a premonition of what was to come, she added: "You can speak in front of these women, they have endured greater horrors than they should have at their young age. Speak!"

"They say the bodies were mutilated in certain parts."

Never will she forget the scream of anguish that rose from Rosande's throat. The mother held the daughter embraced in fervent prayer for hours. It was not quite clear to Sandrine whether she was thanking God or whether she wanted to fend off some terrible curse.

A year passed after these events when word finally came from Morin and César. The letter originated in the New World telling them of the establishment of a successful theater company and asking them all, including Sandrine, to book passage on a Spanish ship as soon as possible.

Time will heal all wounds! Isn't that what Rosande told

her when they said farewell? Mireya looked so pretty. Nobody would ever guess the horror she had gone through. Time also will help her forget, the memory will slowly recede into the far reaches of the mind. Some scars will always remain, but the pain will become less intense. A better life was awaiting them all in the New World. She was sure of it.

CHAPTER
3

She would never see her friends again. Their worlds were too far apart now. They should be setting sail from Marseilles right now. The painted wagon will always remain with her in Montauban as a token of their friendship.

The knock on the door tore Marguerite from a deep slumber she had finally fallen into almost at the graying of dawn. For a moment, she was so disoriented, she did not recognize where she was. She must have fallen asleep after all.

"Madame! Your Ladyship will miss the second prayer meeting!" She recognized the voice of the captain.

"Tell the Reverend ministers I shall join them shortly," she answered through the closed door. Oh! these Protestants are no better than the Catholics. Prayer meetings, vespers, masses, adorations, what have you, all of this was more important than practicing Christian charity, caring for those in need. Still vexed, she called for her lady-in-waiting. It was simply impossible to get into these cumbersome clothes unassisted.

The prayer meeting was followed by the consumption of copious gustatory delights from the inn's kitchen. The innkeeper's wife was outdoing herself with a variety of roast meats, pâtés, crusty, freshly baked, white bread topped with melting goat cheese and fruit preserves brought up for the occasion from the cellar, and all was crowned with white Bordelais wine. The company was relieved to receive Pierrot's assurance that the road would be passable by the next morning.

One more night! She felt as if she was being detained in limbo. She was anxious now to get on with the journey, to begin her new life. No more looking back, no more remembering! Until then she had not realized how much she missed her friends. Yet, Rosande's advice was the only reasonable way to survive: she must go on, embrace her fate. There is so much to look forward to, the reunion with her son, and somewhere, somehow she would find Philippe. Oh, how she looked forward to seeing the surprise on his face! Would he still love her?

"If it pleases Your Ladyship, I beg you to honor us with relating the rest of the most fascinating story of how you established your identity."

She resented the magistrate's polite bow, the fawning smile on his chubby face. Was it her imagination? Or did his smile broaden into a derisive grin? Suddenly, she saw the monk of Saint-Victor before her. Or was it Etienne? Or Hachette? The faces all merged.

But no! He was just a friendly, respectful Protestant burgher from the Consistory of Montauban. But why was he prying?

He is not prying, he just wants to while away the time. Not all men have evil intentions, she reminded herself.

"But you already know the rest of the story," she replied with her most obliging, gracious smile. "You yourselves were kind enough to help me search through the bureaucratic maze of archives and birth registers. I don't know if I ever thanked you enough for your assistance."

"Your Ladyship has honored us beyond all bounds. But it is not praise we are looking for. Only there is one part of the story that is still unclear. You must tell us about the initial clue that set you on the right track, so to speak, of your parentage?"

"Well, do you really want to hear it?" She said tilting her head with a coy expression as if they were playing a parlor game. In reality, she welcomed the diversion from the more painful thoughts that had haunted her during the night. Eager to dwell on a happier episode in her life, she was more than willing to oblige.

"You may remember, at the beginning of the story I mentioned that I had it from good authority that the key that would unlock the secret of my birth would be found in Moissac. In the course of our wanderings through the southern provinces, we found ourselves in the environs of Toulouse. Through a series of unfortunate circumstances, we were separated from Morin and César. Gilles stayed with us since it was considered too dangerous for women to be without male protection. Our reserves were running low and work was hard to find in the wintertime even in the south, it being just about the Feast of the birth of Our Lord.

With nary a penny, no roof over our heads, we had to keep moving to avoid being arrested or being drummed out of the towns as vagrants. We never stayed for more than three days in any town before drifting on to the next one. In this way, we arrived one day in the town of Moissac on the Garonne River. As you can imagine, the local inhabitants, as everywhere, regarded with suspicion any itinerant folk lingering in the town square. It took some persuasion, but I finally located someone willing to direct me to the estate of the Baron de Bécour."

"Ah! the baron is a very fine and upright Huguenot gentleman!" The usually silent minister nodded his approval.

"Yes, a true pillar of the Consistory of Moissac," the other agreed.

"I was, however, surprised," Marguerite continued, "to find a fairly young gentleman. I had expected or maybe hoped, that the Lord of Bécour would be an older man. The man I was looking for, I was told, had passed away several years previously, as you gentlemen undoubtedly know."

"The grandfather of the present Lord of Bécour, also a devout Religionist. Lost his wife in the terrible massacre brought on us by the Medici woman and he died himself within a year."

The mere mention of that most calamitous event that had befallen the Huguenots in the course of their long struggle, the massacre of Saint Bartholomew's Day, set off a chain of venting their general indignation. The magistrate added apologetically: "The same that took the lives of Your Ladyship's sainted parents."

His sanctimonious, doleful way of speaking annoyed her, but she decided to disregard it and continue her story.

"At first he was suspicious of what the purpose of my inquiry might be. After all, I was but a woman in rags, one of thousands of rootless drifters. To convince him that I was indeed different, I produced a few pieces of his grandmother's personal belongings that had been entrusted to me by the physician who had ministered to her on her deathbed. I also related to him the circumstances of her last days as they had been related to me by the doctor, these facts coincided closely with the description in a letter from his grandmother received by his grandfather in early 1573, about six months after the event. The Lord de Bécour was kind enough to show me the letter the family had guarded all these years."

Her voice broke off and she swallowed hard.

"This letter," she continued, "this letter was the most important piece of evidence in establishing who I was. In it, Mathilde de Bécour told about the terrible murder of her mistress and master, though without mentioning them by name, apparently for fear the letter might fall into enemy hands. She told of her escape with the infant child and her attempt to reach the southern town of La Rochelle. She became, however, grievously ill, and had to seek refuge and aid in a village along the way. She did not mention this village nor the area by name. She further told of the good doctor who was attending her and who had promised to post this letter should she die. On every page, she expressed fear for the safety of the child."

How strange that she should be able to talk about this child with total detachment as if it was someone separate from herself. Was it possible that she had outgrown the child that had haunted her so long?

"I have long thought about why Madame de Bécour should have been so adamant in her insistence to the recipient of the letter not to search for the child. Why did she deem it in the child's best interest that it should grow up ignorant of who it was? Even on her deathbed, she had been haunted by the fear that the identity of the child might someday become known. I think few of us can imagine the abject horror she had witnessed on the day of the massacre. She had seen fanatics who would not shrink from the slaughter of children. Only at the end of the letter, she mentioned a yellow butterfly tattoo on the upper right arm of the girl. It was as if she had second thoughts about masking all leads completely to the girl's identity. As you gentlemen know, the tattoo was another important piece of evidence."

"Ever so slowly with the help of many well-meaning people, the pieces of the puzzle were assembled and fit together." With the actor's delight of holding her audience enthralled, her voice took on a dramatic festiveness. She drew out the words slowly, with a hollow, mysterious sound.

"Unfortunately, the Lord of Bécour, who was himself a child when these events occurred, was unable to identify the emblem with the butterflies and the red bend that had been left with the doctor. Only after a long search in the registry at Toulouse was it determined that the emblem had been specially designed for the last Count de Montauban and his wife Isabelle de France on the occasion of their wedding that took place in May of 1570. Further search revealed that a daughter had been born to them at Nérac, the court of the Queen of Navarre, on February 4, 1572, who had been entered into the baptismal record under the name Marguerite de France on February 10 of that year. The record also showed that on the day of the baptismal, the infant's upper right arm was emblazoned with the sign of the yellow butterfly the couple had chosen as the symbol for their household to express their abhorrence of war and their desire for peace, as the document stated."

Marguerite fell silent. She sank back in her chair, drained and exhausted. Motionless, she held her hands folded in her lap and her eyes pressed close together as in fervent prayer.

After a long silence during which the gentlemen cleared their throats and sipped wine, one of the magistrates turned to the captain.

"The town council and the Consistory of Montauban examined the evidence very carefully until no doubts remained that this young woman was indeed the legitimate progeny of our martyred overlord, and thus the rightful heiress to the title and possessions of the House of Montauban. We petitioned our good King, Henri IV that he may recognize the legitimacy of the claim of the young woman. He immediately sent an emissary who on examining the evidence concluded that she was indeed the long lost heiress of Montauban and, not least, a cousin of His Majesty the King."

"There was only one small matter, and Her Ladyship acceded to it very readily," the tacit minister added. "It was the matter of Madame's conversion to the faith of her parents."

"She readily took instruction," the talkative one quickly picked up the story when the other bethought himself for a moment.

"I personally instructed Madame in the precepts and wisdom of our great teacher Jean Calvin. She was a most avid pupil. I was happy to learn that Madame was not totally ignorant of Huguenot beliefs and that she was especially well versed in Holy Scriptures. It seems the good Lord in his wisdom had already predestined her for the position she is to hold from now on."

"Amen!"

Early the next morning the innkeeper arrived from Thiviers. The snow had been removed and the roadway was clear enough to permit safe passage of the horse-drawn carriages. The travelers embarked on the gilded litter emblazoned with the butterflies of the House of Montauban and, followed by the train of attendants, they were soon on what everybody thought was the last leg of their journey.

Marguerite, after rewarding him handsomely for the hospitality they had enjoyed, reminded Pierrot once again not to be remiss in restoring the painted wagon, which the young man promised to do. Taken by her kindness and generosity, he was led to warn her of bands of rebellious peasants. Stories of hold-ups especially of aristocratic travelers along the road just north of Thiviers had become more numerous since the beginning of winter. She thanked him for his concern but assured him she was quite capable of dealing with anybody who had a legitimate grievance.

The journey progressed with arduous pace over vast barren stretches of snow-covered wastes, broken only by the denuded tops of hedgerows and the stark presence of the windmills. The train of carriages passed through Limoges and continued through Touraine, a region strewn with half-ruined fortifications erected in more ancient times. They reached the Loire Valley and Orléans without a single encounter with the dreaded brigands.

"What was it the innkeeper's son at Thiviers said about bandits along the road?" One of the magistrates leaned toward Marguerite.

"He said to watch out for the Croquants, who are becoming as frequent in these parts as in Périgord," she replied.

"Well, I guess God has spared us from being waylaid by the thieves this time," remarked the magistrate.

"I hope our new King will do something about these criminals and have them all hung," said the other. "Wouldn't you agree?"

"I hope quite the contrary, gentlemen," Marguerite declared. "These men are not criminals, if they are driven to a life of crime, please remember it is desperation that goads them. The peasants in all parts of France have suffered far too long the iniquities of exploitation by landlords who impose unreasonable obligations based on the presumed rights of the gentry. The peasants are breaking their backs, yet they go hungry and their children are feeble from malnourishment. Very few landlords will lighten the peasants' obligations if a harvest is poor because of inclement weather in one year. They will collect what they deem their due no matter how meager the leftover for the peasants may be."

Marguerite searched through her baggage and finally produced a paper scroll she presented to her companions.

"I have here a petition entrusted to me by a certain Jacques Corbu, you may have heard of him, he is the leader of the peasants of Périgord in the province of Béarn. This petition, which I have promised to present to His Majesty the King, contains their grievances against the landlords in great detail. If the King is as wise as it is being said he is, he will understand why so many of his subjects have taken to burning chateaux and robbing travelers along the highways. In part, these actions are prompted by the hope of drawing attention to their plight. If His Majesty's reputation for magnanimity and benevolence is justified, I am sure he will hear the cries of his people."

"Madame, I cannot agree with you that resorting to crime can ever be justified, although your warm-hearted concern for the unfortunate poor is truly in the spirit of the Calvinist religion."

Again that sanctimonious smile. Will they ever understand? she thought. Will they ever do more than pay lip service to concern for the wretched masses?

The King will understand, she was sure that Henri de Navarre cared about his people. A sudden sense of confidence for the future of the kingdom filled her as she gazed on the changing landscape.

The road had entered a region of soft rolling mounds of fields, only occasionally dotted with clusters of trees—a fertile, tilled landscape overlaid with snow but unmistakably familiar.

Marguerite's heart throbbed in her throat. May be it was a mistake to come back to this place. Would anybody recognize her? Past, present, and future merged as the majestic spire of the Cathedral of Chartres came into view, loftily holding sway over the countryside for miles around.

CHAPTER

4

ears of joy filled Marguerite's eyes. A soothing warmth engulfed her whole being. Gone was the dread, the fear that had possessed her as the journey was nearing its destination, once, in a different life, the place of her darkest hours, the place whose name had become attached to hers in the fateful epithet of the Witch of Chartres, a place of horror and barely healed wounds. Now all fears had dissipated under the baldachin of the glorious spectacle of the crowning of the King of France. Nothing, but nothing would dampen the exuberance she felt in her heart on this day.

Pride and admiration filled her as she beheld the man who knelt before the altar in the grand cathedral like a humble petitioner, bareheaded and clad in a simple, unadorned doublet and breeches of dove-gray velvet. A glimmer of grandiose solemnity, a faint reflection of the kaleidoscope of colors broke through the stained glass—an auspicious glimmer of hope for peace.

There was something deeply moving about the procession of the grand nobles, the princes of the blood, the peers of the realm, and the princes of the Church, each in a place fixed by a timeless order established centuries ago. The nobility of the highest order was followed by military men —from the marshals of France, various grades of officers to rank and file soldiers of the royal army—a motley throng forming a shield around the monarch. An atmosphere of hope that peace would finally come to the realm, that the factions would be reconciled and bloodshed and strife would end permeated the ceremony.

As if to bolster this hope, shouts of "France has a King at long last!" rang out from the jubilant crowd outside and was echoed in the grand nave of the cathedral where the same crowd once mourned the death of that arch leaguer and conspirator against the crown, Henri de Guise.

"How times change!" she thought. No! she did not want to think about the past. Only the here and now counted. She too placed her hopes for the future in this monarch. He had already done so much for her. How quickly he had put her at ease during their first encounter a few days before! Like an old, long-lost friend he had greeted her. She was immediately won over by his easy-going charm, his jovial bonhomie, just as he was so obviously taken by her beauty and grace.

"My dear cousin," he said, "I have only one regret that I have been deprived of your radiant company all those years."

"You may join my regret to yours, Your Majesty, that I have been deprived of true gallantry such as yours all these years," she replied beaming her brightest smile at him. Where in the world did I learn to talk like that, she thought. Was Rosande right? Was it indeed bred into her lineage? How ridiculous! But the banter gave her a certain pleasure.

"The gentlemen from Montauban have told me that you have been initiated into the Reformed religion and have become a loyal adherent of the Huguenot faith," Henri continued in a more serious vein.

"You have heard correctly, Sire." Leaning over, she whispered close to his ear: "As you know yourself, Sire, a wise ruler must be guided by the wishes of his subjects."

She did not flinch as their eyes met and rested in each other for a moment of tacit understanding.

Their exchange had been interrupted by rasping and throat clearing behind Henri's back. Marguerite recognized the woman who had been introduced to her as Gabrielle d'Estrée, the King's mistress. She placed both hands on his shoulders. Earlier that day they had passed each other in the corridor of the royal residence and Marguerite had been awestruck by the woman who was decked out in raiments of splendor such as she had never seen before. On inquiring who the lady was, she was told by one of the royal archers that she was no lady, but merely the King's whore. She was outraged by the disrespect but later came to understand that Henri did not care much what anybody thought or said. His utter devotion to the woman and the escapades he contrived to be with her was constant grist for the mill of gossip and legends that were woven around his personage.

"I hear Your Ladyship grew up as a peasant," Gabrielle addressed her in an awkward attempt to enter the conversation.

"You heard right, Madame," Marguerite replied trying to sound pleasing. It would hardly be politic to make an enemy of this woman. Besides, she had taken a liking to her, especially after the soldier's remark, she felt almost protective of her.

She was not in a mood to pass the time with idle chatter and since the topic of peasants had come up, she resolutely seized the opportunity to make good on her promise to put in a word on behalf of the King's less fortunate subjects.

"My upbringing among the people has taught me much about their longings and I know how deeply beloved Your Majesty is among the poor of this realm. My acquaintance with the misery of the masses, having myself lived in poverty for so long, prompts me to intercede with Your Majesty on their behalf. I have here, Sire . . . ," she pulled a scrolled paper from the sleeve of her gown and tendered it before the King, "if it pleases Your Majesty to take notice of this petition, an appeal to Your Majesty's well-known kindness from the peasants of Périgord."

"Oh, I know about the Croquants!" He unrolled the scroll and gave it his careful attention. "There has been a lot of trouble lately in that part of the kingdom, which is particularly close to my heart as part of my ancestral land. No matter, burning and looting cannot be condoned."

"If Your Majesty pleases to understand that these are acts of desperation, a way of gaining attention. For so many years, all other efforts to obtain justice, to gain relief from the excessive tax burdens placed on starving people, all proved fruitless."

"Ah, my dear cousin is as compassionate as she is beautiful! I am touched by your compassion for my unfortunate subjects. Once peace has been established, no one shall go hungry in the Kingdom of France. As I have said so often, I hope that one day there will be a chicken in the pot of every household of the realm. Meanwhile, I give you this solemn promise, I shall make it my first order of business to appoint a commission of royal emissaries to visit the provinces as soon as my royal government is constituted in the capital city of Paris. These noble lords are my witnesses," he proclaimed with a solemn gesture toward the gentlemen in the room, "I shall issue a decree remitting all back taxes owed by the peasants to their landlords. If it had not been my destiny to be King, I would certainly be a Croquant myself."

Such was the benevolence of the man who was now bowing his head to receive the royal crown of the Kingdom of France! So absorbed was she with the person of the King, she was unaware of the sensation her presence in the pews, reserved for the Huguenot nobility, caused among the noble guests and in particular among the gentlemen. Even the women turned their heads, whispering, guessing who the beautiful stranger might be.

She had groomed herself with great care, had chosen every detail of her attire, not out of vanity, but out of a sense of occasion. Her usually tousled curls lay in tight-knit braids like a crown around her head, held together by a net interwoven with thick strands of gold. Her gown of luscious, ruby red velvet and rich gold embroidery rivaled in magnificence the vestments of the King's sister, Madame Catherine de Navarre and Bourbon, who was seated at her side. In the absence of Henri's wife, Marguerite de Valois, the infamous Queen Margot, whose scandalous conduct precluded her from being invited, the two Huguenot princesses were the highest-ranking women present at the ceremony.

Somehow, she still found it hard to believe that all this was happening to her. Any moment, she expected to wake from a fabulous dream. But, there was no doubt, she was awake! It was all real, the way she felt carried along by the surge of enthusiasm and adulation flowing from the audience. She too rose to her feet when the Archbishop of Chartres placed the crown of the kings of France on the head of the kneeling man and she applauded when it was said that Henri had earned the crown threefold—by right of succession, by right of having fought for it longer and more persistently than any of his predecessors, and by right of popular acclaim.

Most fervently did she join in the chorus of "Long live the King! Long live the King!"

Only unwillingly did she follow Madame Catherine, who rose at the start of the Mass, signaling her to leave as well. One by one, the Huguenot nobles and dignitaries filed through the side door. Why did they have to make a grand display of their differences? She felt intensely uneasy about what she thought was a tactless gesture. Just a moment ago, everything felt so good, now a profound annoyance overcame her. Why could not she, at least, muster the courage to remain?

Nobility has its obligation, an often irresistible obligation, to conform. She thought of Philippe and how she had chided him for conforming to the dictates of conventions. Only now did she understand his predicament. Still, she was determined not to submit without protest.

A reformed prayer meeting was held in Madame Catherine's apartment, after which Marguerite approached her cousin.

"Madame, I am certain that this day will mark a new beginning for France. I firmly believe that His Majesty, your brother, will restore peace and prosperity to the kingdom. He is a strong and beloved leader, but wouldn't you agree, he needs everybody's help? What I mean is, would it have been so terrible to sit through one Mass, just on this occasion?"

"Oh, Marguerite! My dear naive cousin! I observed your demeanor when we, the members of the Reformed Religion, left the church before the start of Mass and I saw how displeased you were. Since you are new to our community, you cannot understand our absolute abhorrence of that Catholic rite.

There are also political reasons that make it impossible for a Huguenot to attend Mass no matter what the circumstances. Had we stayed, the Catholics would have celebrated this event as a victory. We can never let this happen, or we are truly lost. It was painful enough having to acquiesce in my brother's conversion."

Marguerite just nodded, resigned to the princess' reasoning, albeit without being convinced of its wisdom.

It was then that she first began to feel that noose, spun of gold, tightening around her neck and it became clear to her that from then on she had better maneuver very carefully around the pitfalls of privilege and status, lest she trip and break her neck.

"Please don't make such a sour face. It isn't all that bad! Come let's enjoy! This day calls for a double celebration—the coronation of the King of France and the homecoming of our dear cousin, Princess Marguerite."

Catherine locked her arm into Marguerite's and pulled her toward the balcony. The square below overflowed with a jubilant multitude finding no end in chanting: "Long live the King! Long live Henri IV!"

"Come on, let's greet the people!" Catherine almost had to pull her out into the brisk February air. "They love to catch a glimpse of the royal family."

Reluctantly, Marguerite followed. Then she too waved at the crowd acknowledging the applause. In the middle of the square, people chanted and danced around a huge bonfire, its leaping flames straining to reach the pallid sun in the gray winter sky like a pyre, a stake!

Marguerite stared at the flames. The faces in the crowd merged with those of another crowd. Their jubilation turned into hostile calls of "Burn the witch! Burn the witch!" A cold chill sent shivers through her body. Her chest heaved with short, quick gasps of breath, her blood rushed madly through her veins. Then everything went blank before her eyes.

The first thing she saw when she regained consciousness was Henri's concerned face.

"What happened?" she asked.

"Catherine was concerned about your well-being and called me immediately after Mass. You needn't worry, just a brief fainting spell, probably from lack of food, and then all the excitement of this day." Henri helped her to her feet.

"You must join us at the banquet and partake of a good meal. That will restore your strength."

"Unfortunately, we have to forego the bacchanalia that usually follow the coronation of a king of France." He laughed his short, jovially sarcastic laugh. "More lavish festivities await us once we have established ourselves at the Louvre in Paris."

The banquet, which may have been modest by royal standards, was a more lavish affair than Marguerite had ever witnessed. Henri announced his plans.

"Early tomorrow morning, I shall have to take leave of my princesses—my royal capital remains to be claimed. As soon as the city has been reduced to the royal will, I shall send for the ladies to set up court at the Louvre. The day is not far way, I am certain. To victory!"

He raised his cup, confident that his long struggle for his capital city would soon near its end.

While the King moved on to Paris, the royal court set up residence at Rambouillet, there to await the royal call. Marguerite took a temporary leave of her cousin, Madame Catherine, with the promise to rejoin her within a few days' time. Her entourage went ahead to Rambouillet, but she, accompanied only by Captain de Bucheron and two guardsmen, departed Chartres on horseback by way of the southern gate.

What fateful desire caused her to go on this pilgrimage? What providence decreed her to return to the place of her childhood? What whim prompted her to reveal herself to the people of Bonneval? Was it pride or ostentation that guided her on the journey into the past? Or was it simply a wish to show kindness to the few who had been kind—a deep longing to embrace the woman who had been her mother? Was she compelled to seek out the inn at Bonneval just to be once again in the place where she had first met Philippe? Certain is that she went without thought of the consequences such a visit might bring.

The familiar sign with the beautiful white horse had weathered and pieces of the wooden shingle were chipped off, but the inn itself looked just as she remembered it. Dusk was about to descend as she entered the dimly lit hall, its low ceiling even more oppressive in the spectral gleam of twilight.

There was something comical in Thierry's obsequious bidding her welcome. She was barely able to suppress the urge to burst out laughing. Even after she had revealed who she was, he refused to believe that the elegant woman in the riding costume could be the troublesome foundling Sandrine whom they had given up for lost or dead.

"Now, tell me, Thierry, why would somebody impersonate a wretched waif like Sandrine? What could anybody gain from making such a claim?"

"A point well taken, Your Ladyship," he finally conceded that she must be right. "Besides how else would Your Ladyship know my name?" he added sheepishly.

"Why, yes indeed?" she replied with that same tone of superiority that had enraged him so in the past. "Wipe that worry off your face! You needn't be concerned about the purpose of my visit. I have come only to see Maman. Where is she? Why doesn't she come out to greet me? Are you still keeping her in the kitchen?"

"Come this way!" he said gravely, pointing the way to the private quarters.

She had to duck her head to enter the chamber. A single candle flickered on the night tabled. Berthe Legrand was propped up in bed by a thick pile of pillows. She held her hands folded as in prayer. Her eyes were closed and her head tilted to the side. There were two other persons in the room, at first only shadows, but as Marguerite's eyes became accustomed to the dark, she recognized Doctor Morel and his wife.

As if she had been expecting her, Régine Morel embraced her furtively and guided her to the bed. "I am afraid, she is not well. She will be so happy that you have finally come. Her greatest fear has been that she might die without knowing where and how you are."

Marguerite sat at the edge of the bed and took Berthe's limp, calloused hands into hers. She searched her face for a sign of life, of recognition. The eyes remained closed in the furrowed mask, prematurely aged by toil and anguish.

Softly she entreated: "Maman! Maman! It's me, Sandrine. I am here."

Slowly, the woman's eyes opened and a pained smile appeared around her mouth.

"Sandrine! Sandrine!" she whispered with the utmost strain. "My wish has been fulfilled, to know you are alive! Now I can gladly die."

"No, you can't die! I won't let you!"

Three days she held vigil at the side of the woman who had loved her like a daughter, but who had been too weak, too frightened, to protect her against the evil in the world. She held her in her arms, telling her about all the things that had happened to her. She told her about Philippe and Noël, how she had lost both, but now she would get them both back, and Berthe would come to live with them. Only a few times did the woman give a sign that she understood. Then, imperceptibly, she slipped away.

The March winds blew mercilessly—the ice saints the people called them—when Berthe Legrand was laid to rest in the cemetery behind the parish church of Bonneval. The entire village was gathered in the mourning. Thierry wept inconsolably. To Sandrine, it seemed somehow strange to think of him as the bereaved widower.

She should have departed then, leave the villagers to themselves in their observance of the funeral rites. There was nothing else for her to do after Berthe was gone. This was no longer her world. Yet, she tarried, followed the casket to where it was lowered into the ground.

Everybody saw her, recognized her, knew who she was, knew she was alive. The years had not erased the ill feelings. Silent stares met her from the horrified villagers as if she had returned from the dead.

Whispers. "There she is!"

"What does she want here?"

Only one was bold enough to block her way as she exited the cemetery.

"Welcome back, my dear departed wife!" There it was, that smirk. How he had aged! He was an old man, but contempt still contorted his mouth. A glance ahead reassured her. Her armed escort lingered in front of the church. Without deigning to answer the wretch, she walked on.

"Not so fast, my dear! We have things to discuss." He got a hold of her sleeve. He dared to touch her with his filthy hands!

"So you have come up in the world, you sly, little bitch!"

"Etienne, leave her alone!" Thierry placed himself between

them and pushed Etienne's hand away from her. "Have you no respect for the dead."

"Berthe is in the ground, she won't hear us. I think I'm entitled to some compensation for the trouble this strumpet put me through. Whether she is a rich countess or not, she is still my wife, and it should be worth something to her for me to hold my peace."

"A marriage that was never consummated. Remember? You gave testimony to that effect yourself in a public court of law. An annulment should hardly pose a problem." She threw back her head, gathered up her skirt, and without flinching, endured the gauntlet of piercing eyes that lined the path from the cemetery to the church square.

"A thousand curses on you! I'll get my revenge, I swear!" Etienne's furious screams rent the subdued air of mourning. Marguerite kept on walking. Bonneval was behind her forever.

She stopped briefly at the inn, to say goodbye to her friends, the Morels. Maybe she could persuade them to leave this area and move to a place like Montauban where they could live in a community of Reformed Brethren. Her entreaties fell on deaf ears.

"Why won't you leave this village? Haven't these fanatics done you enough harm? They burned down your house, next time they will burn you!"

"We are putting our trust in our new King. Even though he had to abjure his religion, he won't let the Huguenots down. You said it yourself, his greatest desire is to heal the wounds caused by this long war and see to it that all his subjects live in peace and harmony," Doctor Morel tried to reassure her.

"We are too old to pick up and start a new life in a far-off, unfamiliar province," Régine Morel added, placing her hand on her husband's arm. "Besides we can still be of service to the people around here."

"A fine thanks you got for all the good you've done. These superstitious peasants don't know gratitude. Another bad harvest, another unexplained death, and the blame will be laid at your doorstep."

"Sandrine, we understand why you should harbor such hard feelings, but there are many good people here. You mustn't condemn everybody equally."

"Thierry has been very kind to us in the time of our need, when a fanatic few put the torch to our house, Thierry had the courage to shelter us. He has changed a great deal."

She paused for a moment, breathing a deep sigh as if she were struggling to get something off her chest. "It would mean a lot to him, especially now, if you could find it in your heart to forgive him. Just a sign that you don't hold the past against him."

When she saw her stiffening, she added more emphatically: "If Our Lord, Jesus Christ, could forgive his enemies, shouldn't you do so?"

Everything within Marguerite cried out "No!" Never will she absolve this man, never forgive his crimes against a helpless child. Had she been an adult, she might have been able to endure, even forgive the torments, the anguish, the violence, but not the child. In her heart, she would hold a grudge against him forever. Only to please the Morels to whom she owed so much and for the sake of her mother Berthe did she quickly place her arms around Thierry as she bid him farewell.

CHAPTER
5

arguerite's impatience for something to happen grew with every passing day. Life at the royal court was like wasting away in the doldrums. Or was it purgatory? After weeks of idleness, hours of enduring the daily frivolities of the courtiers, she almost reached the breaking point. The ample time of doing nothing imposed on the courtiers at Rambouillet was unbearable for one not reared to inactivity and leisure. She tried to spend as much time as possible in the library, but court ritual frequently required her presence even if the hours were spent sitting and waiting. She derived little pleasure from card games or needlework. Nor did she find much solace in the endless prayer meetings fervently organized by Madame Catherine, who, despite her brother's conversion, held stubbornly—Marguerite thought fanatically—to the faith of the Reformed Religion.

She had not given it much thought before, but she was certainly surprised to find that the main topic of conversation among the ladies and courtiers was, not the affairs of the kingdom, nor the progress of the war or Henri's struggle for his crown, but the affairs of the bedrooms at the court. Gossip was the big news that animated the spirits of the royal circle. She wasn't very much interested, but found time went by more quickly if she participated in the game of guessing who was bedding with whom.

One thing was obvious. Neither Princess Catherine de Navarre nor her constant companion, the Count de Soissons, made any attempt to conceal that they were lovers. Their affair had to be kept from the King though, she was told by the Countess de Guiche, Catherine's confidante, for His Majesty was adamantly set against their union. He had other connubial plans for his sister, the Countess confided with the knowing tone of the intimate.

The Countess de Guiche for her part, Marguerite learned later, had in her youth been one of Henri's most ardently beloved mistresses when he was just plain King of Navarre. She was then known as the beautiful Corisande, but Henri's ardor cooled quickly when she lost the flower of her youth and her once exquisite body began to acquire more mature dimensions.

"Henri is a very kind and generous man, a gallant lover," the Countess explained, "but when the affairs of the heart conflict with the affairs of state, he can be ruthless and unfeeling—the latter will always take precedence. Poor Madame Catherine will probably have to marry some ogre whose only desirable quality is his political usefulness to the King."

Marguerite protested. She found it hard to believe her most

benevolent monarch should be so heartless.

"Just wait and see," the Countess replied with the smile of experience.

One morning while on her way to attend Madame Catherine's levée, Marguerite found the court buzzing with excitement. News had arrived: Henri had finally taken possession of his capital. As the story was related, in the morning of the 22nd of March in the year 1594, even before dawn, the King, with only a handful of his men, walked into the city of Paris. Without encountering much resistance, he reached the Louvre where he immediately took to reorganizing the governance of the city.

Madame Catherine exhorted the courtiers to be ready for the King's call. Yet, another month went without the royal order for the court to move Paris. Marguerite was dismayed as she found her hopes for immediate relief from the boredom at Rambouillet dashed again. This time the waiting became even more unbearable since every day started with the hope that this would be the day the King's orders would come, only to be dashed by evening.

Meanwhile, the courtiers nourished themselves on bits and pieces of news from Paris and the King's progress of submitting the city to his will. They spent much time discussing the meaning of this or that episode relayed to them by a constant stream of messengers from the capital. The Huguenot courtiers were disturbed by stories of unreconciled priests and monks who were still inciting the faithful to regicide in their daily sermons. Their grave conclusion was inescapable, the time for peace and toleration had not yet come.

Marguerite listened patiently though without paying much attention to Catherine's expositions about the future. She nodded without saying a word, for she did not feel close enough to the Princess to confide in her and share with her the secret apprehension about returning to the city where she was still wanted for murder.

Then one day, her interest was stirred by something Catherine was babbling. Her cousin's voice had changed, all the artificial frivolity in her tone was gone.

"You know, I was in Paris only once before in my life as a child." The Princess's serious demeanor made Marguerite listen up. Their eyes met and Catherine moved closer to her, whispering as if she wanted to share a dark secret. "Even then, as a child, I didn't think it was good for this marriage to take place, the marriage between my brother and Marguerite de Valois— not so soon after my mother's death at any rate. My mother— she was a Valois princess herself, you know—she always said the offspring of Catherine de Medici cannot be trusted. I have no proof, but I am certain, my mother, the blessed Jeanne d'Albret, Queen of Navarre and most devoted defender of the faith, was poisoned by that Medici woman. But who would listen to an eleven-year-old girl? That's how old I was then when the terrible massacre occurred. Fortunately, nobody paid much attention to me then either. . . while the slaughter was raging in the corridors of the Louvre."

"You witnessed the killings?" Marguerite's mouth fell open. To think that she was face to face with an eyewitness of that terrible day!

"I didn't see anybody being killed, but I heard their screams. I was too frightened and hid in a closet in the servants' quarters at the Louvre. But I was present at the wedding, the most magnificent spectacle ever—gaudy and frivolous, my mother would have called it. There was no end to the festivities for three or four days."

"What else did you see?" The words fell from Marguerite's lips almost inaudibly.

"I saw the blessed Princess Isabelle de France at the banquet. She had always treated me kindly and I loved her dearly. I looked at her and thought she was the most beautiful woman at the wedding, more beautiful even than the Princess Marguerite de Valois." Catherine placed her arms gently around her cousin. "She was so young, about the same age as you are now. When I first saw you, I thought she had come back to life."

Then Catherine rose abruptly.

"A thousand times, I imagined myself wreaking bloody revenge for the crime committed against the Huguenot brethren!" she proclaimed. "But that wouldn't go well with Henri's more conciliatory attitude. Now, I just want to return and see all of Paris at my feet."

Knowing how anxious Catherine was to make her entry into Paris, Marguerite was surprised at her almost violent reaction when, at long last, the royal emissary, Baron de Rosny, was announced.

"Tell the Baron to get himself from hence, and if he should dare come into my presence, I shall have him expelled by force of arms," she shrieked.

Marguerite looked to the Countess de Guiche, but she just rolled her eyes and gently shook her head as if to say, better not interfere.

"What nerve that man has to appear here and expect me to receive him!" Catherine turned to her friend. Still sobbing with indignation, she sank to her knees and placed her head in the Countess's lap.

"Baron de Rosny has been the King's closest friend since boyhood," the Countess explained to Marguerite while she stroked Catherine's hair. "The Baron, on instruction from the King it must be said, did Madame a bad turn. You see Madame and the Count de Soissons had exchanged a written agreement of marriage, secretly, since they knew the King would oppose their union. Well, the ingenious Baron, persuaded her to hand over the document to him under the pretense that he would intercede on the lovers' behalf with His Majesty. As we found out later, it was all a ruse. He did indeed hand the paper to the King who destroyed it promptly."

"That underhanded, double-dealing swine!" Catherine was completely beside herself and Marguerite was at a loss what to do. In her heart, she felt deeply the injustice that had been done to the poor Princess.

"He acted on orders from the King," the Countess reminded the Princess once again.

"What a terrible thing to do! How can anybody be so treacherous? It is hard to believe that His Majesty should stoop to such despicable tactics!" Marguerite exclaimed. "Maybe it was all a misunderstanding. Do you think it would serve any purpose if I spoke to His Majesty? He seems well disposed toward me."

"I assure you, there was no misunderstanding. Marrying off relatives is a way kings repay their political debts. You are right in so far as you presume that the King is well disposed toward you, beauty has its privileges," the Countess agreed not without a tone of bitterness. "But if you want to keep it that way, you must learn to keep your opinions to yourself, and you must subordinate your personal feelings to the royal will. A woman is an ornament and even a beautiful woman can become irksome if she meddles in affairs of state."

That evening, Marguerite entered Catherine's chambers for the daily prayer meeting and found her laughing and jesting with a gentleman she had not seen before. Considering what had gone before, she was not a little surprised when he was introduced as the selfsame Baron de Rosny, the King's emissary whose arrival had aroused such hysteria. The Countess de Guiche's very practical stance that one does not send an emissary of the King packing, no matter how odious his sight may be or what one's personal feelings are, had prevailed.

The Baron was no stranger to courtly society and seemed to enjoy great popularity among the ladies. The reason for this became obvious in the course of the evening. There hadn't been that much gay laughter at Rambouillet since the royal court had arrived there, and even Marguerite found herself not immune to Rosny's gallant charm. After supper, a gathering was held in the main hall, and the Baron more than satisfied the company's curiosity with stories, relating in minute detail how King Henri had made himself master of Paris.

"The city was taken exactly the way His Majesty had desired—without armed struggle or bloodshed. There had been many opportunities to take the city by storm in past years, but His Majesty always spoke of Paris as a woman he ardently desired, but would not take by force. Like a gallant lover, he wanted her to surrender herself to him of her own free will. He wanted to avoid at all cost the loss of human lives."

He paused to acknowledge the enthusiastic acclamation that greeted his words.

A strange way of looking at it, Marguerite thought. She was tempted to ask about the thousands who died during the siege, but she held her peace. She had learned her lesson from the Countess de Guiche—nothing would be gained with sowing more contention now that the King had triumphed over the recalcitrant Parisians.

"The first order of business was to clear the city of the Spanish garrison and of the so-called Sixteen, actually there were more of those Papist rogues, who had ruled the Parlement of Paris for so many years," the Baron continued.

"It seems the Duke de Mayenne got a whiff of which way the wind was blowing and quietly slipped out of town only hours before the royal entry. He might try to organize further resistance from a base in the provinces, but many former Leaguers have already made peace with their King—on very generous terms, I might add. Throughout the negotiations with his former enemies, His Majesty has shown himself to be of a generosity these wretches hardly deserve."

"What will happen to those who refuse to come to terms?" somebody asked.

"There are very few who are still holding out—some members of the House of Lorraine, Mayenne, the Duke de Mercoeur, and the young Duke de Guise, of course. But even the queens of the League, Mesdames Montpensier and Nemours have graciously accepted a royal invitation to visit the Louvre. So far only the Duke d'Evreux and his son, the Count de Treffort-Salignac, have been incarcerated in the Bastille. Henri offered peace but was stubbornly refused by the Duke. His Majesty intends to make an example of those two unrepentant Leaguers—he will be put them on trial for treason for which the penalty is of course death. Some of the friars and priests especially the Jesuits are continuing their tirades. A few have even placed themselves above the Pope and claim that nobody, not even the Pope, has the power to lift the ban on, as they say, the heretic. All this will soon be over, once the word arrives from Rome."

Marguerite no longer listened to the Baron's confabulations. A dagger had been plunged into her heart. Philippe in the Bastille! She was certain it was his father who would not make peace with the King. If it wasn't for the influence of this stubborn old man, Philippe would have joined Navarre long ago. How can she waste all this time in idleness with Philippe in need? She had to leave for Paris immediately. She had to talk to the King.

This time she won't let the Duke d'Evreux get in the way of her happiness! Let him be tried for treason, he deserves it—but not Philippe!

The presence of the two women in the royal apartment disturbed her and for a moment she became transfixed to the spot where she was standing. She expected to find the King in the company of a host of courtiers and attendants when she stormed past the guards and forced her way into the royal drawing-room, but she was not prepared to find him engaged in a game of checkers with Madame de Montpensier and Louise de Montreuil!

"My dear cousin!" Henri shook his head while making mock scolding noises with his lips. "There is a certain etiquette that must be observed at the royal court. You must be announced before you are allowed to enter the king's chambers. How should these hapless fellows know you are not an assassin?"

Marguerite bowed down deeply and bent her knees in a curtsy.

"I beg Your Majesty's forgiveness, but if I acted rashly, it is due to an urgent matter. A private conference with Your Majesty is urgently requested."

"That you shall have if the matter is that pressing. You know I cannot resist a beautiful woman in distress," he said, ever the gallant admirer of feminine charms.

"First you must meet your cousin the Duchess de Montpensier and the Baroness de Montreuil, two charming ladies who have graciously granted me the pleasure of their company this evening. Evenings can be so tedious in this place."

With an elegant bow toward the ladies seated at the gaming table, he announced: "Mesdames, may I present my dear cousin, Princess Marguerite de France, the Countess de Montauban."

The women curtsied and scrutinized each other with the

cautious curiosity of cats while they exchanged the customary pleasantries. Madame de Montpensier appeared rather more subdued than when Marguerite had seen her last limping through the streets of Paris.

But it was Louise de Montreuil who drew her attention. Marguerite was unable to take her eyes off her. A thousand times had she rehearsed in her mind an encounter with the woman who had saved her son's life. Only now, she was unprepared. It happened too soon, too unexpectedly, and in the wrong place. Yet, the longer she stared at Louise, the more everything and everybody in the room was blotted from her consciousness. Even the purpose for which she had so urgently sought out the King was, for the time being, forgotten.

She did not know what possessed her. Some magnetic force was drawing her irresistibly toward Louise. With an ingratiating smile, she said softly: "My dear Baroness, I knew fate would bring us together. You cannot imagine how much I have yearned for this moment, all these years. May I embrace you?"

She extended her arms and before the startled Louise was able to answer she kissed her on both cheeks.

"Your Majesty, I want you to know this woman is an angel, a saint. Even when I first saw her I was immediately struck by the gleam of goodness in her eyes. And I was not deceived. She saved the life of one who is more precious to me than my own life. Madame may be assured of my eternal gratitude."

"The Princess is most kind, but I am afraid, I don't understand the meaning of her words. I don't seem to recall having had the pleasure." Louise took a few steps backward.

"Cousin, we are aware of the Baroness's outstanding qualities of heart and mind, but you are holding us all in unbearable suspense," Henri intervened. "You must explain your meaning."

"Most willingly, Sire," Marguerite obliged. "If the Baroness pleases to think back to the summer when the city of Paris was besieged by His Majesty's army. She found an infant child at her doorstep, a child famished and ill, close to death. She was gracious enough to take the child under her care and nurse it back to life."

"Yes, this is true enough," Louise confirmed hesitantly. "The boy has been in my care ever since. But. . .how . . .?"

"I was the one who placed him at your door. I watched you and your companions doting on him. Without you, he would surely have died, for I had nothing to give him anymore."

"You must be Sandrine!" Louise drew out the words slowly. "Unless this is some strange trick."

Marguerite pulled the sleeve from her right shoulder and presented to Louise's view the mark of the yellow butterfly.

"I am sure you must have seen this drawing before. Please, tell me is he well?"

"But Philippe said the mother was a peasant girl!" Then after some thought, Louise added laughing: "He always did suspect she was a princess under an evil spell."

"Please, I must know! Is my son alive and well?"

"He is a very beautiful boy, looks much like his father. He has given us nothing but joy." Marguerite flung her arms around Louise's neck and under tears murmured over and over: "Thank you, thank you! How can I ever thank you enough!"

"Sire!" Madame de Montpensier, who watched the emotional spectacle with a skeptical eye, turned to King. "Am I wrong to presume that the line of the Montaubans had become extinct years ago?"

"We all thought the line was extinct, but then the hand of Divine Providence restored to us the last descendant of this noblest house."

"Sire, if you pardon me for being so straightforward, but

how can we be certain this woman is not an impostor?"

"Madame needn't worry. I have satisfied myself of the legitimacy of the woman's claim to the title and possessions of the Montaubans. There is absolutely no doubt. Besides, just look," he added, "the resemblance, wouldn't you say she is my cousin Isabelle come back to life. Most uncanny, don't you agree? Just as she appeared at our most ill-fated wedding. It almost seems as if time has stood still."

Henri turned his attention back to the other two women who still held each other embraced. Taking them both by the hand, he insisted: "Mesdames, let us sit down, right here, and sort things out."

The exchange was interrupted by the entry of Princess Catherine de Navarre. Henri rose to greet his sister.

"Madame, you have arrived at the right moment. We just heard of a most extraordinary happenstance. You will find our discussion most interesting. Won't you please sit with us, I believe you know the ladies."

The Princess cast a jaundiced look at the two Catholic ladies, nodding only slightly, and then turned to Marguerite: "I have been concerned about Her Ladyship's absence from this evening's prayer meeting."

"Never mind that right now, dearest sister!" Henri waved his hand impatiently. "We are unraveling a most fascinating story. If I understand it right, the Baroness has been kind enough to adopt a child into her household she found at the doorstep of her mansion in Paris at the time my army was forced to besiege this noblest and most stubborn city. Princess Marguerite just informed us that she is the mother of the child, and she was the one who placed the infant at the doorstep of the Hotel Montreuil, counting on the Baroness's goodness of heart to take him in, I presume. My apologies to both ladies for the hardship you had to endure due to the exigencies of war. Let's continue with the story. As you entered, Catherine, the Princess was expressing her gratitude to the Baroness. I believe, dear cousin, you owe your sovereign an explanation who fathered the child, and also who is this Philippe?"

"Count de Treffort-Salignac!" the women called out in one voice.

"Ventre-Saint Gris! That devil! Two beautiful women to mourn for him!" Henri slapped his thigh with boisterous delight. "I always told him he should be on the side of his King."

"Sire! When I requested a private conference it was to appeal to Your Majesty's legendary spirit of clemency in the matter of the Count," Marguerite quickly seized the opportunity.

"My legendary spirit of clemency!" Henri rose. He was no longer chuckling. "You needn't flatter me, cousin. What I don't need is more flatterers. There are enough in this palace. Now, as for the Count, it is my will to make an example of him and the Duke d'Evreux to show to the world who is master in this kingdom. Truly remarkable is the fact that I am immediately beseeched by two women—the Baroness came especially for this purpose out of seclusion in the backwoods of Picardie, and my dear cousin, heiress to the good name of a devout Huguenot family is pleading for mercy for an unrepentant Leaguer!"

Abruptly, he turned on his heels and faced the Baron de Rosny, who had followed the disclosures with bemused interest.

"Is there no limit to the folly of women, Maximilien? What do you suggest I do?"

"I think Your Majesty, this Count deserves to lose his head, then the ladies won't have to draw a lot over the scoundrel."

"The Baron's insinuations are as outrageous as they are insolent," Louise de Montreuil shouted.

"Oh yes! Please forgive me, I forgot, Madame prefers to

share her bed with the bourgeoisie."

"Now! Now, Maximilien!" Henri, barely able to keep a straight face, placed himself between the two belligerents. "I think you owe the lady an apology. This is enough for one night. I hope the affairs of state we will face me tomorrow are not as tangled as the affairs . . ."

"Don't say it, Henri!" Madame Catherine shouted. "I think the women in this room have suffered enough abuse for one evening. If the gentlemen require more diversion, they should seek the company of their mistresses!"

"Well, spoken, my little sister. I had better rush into the arms of my fair Gabrielle. I am sure the mistress of my heart feels neglected already." Henri graciously kissed her hand and dismissed the company.

Nearly two weeks elapsed without an opportunity to raise the question of Philippe's incarceration again. Henri seemed intent on avoiding the topic altogether. Several times, at the royal levée or at dinner, she turned to him, but every time the King placed his finger on his closed lips. His time was either taken up in conference with his counselors or in pursuit of frivolous amusements. There were games of tennis and croquet, and of course, the hunt. Almost every night there were ballets of which Henri could never get enough. The King took an almost childish delight in the dancers' movements and would not be spoken to during the performances.

Never was the time right to gain the King's ear in the matter that weighed on her heart. Yet, she waited patiently for her opportunity. The flowers in the garden of the Louvre burst into full bloom. Spring slid peacefully into summer. A caressing balm filled in the air. Every day it became more painful to keep up the amiable, smiling mask she was required to wear for the King did not like to see frowns at his court. It mortified her to think that she was in the same city as Philippe, and yet they were separated by an entire world.

If at least she could go out into the city, wander through the streets, visit her old friend Arsène Rigoud. From the first she looked for an opportunity to get away—Arsène will be so proud of her—but so far it had proven impossible to escape the golden cage that held the royal entourage imprisoned.

Her only consolation was Louise. She visited her under escort at the Hotel Montreuil as often as possible. The two women spent hours in conversation. Marguerite could not hear enough about her son's progress, and Louise never tired of describing every detail in glowing terms. Her new friend was so obviously enamored with the child, she did not have the heart to ask her for his return.

Louise also told her about Philippe, the torment he suffered not knowing whether his love was alive. Louise was certain it was only the Duke d'Evreux who stood in the way of reconciliation with the King. She knew Philippe had lost all interest in the struggle or serving in the League, but he also seemed to care very little about what was to happen to him. He had often said without Sandrine his life was meaningless.

"I hope Raphael loves me as much as Philippe loves his Sandrine," Louise confessed to never having seen a man as deeply, yes madly, in love as Philippe.

"I have lived only for Philippe and our son. The thousands of obstacles in my way were nothing, eventually, I knew I would be reunited with them. Now it seems that all has been for naught!" Bitter tears welled up in Marguerite's eyes. "How can the King be so cruel?"

"I am sure, once you speak with the King alone, away from his courtiers, he will show himself to be more kindhearted," Louise tried to console her although she was all too familiar with political intrigues not to suspect that Henri was playing some underhanded game.

"Wouldn't it be wonderful if we had a double wedding, you and Raphael?" Marguerite mused.

"Please you mustn't even mention it," Louise shook her head with a sad smile. "We are very happy the way things are, although it will be difficult to keep the suitors away when it becomes known that I am no longer the betrothed of the Count de Treffort. Fortune hunters, that's what they all are! I must return to Bonneterre tomorrow. Raphael and the children are waiting. We have two children and another one coming." She proudly padded her belly. "I want to fill the entire manor with Raphael's children!"

Seeing the pained expression on Marguerite's face, she added: "We have raised and loved Noël like our own, but he is yours and Philippe's. When I arrive home, I shall prepare to have him sent to you here at the Louvre."

Marguerite found no end in hugging and kissing her new friend.

"You must understand the change will be difficult for him at first, but love and time will heal any hurt he might feel. Of course, you will visit us when everything is settled. I want you to meet Raphael. He has heard so much about you, I know he will be delighted to see that this fabulous woman of Philippe's dreams is real and not a figment of the Count's imagination."

Her loneliness intensified after Louise's departure. But at least she had the consolation of looking forward to being reunited with her son. A mixture of excitement and apprehension filled her. She rehearsed in her mind what she would say. She didn't have much experience with children and wasn't sure what a four-year-old was like. Well, she would learn all that and much more. She thought about his name. Noël somehow did not seem fitting anymore for the heir of the House of Montauban. She would rename him after her father and have his name entered into the official register as Arnaud de Montauban.

The matter of Philippe's release was going nowhere. Henri was engaged in endless negotiations with an endless line of petitioners—noblemen, of the grander as well as lesser sort—who were filing daily in and out of the stateroom. By the hundreds, they presented themselves at the Louvre to pay homage to their King. Most emerged from the royal audience with satisfied mien and clutching titles to fiefs bestowed on them.

Only one fellow, so boisterous in his behavior she could not help but notice him, seemed rather dissatisfied with the bargaining. He stormed from the stateroom spewing curses and thunderous protests. His giant stature and flaming red hair and beard made him look like the descendant of a Viking invader.

That very afternoon, the day on which she had observed the cursing Viking slam the door of the stateroom behind him, a page arrived with orders to escort her to the King. She found Henri in the private enclosure of the palace garden crawling on all fours with several of his brood riding horseback on him. Their mother, Gabrielle d'Estrée, was sprawled out on a canapé, surrendering herself to the sensuous breeze from a huge fan kept in motion by two servants.

Henri shook off the jockeys and rose to meet his visitor: "How nice to see you, dear cousin! You look more radiant than ever. Isn't this a wonderful way to forget the troubles of a king? Have you seen the bloodsuckers line up in front of my door? They are ready to carve up my entire kingdom for themselves. Unfortunately, I need them."

"Sire, you called me with a specific purpose? Do you have any news for me about the Count de Treffort?" she asked impatiently.

"Oh, yes! Of course, the Count de Treffort-Salignac!" He excused himself from his mistress and the children and led Marguerite on a walk along a gravel path under an espalier of roses.

"I am a great admirer of the Count de Treffort," he began locking his arm into hers. "Saw him in action at the battle of Arques, an exemplary soldier! Twice before he had become my prisoner, and twice I let him go. The last time we met, I warned him, should he ever become my prisoner again I would not be lenient. He knows very well how much I value his talents. I was ready to meet the most exorbitant conditions he might make if only he would come over to the royal side. But, no, he clung to the League. While there was almost no resistance to the royal entry into the city, there was an altercation in front of the Hotel d'Evreux. I offered my hand and it was refused. Now I must make an example of these two gentlemen."

"I am certain the Count's sympathies have been with Your Majesty for a long time. Only his father is a stubborn fanatic."

"You seem very sure of the thoughts and inclinations of a man you say you haven't seen for several years."

"All I know is if Philippe dies, my life is not worth living. Please, I beg Your Majesty, just one more time, to show yourself magnanimous and release him, for my sake!"

She fell on her knees and fervently pressed her lips to his hand.

"Dear cousin! What passion for a mere mortal! Do you think he deserves such love and devotion? You seem to think so. But what about the family? You said yourself the Duke is a fanatic. And you are right in that. I remember very well, the day of the great massacre on Saint Bartholomew's Day, the Duke d'Evreux and his men were among the most bloodthirsty of the henchmen storming through this very palace. They almost outdid the Duke d'Anjou and the Guise clan in the carnage they visited on my Huguenot brethren. Please forgive me for mentioning this tragic episode which must cause you great sorrow as it does for me. I too lost many of my closest companions. The guilty have never been brought to justice, and it is not my intent to seek them out now. But just think it has never been determined who was responsible for the death of your parents. The Duke was there."

"Sire, while I deeply mourn the death of my parents, it has nothing whatsoever to do with my concern for the life of the Count, who has very little in common with his father. I know him to be kind and compassionate, just and upright. Your Majesty cannot wish to waste the life of such an outstanding subject!"

"There is one way to save his life," Henri said slowly as if the thought had just occurred to him. He folded his hands behind his back.

"I give you my royal word, Philippe de Treffort will go free if in return you agree to take the hand of the Marquis de Launay in marriage."

Marguerite looked at him as if he had spoken in a foreign tongue. Slowly the meaning of his words began to sink in, but she still thought this must be one of his jokes and she almost began to laugh. Then she remembered the scene at Rambouillet, Princess Catherine's fury at Rosny. He will stop at nothing to marry off his kin to suit his political purposes, the Countess de Guiche's warning rang in her ears.

"Your Majesty expects me to marry another man?" she gasped.

"You will not only save the life of the Count, but you will also serve your King. The Marquis de Launay is a wealthy, powerful nobleman of ancient lineage. He is also a fervent Huguenot, and, I am sorry to say, he has not yet reconciled himself to his King's abjuration of the Reformed Religion. A marriage alliance with the royal house will appease his rebellious spirit and his wealth will help the royal coffers which are, at the moment, none too plentiful, I am afraid. When the marriage has been concluded, the Count will go free. The Duke can go as well, he is too old to cause further trouble."

He placed his arms around her shoulders in a fatherly gesture and added laughingly: "You can always keep the Count as your lover. I am already jealous of that lucky devil!"

Marguerite bethought herself for a moment. In all the excitement of the last few weeks, she had forgotten to take care of having her marriage to Etienne annulled. News of a wedding was certain to reach Bonneval and Etienne would not hesitate to decry her as a bigamist. This would also bring up her conviction for witchcraft at Chartres, and there are still people in Paris who are seeking to bring the murderess of the monk of Saint Victor to justice. She had better level with the King—at least in part.

"Sire," she began slowly. "There is one small matter that might get in the way of Your Majesty's plan. Without burdening you with the circumstances, the fact of the matter is that I, that is I in my former existence as Sandrine Legrand, am formally married to one Etienne Grosjean of Bonneval. No, wait! The marriage was never consummated and it should not be difficult to obtain an annulment."

"Ventre Saint Gris! Cousin! You are a ceaseless wonder!" Henri burst out, half angry and half-amused. Strange that he should use the same words as Arsène, she thought.

"I love diversions and twisted plots, but at times they can be a nuisance."

So absorbed were they in their discussion, they did not

notice that they had completed the circular path around the garden and arrived now again in front of the pavilion.

"Sire, you promised the children another round of horsy before Vespers!" Gabrielle waved to her royal master.

"Yes, of course! Please, I shall be only a moment!"

Turning back to Marguerite, he shrugged his shoulders with a helpless grin: "Madame, I am afraid the continuance of our discussion must wait for another time. As you can see, important affairs of state require my immediate attention."

He had already started for the pavilion when he turned and called after her: "I will be away from Paris for a few days. On my return, I must have your answer."

"Oh, you don't know the half of it!" Marguerite mumbled under her breath. She raced through the maze of corridors as if chased by a hundred demons. Breathless, she reached the wing where she occupied a suite of rooms. She promptly dismissed the servants. Alone in her chamber, she flung herself on her bed and buried her face. Is there no end to the pain in this life? Will the anguish of her heart ever cease?

If only Louise were here. She was a woman she could confide in. A woman of such admirable strength, in the way she defied conventions! She was secure in her position, not dependent on the good graces of a treacherous King.

Yet, she was incapable of hating him. Didn't he just do what the governance of the kingdom required of him? He did what kings and nobles have always done. Marriage was not a bond of love between two people, but a political alliance. His marriage to Marguerite de Valois is a perfect example. It just had never occurred to her when she aspired to the position that was hers by right of birth that she would become entangled in a web of politics, a pawn in Henri IV's strategy to consolidate his power.

The King was probably right, and judging from her

observations of the morals of the courtiers and nobility, why not have Philippe as her lover? This was not how she had imagined it to be! All the misery she had endured, her fight for her birthright had only one goal: so she should be worthy of being Philippe's wife. The thought of another man touching her body made her recoil in horror. Even if she was free to take a lover, her husband under the law could always, whenever he pleased, exercise his right as her lord and master.

Did Henri consider even for a moment the personal sacrifice he was demanding of her? Probably not. Princess Catherine's story came again to her mind. Most certainly not! Why should he be concerned with the violation of her body, the humiliation she would feel in the bed of a stranger. Such intimately private woes were not the concern of a great statesman whose sight was fixed on the future of France. Individual happiness counted very little in the grand, universal scheme of things.

A sudden calm came over her and the flow of tears ebbed. Not that she had reconciled herself to her fate, but she recognized that the time for tears had passed. Too many times had she protested against injustice by giving herself over to weeping and despair. Even if she had to face defeat in the end, at least she would not submit to being slaughtered like a meek lamb!

She rose and walked to the open window. The half-open curtains fluttered in the warm summer breeze. Sprawled below her was the expanse that was the city of Paris. Even at night, the noises of feverish activity never ceased, a buzzing anthill, an indistinguishable mass of creatures struggling to stay alive. Out there in this heap was the one who was able to help her, her mentor and friend, Arsène Rigoud, king of beggars and thieves.

There must be a way to leave this palace. She was a free person. Why should she not come and go as she pleased? Cousin Catherine may miss her at the prayer meetings, but so be it! She had never really warmed to the Reformed ritual. The constant recitations and sermonizing of the ministers wore her patience thin as much as had the Catholic practices.

Taking strength in her resolve, she called her lady-in-waiting. She needed to change into something simpler, less cumbersome, or ostentatious than the current fashion. She chose a dress of black satin, devoid of ornaments except for a white lace border, the fine material and expert craftsmanship still betrayed the wealth and position of its wearer. She pulled a light knit shawl over her head and shoulders and started for the door. Outrage followed upon surprise, the exit to her apartment was blocked by two crossed halberds.

"Guard! What is the meaning of this?" she demanded to know.

"On orders from His Majesty, Madame is not to leave her quarters without an escort."

"This is outrageous! Well, then you will have to escort me to the royal apartment!" A quick duck and she was on the other side of the halberds. The baffled guards in heavy breastplates were hardly able to keep up with her as she sailed toward the King's quarters.

"I am dismayed that Madame must be reminded again of the etiquette prevailing at the royal court!" Henri called out sharply on seeing her burst into the room where he was engaged in conference with his councilors.

"Surely, my tempestuous cousin has not forgotten that it is customary to request permission to be admitted into the King's presence!"

"If it pleases, Your Majesty, I demand to know why I am held a prisoner!"

"Hardly the right word, Madame!" he replied. His anger almost immediately melted away and his gallantry got the better of him.

"Madame is free to move about anywhere within the confines of the Louvre, but I don't think it would be wise to venture beyond. The order was given to protect you from your impetuosity, shall we say? I would not want any harm to come to Your Ladyship during my absence."

"Your Majesty's concern for my well-being is most touching. May I be granted permission to go on an outing into the city?"

"Granted! So Madame doesn't deem me unkind or heartless, an escort shall be assigned for Madame's protection."

Having said this, he considered the conversation terminated, but since he failed to dismiss her formally, a situation ensued in which she was left standing, not having anything more to say, but unable to leave. When he finally realized the awkwardness of her situation, he apologized profusely: "I beg your forgiveness, I am neglecting my manners."

And with an elegant gesture toward the gentlemen assembled around a huge wood-hewn desk: "I believe Madame is acquainted with most of the gentlemen."

Then suddenly, he seized her by the hand and pulled her forward: "There is, however, one gentleman who has not had the pleasure of Your Ladyship's acquaintance. My dear Marquis de Launay may I present Marguerite de France, the Countess de Montauban!"

My God, this must be a bad dream! It was the crimson Viking! Her surprise was all the greater when the Marquis revealed himself to be a flatterer, almost rivaling the King in gallantry. Maybe she had judged him prematurely and he was, despite his bulky size, a man of gracious manners and good breeding.

But even if he were the most graceful courtier in the world, she did not love him and did not want to marry him. Her whole being revolted against such a prospect.

CHAPTER
6

Somebody had gone through the trouble of repairing the hinge on the wrought-iron gate to the court of miracles of Saint Honoré. When she had first entered the realm of beggars and thieves during the siege, the gate had been flapping back and forth, sounding an eerie melody in the stillness of the deserted courtyard. Now human life had returned to the dregs of the city. Life, however miserable and degraded, had resumed in the hollow alleyways where a few years before the hand of death had held its ghastly sway.

Everywhere in the city beggars and paupers littered the pavement, tucking at passers-by, seeking alms. Countless times in a day the same scene was enacted: a thief races through the crowded alleys pursued by irate screams of a victuals vendor.

Even children, and cats and dogs, had returned—she wondered where they had come from—swelling the army of the destitute. Oh yes, life in the streets of Paris moved again along its normal paths—filth and vermin, hunger and disease, were still the natural backdrop to the pitiless drama of survival.

Marguerite traversed the cobblestones of the courtyard. She lifted the seam of her dress slightly so as not to sweep up the dirt. News of the presence of a lady spread quickly. Window frames filled with curiosity seekers, some leaning far out to catch a glimpse of the rare sight. Her path to the portal of Arsène Rigoud's headquarters was lined with suspicious characters. Only reluctantly did her escorts follow her order to remain outside, their eyes followed her nervously as she disappeared through the heavy wood carved door. Inside, two thugs blocked her from entering the hall crudely marked "Throne Room."

"Madame cannot go in there, the court is in session. Unless you have come to pay tribute."

"Tribute to whom or what?" she laughed.

"To our king, Arsène Rigoud. Whatever brought Madame here, this is the territory of the king of beggars and thieves. In here his will is the law."

"In other words, he is extorting the people in line for a share of their earnings!"

"The contributions are voluntary, Madame, not extortions. We offer them protection from criminals of which there are many in this city."

"I'm sure of that. If you don't mind, I would like to watch the proceedings from the back of the room." She started to walk past but the two massive bodies presented an insurmountable obstacle.

"I assure you, it's all right. I'm an old friend of the king. He will be very angry if you turn me away."

Arsène was seated on his "throne," an upholstered bench, an imposing figure with tangled hair like Poseidon ruling over his subterranean realm. He rose and descended from the elevated platform. Good old Arsène, she thought, nothing ever escapes him. His attention may be concentrated on his subjects, on accepting their offerings, mediating disputes, but his sixth sense never ceased working, he was always aware of the slightest disturbance in the farthest corner. A shuffle between a well-dressed woman and his bodyguards surely deserved his special attention.

How fabulous he looked! No longer a hollow skeleton in rags. His towering frame was padded with muscle and meat. His hair, glowing white touched his shoulders over which a purplish red cloak was draped. He strode toward her with a dignified and commanding air. There was no doubt who was the king here.

Suddenly, he quickened his step as an air of recognition came over his face.

"Sandrine! Sandrine!" She felt gathered up in his arms and twirled around. Wild applause from the miscreant audience accompanied this unabashed outburst of joyous emotion from the king of thieves. He set her down and looked her over very carefully, shaking his head: "You did it! You did it! I knew you would. Just look, what a beauty you have become!"

Turning toward the riffraff staring at them, he called out: "The court is adjourned, until tomorrow morning!"

They sat together for the rest of the day and talked, oblivious of time, until dusk dimmed their glowing faces. Arsène questioned her like an interrogator. He wanted to know every detail of what had happened to her since they had parted at Saint Cloud, some four years before.

"But we are only talking about me," she said finally. "What

about you? It seems everything is going well. But is it?"

"It took a long time to rebuild my realm after the siege. Thousands of beggars and thieves poured back into the city, I don't know why, since there were shortages and misery for a long time afterward. Even now, we have to fight against hunger and disease constantly. The situation was complicated by the fact that the return of the people also brought back large numbers of the lowest criminals, murderers, felons, rabble-rousers. This makes matters more difficult for me."

"You mean, it is more difficult for you to protect these miserable wretches who were in your courtroom this morning."

"Exactly. Some bad elements will kill for a piece of bread or a few écus. But, in general, the court of miracles is back to what it once was. Miracles take place here every day."

"There is a sadness in your eyes, Arsène!"

"That probably comes from being old and alone. Sometimes, I wonder why God has willed me to survive all these terrible catastrophes that have been visited on this city."

"After you were gone, Mellisande rejoined me," he continued after a pensive pause. "Thank God I found her still alive. But she was in a frightful state, almost unrecognizable, infested with vermin, emaciated to the bones. I felt responsible for her condition. I wanted to make it up to her. It took a long time to nurse her back to health, but eventually, she regained her strength, even some of her vitality, if not her beauty. She became my companion—working her old beat was of course out of the question—she was the consort of the king of beggars and thieves. Having her by my side filled me with some inner tranquility, I guess you could call it happiness, as I had never known before. She was so incredibly forgiving. Never a word of reproach. Then, the plague carried her off. A hundred times I have asked, why her and not me?"

Anybody else would have been astounded to see tears in the big man's eyes, but Marguerite knew the tender heart that beat beneath the tough exterior. She placed her hand on his arm.

"There is a reason for everything. Your work in this world is not yet done, Arsène," she said.

He quickly changed his tone. "For one thing, I first had to find out whatever happened to that miserable waif, Sandrine, who caused me so much trouble during the siege!"

There was the old goatish laughter and he slapped his thighs satisfied to have found an answer to the riddle.

A disturbance at the door summoned Arsène's attention. Through the half-open door, Marguerite saw a man in chains who struggled with Arsène's men. For a moment his eyes met Marguerite's. He had the desperate look of a captured animal. One of the men said something about a trial. Arsène ordered the prisoner put away, the trial could wait until the next day.

"Who was this man?" she demanded to know when Arsène returned.

"Oh, just a common murderer and thief."

"Are you going to hand him over to the police?"

"Goodness, no! He will be tried in this court of law and then we shall hang him."

"But shouldn't you hand him over to the authorities if you have evidence that he killed somebody."

"Listen, Sandrine, I don't know why this scum interests you. But if you must know, he did not just kill one person. His name is Jéhan Vignerie. Calls himself king of beggars and thieves of Saint-Marcel on the other side of the river—has been trying to take over my territory for years. I've lost some of my best men in this war. As if that miserable worm were a match for Arsène Rigoud. He'll be tried following the laws of the underworld. His death will restore peace in my realm."

"Let's see now," he continued, trying to be jovial. "You are now the Countess de Montauban. Excuse me, if I don't call you Marguerite, for me you will always be Sandrine, cousin of the King of France or not. But you haven't said anything about the fellow you were so infatuated with, whatever his name was. A Count something, wasn't he?"

"Philippe," she nodded. Jéhan Vignerie soon faded from her consciousness and she was glad to get to the purpose of her visit.

"Ah, I see you are still crazy about him, but all is not well. Let me guess, he is detained somewhere. Now I remember, he was a captain in the League. But rumor has it, our new King has been very generous with his former enemies. These aristocrats always stick together. So what is the problem?"

"Philippe is being held at the Bastille and unless I agree to marry some Marquis I don't know nor care about, he will be put on trial for treason which almost certainly means death. I must see him."

"Hmm, so you want me to arrange a little get-together for you and your lover, maybe an escape. You certainly have a talent for getting entangled in twisted situations," he grunted.

"I don't look to get into these situations!" she protested. "You make it sound as if it was my fault. It's the world, not me!"

"All right! No insult intended. I want to help you, but I don't see how. A cunning fox that Navarre!"

"Please don't insult His Majesty the King. He's only doing what he must for the good of the kingdom. But I must see Philippe. I need to talk to him alone, explain to him why I have to marry this Marquis before he hears it from another source. I hope he will understand. I couldn't bear it if he thought for one moment our love meant nothing to me."

"That thought might have occurred to him before in the course of all those years," Arsène observed not without a trace of sarcasm.

"Getting you inside the Bastille for a few hours is no problem if you want to talk with him, but getting him out is practically impossible. Nobody has ever escaped from that fortress and even my resources are not enough."

"The King gave me his word, he will set him free as soon as the marriage with the Marquis is concluded. If you can get me inside, before the King's return to Paris, I shall be eternally grateful to you. I shall do anything for you."

"Now, now, you don't owe me anything. Let me make some contacts. Come back tomorrow night, I'm sure I can arrange something. You are in luck, the new governor of that fortress is an old friend of yours and mine, Monsieur Perron. You know him, he was governor of the women's asylum. I'm sure he will be delighted to see you again though he may not be too enthralled with the purpose of your visit. Don't worry, I shall take care of everything."

"The world certainly is small," she noted with satisfaction. "I must return to the Louvre now. Madame Catherine will ask questions why I wasn't a prayer meeting."

"Mustn't miss those prayer meetings!" He waved a scolding finger at her. "By the way, it may be difficult, but you must try to get rid of your escorts tomorrow. The fewer people know, the better, or we all stand to lose our heads."

She nodded and gratefully pressed his hand against her cheeks. In a rare fit of emotion, he gently stroked her hair.

"I'm sorry about Mellisande," she whispered. "I wanted so much to thank her. You know she saved my life twice—once in prison, she encouraged me to seek the attention of the governor, and then by leading me to you."

A deep sigh escaped from his lips, but then he quickly pushed her out the door.

"You'd better go now. Come tomorrow after dark to the Châtelet. But take care. It's getting late."

It was the small hours of the day and the city was beginning to awaken when the litter carrying her back to the Louvre made its way through the narrow, twisted streets. She leaned her head back, tired, but content and secure. All was well with the world as long as Arsène was there to look after her. The thought of the feared ruler of the underworld worrying about her getting enough sleep brought an amused, affectionate smile to her face. He hadn't changed one bit. As always, he looked out for every practical, minute detail concerning her welfare.

But sleep was the thing that was farthest from her mind on that day. The prospect of seeing Philippe so elated her she became almost careless with exuberance.

A feverish excitement pervaded all her activities. She cared little that her lady-in-waiting might suspect something unusual when she was asked three times to draw a bath and she spent hours smoothing voluptuous fragrances all over her body. In the end, a cloud of clashing perfumes wafted about her, so she had to take yet another bath to wash off the aroma.

Several hours were spent combing her hair, trying out different hairstyles, and changing in and out of various robes. She finally decided on a charcoal gray riding costume that would not attract too much attention. The wool fabric was a bit warm for the time of the year, but one of the first lessons she had learned was that high fashion and comfort rarely went together. She refused, however, to don the constricting corsets the ladies strap around their waists and hips like pieces of armor that inflict merciless pressure on the vital organs.

The same went for the prevailing fashion in footwear. For someone used to moving about barefoot or in light sandals, the long-toed, narrow leather shoes in the Italian style caused excruciating pain. Fortunately, the skirts were long enough to drape over her feet allowing her to go either barefoot or to wear sandals. She certainly did not want Philippe to feel he was holding a stilted marionette in his arms.

Despite all this activity, it seemed the day would never end. When at long last the hour for evening prayers arrived, she was the first to enter the assembly room. Was she imagining things, or was Madame Catherine scrutinizing her more than usual? Her excuse for her absence from the prayer meeting the night before that she had not been well was not met with much credence. It had not gone unnoticed that she was out all night. Yet, Marguerite felt a singular heedlessness about what anybody might think or the consequences of her actions. Nothing could be worse than what she had already experienced in her life and nothing in this world would keep her away from Philippe except physical force or death.

She sat through the sermon and prayers, trying to avoid giving the impression of being preoccupied or impatient. Silently she prayed that evening with greater fervor than usual, imploring God to shed his grace on the man she loved and guard his life and to let them be together just once. In return for God's favor, she vowed to obey the wishes of her royal cousin King Henri IV of France.

Her prayers were indeed heard that night. In the King's absence, no evening entertainment took place at the palace, and the court ladies retired early to their private quarters. Slipping through the palace guard proved easier than she had expected, and she was soon on her way to the rendezvous at the Châtelet. From afar she recognized Arsène sitting in a simple horse-drawn cart, his head bent as if he was nodding.

Everything had gone so well, she was almost sure her luck had run out when she saw two night-watchmen approach the cart from the other direction. Her heart skipped a beat, something must have gone wrong. But she should have known better. After a brief exchange with Arsène, they continued on their rounds, calling out a few friendly warnings to him not to stay too long in this spot. Arsène thanked them and promised to move on shortly.

Instinctively, she pulled the hood of her velvet cape deeper over her face. He lifted her into the cart, mumbling something about impractical clothing, and directed the horse toward the quarter of Saint-Antoine.

"I am sorry," she said indignantly, "but I don't have anything else to wear. This was the simplest dress I could find. Do we have to scale any walls?"

"No, no! Never mind!"

"Why are you in such a foul mood? Look, if you don't want to do this, you don't have to. I can find another way of getting inside that fortress."

"Like hell, you can. The bridge will be lowered at nine o'clock and you are late. We are lucky if we make it on time."

"At the speed with which you are going, we shall be there in plenty of time if we don't break our necks first."

She looked at him from the side. The image of him saying good-bye at Saint-Cloud appeared before her. He was brooding back then the way he was now. She wondered whether he was pleased that she had come back into his life, leaning on him, practically demanding his protection. For her, it was the most natural thing in the world to do in her moment of need. Maybe it would have been more appropriate for her to ask first how he felt about all this.

"There's something else, isn't there?" she said.

He didn't answer.

"Arsène, I think you are jealous!" The wind almost blew

away her words. He whipped the horse into a wild gallop.

"I think you are jealous!" she repeated.

"Don't be ridiculous, I could be your father, almost even your grandfather."

With a jolt he brought the cart to a halt at the edge of the square of the Bastille. The infamous towers stretched ominously a hundred feet into the night sky, a formidable sight, without grace or beauty. Just then, the bridge was slowly lowering over the moat, said to be over eighty feet wide. It was easy to see why the fortress was considered to be impregnable.

"What is it then?" she insisted. She had to raise her voice above the awesome clanking of the unrolling chains. He still did not answer. She moved closer to him pleading: "I have been waiting for this reunion so long, and now all I have is this one night. Please, don't spoil it for me Arsène. You are my friend and I love you, but it's not the same kind of love I feel for Philippe."

The drawbridge hit the ground in a thunderous crescendo.

"Please forgive me," he finally said. "I have been acting like a fool. You're right, I was jealous; the thought of an aristocrat putting his hands on you drove me mad somehow. This is silly, of course, since you are a noblewoman yourself."

After some consideration, he added, stammering, the words did not come easily: "I don't want you to misunderstand me. It's not what you might think. I know I'm too old for you, but I never had a daughter or a son for that matter, and I didn't know what I was missing until you came into my life."

Before he had finished his confession, she flung her arms around his neck and covered his face with vehement kisses.

"There, go now! The bridge will only stay down for fifteen minutes, time enough to cross the moat. I shall wait here for your return."

He jumped off the cart, lifted her effortlessly, and set her down on the ground. For a moment, she hesitated, but he breathed a furtive kiss on her forehead and with a "God bless you, my child!" prodded her to go.

"You must cross the moat alone. Monsieur Perron will be on the other side. Go now and don't look back!"

She did not look back, secure in the knowledge that Arsène was watching over her. Why then the wild palpitations of her heart? Was it the anticipation of seeing Philippe or fear of being locked in this formidable prison? Deep inside a voice reminded her that she was defying the King's specific orders, making herself an accessory to treason. Hush! She did not come with a plan for the prisoner's escape or to help him elude royal justice. All she wanted was see him, touch him, assure him of her love. If fate conspired to separate them forever, they will have at least this one night to remember.

When she reached the middle of the bridge, she staggered briefly, the exertion of the steep climb made her struggle to keep her balance. Annoyed, she vowed not to let herself be restricted by the ridiculous fashion, and gathering up her skirt, she resolutely marched forward through the gate.

She was still trying to accustom her eyes to the tenebrous surrounding of the courtyard, when the sound of the drawbridge reeling back conjured up the memory of another time and another prison, another gate slamming shut behind her. The same hopeless despair gripped her now. She reminded herself, the circumstances were different then, this time she was only a visitor. In a few hours, she would be back on the other side and freedom.

Only for Philippe, there was no escape. What anguish he must suffer, entombed within these massive, sweating stone walls, accused of being a traitor to the crown!

"Welcome Madame to the royal fortress of Saint Antoine!"

Monsieur Perron, ever the kind-hearted, perfect gentleman, leaned over and lightly touched his lips to her hand.

"Please come this way, Your Ladyship."

She followed the governor through long, dim corridors, a single torch, carried by a guard, lit the way. If Perron recognized her, he gave no sign. She felt a strong impulse to thank him for what he had done for her in the past, but then abided by social etiquette. She observed him from the corner of her eyes, curious why he should put his life in danger by making himself an accessory in this tryst.

Only later did she learn about the long friendship between the bourgeois bureaucrat and the king of the underworld, going back more than two decades, to the time of the great massacre.

After what seemed endless peregrinations through vaulted corridors, lined with rows of unoccupied prison cells, they descended a spiral staircase into a cavernous underground crypt. The governor asked her to wait in the hallway while he assisted the guard in prying open a heavy iron crate.

Cold sweat moistened the palms of her hands; she hardly dared to breathe. Somewhere far off, she heard the governor announce: "Her Ladyship, the Countess de Montauban wishes to see His Lordship the Count de Treffort-Salignac."

She did not hear the answer if an answer was given. Clanking of chains and heavy thumping steps coming closer drowned out the voices.

A bizarre, spectral figure emerged from the darkness—hands and feet shackled in irons, wild growth of hair and beard glowed in the torchlight. He squinted like a hermit emerging into the light after being sequestered in a sunless cavern. The figure bore little resemblance to the image she had carried in her heart, and yet she knew instinctively it was Philippe.

She pushed the hood of her cape back and moved quickly

toward him, restraining herself from physical contact, not out of repulsion, but because she was uncertain of his reaction.

"Philippe!" she called out softly. "It's me, Sandrine."

A light flared in his eyes. He stretched out his arms. "Sandrine? Sandrine?" The chains were holding him back.

She turned a tacit glance toward the governor. He understood immediately and ordered the chains removed.

Time and space vanished as she sank into Philippe's arms. Without a word, they held each other embraced, listening only to the quickening beat of their hearts.

"Madame!" The voice of Monsieur Perron brought them back to reality. "If Madame would like to have a private conference with His Lordship . . ."

"Why wasn't I informed of Her Ladyship's visit in advance?" Philippe demanded to know with an out-of-place imperious tone. "How can I be expected to receive the Countess in this condition?"

"My Lord," Marguerite quickly stepped in, "it is only due to Monsieur Perron's kindness that I am here. This good man is risking his position and the wrath of His Majesty the King. I think he deserves our most profound gratitude."

The governor led them to his private apartment where he bade her wait in a sitting room while His Lordship was being groomed in another room for the occasion. He apologized for not being able to offer refreshments, but the servants had retired, and he, being a bachelor, was not very adept at preparing food. Marguerite seized his hand and pressed it fervently to her cheek assuring him that he had already done more than she could ever repay him.

Almost an hour passed. At long last, Philippe appeared alone, beaming a pearly smile. He had undergone a remarkable transformation, hair and beard had been neatly trimmed. He had a bath. The musty prison smell that had clung to him before was gone. He was comfortably dressed in a fresh white silk shirt with an open collar and widely slashed sleeves and the dust had been brushed from his black velvet breeches.

Although she thought him even more handsome than she remembered, he appeared drawn and gaunt. The corners of his mouth were etched with fine lines of bitterness.

Was she the cause of this? A mad desire seized her to make everything good, to erase the sorrow engraved in his beloved features. They clung together like two souls drowning in an ocean of despair. Something told her that he already knew this reunion was to be of only brief duration.

Almost roughly, as if he remembered something, he pushed her away. Holding her at arm's length, he ordered her to sit down. Silently he probed her face as if he wanted to assure himself that she was the woman he had longed for all these years. It was easy to see, she had blossomed into a self-assured woman of the world. No doubt she was the woman of his dreams, only she was real flesh and blood, not a figment as he had at times come to believe.

A frown clouded his face. But was she still his and his alone? Her circumstances certainly had changed. He recognized the fine fabric and craftsmanship of her attire. Then there was the title by which she was introduced. Was this all to mock him?

"Is something the matter Philippe?" she asked.

"I was just thinking how much you have changed, and yet you are Sandrine."

Then he rose abruptly. Bitterness rang in his voice: "Countess! I always knew Madame had what it takes to make it in the world, but was it necessary to marry some count."

Before she had time to grasp the meaning of his words, he fell on his knees and fervently clutched her hands: "Why didn't you wait for me to make you a countess?"

Several seconds passed before she was able to answer so affronted was she by his accusation.

"You mean to say you believe I slept my way into noble society!" Her voice was shrill and jarring.

"What other explanation can there be?— the title, your clothes, your whole bearing, very much true to form."

"It is true to form, but if you have such little trust in me, maybe it was all a mistake and we don't have anything in common anymore."

She felt the whole world collapsing. If Philippe did not trust her, then all had been for naught. She turned away from him, fighting to hold back the tears.

"Please, if there is another explanation, you must tell me," he pleaded.

"I was about to, but you don't give me a chance. You make it sound as if you were the only one who suffered in all those years. At least you had a roof over your head and always plenty to eat. Don't think it was easy for me to be without you. There has not been one night when I was not lying awake longing to be with you. But I had to find out who I was—for you and our son. I know the change in my circumstances is almost miraculous. I fought for it long and hard, but I did it myself. If you only had let me tell my story instead of making assumptions!"

She straightened herself and tilted her head back with pride: "The title is mine, it is my birthright and so is the wealth. I don't mean to brag but had you asked, you would have found out that I am not only a countess but also a princess of France and cousin of the King."

There was something irresistible in his expression, especially that contrite boyish look he showed now. She ruffled his hair and added playfully: "If you want to reach me, my address is the Louvre."

"You are still not happy about it?" she asked when she saw him furrow his brow. He fell on his knees before her and buried his head in her lap.

"Please forgive me for being so selfish. I am very happy for you. I always knew you were no ordinary peasant, but now I almost wish you were. What I want you to understand is that it doesn't matter to me who you are, who your parents are, and whether you are a cousin of the King or not. All I know is that I love you, and I feel we have been cheated out of five years of our life together."

"Do you think we could have stayed together, or that we could have been married? Not as long as the Duke d'Evreux is alive!" The vehemence with which she spewed forth the last words startled him and bid her hush lest they were overheard.

"Are you afraid he might hear us?" she asked with belligerent derision. "Still the good, obedient son, aren't you? He is far away in his dungeon."

"Sandrine, please, I know what he did to you and I am not asking you to forgive him. He is very ill and may die in this prison, but he will not accept mercy from the King whom he still regards as a heretic and a usurper. No, I am no longer the obedient son, as you put it. I broke with him and the League long ago. When I learned that he was responsible for your disappearance, I simply did not know what to do."

"Then why are you in here, in this hole, and not at the side of your King? Every day I see former Leaguers going in and out of the Louvre making their peace with His Majesty."

"This is very difficult to explain and I don't think we should spend what little time we have together in mutual recriminations. You will understand some day. At any rate, the Duke has refused to answer my questions about the motive for his cruelty against you, only to say that he thought you would bring bad luck to his domain, which is, of course, total nonsense. This much I know for certain, he had no knowledge of our love, which makes his action all the more puzzling."

"You are not alone in your confusion. For years, the question of what could make a human being act so inhumanly has plagued me. What I have learned about the fate of my parents in recent months causes me to believe that somehow the Duke's behavior, not only toward me but his fanatical hatred of Huguenots has something to do with the massacre on Saint Bartholomew's Day."

He looked at her astounded. "Do you mean to say, your parents were victims of that terrible massacre of twenty-two years ago?"

"Yes, they were Huguenot nobles, guests at the blood wedding of Henri de Navarre and Marguerite de Valois. So was the Duke d'Evreux, only, I have it from good authority, he was among the butchers."

The outcry of anguish that rose from the bottom of his tormented soul tore her heart. She gathered him toward her and cradled his head in the softness of her bosom.

"But all this has nothing to do with our love. Nothing in this world can ever destroy our love," she reassured him pressing her lips against the top of his curly head.

"You were there too," he surmised.

"Yes. I was only a few months old and through the courage of a good woman, I survived and was brought to Bonneval, as you know. But we have so much else to talk about. For the moment, at least, let us try to forget this terrible event. His Majesty does not wish to take revenge. The actual murderers can never be determined or be brought to justice."

"I detect great fondness in your way of speaking . . . of the

King."

"You are right, I am extremely fond of him as one should be of the one who holds royal authority."

"It seems more than just the affection of a loyal subject. Is it the person of this King you hold dear?"

"If you want to know whether I find his person charming and appealing, you are right again. He is everything a king should be: generous, kind, benevolent. I also owe him my deepest gratitude. Even amid the many troubles he is facing in the endless struggle for his throne, he considered my claim to being the last descendant of the House of Montauban. Once the claim was verified and I was formally instated, I was most graciously received at the royal court. Oh, Philippe, I only wish you had made your peace with him when there was still time!"

"Psst, we agreed not to talk about this now," he reprimanded her gently. "Everything you have told me sounds so wonderful, miraculous, almost like a dream. You must be very happy."

"Truth to tell, I loathe life at the court—I feel as if locked in a gilded cage. Every move is circumscribed by rules of etiquette, most of them new and senseless to me. I cannot tell you how often I have been told my behavior violates court etiquette."

"I can picture you exactly," he called out as they both burst into laughter. "Tempestuous Sandrine bursting unannounced into the royal apartment!"

"How do you know?"

"Oh, I know you very well, my love. Did I guess right?"

"Well, it happened a few times. Once I was almost stabbed by an indignant look from Madame de Montpensier when I interrupted her game of checkers with His Majesty."

"Madame de Montpensier at the court of Henri de Navarre?" he exclaimed.

"Oh, yes she is quite at home at the Louvre these days. Once the man she had professed to loathe with undying hatred had entered Paris, she either fell for his charm or she decided to go with the times. The story is being told that she swooned when Navarre embraced her. Her only regret, she assured His Majesty, was that Mayenne, her brother, wasn't present to open the gates to the city for him in person."

This story was too much for Philippe, he was almost helpless with laughter.

"But listen to this. This is funny," she continued. "The entire day revolves around the levée and the couchée of the King. Everybody is present in the royal chamber when he rises in the morning and then again when he goes to bed at night. The whole thing is so hypocritical because everybody knows that he does not spend a minute longer than necessary in that bed. As soon as everybody is gone, he slips out and flees into the arms of his mistress. In the morning, you can sometimes see him racing to reach the ceremonial sleeping quarters before the courtiers arrive. It seems few people at the French court sleep in their own beds at night."

Abruptly, their laughter ceased, vanished. Facing each other, their hands intertwined, their eyes became transfixed, a probing seriousness held them suspended.

"There never has been another," she whispered, lowering her head to avoid his inquisitive glance. Slowly he drew her toward him. Their lips touched, gently at first, then with rising, desperate passion, their mouths opened, pressed against each other, dissolving into each other.

Alarmed by footsteps outside, he relaxed his hold on her.

"You needn't worry," she assured him. "M. Perron is very discrete, he won't disturb us."

"Let me close the latch on the door, just to be sure."

When he returned to her, they flew into each other's arms.

They clung to each other as if they never wanted to let go. He released her hair from the netting and buried his face in the mass of golden curls sensuously draping them about her shoulders. Without haste, he peeled away layer upon layer of her dress, leaving only a simple, white chemise on her trembling body— the image of a young girl in a white smock standing motionless on an oxcart on an icy January day flashed before him.

Feeling a bit awkward, she stood motionless watching him smoothed the garment over the back of a chair. He pulled her toward him with deliberate slowness, she clutched her legs around his waist, and as one they moved toward the lounge chair in the middle of the room.

A dimming light shone from two candelabra as the candles slowly consumed themselves, casting the lovers' lengthening shadow against the wall. Cradled in a swaying rhythm of ecstasy, the wave of passion transported them to the heights of fulfillment. Again and again, like a desiccated riverbed lap up the water from a longed-for downpour, Marguerite opened to being inundated by his love.

Not until the first chirping of birds did they nod off into a blissfully exhausted slumber. It seemed only a short while later that the early morning chill roused them from their sleep. Philippe assisted her in getting back into her dress, meticulously fastening the countless hooks. Without a mirror, she had considerable difficulty gathering all her hair inside the net. Impatient with the failure of her effort, she simply gave up. No time for such vanities now.

The first rays of the sun beckoned them to approach the narrow window and leaning against each other in silence, they were overcome with almost devout awe by the magnificent dawn that bathed the city below in a soft pink glow. There was still so much to say, but neither knew where to begin.

"Will you come again?" he whispered.

She shook her head, her hand firmly pressing his.

"You haven't told me everything," he probed.

"It would be too much of a risk for too many people. I don't know when we shall see each other again. Henri knows of our love, but he has strictly forbidden me to see you."

"Why would your generous, affable king be so cruel?"

"Reason of state or something like that."

Philippe was not brushed off that easily. He turned her toward him, full face, held her chin in his hand and forced her to look into his eyes.

"Why are you evading my question?"

"Please Philippe!" she squirmed to free herself.

"No matter what happens, you must never doubt my love for you. The King has promised to release you and the Duke from this prison if I marry the Marquis de Launay."

He stared at her in disbelief. Only slowly did the meaning of her words sink into his consciousness.

"You mean he wants you to become the wife of the Viking? That is preposterous. What kind of wonderful monarch is this who demands such a sacrifice from his kin? And you agree to this plot?"

"I don't see what choice I have, it's your life or marriage to the Marquis. Either way, I lose," she whispered. "You know yourself that marriage has little to do with love among the powerful of this world. Marriage is a way of forging alliances, in this case, to appease a wealthy, rebellious Huguenot subject."

She wasn't sure whether he was still listening. While she was speaking, he had assumed his habitual pacing in brooding silence.

"Please Philippe, I cannot bear it when you are angry. The thought of being another man's wife has mortified me since the day the King put this terrible choice before me. But how could I possibly decline?"

At last, he seemed mollified. He locked his arms around her waist from behind and cradled her.

"Please forgive me. It was unjust of me to blame you. But this changes the whole situation. My God, why can't I do something? Everything within me revolts against accepting such a sacrifice from you. Is there no other way?"

"I'm afraid he is adamant. He needs the Marquis and his money. You know the royal coffers are empty. No matter what happens, no matter how helpless we are in forging our destiny, promise me that we shall never permit a misunderstanding to come between us or life would be truly unbearable. I came back to you in the state I was when we parted," she continued. "No other man has touched me. And you must promise never to doubt that I am yours alone forever, even if it becomes my duty to submit to an unwanted husband."

"My love, you are so strong and brave. I feel like a fool. Of course, our love will endure forever, no matter what adversities may be visited upon us."

Suddenly she pulled away and slapped her forehead with the palm of her hand.

"But wait a moment, how could I forget!" she exclaimed.

"The wedding may not take place so soon which means you will not be released so soon. There is still the matter of Etienne and the annulment which has not yet gone through and the whole thing may bring more trouble."

She related to him in as few words as possible her visit to Bonneval, Berthe's funeral, the encounter with Etienne and his threat of revenge, witnessed by the entire village. She knew it was a mistake to go to the cemetery instead of leaving quietly after Berthe had died. Some foolish pride made her want to impress the miserable churls with her wealth and status, show them her contempt without considering that the villagers still held a trump card against her. Only when she was confronted with Etienne's naked hatred, did she realize how rash she had been. Now she was afraid nothing will stop him from denouncing her to the world as the witch who escaped from the stake at Chartres.

She buried her face in her hands. The situation seemed so hopeless.

"There must be a way out," he declared. "The situation has changed, you have friends in high places, even the King of France is well disposed toward you."

"The King of France has not yet been recognized by the Papal See nor by a large number of his subjects. His position is still too vulnerable and he cannot, and will not, risk his kingdom to protect a convicted witch. Besides this isn't all. There are also the monks of Saint-Victor . . ."

"Yes, I have heard about that," he interrupted her almost impatiently, unable to disguise his irritation at yet another complicating factor that had to do with the Church. "Don't think for one moment that I believe you capable of murder, but these fanatics . . ."

"But I did kill him, Philippe," she stated simply. "Not intentionally. It was in self-defense. He attempted to rape me. But who would ever believe that?"

Philippe resumed his pacing. His mind was working feverishly.

"You could leave the country, go to one of the Protestant German princedoms, out of reach of the power of the Catholic Church."

"Run away and assure your death? You are my life. How can you expect me ever to forfeit your life just to save mine? I would rather we end our lives right here and now, while we are together."

The ominous tone in her voice arrested his step. He stared at her with a blank gaze. She stood fully erect, her head tilted back, her eyes sparkled bold defiance.

He almost crushed her bones, so violently did he pull her into his arms.

"You must never even think it," he murmured. "We shall make it through, do you hear? For the sake of our son, we must and we shall!"

"I don't know. At every turn, there are perils and more perils. Our son may be better off never knowing his parents!"

"There is an old saying, no battle is over until the firing power of one side runs out. You still have much ammunition left."

"We both still have friends who wish us well. Maybe, your friend who helped you get in here could help us to get away together?" he said after some consideration. "Gaspard and Mathieu are still at the Hotel d'Evreux, they can get us out of the city. Once we are in the countryside, we can reach the estate of Louise de Montreuil and from there, the Netherlands or England or the Empire."

"I am sure all these people could be relied upon," she replied. "But could we live as fugitives for the rest of our lives? We would forever incur the wrath of the King and could never return to France. When I took possession of my ancestral estates, I swore an oath of fealty to him. I feel I have a duty not only to him but also to my family, an oath that I cannot betray. No, the only way open is to level with Henri and let the events take their course. The mood among the people has changed, and even if I have to stand trial again, the truth may yet win out. It's a chance I have to take."

"It is ironic, is it not," said added wistfully, "that I should lecture you about duty and family loyalty, the sacredness of an oath."

"And what happens then, suppose you are acquitted?" he asked, but he already knew the answer.

"There is no other way—I must marry the Marquis de Launay. Henri won't relent."

He smiled a painful smile and touched his lips gently to hers. "If I ever wondered why I had to love you of all women in the world, here is the answer. Because never has there been a woman more beautiful, more courageous, and upright than my Sandrine."

"You are an incorrigible romantic! By the way, my name is Marguerite now, I was named for our friend, Marguerite de Navarre." She laughed, her mood returned almost to her earlier exuberance. She covered his face with kisses silencing his protests that he liked Sandrine and for him, she would always be Sandrine.

CHAPTER 7

Monsieur Perron sent word requesting the pleasure of their company at breakfast. The invitation was gladly accepted since both, His Lordship and Her Ladyship, were ravenously hungry. The table conversation at first turned on polite subjects such as the sweltering heat that had gripped the city so suddenly after a pleasant early summer.

"Not since the year of the big siege have we had such a hot summer," Monsieur Perron remarked. "I have always been convinced that great disasters occur at times of rising temperatures. Let us hope this is not an omen."

His observations were interrupted by a knock on the door. The guard showed in Arsène Rigoud who entered with obvious reluctance.

"Oh, I took the liberty of inviting our friend Rigoud," the governor said. "He deserves a good meal after holding watch all night."

Perron took Philippe briefly to the side.

"I extended an invitation to His Lordship, the Duke, to join us, but he declined to leave his cell."

Philippe nodded saying something that this was to be expected. His attention was drawn to the imposing figure just being greeted by the Countess with a warm embrace.

Marguerite, her face still aglow with passion, presented Arsène to Philippe, and the two men shook hands cordially, but with cool reserve on both sides. Especially Arsène seemed unable to suppress a certain discomfort, be it his aversion toward aristocrats, or his knowledge that this aristocrat had just spent the night with the woman he held most dear in this world.

"Only the growling of my stomach persuaded me to enter this forbidding place," he said with an uneasy glance around. "I have tried to stay out of prisons all my life, and so far I have succeeded."

The guests took their seats around the governor's table and soon gorged themselves on freshly baked white bread, topped with butter and blackberry jam, and washed it down with creamy, warm milk. Monsieur Perron remarked that he had spent most of his life in one prison or other as a civil servant, but the most vexing assignment he has ever had was that at the Asylum, the women's prison.

He turned to Marguerite: "Allow me, Madame, to relate to the gentlemen the circumstances under which I had the pleasure of making Madame's acquaintance."

He remembered after all. She nodded her agreement.

Mainly addressing himself to Philippe for some reason, he spoke of Sandrine's attempt to intercede with Monsieur

Hachette on behalf of her gypsy friends who had been arrested for a politically sensitive theatrical presentation, but that louse of a police prosecutor sent her to the Asylum for resisting his advances.

"Of course, I saw her only briefly when she came to the prison. She was one of hundreds of hapless souls who end up in this terrible place every day. A governor cannot get to know all inmates personally," he said apologetically. "But Madame did not resign herself to being entombed, buried alive—these were her exact words. She moved heaven and earth to gain the attention of the governor, which she finally did. Since then I have often wondered what had become of this young woman who had displayed such indomitable will to live, especially since so many did not make it through the siege. I cannot begin to tell you how gratified I am to see Madame has made good in the world."

"Monsieur permitted me to leave the prison," she picked up the narrative. "He expressed the hope that our paths would never cross again, but somehow I knew we would meet again if only to allow me to thank him for his kindness."

"An injustice had been done to an innocent woman by a ruthless bureaucrat who exploited his position of police prosecutor. I have known Monsieur Hachette for a long time. There is no love between us."

"And where is this Monsieur Hachette now?" Philippe asked his curiosity aroused.

"He was removed from office for misconduct and was imprisoned at La Concièrgerie. Later at some point during the siege, he was, at first rather inexplicably, reinstated in his position as police prosecutor. As became known soon thereafter, his claim that he could identify the witch of Chartres, a woman who then was sought all over the city for the murder of a monk, endeared him to the Archbishop of Paris. Curiously, or not so curiously considering how many enemies he had, he vanished without a trace while he was on the witch hunt."

Nobody spoke when the governor had ended his tale. Philippe wondered about the red glow in Sandrine's face and the serious glance she exchanged with Arsène from behind the rim of her cup. There was more to this story than Monsieur Perron knew. Against his will and better judgment, it drove him mad that she should be on such intimate footing with this peculiar, quiet man.

"Well, we won't have to worry about this slime Hachette anymore. I'm sure he bit the dust back then," Arsène assured the company.

"Madame, if I remember correctly," Perron turned again to Marguerite. "It was your concern for the welfare of your child that made you so anxious to leave the prison at the time. How did you find the child?"

"I found him well, thank you, with my friends from the itinerant theatrical company, but later when food became scarce during the siege, I was unable to provide for him adequately and he became very well ill. Fortunately, a kind noblewoman adopted him and has raised him in her household. I am told he is a very fine boy."

Philippe's probing eyes made her writhe in her seat. She rose and thanked the governor for his hospitality and all he had done.

"Please, don't thank me," he fended off her profuse assurances of gratitude. "Thanks goes to our friend Arsène Rigoud. No man or woman ever had a better friend, as Madame well knows."

"Don't get carried away, Joseph," Arsène growled. "Well, time to get back into town. Madame, I don't think it would be advisable for Your Ladyship to be seen riding in an open cart with me in broad daylight. Please, allow me to secure a less circumspect conveyance. I shall return shortly."

"If you talk like that to me, I shall box you in the ear," Marguerite hissed menacingly.

"Your Ladyship will have to get used to it," he grunted and nodding his head in the direction of the gentlemen, he left.

"I don't know what has come over him?"

Monsieur Perron hurried after him.

"Who is this man?" Philippe demanded to know sharply when they were alone.

"I already told you, he is Arsène Rigoud, the most powerful man in the Paris underworld. He is a thief, an extortionist, a pimp, and who knows what else. He is also one of the most decent human beings on this earth and the best friend I have," she declared defiantly, sensing his dislike of the thug.

"Some really fine friends you have there, gypsies, professional criminals!"

"Philippe! Stop it!" she shouted. "These are the people who have been kind to me when I was in greatest need, without them I would be dead. If it hadn't been for Arsène, I most assuredly would not have survived. I would have died of hunger or been burnt at the stake. How can you disdain them, just for being outcasts of society? I have been an outcast all my life, and now that I have found a place in society, I shall not forget those who stood by me in my time of need."

"You are right. I was stupid to be so overcome with jealousy. The intimacy that exists so obviously between you and this Arsène drove me mad. It was silly of me to resent the fact that you shared a bond of common experiences with somebody else. Something seemed to eat at him too."

"Oh, men!" she exclaimed. "Why do they always have to complicate things?"

She moved closer toward him and tried to put her arms around his waist, but his body stiffened and did not respond to her touch.

"He is not my lover if that's what you are thinking," she said calmly. "I already told you there was none. But he is, next to you, the man I love most in this world. I hope the time will never come when I should be forced to choose between the two of you."

"You must trust me, Philippe," she pleaded when he did not answer. "No matter what happens, I am always yours."

Monsieur Perron returned and assured them that Arsène was all right, just one of those black moods he is prone to from time to time.

"You seem to know him well, Monsieur" Marguerite observed.

"Arsène? Oh yes, we have been friends for twenty-two years. Without that man, I would not be here with you."

"He saved your life twenty-two years ago?" The specific number of years peaked her interest. Everything seemed to go back to that terrible year 1572.

"Yes, twenty-two years ago on the 24th of August." He looked at her seriously, pleased to find that she immediately grasped the meaning of that date. "He saved me from certain death at the hands of the Guise butchers. My wife and daughters were not so lucky if one can call it luck to have survived only to be cursed with the memory of the most abject bestiality committed in the name of God."

"Would you like to tell us what happened?" Marguerite prodded softly.

"For the first time, I feel free to tell the story, but you must also remember mine is just one of many tragedies that occurred on that day. I am not a Huguenot, but then no proof was needed, suspicion alone was enough for anybody to fall victim to the fanaticism of the mob."

Monsieur Perron, a loyal servant of the King and devout Catholic but with a profound humanitarian spirit, had harbored several members of the Reformed Religion in his house on that fateful Sunday morning of the 24th of August 1572. Somebody must have denounced them. When he and his wife and two children, daughters of ten and twelve, returned from Mass, they found the bodies of their guests impaled outside the house. They recognized the mercenaries of the Duke de Guise, who, still drunk from the orgy of blood, pushed them inside the house. They tied Monsieur Perron to the doorpost and before his eyes committed the most bestial outrages against his screaming wife and daughters before stabbing them to death.

The murderers refused to listen to his pleas to kill him on the spot likewise. With his hands and feet shackled, they dragged him through the streets. They came to a halt in a square, where they suspended him on a pole, his arms stretched out as if he was to be crucified. The butchers pierced his arms and legs with their blades, screaming with delight, the way young men "sacrifice" farm animals during the carnival season. They were about to disembowel him—he had closed his eyes, half-unconscious he whispered his last prayers—when he heard the firing of several shots and the bloodthirsty screams of his tormentors turning into ghastly howls of agony. Then there was silence.

When he finally dared to open his eyes, he saw his attackers on the pavement in a pool of blood. He became vaguely aware of the presence of a huge man with the broadest shoulders he had ever seen, who bent over him, cutting him loose. Then he felt lifted and carried from the scene of the carnage.

Arsène Rigoud nursed Monsieur Perron back to a life he did not want anymore. Since then a close, mutually beneficial, though unsentimental, friendship existed between the two men. Monsieur Perron would never turn down a request from the underworld king, but in this case, he was especially obliging.

Arsène had told the young woman's story in his terse, matter-of-fact way and Perron immediately felt a special bond with her. Like himself, she was a victim and a survivor of that terrible outrage. She may not carry the weight of remembrance of the bloodbath that stooped his shoulders and bent his back with pain, but her life too was irrevocably linked with this ghastly event.

When Monsieur Perron had ended his story, Marguerite clutched Philippe's hand. She saw how mortified he was to learn about the crimes of the Guise faction. He too was a victim, an unwitting pawn in the brutal struggle for power between ruthless men. Even though he now recognized that the League was a sham, he was still, by the twist of a cruel fate, inextricably tied to an unrepentant old man who would sooner sacrifice the life of his only son than recant and make peace with his King.

At that moment word came that Madame's carriage had arrived. Monsieur Perron excused himself, discreetly providing time for the lovers to bid farewell.

"If we see each other again, it will be elsewhere, not here," she said in parting. "My dear cousin, Madame Catherine, is not likely to let me out of her sight again."

For a brief moment, she leaned her head against his chest.

"We must never lose hope, Philippe. No matter what happens, we shall always have our love."

When he did not respond, she burst forth, "Good God, Philippe, as if the situation was not difficult enough! Please don't you make it more so!"

He enclosed her in his arms and rocked her gently back and forth.

"If there only was something I could do. This helplessness is simply maddening. Why can't the world leave us alone? All I want in this life is to love you. I have long ceased to care about this war or politics. If I had been free to act, I would have joined Navarre five years ago when I realized that the cause of the League was being perverted by knaves who cared nothing for the Church or for France, and who tore the country apart for personal gain and power."

"You must understand that the only thing I was able to do was to withdraw from active service in the League army. Then when I found you gone, my life became aimless and empty. When Louise told me how the child had come to her, and there was no doubt that the child was ours, I came to Paris in hopes of finding you here. I resisted pressure from my father and Robert, that fool, to rejoin Mayenne's forces. The news of Henri's coronation at Chartres threw the die-hard Leaguers into a panic. My father arrived in Paris with a troop of armed guards. Despite his ill health, he prepared a last-ditch defense of the city at the Hotel d'Evreux. I was there when the skirmish ended and was arrested with the Duke. Not knowing whether you were alive, I didn't care much what was happening to me. So I hardly protested when they took us both away. Besides how can I permit an ailing old man, my flesh and blood, to be incarcerated alone in this fearsome prison?"

He took her hands into his and continued: "I wanted you to know my motive or lack thereof. It wasn't fanaticism, recalcitrance, or anything of the sort, that kept me from taking the oath of fealty to Henri IV, but the chains that still tie me to my family, and maybe even a secret wish to die. That was when I did not know whether you were dead or alive, whether we would ever see each other again. Now I have again reason to live, for you if not with you."

"First you have to get out of here alive. Patience, we must be very patient, my love. Everything will turn out well in the end."

Her voice trembled as she tried to speak with greater conviction than she felt in her heart. Their lips met in a long, last kiss just as Monsieur Perron entered to announce everything was ready for Madame's departure.

Philippe called her back one more time.

"If you please, I would like you to do me one favor. Call for Gaspard and Mathieu at the Hotel d'Evreux, I wish them to act as your bodyguards. I shall rest easier knowing you under their watchful eyes."

She nodded. Then, in a sudden hurry, she tore herself away, and without looking back, she was gone.

CHAPTER
8

Marguerite's moods oscillated between utter dejection and sublime elation. For hours she lay awake at night in her luxurious mahogany bed at the Louvre, netting the satin pillow with bitter tears. All the glamour of the court, her wealth and her status did nothing to brighten what she saw as a hopelessly bleak future.

The thought of Philippe pained and warmed her heart. Her tormented soul found at least temporary consolation in the memory of the night they had together at the Bastille, a night of renewal and fulfillment of their love. She now knew the bond of love that was first spun between them in the barnyard at the inn of Bonneval could never be severed.

She paid little attention to Madame Catherine's reprimands

for having everybody worried, as she put it when she simply disappeared without a trace. Thank God, she had the good sense of returning before the arrival of His Majesty, the King.

Poor little princess, Marguerite thought, how can you be so naive? Didn't she know there was no punishment, no matter how severe anyone, including the King, could mete out that had not already been inflicted on her countless times? No punishment could darken the memory of her night of love.

Every night she unburdened her thoughts and feelings in long letters to her beloved which were delivered to the Bastille by the faithful Mathieu, who in turn brought Philippe's reply to her. Monsieur Perron acceded to Philippe's request for ink and paper so that a constant, flow of secret communication ensued between the lovers.

Marguerite learned that Philippe was no longer kept in chains in the underground dungeon. Monsieur Perron had the prisoner moved to a cell in one of the towers from where he had a bird's eye view of the city and the Louvre. The kind governor provided him with plenty of reading material to occupy his mind.

Philippe's confession that he had carried the book of Marguerite de Navarre with him everywhere pleased her enormously—why, he practically knew every line by heart, so many times had he read the stories. He was afraid the edition she gave him was worn and he would hate to have to replace it. Evenings, he usually spent in the company of Monsieur Perron who was happy to have found a worthy chess partner. Many of their games lasted for days before one was declared checkmate.

The news she had to relay to him concerning events at the court and outside was hardly suited to cheering to his heart. She tried to temper the tone of her report, but was often unable to conceal her trepidations. This was especially true since Mathieu had alerted her to his father's presence in Paris.

Etienne seemed to have reached the ear of several churchmen, who were still unreconciled to Henri de Navarre's assumption of the French crown and was providing them with new fuel for their diatribes against the King: the heretic was harboring a witch in his palace.

Henri did not dare proceed with the wedding plans without an answer from the Pope to the petition requesting the annulment of the marriage of Sandrine Legrand and Etienne Grosjean of Bonneval. Though neither the intended bride nor the groom adhered to the apostolic faith, she understood that the King, who was himself anxious to be received into the good graces of Church, had to avoid at all cost the appearance of defiance of the Church's authority. The Holy Father might seize on any pretext not to grant him absolution and lift the ban of excommunication that still stood in the way of his full recognition as King of France.

As if all this were not enough—she tried hard to understand the King's predicament—Henri was placed in the position of a juggler struggling to keep several balls in the air at the same time. Besides the troubles with the Church, there was also the still recalcitrant Marquis who needed to be humored lest he tire of the deal and refuse to go along with the marriage alliance. It seemed, therefore, only natural that Henri should engage her cooperation by obliging her to entertain the Marquis. Since her intended had a virtually inexhaustible thirst for physical activity, this entertainment took mostly the form of strenuous exercise. Hours were spent riding in the countryside at top speed, playing tennis, or rowing on the river. She needed all her energy to keep up with him.

What she did not tell Philippe was that she welcomed these activities. They relieved her, at least temporarily, of the unbearable tension caused by the long wait for the Pope's reply. She also found to her surprise the Viking's company not altogether distasteful, especially since he treated her like a good sport and exhibited no amorous inclinations toward her. She soon noticed the constant presence of a young lady in his entourage who commanded much more of his attention than she did. Through a network of servants, she was pleased to learn that the young woman was the Marquis's mistress and mother of a sizeable brood. Although she was not a suitable marriage prospect, he seemed most devoted to her.

Philippe warned her not to overindulge in physical activity. He feared she might injure herself if she applied herself with too great intensity. He tried to keep his body agile through exercises, he even engaged one of his guards in a round of fencing from time to time. He still felt his muscles weakening from the lack of sufficient movement. Then he assured her he did not mean to complain, his condition at the prison had improved immeasurably since her visit.

For several days no letter came from her. Then an apology. She had been unable to write because the court had moved to Fontainebleau for the hunting season. Now she was a virtual prisoner at the Louvre. Etienne had gathered a mob of Parisian riffraff and friars, who were demonstrating outside the palace every day. The chorus of shouts demanding that the witch of Chartres be handed over was heard from morning till night. She was told of scenes of mass hysteria at the churches in the city, the pulpits rang with screams for the King's head.

One day she looked out on the mob from behind the window and to her delight recognized Arsène's towering frame in the crowd. She also spotted several of his myrmidons eyeing those who incited the mob. Although Arsène's presence gave her the sense of security it always inspired, she could not shake a vague sense of intimation of coming disaster.

Henri continued to be most gracious and well disposed toward her. She had told him the story about the trial at Chartres and how she defended herself against being raped by the monk from Saint-Victor. Henri had promised to protect her with all his power. Unfortunately, his power was not that firmly established, and he doubted that he could withstand the pressure from the mob and the Church for too long.

Guess what, she wrote more cheerfully a few days later, today the Duchess d'Evreux and the Abbess of Sainte Hélène accompanied by the Count de la Croix, in priest's frock and moving about rather well on his artificial leg, came to the Louvre and were most graciously received by His Majesty. They petitioned the King for clemency toward the Duke and the Count. Still, the King remained firm.

She heard the ladies and Robert were staying at the Hotel d'Evreux, but for the last several evenings, they had braved their way through the riotous throng in the street to follow the King's invitation to dine at the Louvre. She kept in the background, not sure whether it would be wise to make her presence known.

Robert inquired about the mob demonstrations outside and Henri informed him that somebody seems to have started a rumor that the so-called witch of Chartres was within the royal palace. From her seat at the end of the table, she could see the discomfort in Robert's face as he exchanged ominous glances with the Abbess. Then she saw the Count turn to the King.

"Well, is she?" he asked. "I beg Your Majesty's forgiveness, but is this witch in Louvre?"

"You are a man of the Church, my dear Count, how do I know you can be trusted?" the King replied.

"If I told you that I had something to do with the rescue of said lady, who I know is no witch at all, from her tormentors at

Chartres, would that convince Your Majesty?"

"I think I have good reason to believe you, dear Count. This may seem to have nothing to do with the matter at hand, but I would like to tell you of an episode that occurred several years ago and that prompts me to believe you are well disposed toward the woman they call the witch of Chartres. As I said, several years ago, during the battle of Arques, the Count de Treffort-Salignac became my prisoner of war. I liked the young man and had come to respect his military talents. So, of course, I did my best to woo him to the royal side, offered him position, wealth, everything. I sensed then that in his heart he was already convinced of the legitimacy of my claim to the French throne, and that he was ready to join forces with me had it not been for his concern for the welfare of a seriously wounded friend and his desire to return to his bedside as quickly as possible."

Henri paused for a moment to gauge the Count's response, who did not fail to show himself moved.

"Friendship and loyalty are virtues I hold in greatest esteem. I, therefore, have reason to believe that you would not wish any harm to come to such a friend. The lady in question is my dear cousin, Princess Marguerite de France, Countess de Montauban, a close friend of said Count."

Henri extended his arm in the direction where she was about to steal away from the table. All eyes turned toward her. She looked at the Abbess Catherine for help. For a brief moment, she saw a spark of recognition in her eyes.

"The lady I am thinking of had a different name, but there is a certain similarity," Robert said slowly, staring at her as if she was an apparition from another world.

During the ballet performance after the lavish multi-course dinners—entertainment at the palace went on as if nothing was happening—Marguerite found herself seated next to the

Reverend Sister Catherine who clasped her hand reassuringly.

The next day finally brought an opportunity for a private conference with the three visitors in her quarters. Giving in to the Abbess's urging, she related in as few words as possible how she had fared in the time since her disappearance from Chateau d'Evreux. She also assured them that Philippe and the Duke were well and would be released as soon as a somewhat complex situation was resolved to the King's satisfaction. Robert expressed his pleasure that she was after all one of them.

"I have to give the devil his due," he said with a deferential bow toward her. "From the beginning, Philippe insisted Madame was not an ordinary peasant girl."

She decided she had better let this expression of class presumption slide for now. Robert was a good person, but he would not understand her objections to what was to him a compliment. She thanked him for his kind offer to testify on her behalf should the mob get its will and have her put on trial.

The reunion with the Abbess was a godsend in this time of anguish. Sister Catherine told her how pained she had been when she found her gone, not knowing where to search for her. She had been all the more concerned since she knew her time had been drawing near. She had to tell her all about the child, how and where it was born. To her surprise, Catherine was unaware that her nephew was being raised by Louise de Montreuil.

They talked and talked endlessly through the night. The Duchess found no end in embracing the woman her son loved with such abandon, thanking God that they had finally been brought together. At last, she said, she understood why her son was so inconsolable when he thought he had lost her forever.

On hearing of the circumstances of the murder of the monk, both women professed outrage and swore to do everything in their power to further the cause of justice. The Abbess remarked that it was the failure of the Church to extract from its midst those bad apples who poisoned the Holy Faith that gave rise to the Reformed Religion in the first place.

You see, my dearest Philippe, Marguerite wrote, when I shall finally have to drink from the bitter cup and walk the path of thorns, I can take comfort in the certainty of not being alone, as I was in the darkest days at Chartres. The prayers of so many well-disposed people will lighten my burden.

Philippe expressed his delight to learn of her meeting with the members of his family and Robert, that old, good-natured fool.

A few days later, she told him of another visitor. Raphael Floris, the emissary of Louise de Montreuil, came with the happy tidings that their son was well and growing. However, she thought it better not to tell Philippe that the child was actually at the Hotel Montreuil in Paris. Raphael had lodged him there to keep him away from the tumult that was going on every day outside the royal residence at the Louvre. As much as she yearned to hold the boy in her arms, she feared it may confuse him if he heard the accusations that were being hurled against his mother.

Again a break of several days in the flow of letters. As the mood in the streets grew uglier, she found it increasingly difficult to put her thoughts and feelings to paper. The preachers' continued their relentless diatribes, whipping the crowd into a state hysteria as they had done during the siege. How could she describe this to Philippe without causing him more anguish?

Then a brief note. Etienne was found dead the night before in a ditch near the river, apparently the victim of a stabbing. This takes care of the annulment, she concluded without regret. However, the events were closing in on her. The pressure on the

King to hand her over to the judiciary intensified daily and the longer he waited the more he risked becoming embroiled in a struggle with the Archbishopric of Paris or even be denounced as an accessory to murder.

"Please try to understand, my dearest Philippe, for the King there can be no choice. My fate pales into insignificance next to his formidable task of healing the wounds that have inflamed the body of France for so long. Pray for me, Philippe as I do for you."

Scribbled almost illegibly on the bottom of the page: "I love you. Forever yours, Sandrine."

Then the flow of letters ceased.

CHAPTER
9

Intermittent light rain netted the parched pavements of the city. From the rooftops rose a soft white vapor and mingled with the dense, hot air. Marguerite watched the raindrops dancing on the surface of the river before dissolving in the vastness of the pool of water from the window of her prison cell at the Concièrgerie high above the river.

A placid acquiescence in whatever may lie ahead had taken hold of her. Nothing touched her now, not the oppressive late August heat, not the restless crowds crawling like ants in the streets below, not their unremitting cries of "death to the devil's handmaiden!" The fanatical hatred of the friars promised an end to starvation and disease once the heretic and the witch were excised from the city.

Although her situation could be described as neither happy nor auspicious, as matters stood, she had little cause to complain. The almost obsequious respect accorded her by her jailers and interrogators provoked her quiet scorn. The mood of the crowd was more volatile. She gauged its temperature from the incessant shouts that echoed from the square below, fragments of "heretic" and "witch" interspersed with demands for justice for the murder of the "Man of God from Bonneval."

What irony! For a fleeting moment in his drab life, this crude peasant, who had never ventured more than twenty leagues from his village, had become the hero of the rabble of Paris. Who his murderers were, how well-intentioned their motive— she had a pretty good hunch where the order had come from and who carried it out—this deed, though freeing her from an odious bond, had complicated her situation immeasurably.

Most painfully did she feel the effect Etienne's murder had on Mathieu. Never had she expected him to reproach her with such bitterness.

"Wherever you go, you sow death and destruction, Sandrine! You bring nothing but sorrow and pain especially to those who love you most!" he said. She did not know how to reply for in her heart she felt the awful truth of his accusation.

Was it any wonder that Mathieu should feel the way he did? Had she not been insensitive toward his feelings all along? Even when they were children, she had always taken his devotion to her for granted. She had been his refuge and his solace. She had cradled him when he came to her, fleeing from his father's violent rages. There hardly was a time when he was not bruised and battered, suffering from a broken nose or rib. The more his hatred for his father grew, the closer he drew to her, willingly making himself her slave in the games they played. He suffered her whims, her deriding him for not thinking as fast as she did. It didn't seem to matter to him that she could outrun him, outclimb him, outdo him in almost anything, her companionship seemed to make up for everything. The violence and abuse Etienne did to Sandrine, Mathieu felt as if it had been done to him. He did not hesitate to break with his father and leave the village once she was gone, driven out by the hatred of the villagers. Even now, after he had vented his anger, seeing how shaken she was, he felt compelled to mollify her.

"I have no reason to mourn him after what he did to both of us," he said sadly, "but something inside me keeps reminding me that I am flesh his flesh and blood and that I should not have permitted him to die like a dog in the gutter, even if he deserved no better."

"But there is nothing you could have done to prevent it," she replied. "Nobody knows who his killers are. During the last few weeks, he became so well known in Paris, he was an open target for anybody who disagreed with him."

"You don't know who his killers are?" He looked at her, not sure whether to believe her. "Aren't you the one who benefits most from his death?"

"That all depends. If you mean I got rid of an unwanted husband, you are right, and I can't say I'm sorry for that. But look what else his death has brought me. Tomorrow, the King will deliver me to my accusers. Etienne's death has made further stalling impossible. He should be very happy in his grave, for his vengeance can still reach me, even from beyond."

"You forget his body is still with the coroner and his soul will find no rest until he is placed in the ground. Tomorrow, I shall take him home to Bonneval. The least I can do is fulfill my duty as a son and give him a Christian burial." He bowed stiffly and turned away from her. "I won't be back for the trial."

"Am I going to see you again?" she called after him.

"You have many good and powerful friends who will protect you from the worst. You don't need me."

"I need some time alone, to think. Maybe I'll stay at Bonneval, at least for a while," he added. "If and when Count Philippe is released from prison, I shall reenter his service. He is a very good man."

She held out her arms, wanted to embrace him, but her arms dropped empty to her sides. Something irretrievable vanished with him. Her last link to Bonneval had been severed.

The chanting and shouting in the square were for the moment drowned out by a raging thunderstorm. Then as quickly as it had arisen the storm receded without leaving much relief from the heat.

Numbing fatigue made her lie down on the cot. The world receded from her consciousness. The eyelids felt sore and heavy. Mathieu's last words briefly came back to her mind. How right he was, Philippe was a very good man, the very best. Her thoughts trailed off into a semi-conscious state—who knows what tomorrow holds in store, as long as they both were alive, there would always be hope. Imperceptibly, she sank into a deep, dreamless sleep.

The trial of a certain Sandrine Legrand, alias Princess Marguerite de France, Countess de Montauban, the accused in the murder of one Brother Hippolyte of the Holy Order of Benedictines at the Abbey of Saint-Victor on the night of the 17th of July in the year of Our Lord 1590, the year of the great siege, opened on the 24th of August in the year of Our Lord 1594 in the city of Paris, twenty-two years to the day when she had been rescued from certain death through the courage of a devoted woman.

Because of the sweltering heat, the court convened in the small hours of the day. A solemn procession of magistrates in ample black velvet robes and stern miens accompanied the prisoner on the short walk from the Concièrgerie to the Palais de Justice. The din of the bell from the gothic spire of La Sainte Chapelle mingled with the monotone, flat intonations of the hooded friars, who brought up the rear, invoking the help of Almighty God in their task of wreaking vengeance against the enemies of God. Tense excitement ran through the huge crowd that had gathered since the previous evening and had staked out their place during the night.

A brief shuffle broke out when some onlookers protested the row of town guardsmen blocking the view of the square, halberds at the ready. But it was quickly brought under control. A detachment of royal arquebusiers in full view on the rooftops around the courtyard discouraged more unruly behavior.

Then hushed silence. Only the faintest whispers were heard as the people strained to look over the shoulders of the guards to catch a glimpse of the accused murderess and witch. The sight of the young woman in an unadorned black, velvet gown, her head bare and her hair pulled back severely into a knot, walking calmly in measured strides across the courtyard, evoked expressions of hushed awe among the throng. When she had passed, the opinion was ventured in some quarters that only an angel, or the devil incarnate, could be endowed with such unearthly beauty.

Inside the courtroom, the visitors' gallery was packed to the rafters. The court announcer rapped his cane three times and he called out: "Silence in the court."

The members of the Parlement of Paris took their seats. The chief magistrate declared the court in session and asked the accused be brought before the tribunal.

Marguerite took her place on the accused's bench. An eerie sense of being caught in a drama that was repeating itself seized her. She was almost prepared to surrender to an inevitable fate, when her glance fell on the box reserved for aristocratic visitors. A remarkable group of personages was assembled there: the Duchess d'Evreux and her daughter, the Reverend Mother Abbess Catherine, in the company of the Abbé Robert de la Croix, who seemed on excellent terms with Madame de Montpensier at his side; slightly to the left, apart but in the same section, was Madame, the King's sister, Princess Catherine de Bourbon and Navarre, in the company of the ruddy Marquis de Launay. A faint smile forced itself on Marguerite's face. It took her trial to unite the most fanatic Catholics and Huguenots on one bench. Also in attendance were the ubiquitous Count de Soissons and Countess de Guiche.

This time things will be different, she told herself. This time she did not avoid the hundreds of curious eyes trained on her. Her face was in perfect repose as she searched the audience for other familiar faces.

On the commoners' side, she acknowledged the presence of Thierry and the Morels. Raphael Floris sat in the front and flashed a sign of encouragement. Gaspard was there, no doubt to act as the eyes and ears of Philippe. Only one face she searched for in vain.

Although the presence of so many well-disposed people heartened her soul, she was disappointed not to find Arsène Rigoud among them. Of course, she knew there were many reasons why it would be wiser for him to stay out of a court of law. For one, his professional code dictated that he not venture into the precincts of the authorities. Didn't he tell her once of an unstated, mutual understanding between the underworld and the authorities that defined a certain line within the city neither party would cross? His imposing stature would no doubt draw immediate notice, and his friends from the police would hardly be pleased to find him in the halls of justice on whatever business.

Her assumption about Arsène's reason for not showing himself proved right, only much later did she learn that he was there during the entire trial. Even at the risk of being apprehended outside his regular haunts, Arsène Rigoud did not miss a single moment of the proceedings. He sat, cloaked in monk's garb, in the far corner, high up in the gallery, vigilant, scanning the courtroom, nothing and nobody escaped his discerning eye.

The court came to order and the prosecutor read the indictment. One Sandrine Legrand of Bonneval was charged with forcibly entering the premises of the Abbey of Saint-Victor in the city of Paris on the night of the 17th of July in the year of the great siege 1590, with intent to commit burglary. In the second count, she was charged with the murder of Brother Hippolyte of the Benedictine Brotherhood as he attempted to arrest her for criminal trespass. Upon being apprehended on the grounds of the Abbey by two monk soldiers guarding the gate, so the indictment stated, she wrested said Brother Hippolyte's sword from him, then assaulted him with the weapon and stabbed him in the chest until he was dead. The prosecutor reminded the justices of the accused's previous conviction for witchcraft, passed against said Sandrine Legrand by the magistrature of the town of Chartres after she had confessed to consorting with the devil. There was no doubt about the devilish nature of the condemned woman since she eluded execution of justice, death by burning at the stake, by vanishing before the eyes of the entire town of Chartres—a daring escape that could only have been performed with the connivance of Beelzebub himself.

Marguerite lowered her head to suppress sardonic laughter, but the very next moment, she blanched when she recognized the first witness being escorted into the courtroom. The deaf-mute monk bowed before the magistrates with an unctuous, subservient grin and laboriously took his place on the witness bench. How could she have forgotten about this ogre so completely? It was, after all, he who had stated that his confrère had been murdered by the witch of Chartres; it had been he who had roamed the streets of the city with his cohorts day and night. She shouldn't have given Brother Hippolyte if that was the worm's name, a chance to identify her, not after he had told her he knew who she was. If only she had made sure that he was finished off right then and there. With hundreds, probably thousands of monks in Paris, it was her luck to be confronted with one who had seen her at Chartres!

Brother Agrippa, for that, was the deaf-mute monk's name, was accompanied by a Benedictine friar who interpreted the meaning of his grunting sounds and hand movements to the court and relayed the prosecutor's questions by writing them on a small slate tablet. The result was a tedious exchange that tried the patience of the judges and audience alike.

From the gesturing and shouting between the prosecutor and the two monks emerged the picture of a devious wench trying to break into the Abbey, who, when confronted by the friars assigned to guarding the gate, tried to distract them with beguiling allures; when the two holy men resisted the temptress, a scuffle ensued, Brother Hippolyte attempted to push her away, but she clung to him tenaciously. His fatal mistake was to let her know that he recognized her, for it was then that she availed herself of his sword and slew him without mercy. Fortunately, the deaf-mute indicated, his companion remained lucid long enough to write, the words "Witch of Chartres" on the blood-soaked gravel path where he duly expired.

Asked by the presiding judge where he had been keeping

himself while his companion fought for his life, the deaf-mute indicated that he was alarmed by the accused's lewd suggestions and immediately went to seek help. On his return, he found her gone, and the friar breathing his last.

"Lies! Lies! Nothing but lies, and you know it!" All eyes turned toward the prisoner's dock where Marguerite stood glowering at the witness, her voice trembling with indignant rage. "You know you did not go for help, you went to stand guard . . .!"

She was quickly restrained and forced to sit down.

"Quiet in the courtroom!" the presiding magistrate warned the audience among whom a debate about the incident threatened to turn into fisticuffs. He turned toward the accused: "Madame, I must remind you that such outbursts can only serve to prejudice the case against you. Your Ladyship's testimony will be heard in due course, until then we must proceed in an orderly manner."

Appeased by his mild manner, she sat down promising to curb her temper and let the testimony take its course.

A lifetime seemed to separate her from the miserable waif who had been condemned as a witch. But for as long as she lived, a bond of kinship would unite her with all the defenseless women who, denounced as witches, were churned up in the merciless machinery of injustice.

The witness ended his testimony and was asked to step down. Since the deaf-mute monk was the only known eyewitness to the incident, the prosecutor's request to introduce another witness created a commotion bordering on a riot in the courtroom.

"Is this witness privy to the events of the night in question?" The judge asked with obvious weariness that something unforeseen might force the hand of those who were entrusted with passing the final verdict on the affair. "The original deposition to the court mentions only one witness."

"Your Honor, the witness was made known only this morning, but his testimony is vital for establishing the link between the accused and her prior conviction at Chartres."

"My learned friend, the identity of the accused is not in question. Madame, the Countess, has freely admitted she is indeed identical with Sandrine Legrand, the woman who was convicted of witchcraft at Chartres five years ago."

"Your Honor, though this witness was not present at the scene of the crime, his testimony has an important bearing on demonstrating the criminal character of the accused."

The presiding judge conferred briefly with his colleagues, and then declared the court adjourned until the afternoon, to give the tribunal time to decide whether to admit the surprise witness.

CHAPTER 10

Marguerite did not touch the food that was put before her. She strained her ears to hear something of the judges' discussion in the adjacent chambers. But the walls were too thick for anything coherent to penetrate.

When the session resumed, the presiding magistrate raised his gavel and announced that the witness would be permitted to testify. Instead of the expected storm, a stark silence settled over the courtroom as if everybody present sensed something terrible was about to happen.

"The prosecution calls Monsieur Hervé Hachette!"

Marguerite thought at first surely her ears must be deceiving her. When there was no doubt that it was indeed the odious name of the one she had not expected to see again alive, she convinced herself that this must be a cruel hoax by the prosecution to break her nerve.

Her throat narrowed and she felt as if the life's breath was being squeezed from her.

Only half-consciously at first, then more clearly, she became aware of an irregular thumping sound approaching from outside the courtroom. All eyes turned toward the door as it opened to admit the witness.

Marguerite dug her fingernails into her palm to prevent herself from fainting. Were she to pass out, it would most certainly be taken as an admission of guilt. There was no doubt, the twisted shape of the little man, hideous and pale, in black bourgeois garb, breathing heavily and toiling to propel himself forward on two crudely fashioned, wooden crutches, was none other than Hervé Hachette.

Trying everybody's patience, he finally came to a halt in front of the judges' podium. Marguerite had a clear view of him. He was still panting when he bowed to the venerable gentlemen. His attempt at a gracious smile turned into a grotesque contortion of his facial muscles.

Before the presiding judge could say anything, Hachette suddenly swung around, raised his stick at the accused, his voice hardly human, he shrieked: "There sits the accursed witch of Chartres! God in his mercy has kept me alive to see the day when she will burn in hell at last!"

"If it pleases the esteemed gentleman of the prosecution to instruct his witness to speak only when questioned," the magistrate shouted. "Let the witness take his seat in the witness dock and be administered the oath on the Holy Book."

Marguerite's face had drained of all blood. Her heart hardened. She returned her tormentor's stare without expression. How he survived mattered little just then. The reason for his appearance could be easily surmised. As in the case of the deaf-mute monk, it was his word against hers. No matter what this worm would say, she would have to sway the judges, expose his lies and those of the monk. She prayed that Arsène would not hear of Hachette's return. This would be a most unpropitious time for finishing the vermin off.

It would no doubt have caused her great concern had she become aware of the unobtrusive drama that was being enacted in the gallery or had she known how close her fears came to being realized. The instant Hachette's name was pronounced in the courtroom, Arsène instinctively felt for the dagger inside his boot. Like a wolf before launching his strike, he surveyed his prey. Suddenly a familiar voice whispered close to his ear: "I would not do that, you will only get her deeper into trouble. The peasant was enough." Arsène recognized the voice of Joseph Perron and relaxed his grip on his dagger.

"Joseph, my friend, when did you get here?"

"I heard yesterday that Hachette was alive and was to testify at the trial. This is not the right time for vengeance, not while the trial is in session."

"You are right, my wise friend. I realize now the move against the peasant was a tactical error. Another dead witness would surely turn everything against her. But if he makes one threatening move, I swear, this blade will reach his chest faster than he can say Amen. How did this miserable slime get away with his life anyway?"

"I am sure we shall find out very shortly. At least on this matter, he can be expected to tell the truth. But you must hold your peace."

The two men fell silent and fixed their attention on the cripple on the witness stand.

Marguerite meanwhile resolved she would not let this

wretched carrion, risen from the dregs, get the better of her. She absorbed every word of his testimony and prepared her refutation of his lies. A sacred oath on the Holy Book meant nothing to this godless worm, and she was not at all surprised to hear him relate a course of events that had very little resemblance to what had happened.

The prosecutor asked him to state his name and place of residence. With self-satisfied mien, he acknowledged the audience's startled reaction when they heard his domicile was the Cemetery of the Innocents.

"Isn't this an unusual place for anybody to live, except maybe the gravedigger?" the prosecutor asked.

"You mean living among the dead? My gracious Lords," he turned to the magistrates, "I have lived, if one can call it that, surrounded by death and decay since the day the caretaker of the cemetery, a kind man, found me with barely a breath of life left under a pile of corpses he was about to toss into a ditch for mass burial. That was exactly four years ago, four long years of agony. How did I get to be in such a deplorable state? you might ask. Stabbed and left for dead at the cemetery I was by the accursed witch and her henchman, the notorious criminal, Arsène Rigoud."

Hachette gave off an eerie squeak with every word he pushed over his lips under the utmost strain.

Mention of the name of the underworld king set off a renewed uproar among the spectators and they were brought under control only at the point of the guards' halberds. Hachette gloated over the effect his statement produced, and he waited patiently for the storm to subside.

"In the summer of the year 1590," he continued under prompting from the prosecutor, "I was the only person in all of Paris able to identify the witch who was wanted for the murder of the sainted Brother Hippolyte. After a long, elusive search of every corner of this city, I finally had tracked her down and was about to arrest this witch and dangerous criminal so she could be brought to justice and the people of this city would no longer have to live in fear and misery. At that very moment, I was cut down by her accomplice Arsène Rigoud, who came up from behind."

"How do you know it was Rigoud if you were struck from behind?" the chief magistrate interjected.

"Your Honor, the reason why the witch was able to elude justice during that long summer of the siege was that she had found refuge at the court of miracles of Saint-Honoré and enjoyed the protection of the notorious criminal who calls himself king of beggars and thieves."

"But you did not die," the prosecutor prompted him in a kindly manner.

"No, Your Honor, I did not die. I was close to death, but the hand of Divine Providence preserved me so I could testify before you in this courtroom today. For many months, my life hung in the balance. I would surely have died had it not been for the kind care I received from Monsieur Daumier, the keeper of the cemetery. The injuries inflicted on me are only now healed well enough for me to get about, though with great difficulty and pain. I appear here before you, Most Honorable Gentlemen, to cry out for justice."

"You say you were the only man in Paris then able to identify the woman wanted for the murder of Brother Hippolyte. Will you please relate to the court under what circumstances you became acquainted with the accused."

Before Hachette could answer, the judges' spokesman declared that they had heard enough for one day and adjourned the court session until the following morning.

Marguerite was grateful for the reprieve for she was barely able to contain her anger over the hypocrisy and lies of this witness. Something about the way the exchange between the prosecutor and Hachette was conducted made her wonder whether it had not been rehearsed and the whole thing was staged for dramatic effect. At first, she had presumed that the prosecutor was a state advocate assigned to the task, but now she was beginning to suspect that he was in the pay of the Archbishopric of Paris.

On her return to her prison quarters, she found Raphael Floris waiting for her. She was always pleased to see him, but she was even more deeply touched when she learned that his visit was prompted by the same concern she had about the prosecutor.

"I have made some inquiries about this gentleman," Raphael said. "He is a renowned professor of law at the Sorbonne, and until recently he was known as a fanatical Leaguer with close connections to the Sixteen. Outwardly he had made his peace with the new regime, but the eyes and ears of Paris tell of frequent comings and going at the Archbishopric, even after his reconciliation with the King. One of my sources saw him leave the episcopal residence as recently as three days ago."

"May we then presumed that he knew of Hachette's appearance in advance."

"Most certainly. The problem I see is, although the judges are favorably disposed toward Your Ladyship, the threat of excommunication for a not-guilty verdict can be very persuasive and will work in Your Ladyship's disfavor. We cannot rely on the good will of the judges alone."

A gratifying warmth touched her to hear him say "we" as if it was the most natural thing that he should be involved in her fate.

"We must create a counterforce to the pressure exercised by the Church," he continued, "a force more powerful than the clergy. We must gain the support of the populace. To win in Paris, the people have to be on your side."

"My dear Monsieur Floris, I am sure your assessment of the situation is correct, but the people of Paris have always held firm where the Church is concerned. Remember the demonstrations in front of the Louvre, only a fortnight ago? The mob forced the King's hand and as you must be aware, the mob is guided by irrational superstition."

"True, dear Countess! But the mob is not only superstitious, it is also fickle. Believe me, I can feel it in the air, in the courtroom, outside in the streets, in the taverns, the people's mood is shifting, the sympathies of the people are turning toward Your Ladyship."

For a brief moment, she let herself be enticed by his argument. His enthusiasm fanned the flicker of hope still alive in the far reaches of her soul into a searing flame.

"What do you propose we do?"

"In the end, it is Your Ladyship who must carry the burden of persuasion, with competent counsel, of course. You will have to capture their hearts, excite their emotions. I am not saying we should distort the truth, on the contrary, we must tell the undisguised truth. Madame, you are an actress, use this skill to present the truth with dramatic force!"

"I agree with you wholeheartedly. Only there is the problem of finding trustworthy counsel. Paris is full of lawyers, but most are former Leaguers."

"Look, no further, Madame!" Raphael described a mocking gesture in the air, in the manner of the courtiers, swinging his right arm far out and then bringing it back in front of him with a deep bow of the head. "Raphael Floris, counselor at law, at

Your Ladyship's service." His droll expression made her burst into laughter.

"Madame does not believe my credentials are good? Among many other subjects, I have studied jurisprudence for many years. I even passed the examinations—that was in Salamanca, but what does it matter, Roman law is the same everywhere." Her laughter was so infectious he was unable to continue in the dry, mock-academic tone.

"Laughter is a balm for the soul, Madame!" he declared.

Only with Philippe had she ever felt free to give way to unbridled mirth.

She felt perfectly at ease with Raphael who seemed like an old trusted friend. His pleasing manner was neither self-serving nor subservient. He moved among the high-born, self-confident without overstepping the boundaries of social distinctions. What she perhaps admired most was the sense of pride he projected in what was considered his humble birth and his refusal to let his origin affect his sense of self-worth.

"You should have been an actor!" she called out as he amused her by enacting with some exaggeration the courtroom scene as he envisioned it, alternating quickly between the roles of prosecutor, witness, defense counsel, and judge, endowing each with a particular manner, mien, and tone.

"I tried acting once, briefly, while I was starving in Bologna."

Suddenly, he stopped clowning and became very serious.

"Madame is, of course, aware that once we are in the courtroom, it will not be a game, but a struggle of life and death."

She took his hand and pressed it warmly. "I am very grateful to you for being the bearer of hope, your presence will lighten the heavy task ahead. With your help, I feel almost certain that I cannot but be exonerated."

They parted with a handshake. As he was about to pass through the door, she called him back: "Noël is well, I trust?"

"Oh, yes, Madame needn't worry. He is in the care of his two doting nannies at the Hotel Montreuil."

"Does he know?"

"I have tried to explain as best I could. He is young, but he seems to understand that there are evil people who want to do his mother harm. If Madame wishes, I shall ask him if he would like to be present at the trial."

"The thought has occurred to me, but I am not sure what effect it might have on him to hear these terrible accusations, especially since we are still strangers. If only we had time to get to know each other, it would be different. As things stand, I am afraid he would be too confused. But I am relying on your judgment, you know him so much better than I do."

Her voice trailed off. She suddenly felt faint.

"Please, you must excuse me now. It was a long and strenuous day."

"Certainly. I hope this visit did not place too much of a strain on Your Ladyship."

"No, not all! Please, you have nothing to blame yourself for. You are a messenger from God. Good night, Monsieur."

CHAPTER 11

The next morning, the resumption of the trial was delayed for an hour. No reason was given. The restive spectators were so closely pressed together in the gallery, they were hardly able to breathe. Many had camped out overnight in the courtyard—the police seemed either unable or unwilling to remove the loiterers—when word had spread of sensational revelations from a witness who had miraculously been resurrected from the dead.

Marguerite scanned the gallery. She for one did not mind the delay caused, as she knew, by Raphael's presentation of his credentials for her defense—for it allowed her to establish a tacit rapport with the audience. Her instinct told her she only had to win the hearts of the people inside, the mob in the street would follow.

As her eyes moved along the rows of indistinguishable faces, her attention was drawn to the bulky figure seated under the rafters. His cloak was pulled tightly around him, a hood concealed his face. She recognized the outline of Arsène as one recognizes an intimate friend from distinctive body movements or even from a particular tilt of the head or body even while sitting still. Try as she may, he resisted her silent entreaties for a sign of recognition, but that only deepened her conviction that the figure was indeed Arsène.

The thought of how to get word of Hachette's reappearance to Arsène had plagued her. Hachette's lies involved him as much as her. Now she prayed that he would not act rashly and finish expediting the vermin to eternity while the trial was in session.

Just then another familiar figure, Monsieur Perron, came into view next to the cloaked man. The governor's presence considerably eased her fears of what an impetuous Arsène roused to anger might do. Perron's level-headed influence was likely to keep Arsène's temper reined in.

At last, the entry of the magistrates was announced. Raphael took his place next to the bench of the accused, greeting her with a reassuring nod of the head. Not a sound was heard in the courtroom when the presiding magistrate recalled the witness to the stand and began by reminding him that he was under oath and had to tell the truth.

The prosecutor asked the witness again to relate to the honorable gentlemen how he came to know the accused. Hachette's breathing was even heavier than the day before. Each word he spoke was accompanied by a squeaking and rattling sound from his throat, alternately shrill and raspy. His twisted body seemed in constant pain. She tried to fight back a sense of pity, she felt rising within her. No, absolutely no sympathy for the fiend!

Never forget for one moment, she told herself, that given the opportunity he will destroy you mercilessly and completely. Just listen to his words! Lies! Nothing but lies! Even at the risk of eternal damnation, he did not shrink from swearing a false oath. Undeterred, he spewed forth his spiteful, monstrous lies.

Never, by her life, and God was her witness, did she engage in the lewd behavior he described. Never did she, when alone with him, offer her body to him in return for the release of her friends, whom he described as a band of thieving vagrants, fond of blasphemy and heresy. Never did she confess to him that she was the witch of Chartres or threaten him with evil spells if he did not do as she demanded. Nor was it true that he condemned her to the Asylum out of a sense of duty to shield himself from her corrupting, immoral influence.

She looked around. Did anybody believe these lies? The engrossed faces of the spectators gave no clue.

"My dear Monsieur Hachette, will you now be so kind to inform the court how you came to be in such a deplorable condition." The prosecutor's goading voice vibrated hollow in her ears, fluctuating as in a dream. With the utmost determination, she fought her mind's yearning to seek refuge in the murky realm of oblivion, to shut out this testimony from her consciousness. She could feel Hachette's eyes boring into hers like daggers as he slowly repeated how he led the witch-hunt and how he attempted to arrest her.

"This was already heard in the previous session," the presiding judge interrupted the witness impatiently. "The witness' testimony shall be regarded as concluded if there is nothing new to add!"

Marguerite believed to detect in the judge's reprimand a sign that at least this gentleman was not swayed by Hachette's story and was getting impatient.

"With the honorable gentlemen's permission, I wish to interrogate the witness to clarify a point," Raphael shot up as Hachette was about to step down.

"Monsieur Hachette, will you please tell the court why you were incarcerated in the Concièrgerie from March to July in the year 1590, the same year when the events in question purportedly took place?"

"I was the victim of evil rumors against me. I would not be surprised if the accused had something to do with that as well," Hachette replied annoyed.

"If it pleases the court," Raphael continued while approaching the judges' bench without further regard for the witness, "I have here an order for the arrest of one Hervé Hachette, police prosecutor, which is signed by the then-chief magistrate, who is unfortunately no longer with us. God rest his soul. The order states: Hervé Hachette is to be removed from office and held at the Concièrgerie until he can be brought to trial for corruption, for taking and soliciting bribes, and general misuse of office. Specifically, according to this document, he was charged with lewdness toward young women in distress. Honorable Gentlemen, the trial never took place because the great siege intervened. Gentlemen, Hervé Hachette remained incarcerated until he contrived his release by convincing the Archbishopric that he could find and identify the woman he calls the witch of Chartres. Thank you."

Veritable pandemonium broke loose in the gallery when Raphael had finished. The court was quickly adjourned until the afternoon. The accused would then have a chance to refute the testimony given and present her side of the case.

Marguerite felt caged, trapped. The narrow space of the room enclosed in naked stone walls where she was awaiting the resumption of the trial enclosed her like a snake pit. An eternity seemed to pass before she was finally escorted back to the courtroom. One more delay for no apparent reason. She tried hard not to let her frayed nerves get the better of her. She scanned the gallery furtively, as had become her custom. Her vision was blurred though like a clouded prism. On a half-unconscious level, she was aware of Raphael addressing her, but she was unable to grasp the meaning of what he was saying. Then suddenly, the delicate features of a young boy forced themselves into focus before her. The eyes of mother and son met, rested in each other, his wide and serious, set in a sallow, delicate face. She attempted a smile. Did he know who she was? Raphael must have told him what this whole spectacle was about.

Just then she became aware that he was flanked by the Duchess d'Evreux and the Abbess. She acknowledged the ladies' encouraging smiles, then turned to Raphael.

"The Duchess and her daughter have visited Hotel Montreuil several times in the last few weeks," he whispered. "Noël has taken to them and looks forward to their visits. They dote on him as may not be good from a pedagogic standpoint, but at the moment that hardly matters. One can only be astonished by the many questions he asks of everybody, a very bright boy, very deep in his thinking. We thought it good for him to hear Your Ladyship's testimony so that he can hear the truth directly from your mouth."

The presence of her son imbued her with a sense of mission. Her tongue loosened and her testimony poured from her lips in an eloquent stream. She felt the hearts and minds of the hundreds of people present reaching out to her, but she spoke only to one: a five-year-old boy who sat perfectly still for the duration of her testimony. She was sure that somehow, on whatever level, he sensed that she was addressing him, that only he mattered, that only to him did she feel obligated to give an account of her life and its vicissitudes.

She began her story by taking him back to the years of her childhood in the village of Bonneval, the abuse she endured there, her forced marriage to the peasant Etienne Grosjean and the circumstances that led to the accusation that she was a witch. With almost detached pathos, as if she were reading aloud from a tale of horror and suspense, she told of the shame of that wedding night, the villagers' thirst for her blood, the tortures she suffered at the hands of the Dominican friars, the confession extracted from her after months of resistance, and ultimately the trial before the magistrates of Chartres, her conviction of witchcraft and condemnation to be burnt at the stake.

On the matter of the miraculous escape, she remained deliberately vague, careful not to implicate those who had risked their lives for her. She also thought it impolitic to give public testimony of the Duke d'Evreux' cruel behavior toward her, but rather continued the story with lavish praise for her gypsy friends, itinerant actors and acrobats, whose kindness saved her life in the hour of her son's birth.

After a brief pause, she recalled their move to Paris and the great success of a play about David and Goliath in which the audience saw a parody of the struggle between the Catholic League and the royal forces. When the male members of the company were arrested on charges of sedition, she attempted to gain their release by pleading with the police prosecutor. It was, she felt, the least she could do to repay the kindness of the people who had received her and her child into their family.

"Before this court, this man's word stands against mine. This man's words are nothing but the basest lies!" Her voice trembled with righteous indignation. She stretched her arm heavenward, as if to invoke the help of the Almighty, then she lowered it slowly until her finger pointed like a dagger at her accuser.

"What you have heard are the lies of a jilted lecher who would pursue those who will not submit to him with an undying hatred. Even on the day he claims to have intended to place me under arrest, his true intent was to force me into his bed at knifepoint. Just when I had resolved to die rather than be thus debased, a fortunate circumstance brought a friend to the scene and delivered me from the hands of this evil man. Not for one moment did this man intend to have me brought to justice as he claimed. God is my witness, I cannot but speak the truth!"

She fell silent and sank back into her seat. Her forehead was bathed in sweat, her clothes clung to her body in the stifling heat, the air in the courtroom was so heavy she almost fainted.

The windows were wide open but admitted little relief since there was barely a breeze outside to temper the sultriness of the afternoon.

The putrid odor that exuded from hundreds of sweating bodies pressed together combined with the merciless heat of summer and had already caused several spectators to pass out. Nevertheless, most remained riveted to their places, patiently suffering the discomfort. Neither lack of space nor lack of air could make them abandon their chance of directly hearing the details of a human drama as sordid and sensational, a tale of treachery as they were not likely to hear of again in their lifetime.

A brief break was called in the proceedings to allow the water carriers to pass through the crowd. A clerk handed a cup to Marguerite. She took a few big gulps and offered the cup to Raphael, who took it over to Noël.

The presiding judge asked if the accused desired a recess until morning. She shook her head and Raphael informed the court that it was his client's will to conclude the testimony that very day.

"If it pleases the court," the defense counsel continued, "Her Ladyship is now ready to answer the charges against her in the matter of the death of one Brother Hippolyte of the Abbey of Saint-Victor during the night of the 17th of July in the year of the great siege 1590."

And turning toward Marguerite: "If it pleases Madame, to relate to the court the circumstances under which Your Ladyship happened to find herself near said monastery on the night in question."

Here was the moment of truth, the test of fire. To discredit Hachette was not so difficult—even while he was testifying, she sensed only scant sympathy for him in the courtroom—but the murder of a member of the Church was a matter that nobody took lightly. She knew it took more than courage to take on the power of the Church, it took tact and cunning she was not sure she possessed.

She took a moment to collect her thoughts. Then she rose slowly and with deliberate strides, mindful not to seem haughty or impertinent, she stepped forward placing herself between the judges' bench and the visitors' gallery.

"Many of you remember, I am sure, the siege, that terrible summer when famine and deprivation, disease and starvation turned Paris into a city of the dead and dying," she commenced, her voice, at first thin, almost plaintive, rose gradually, becoming mellifluous, as she felt her power extending over the crowd.

"You will also remember that Paris had become, within a few weeks, a city without children. Yet, the preachers told the bereaved mothers to hold out, to resist those who were ready to fling open the gates and surrender the city to the man they called "the heretic"—now our most beloved King Henri—and consoled the starving wretches with promises of rewards to be reaped in heaven. These same preachers and friars were the only denizens of the city who went about the streets with strong and well-fed bodies. It was easy for them to hold out with their stuffed bellies! But what about the rest of us? Like thousands of mothers in Paris, I was faced with the imminent death of my child, his life was hanging by a thread and the thread was wearing thinner every day. Obtaining food for my child became a single-minded obsession. All resources had been exhausted and we stared starvation and certain death in the face. Driven to the brink of despair, I devised a way to secure small amounts of food every night from the ecclesiastical and monastic larders that were bursting with stocks of food, withheld from the destitute people. Call me a thief if you will! I believe the real thieves are those who hoard food for themselves in time of need and keep it from the starving masses. It was in this way that I, the mother of a dying child, arrived at the gate of Saint Victor on the night of the 17th of July in the year of Our Lord 1590. My purpose was, and I admit it freely, to raid the well-stocked pantries that had kept the monks' bellies rotund, their cheeks shining in a rosy hue, and, as I was to find out, their carnal lust well-nourished."

She paused to let the last words, delivered with grating slowness, sink into the minds of the spellbound audience. Shouts were heard that the monks always pilfered the poor. The friars in the audience tried to protest but were prevented from rebutting the hecklers by the call for order in the courtroom.

"I cannot deny that Brother Hippolyte if that was his name, died at the hand of the hungry, miserable waif I was then," she continued. "But what reason should I have to kill this man? Consider the situation of a young girl, all strength drained from her famished, emaciated body, being assaulted, dragged behind the cloister walls by two strong, well-fed men determined to have their way with her. The one, whose testimony you heard yesterday, left to make sure nobody was approaching so the other could feast on his prey undisturbed. The attacker nearly succeeded in his purpose had it not been for one mistake, a mistake that cost him his life—he ungirded his sword and placed it carelessly within reach of his victim. I used the weapon to hold him at bay, but so sure was he of himself, he continued to advance, with disdainful laughter, and walked straight into the blade I held extended in front of me. If self-defense be murder, then I am a murderess! This is the truth, so help me God."

Silence followed her as she walked slowly back to the accused's bench. The presiding magistrate had just enough time to announce the session adjourned till morning when the verdict would be delivered, when all hell broke loose and the crowd pushed through the balustrade that fenced off the visitors' gallery from the area of the proceedings. Marguerite was quickly surrounded by the guards and hustled out of the courtroom. Only once did she look back before the door closed behind her. With relief she noticed Raphael carrying Noël in his arms and guiding the ladies out through a side door.

It was difficult to assess what was causing the excitement of the masses, whether the mood was for or against her. Only later did she learn of the flight of the friars from the courtroom, narrowly escaping an angry mob bent on revenge.

All through the night, an indistinct clamor from the courtyard and the streets reached her in the prison cell where she held an anguished vigil. Since the window faced the river, she did not become aware that the noise came from an assemblage of hundreds of women, some of them carrying children, many of them mothers who had lost their children to the famine, who held a vigil in the square in front of the Palais de Justice. She did not see the women venting their anger against the preachers, nor was she able to understand the words of the repetitive chant that filled the night until the early hours.

Only later did she learn that, in an instant, the defamed witch of Chartres had become the heroine of the women of Paris—for the washerwomen, fishwives, seamstresses, street vendors, domestic servants, prostitutes, beggars, shopkeepers, wives of middling and wealthy merchants, and factory owners, from the wretched and downtrodden to the elegant, well-to-do bourgeoise, she, the hapless victim of an unassailable power that held sway over each one of them, in one way or other, had become the symbol not only of the degradation felt by each one of them but of resistance. She was one of them. She had been there with them at the time of greatest distress, had suffered the privations, experienced a mother's sorrow and anguish, fought a daily struggle for survival just as they had. The insult and injury that had been inflicted on her, was an insult and an injury against all women. She could not have found a more powerful band of allies than the women of Paris.

As had been seen many times in the past and under various circumstances, Parisians are nothing if not great revelers. At the spur of a moment, the voluble populace of this city can give itself over to the most unbridled bacchanalia, turning the entire town into a stage for excessive dissoluteness—the singing, dancing, and drinking and general merrymaking could last for days.

The not-guilty verdict in the case of Marguerite de France, Countess de Montauban alias Sandrine Legrand precipitated a wild outburst of revelry. The celebration lasted three days, in some parts of the city the festivities extended to a week, during which all normal activity was suspended. This was one of those occasions when class distinctions became effaced, when scenes of unabashedly maudlin displays of affection between strangers of different classes, punctuated by assurances of brotherly love, could be observed everywhere. The general elation, enhanced by the free-flowing wine and gin, roused the people to toast the health of the King, the great benefactor who had lifted their heroine from the dregs. Throngs of thousands converged on the square in front of the Louvre where the chanting and dancing turned into a demonstration of almost frenzied adulation of the House of Bourbon.

Marguerite was at first too overwhelmed to take note of the joyous multitude in the streets. She leaned on Raphael's arm and let him guide her down the marble steps of the Palais de Justice. Her mind was still enveloped in a haze when they reached the bottom of the stairs and she did not immediately understand the meaning of the well-appointed carriage from which emerged the Marquis de Launay.

A sudden awareness of the meaning of the Marquis' attentiveness—as if she was already his possession—made her faltered and she grasped Raphael's arm with the vigor of someone struggling against being churned up by the ground moving underfoot. All she could do was beseech Raphael to carry a message to Philippe and assure him of her undying love for him before she gave herself over to the inevitable.

Unaware of the anguish his presence caused her, the Viking rushed to meet her with a gracious smile and a message from His Majesty the King who was anxious to congratulate his cousin in person. For a moment, Marguerite remained suspended between two worlds, then Raphael receded respectfully into the background as the Marquis extended his hand to guide her toward the carriage where a footman was holding the door ajar.

"Monsieur Floris, I shall expect you at the Louvre tomorrow morning with the delivery," she had just time to call out before a mob of admirers caught sight of her and surrounded the carriage, blocking from view the person who was the last remaining link between her new life and Philippe. Her companion was about to order the crowd disbursed, but, either out of gratitude or to delay the moment when she would be alone with the Marquis, she insisted on greeting them.

"My dear Marquis, these are the people who saved my life. We mustn't be ungrateful." Disgruntled, but realizing the imprudence of resisting her wish, he acquiesced, shielding her from behind as she moved through the throng. She answered their cheers with handshakes and embraces all around. Her march through the crowd continued undaunted even when the mass of people drew so close—hands reaching out and seeking to touch her as if some magic power emanated from her body —that at several points she was in danger of being submerged under the pressing human wave.

Finally, several young men lifted her onto their shoulders and carried her aloft in a triumphal march to the royal palace. The Marquis caught up with them just as she was being set down in front of the gate to the Louvre. He quickly lifted her into his arms and rushed inside.

The crowd had become so insatiable and was not easily turned away. They hailed her to the balcony again and again. From time to time, the King himself joined her to wave at the jumbled, faceless mass of humanity. A thousand parched throats shouted endlessly: "Long live the King! Long live Henri IV! Long live Princess Marguerite!" It was a great day for the House of Bourbon and Navarre. Paris was at the King's feet.

CHAPTER 12

If the city of Paris knew how to celebrate, the royal court knew to do her one better. The grand halls of the Louvre were lavishly decorated for the festivities crowned by a sumptuous feast of countless courses of meat and fowl, served in huge piles to satisfy the most gluttonous appetites. Henri ordered the best vintage from the royal cellar and before long Marguerite had the distinct impression that she was the only clear-headed person left in the palace.

The culinary excesses did not even cease with the beginning of the theatrical diversions, endless skits and ballet performances. Highlighting the evening was the performance by an itinerant theater group of a play called David and Goliath. There were many imitations of this now-famous play, and as Henri told her later, he meant to please her when he invited this group to the Louvre.

That evening, however, Henri evaded any attempt on her part to find a moment alone with him. Finally, Marguerite garnered a seat next to the King when he was absorbed by the presentation of his favorite corps de ballet. She had observed him and the Marquis de Launay in several private conversations. If something was afoot that concerned her, she surely wanted to know.

"Your Majesty seems to be avoiding my company," she said reproachfully.

"Ah, cousin! No talking during the ballet!" he said. "Come sit here and delight in the graceful movements of the human body."

The finality of his tone permitted no further discussion. She had no choice but to watch the awkward jumps and contortions of the performers who could hardly be regarded as the flower of their profession. But far was it from her to ridicule the King's well-known crudeness in artistic taste.

With the last sustained stance, Henri jumped to his feet applauding with a boisterous enthusiasm that was dutifully aped by his courtiers. Marguerite, irked by what she regarded as the King's childish delights when she felt her fate was in the balance, almost rudely insisted on gaining his attention when the clapping had finally abated.

"Your Majesty, I must have a conference with you about a matter of great urgency."

"Cousin, you have yet to learn how to address a king. But I must say impatience becomes you. Your beauty glows with special fire and, as you know, I can never resist a beautiful woman for long."

His gallant banter increased her anger, but now that she at

least had his ear, she managed not to let it get the better of her.

"Sire, I must know what is to become of the prisoner in the Bastille. Your Majesty will graciously recall that we had an agreement concerning the Count de Treffort-Salignac."

"I never forget a promise I make, Madame," he replied stiffly. "I hope Madame abides by the same code of honor. As far as our agreement is concerned, the terms have not yet been fulfilled on Madame's part. By the way, the fulfillment of these terms was the subject of my discussion with the Marquis de Launay this evening. He seems quite enamored of the prospect and wishes the wedding to take place with due speed. Arrangements are being made, no need to worry. The ceremony will take place at La Rochelle. Paris is hardly a suitable place for a Huguenot wedding. Unfortunately, I shall not be able to attend personally. I am sure Your Ladyship will understand the delicacy of my position. But our dear sister, Princess Catherine will accompany you on your journey. She is quite excited that her cousin will marry into one of the most illustrious Huguenot families in the realm. As a good Huguenot, she likes to see the cause strengthened. May we all live together in peace!"

He seemed to tire of his chattiness and his attention turned abruptly toward the fair Gabrielle, who never seemed very far from his side.

"But what about the Count?" Marguerite called after him. A sudden fear gripped her that the King's evasiveness was a sign that he planned to go back on his word.

"The Count de Treffort-Salignac and the Duke d'Evreux will be released the minute I receive word that the knot has been tied at La Rochelle."

"But it could be weeks!"

Her anguished tone made him turn back. "Shall we go for a stroll in the garden, cousin?" The tendered arm was gratefully taken.

"Your Majesty," she began under tears when the depth of the garden finally shielded the curious pair from the glances of the courtiers, "you have my word, I shall marry the Marquis, I only need some time to take care of a few personal matters here in Paris. Would it be so terrible to let the Count go free now?"

"I seem to recall that Madame once gave her word not to seek contact with the Count." The King's scornful tone put her on her guard.

"I underestimated you, dear cousin. You seem to be admirably connected. Gaining access to the Bastille is no mean accomplishment. Fortunately, your King is a sentimental old fool in matters of the heart. In this respect too, you are a true Bourbon, braving prohibitive obstacles for a night of passion. I shall be lenient, neither you nor the Count nor those who arranged for the all-night tryst shall be punished. Just remember, you can never deceive your King!"

He waved a stern finger at her. A mixture of shame and gratitude turned her face glowing red.

The unexpected revelation took the wind out of the sails on which she thought she was gliding along since her release. Somehow she had deluded herself that her vindication provided her with special leverage vis-à-vis the King. Utterly defeated, she realized the futility of further pressing for Philippe's immediate release. She was ready to drop the matter when Henri said: "Give me one good reason why I should release this blasted Count now?"

She was not about to let this opportunity pass, even if he was playing with her.

"Because he is a brilliant military strategist and sooner or later he will become a valuable ally and a loyal servant of the Royal House of Bourbon. Also, he and his family control a large part of Normandy, a strategically important area."

"No, no, not good enough," he shook his head impatiently. "I already have enough men who can plan and fight wars, I need men who can plan peace. As for the landholdings of d'Evreux, what could stop me from seizing them tomorrow and having the two scoundrels executed? No, you must do better than that!"

Ah, this was a challenge, a battle of wits —something like a riddle, if she found the right answer, her wish would be granted. Myriad ideas raced through her head. What was most likely to please him? She looked at him as he stood waiting with that broad devilish smile. With no time for thorough reflection, she burst forth instinctively: "Because Your Majesty wishes to reward his humble cousin for gaining him the affection of the people of Paris and because nothing is dearer to her than the life of the Count de Treffort-Salignac."

"Ventre Saint Gris!" The force of his hand landing on her back, a gesture he usually reserved for his soldiers, made her cringe. "Spoken like a true Bourbon! Once we Bourbons aim for a goal, nothing will deter us from reaching it, we go straight for it. Although your answer pleases me, I am puzzled how Madame gained her King the affection of the people of Paris when it was he who reduced this city unopposed?"

"This is exactly it! Your Majesty reduced the city, the people tolerated the imposition of your regime because they were weary of war, were weakened by hunger and disease, and their tolerance for the bombastic, empty promises of the preachers had worn thin. Since yesterday, Your Majesty is not only lord of the city but also of the hearts of its citizens, because of your kindness and generosity toward one who was, and in a way always will be, one of the people."

When she finished, he burst into the knavish laughter for which he was renowned in every corner of the kingdom.

Throwing up his hands, he exclaimed: "Checkmate! Madame, I declare myself defeated, and throw myself at Your Ladyship's mercy. I guess I have no choice but to release the two prisoners in the morning. One proviso though, the two gentlemen shall be banned from the city of Paris for three months. And no trysts in the meantime!"

He never had a chance to lift his finger sternly in reprimand to underline his last words as was his habit, for he needed both hands to disengage himself from the clutching arms that threatened to squeeze the living breath out of him.

"I always knew that Count de Treffort-Salignac had a lucky star," he mumbled. He turned quickly to rejoin the court party, leaving her sobbing with happiness in the darkness of the garden.

CHAPTER 13

On a beautiful day in early September of the year of Our Lord 1594, a train of magnificent carriages passed through the Louvre Gate and proceeded southwest toward the fortress city of La Rochelle. Heading the procession was the coach of Madame Catherine, the King's sister, easily recognizable by the emblem of the House of Bourbon and Navarre emblazoning its sides. Close behind followed a lighter carriage, embossed with golden butterflies of the House of Montauban. Madame Catherine waved to the crowd along the way leaning out of the open window. Anybody who wanted a glimpse of the occupant of the Montauban carriage was to be disappointed. The curtains remained drawn for most of the journey. Inside, the future Marquise de Launay preferred to be alone with her tears and thoughts.

Time heals all wounds! The words of Rosande, spoken on another occasion when the future had appeared as a dark, unfathomable hole, came to Marguerite's mind. Maybe there was something to the old folk wisdom. Like a person tossed into a turbulent sea reaches for a life-saving raft, she latched on to any consoling thought. Time! How much time would be required? Could anything less than a lifetime heal her wounded heart? Even if the passage of time were to dull the pain, nothing, she was certain, absolutely nothing could ever fill the gaping void left by her loss of Philippe.

In the eyes of the world, she was the luckiest of women, the restored heiress to a great noble name and a vast fortune. She was about to be joined in holy matrimony to one of the wealthiest and most powerful nobles in this part of the kingdom. And did she not count the King of France among her admirers? She had every reason to rejoice, but all she felt was defeat.

As the carriage train entered Poitou, at every stop throngs of well-wishers reached out to press her hand, to touch the seam of her garment. She tolerated it all with a sense of lassitude. Even at La Rochelle, she would not permit herself to be drawn into the festive mood that pervaded the city scintillating with wedding fever.

As she was awaiting the dreaded day, she spent many idle afternoons in the company of Princess Catherine sitting on the balcony of the Launay residence overlooking the town square. Below them, a never-ending stream of carriages brought the wedding guests to the town—the flower of the Huguenot nobility, as Catherine would say in her flowery style—flocking to their Jerusalem, carried on wings of faith and hope for the future the union between the Houses of Montauban and Launay inspired.

Catherine's rhapsodic exclamations were almost too much for Marguerite to bear. Yet, as she sat on that balcony observing the activities in the town square of La Rochelle something began to stir in her. Against her will at first, but gradually more relenting, she felt swept up in the enthusiasm. The image of her mother, however indistinct, appeared before her. At times she thought she could see her nodding her approval, at others, she seemed to exhort her to have courage.

She did not remember the exact moment when it happened, but at some point, the meaning of the momentous step she was about to take had for thousands of people came to her like a sudden revelation. The resurrection of Huguenot power, the formation of a solid Huguenot block across the entire southwest of France, from the Pyrenees to Poitou, was again a possibility. Henri's intent may only have been the taming of a recalcitrant nobleman he needed as an ally, but the people the King once led and then left in a state of dejection chose to view the marriage as compensation for what they had lost when their leader became a Catholic.

Princess Catherine did not have to remind her of the historic importance of the wedding.

"The Huguenot cause will live forever!" she proclaimed, embracing the bride with Bourbon vehemence. Then one day in a more reflective mood, she remarked: "If only your dear mother, Princess Isabelle, could witness this day. She would be so proud! The good Queen of Navarre, my mother of blessed memory, who was herself a most devout Huguenot, often said that no one was a more fervent believer than Princess Isabelle de France, and no one was more willing to die for the true faith."

The words, almost carelessly spoken, "no one was as willing to die for the true faith" became imprinted in Marguerite's mind. Her mother's fate came to preoccupy her thoughts. It was as if her own identity slowly merged with that of Isabelle de France. A nascent conviction deepened in her that fate had her survive the great massacre of Saint Bartholomew's Day to redeem her mother's death. Although she had little interest in the finer points of theological truths, she believed human destiny was guided by a divine hand and that it was her destiny, her purpose to assure that her mother's spirit would live on.

The wedding took place on the 15th of September in the year 1594. Marguerite ascended the steps to the altar at the church of Saint Sauveur, not as the sacrificial lamb as she had pictured herself earlier, but as the proud paragon of a noble family, with a deep sense of responsibility that at this moment dwarfed all personal longings. So convinced had she become that she had been selected by divine ordinance for this special task, she felt a certain joy when she joined her hand to that of the Marquis de Launay. Later that night she submitted to his embrace, placidly, but without revulsion and with a firm sense of serving a higher cause.

She would never love her husband and she consoled herself with the thought that he was likely to grow tired of an unresponsive bed partner once an heir was produced. But her hope that he would be too preoccupied with Mademoiselle de Crée to bother much with her at all was soon disappointed. The Marquis was quite enamored of his beautiful bride and she had underestimated his tremendous capacity for dividing his attention between several women. In intimate moments, the boisterous giant even revealed a gentle, sensitive side.

Philippe's name was never mentioned between them. She was not even sure he knew anything about him. But then one night, to her great surprise, while resting next to her, he said with a sigh: "I wonder how it might have been if we had come to know each other under different circumstances. How I wish we could be true lovers without the encumbrance of marriage. I envy the man who is in your thoughts when I make love to you!"

"How can you be envious? You have what the other has lost," she replied.

"Yes, but somehow I always sense his presence. I always feel like the usurper of another man's bed."

"What a silly notion!" she exclaimed, albeit not very convincingly.

The subject was never touched again, and she lay stiff and silent in the performance of her duty.

For several weeks after the wedding, the Marquis and Marquise traversed the extensive Launay possessions in the province of Poitou, moving from chateau to chateau. At every stop, the household settled down with great pomp. Mademoiselle de Crée and her brood of Launay bastards always brought up the rear.

Marguerite wondered about the great love this young woman of minor nobility must feel for Aiméry de Launay. She was always at his disposal, yet without hope for legitimate status for herself and her children since she lacked wealth and pedigree. The grace with which this woman endured the degraded position made Marguerite feel like the usurper. Several times, she had been tempted to approach her "rival," but refrained at the last minute for fear of intruding or having her intentions misunderstood.

The situation was, at least temporarily, resolved by an urgent request from the King for the Marquis to lead a campaign against the Spaniards who were still operating an army on French soil near the border with the Low Countries. Reports were circulating that the armies of Philip of Spain were daily penetrating deeper into France and that a full invasion may be imminent.

The Marquis immediately gathered a small army and prepared to march north. It was understood that Mademoiselle would follow the troops, while Marguerite was neither invited nor consulted on the matter.

Later she would laugh by herself remembering how irked she had been by the Marquis's readiness to accommodate her wish to return to her estates in the south under the pretext of having to put her affairs in order. She suspected that he was tiring of her and took this as a sign that an arrangement could be made that would release her from further marital obligations.

Two months passed without a word from her husband. She neither knew where he was nor when he would rejoin her. She was free to arrange her life as she pleased, and she might have forgotten that she was married at all had it not been for the life that was growing under her heart.

Life at Montauban brought fulfillment of almost everything she had dreamed of. She settled into the role of lady of the manor with great ease. The Huguenot barons welcomed her the way one receives back a wayward child. If they found certain aspects about her unconventional, like the presence of a five-year-old son born out of wedlock, they blamed the Papists who had almost destroyed her life. Those tenants of the estate and servants of the manor who remembered saw in her a miraculous reincarnation of Countess Isabelle.

When not occupied with official business, she took long, solitary walks through the vineyards that sloped gently toward the river Tarn. It took her some time to get used to the idea that all the land, as far as her eye could see, was hers. Gradually she began to feel at home in this hospitable land of her ancestors. For the first time in her life, she felt a sense of belonging. It gave her a deep sense of satisfaction to have a place she could call home, to carry responsibility, to serve the family name, which at times made up for the gaping emptiness in her heart.

One cool, clear afternoon in early December, she was out on her favorite walk through the vineyards. A shrieking flock of geese overhead distracted her from her musings and for a moment she became entranced with the perfect patterns their winged formation drew in the sky. Hundreds of birds in constant motion and equal distance from each other, not one drifting into the neighbor's space, each part of a unit, yet soaring free. What an admirable arrangement, she noted, a community of perfectly free individuals in working harmony for the common good! Her eyes followed their flight until they vanished.

The burnished brilliance of the sun setting over the river valley tore her from her reveries. Alarmed at being late for supper, she hastened back to the manor house. She reproached herself for having lost all sense of time. Although she was free to come and go as she pleased, she would never forgive herself were she to miss the dinner hour with Noël.

Preoccupation with other affairs had kept her from reaching out for her son. When they arrived at Montauban, she set up a strict schedule of common daily meals so that they would have at least some time to share. To her disappointment, he maintained a guarded reticence in her presence. She tried to blame the nursemaids, the stolid twin sisters from Picardie, who doted on him with self-effacing devotion. In more rational moments, she discarded the idea as the silly jealousy that it was and in reality, she was relieved that her son's welfare was in such good hands.

Time would draw them closer if she only let things take their natural course. Patience, she told herself, she had to exercise patience. In the end, she was sure, she would be rewarded with his love.

She looked for the slightest signs, but she had learned not to be too quick to see a change in his sullenness. Once before her hopes had been raised. One evening he suddenly broke his silence at dinner and, without looking at her, asked about the blue wagon stored in the carriage house. The question came so unexpectedly, it took her a few seconds to understand what he meant. Then she remembered the arrangement she had made with Pierrot from the inn at Thiviers. In all the turmoil of the last months, she had completely forgotten about it.

She almost leaped up from her chair, took the boy by the hand, and rushed with him to the carriage house. And there it was: the caravan of the Oranto Brothers' Theatrical Company, restored, still giving off a faint smell of fresh paint from the glossy colors on the basic blue as bright as the southern sky. She was told that a young man from Périgord delivered the wagon several months before, around the time of the grape harvest, presumably by order of the Countess. The foreman saw nothing wrong with accepting the delivery since the man did not ask for any compensation.

"There certainly was nothing wrong at all!" Marguerite beamed and bade the man take special care of the wagon from now on.

Noël became so enamored with the painted wagon, she had to tell him again and again about the itinerant gypsy actors, the owners of the wagon, who had gone to the New World. His fascination was complete and the wagon almost became an object of veneration when he heard of the circumstances of his birth in that same wagon on a bleak Christmas Day along a snow-swept highway in Normandy. The wagon became his favorite play area, and whenever he was late for a meal or a lesson, one was sure to find him huddled inside this private realm. But toward his mother, he soon resumed his sullen attitude that remained an insurmountable barrier between them.

That evening when Marguerite hurried back late from her walk, rushing anxiously along the narrow winding path, impeded by wild-growing barren twigs of the vine, she was greeted by excited servants with the news that Noël was nowhere to be found. Yes, they had searched the painted wagon, but he was not there. The twin sisters from Picardie wailed in a chorus of self-reproach. They had left him to play near the wagon but had not let him out of their sight for more than half an hour while they were tending to other chores. When they returned to look for him later he was gone. Something terrible must have happened, it was not like him to stray. The yard was empty, no children anywhere, and none of the servants saw anything suspicious.

Search parties went out to the surrounding villages where Noël often went to play with the children of the tenant farmers. After some coaxing, one of the villagers reluctantly admitted seeing a stranger, a foreigner, in the area in the late afternoon hours.

What made him foreign?

His appearance, they said, it was not like the men from around these parts.

Did he seem to be from France?

No, he looked more like a Spaniard—straight pitch-black hair and a Spanish mustache. But his clothes were not Spanish, more like a gypsy's.

Did anybody speak with him?

No, he might have been a thief or a brigand.

Were there others?

No, he was alone as far as one could see.

A little girl, who sometimes played with Noël, finally, motioned to Marguerite. She pointed in the direction where the brook cut through a wooded area. It was there that she saw Noël go with the stranger who was leading a horse.

To everybody's relief, the search party sent to explore the area around the brook brought back the boy as well as the stranger and his horse. The man did look exotic, wrapped in a long crimson wool cape, knee-high soft leather top boots, his hair so deep black it glistened in the dusk, and, unlike the short-cropped hair of the men of the area, his fell to his shoulders. His face was clean-shaven safe for a thin, twirled-up mustache.

Although he had changed, had grown to be a man from a shy lad of eighteen when she had last seen him, Marguerite gave off a scream and rushed to embrace her friend Gilles. But then she bethought herself and heaped a barrage of reproachful epithets on him. He patiently heard her out, then professed his guilt, and offered his most sincere apologies for having caused her so much anxiety.

"Madame, I have acted selfishly and thoughtlessly when I invited the boy to accompany me on a walk after we met in the yard near our wagon. I cannot tell Your Ladyship how excited I was to find the wagon here, in such a perfect state of repair. I must have lost my good sense. The boy and I had so much to talk about we lost track of time."

"I should very much like to learn what kept the minds of the two of you occupied for so long," she replied already appeased by the safe return of her son and the reunion with her dear companion of old. "But you must be starved, at least I am. Let's go inside, dinner has been waiting for hours."

The visitor's protest that he would be satisfied with taking a bite in the kitchen brought him a sharp rebuke from the hostess. After another exchange of protests and assurances, the three of them, mother and son and the gypsy, finally sat down to a tepid dinner in the dining hall. Long after Noël had been taken to bed, the old friends lingered over the repast and did not part until almost midnight.

Gilles had to tell every detail of what had happened since the day when he set sail for the New World with Rosande and Mireya and she departed for the royal court of France.

Marguerite was pleased to learn that the voyage to the New World went as well as could be expected—they all suffered from sea sickness at first and once the ship came under attack from English pirates. They disembarked at Panama and luckily had not much trouble determining the whereabouts of Morin and César who were already well known as acrobats in the coastal towns along the isthmus.

Once they were all back together, they continued their travels, venturing here and there into the interior of the country. But the oppressive climate and a network of roads not suited for a wheeled wagon caused severe hardships. Their situation was made worse because they had to perform in a language whose finer nuances none understood, so that the subtleties of double-entendre at which they excelled and with which they would thrill French audiences, were lost.

After many months of wandering, in the course of which they became acquainted with a fascinating, hitherto unknown world, they settled in the port city of Cartagena. The theater they tried to set up came to naught, however. Morin, who as she will recall, always had a nose for business and was always engaged in deals of some sort, was also lucky at cards. After one whole night of gambling, he emerged the proud owner of a tavern. The run-down establishment was located in a rather disreputable area of town, but they all worked together, refurbished it, and Morin was soon able to turn a good profit. Sailors of every description and from all over the Caribbean sought out the place for its excellent food and entertainment provided by Morin playing his hurdy-gurdy and a group of female dancers and singers.

As for Mireya, she was fortunate enough to capture the heart of a wealthy plantation owner. Soon after they settled in Cartagena, the wedding took place and she was spared having to live in the raunchy atmosphere of her parent's inn. César soon got restless. He never was one to settle in one place for long—she will remember, how impatient he was to leave Paris—so he followed the lure of gold to Brazil.

"He is not very likely to stay there for long," Gilles mused, "but the New World is so vast and opportunities for making one's fortune are everywhere. No need to worry that César will run out of prospects to pursue or new places to explore."

He paused. A draft chilled the vaulted hall. Gilles rose to stoke the glowing embers in the fireplace.

"And you, Gilles?" she asked softly. "What brought you back here? Could you not find a place and fortune that suited you in the New World?"

He stared pensively at the tiled floor as if he was not sure what to answer.

"No, not me." He shook his head determinedly. "I always longed to return to the sweet land of France. The New World offers much to those who are adventuresome and enterprising. I am neither. I am satisfied that those dear to me are well provided for, but I am no longer needed there. Somehow, I was hoping that I might be needed here. Please forgive if I am too intrusive with my desire to remain near Your Ladyship."

"But of course, you may stay here, my house is always open to you. Whatever is mine, I share with my friends!" she burst forth trying to laugh away his serious mood.

"No, no! I don't mean to indulge your hospitality," he protested. "What I want is to serve Your Ladyship, in whatever capacity you may see fit."

"I wish you would permit me the pleasure of repaying you for what all of you have done for me by this small token of accepting my hospitality."

"But you have already repaid us a thousandfold. Now my only wish is to be near you and the boy and to serve you."

"I cannot have you in my house as a servant," she protested.

"You know I am very good with horses. Maybe I can take care of Your Ladyship's stables," he suggested glossing over her indignation.

"Very well, if it pleases you, you shall be my valet d'écurie who takes care of the horses. You shall also be my son's riding and fencing instructor. Noël has so far had very little of the education a young aristocrat his age should receive. As I recall you are also a master in the art of elocution and dance. Where could a young man receive better instruction in being a courtier than under the tutelage of an actor?"

She began to warm to the idea. "Yes, what we need is exactly a man of your talents. Pass your skills on to my son and make him a gentleman! Teach him to speak, to dance, to learn the art of fencing, to comport himself."

"I believe your assessment of my skills is vastly exaggerated, but I shall try my best nonetheless to please Your Ladyship," he replied with a bow.

He leaned forward and with gratitude pressed his lips against her hand, but she pulled him toward her and held him in a warm embrace.

The residents of Montauban at first viewed Gilles's presence with raised eyebrows. But his gentle manner soon reconciled them to the foreignness about him and he found acceptance as someone belonging to the Countess's former existence, which, as everybody knew, had run a somewhat irregular course, not through her fault, but brought on her by the hated Papists.

Besides, the peasants and townspeople of this area always appreciated a good horse trainer.

Happiest of all was Noël. Though he still stubbornly refused to follow the wishes of his mother and be called Arnaud in honor of his martyred grandfather, a remarkable change came over him in the company of his tutor, and by Christmastide, the time of his fifth birthday, he had turned into a bright, almost cheerful lad.

The relationship between mother and son was unfortunately strained further by a particular incident in the village that left the boy upset and in tears. For days he refused to leave his room or speak to anybody. Only Gilles was finally able to elicit the cause of his strange behavior. A child, with whom he had gotten into a fight, had called him a bastard. The incident had brought home to him the fact that everybody knew that his mother was the wife of a man who was not his father and that she had never been married to whoever his real father was. How could he face his playmates and the world ever again?

Marguerite had attempted several times to talk to him about his father but he had only responded with indifference that concealed his shame about his illegitimate birth and anger at the woman responsible. Not even Gilles could appease him and make him consider his mother's feelings. She was grateful that Gilles was looking after the boy's welfare and on occasion act as a mediator between mother and son. As he grew older, he would come to understand, so she hoped.

For the time being, she was content to leave the boy's upbringing in the hands of Gilles. To take her mind of this and other matters that still mortified her, Marguerite steeped herself in learning the management of her estates. She made almost daily rounds of the wineries, the dairy farms, listened sympathetically to the grievances of the tenant farmers, the sheep and cattle breeders, the wheat and barley growers. She brought comfort to the sick and aided women in child labor. She never forgot, nor did she try to hide the fact, that she once was one of them.

Her days were thus filled with a great variety of tasks. Only the nights still stretched before her like a boundless, barren landscape of torment. She was grateful for every hour of forgetful slumber that was granted her but all too frequently roused to resume the terrifying vigil.

CHAPTER 14

While Marguerite was thus entwined in a web of regret and recrimination, something occurred, that took her preoccupations in yet another direction. Even her heartache over the separation from Philippe became secondary when a chance discovery admitted her into the world of the brief and tragic life of Isabelle de France.

Her mother's life and death had gradually become known to her in broad outline through bits of information gathered from those who had known her, but she knew nothing of her feelings, her thoughts, of her hopes and dreams. All she had been able to assemble were the lifeless, disparate pieces of a shattered picture.

One evening while sorting through the personal effects in

what was her mother's suite that had been left undisturbed and uninhabited, her attention was attracted by a rectangular box she found buried at the bottom of a chest full of clothes and knick-knacks. The box was of inlaid with wood, very much like, only larger than, the box that had contained the emblem Mathilde de Bécour had left with the Morels at Bonneval.

The box was locked and she had to try several keys lying next to it before one would open it. Apprehension and delight made her heart race as she stared at the thick bundles of parchment, neatly tied together and filled with dense, evenly drawn characters, beckoning, so it seemed to her, to be unraveled.

Her guess about the nature of the papers was shortly confirmed by the bold heading on the first page: Diary of Princess Isabelle de France, daughter of Marguerite de Bourbon and François, Duke de Nevers, both of blessed memory.

Marguerite had learned that keeping a diary was a practice, a whim, cultivated by many young noblewomen, but when Isabelle recorded the events of her life and entrusted to paper her thoughts and feelings, whether she intended it or not, she was establishing a link with posterity. As Marguerite began to read, she could not suppress the feeling that Isabelle was speaking directly to her and by the light of a single candle, she was slowly drawn into her mother's world.

The preamble to the diary in which the writer, following established custom, introduced herself contained a concise autobiographical sketch. Marguerite dwelled on that part for a long time, memorizing every detail, studying every word, and searching for hidden clues. What she uncovered was her family history. The actors in the diary were not mere characters in a book, but people of her flesh and blood. Memorizing every little fact recorded would mend the broken link and make her a link inthe chain of generations. She was an outsider no more.

Isabelle de France, so she learned, came into this world on the 19th of August in the year of Our Lord 1550, the third year of the reign of King Henri II, on her father's estate at Chevenon in the province of Burgundy. Her father was Duke de Nevers, scion of a noble house of ancient lineage and peer of France. Her mother, Marguerite de Bourbon, was the issue of one of the most illustrious noble families in France, a princess of the blood, related to the royal family itself.

Born of such exalted parentage, Isabelle remembered her childhood as a charmed, unclouded existence, a long, peaceful summer that abruptly came to a tragic end when her parents were carried off in quick succession by the plague, leaving her orphaned at the age of twelve.

In the following years, she was found at Nérac in southwestern France, at the court of her aunt, Jeanne d'Albret, the Queen of Navarre. Her sorrow over the loss of her parents was alleviated by the Queen's warm concern for her welfare. Isabelle professed that the influence of this strong-willed, upright woman of deep Calvinist convictions initiated her into the Reformed Religion and she became as ardent a Huguenot as her aunt.

Shortly after she arrived at the court at Nérac, Isabelle became the object of the precocious amorous pursuits of her cousin, Henri de Navarre, almost three years younger than she, to whom she referred in the diary mostly as the Prince of Béarn. His ardor was cooled by a stern reprimand from his mother. Thereafter the cousins became almost inseparable companions and since Jeanne strongly believed in equal education for boys and girls, the two shared in their studies, competed in the exercise of their mental capacities as well as in physical endurance contests. Isabelle was as fond of the hunt as he was, but with the critical eye of the older child, she judged his competitive spirit to be excessive. Again and again, she expressed her conviction that he was destined for greatness.

One particular passage was filled with such sisterly admiration and almost prophetic forethought, it brought tears to Marguerite's eyes as she read:

"There is no doubt in my mind that my cousin Henri of Navarre, the Prince of Béarn, is destined for greatness. To say he is destined for greatness is not enough. Words fail me to describe the heights of glory he will attain one day. But his glory will not come from self-indulgence or the pursuit of personal gain and power. The power that will be his, he will wield for the benefit of his people, for the liberation of his people from oppression and persecution. He will be our Moses, our Joshua, he will be our spiritual and military leader in one person. He will lead us to the promised land of freedom in the sweet land of France, he will lead us in a holy crusade against the abominations and idolatry of the Roman Church, and he will rule over the kingdom of true faith in the reign of our Lord Jesus Christ on earth."

Marguerite wondered whether Isabelle would look with pride on Henri if she could see him now as King Henri IV of France. His career had always been more that of a Joshua than of a Moses, but in the end, he became King of France through the only course open to him, by bowing to the desire of the majority of his subjects and abandoning the "true faith" and adopt the "Roman abomination." Although the youthful diarist breathed the same kind of absolute moral righteousness the Queen of Navarre was noted for, Marguerite could not help but feel had she lived, had they both lived, Jeanne and Isabelle would have seen the wisdom of Henri's decision. Even a Jeanne d'Albret, so it seemed to Marguerite, was not likely to have withheld approval of her son's conversion if that was the price he had to pay for his throne and the peace of the kingdom.

The pivotal event in Isabelle's life occurred in the summer of 1565 in her fifteenth year. That summer the royal court of France, in its second year of a grand tour through the provinces, came to the court of Nérac on its itinerary through southwestern France. It was this event that prompted her to begin the diary, for the first entry conveyed in great detail the excitement at Nérac caused by the presence of the royal family—especially the boy king Charles IX and the Queen Mother, Catherine de Medici—and their entourage of hundreds of courtiers, soldiers, and servants, even foreign representatives to the court.

"The announcement of the approach of the royal cortège from the south made everybody at Nérac scurry to the ramparts hours before the first drum rolls and fanfares heralded the court's arrival. We searched the horizon for a glimpse of the banners displaying the royal colors. At the first sign of the approach of the royal company at several leagues' distance, the Queen of Navarre and the Prince of Béarn rushed out to greet His Majesty. I stayed on the ramparts with my four-year-old cousin, Princess Catherine."

Isabelle did not let her excitement get in the way of a discerning assessment of the royal ménage which was almost too unwieldy in size to be comfortably accommodated at Nérac, especially since none of the courtiers seemed inclined to make do with less comfort than they thought was their privilege. Isabelle thought the royal children a rather disagreeable brood, of exceeding complacency and affectation. She described the King as a capricious boy her own age, who tended to vacillate between fits of violent ranting and artificial joviality.

Marguerite was most impressed to read Isabelle's description of the then Duke d'Anjou, Catherine's third and favorite son, who later became King Henri III and found such a violent end for all his sins. Isabelle intensely disliked the boy whom she described as the most effete of the lot who frequently displayed streaks of vicious cruelty.

The only one of the children whom she seemed to find in any way appealing was the King's sister, Princess Marguerite de Valois, who was then a thin, sallow twelve-year-old, withdrawn but already endowed with a haunting beauty. Isabelle regretted that her overtures toward the princess met with a cursively polite but inanimate response. She wondered what it was like to be the daughter of Catherine de Medici and with precocious astuteness, she noted: "It seems that to survive the fierce rivalry among the princes at the royal court, a rivalry the Queen Mother quite obviously constantly incites and fans, Marguerite de Valois must have learned at a tender age that to avoid being destroyed by her brothers' viciousness, she had to resort to manipulation, intrigue, and deceit; true feelings must be concealed behind an inanimate mask of charm and obliging graciousness."

The Queen Mother herself was a woman of monstrous dimensions in Isabelle's eyes. She observed the royal guest at close range during dinner in the grand hall, studying her features intently but finding it difficult to determine whether a human heartbeat under the severe, frozen mask of powder and rouge. Her vestments were so elaborate and constricting, forcing her to move like a life-size marionette doll. It is almost a miracle, she noted, that the Queen Mother and the other ladies of the court did not faint or suffocate in the summer heat. She compared the royal ogre with the Queen of Navarre, a head-strong and severe woman herself, but how different was the warmth and vivaciousness of her expression.

The two queens had been closeted together all afternoon and Isabelle speculated that maybe Catherine was trying to quell rumors that she had entered into a conspiracy against the Calvinists in France with the Spanish minister and the Papal

Nuncio when she met with another one of her daughters, the Queen of Spain, in the coastal town of Bayonne in the far southwest corner of France.

Isabelle professed herself ignorant of politics, but her instinct told her that no Huguenot should trust this Italian woman even if she did indeed foil, as she claimed, a plot by the King of Spain to kidnap Jeanne d'Albret and to make the province of Béarn a Spanish possession. This was one of many rumors making the rounds at the time. Nobody knew who set the stories of treacherous plots and atrocities into circulation, but they never seemed to cease.

Isabelle's distrust of the "Italian" woman had already been stirred the previous year after the return of Jeanne d'Albret and the Prince of Béarn to Nérac from a stay at the court. Mother and son had joined the ambulatory court at Macon while it was on its way south and they were present at the King's entry into Lyon. The joy of the warm official reception accorded the royal party had been tempered by the presence of the plague in the city. Everywhere houses that had been sealed and whole quarters that lay deserted. The constant wailing of the death knell imposed a somber mood on the customary festivities, the balls and tournaments, staged for the royal visitors. Hysteria broke out among the courtiers when a young woman in the entourage of the Queen of Navarre was stricken with the dreaded disease and died. Jeanne d'Albret petitioned Charles IX to permit her to return to Nérac immediately. The request was granted, but an altercation arose with the Queen Mother who insisted that the Prince of Béarn had to stay with the court. Fearing that the plague was a sign of divine displeasure with the House of Valois, Jeanne was determined to take her son back to Nérac if she had to kidnap him herself. Jeanne later told her niece that she knew very well Catherine de Medici's motive for desiring Henri de Navarre's presence at the court. The court was about to travel through the southern part of the kingdom on its way to Bayonne. By traveling in the company of the Huguenot princes of the blood—the Prince de Condé, Navarre's first cousin, was also of the party—the Queen Mother thought she could appease the Huguenot inhabitants of these areas.

Jeanne, however, was not inclined to make the life of her old rival easy, especially not if the life and safety of her son were at stake. She dressed him in women's clothes and set out for Nérac before dawn.

"Maybe the ladies are trying to settle their differences," Isabelle wrote of the animated dinner conversation she observed.

How surprised she was when several days later, in the course of rounds of balls and masquerades, ballet performances and tournaments, begrudgingly consented to by the Queen of Navarre, whose sterner religious tastes abhorred such extravagances, the Queen Mother suddenly stopped in front of Isabelle during a chaconne and, without inquiring about her name or origin, she requested that she may grant her the pleasure of joining her entourage on the court's journey back to Paris. Isabelle had heard of Catherine's predilection for surrounding herself with an appanage of beautiful young maidens. Speculation had it that she wanted the court to project an air of youthful gaiety and hoped that the presence of attractive young women would in turn engage the loyalty of handsome young warriors. But why ask her, a Calvinist?

The request was so unexpected, she knew not what to say. Her embarrassment was heightened when her eyes fell on a captain of the Queen's guard, whose dark gaze had been firmly fixed on her for some time. She managed to say something about the graciousness of the invitation and the great honor, but the Queen Mother had already moved down the line. Still flustered, she found herself face to face with her next dancing partner, the captain whose name she later learned was Charles Treffort.

From then on he never seemed far from wherever she happened to be. He never approached her, but she felt his burning eyes follow her everywhere.

"She knew him then!" Marguerite exclaimed to herself. Dark foreboding gripped her as she read on.

For several days Isabelle was in a state of inner turmoil. The Queen Mother's invitation placed her in a painful dilemma of having to choose between the glitter of the royal court and the tranquility of Nérac. She did not know where to turn for advice, for even her aunt, the Queen of Navarre, told her an invitation to the royal court was an honor so rare and distinguished no young woman could turn it down. The Prince of Béarn wished he could accompany her. Only the little Princess Catherine begged her not to go.

Only to her diary did she entrust the strange sensation that made her heart beat faster every time she thought of that strange man who so persistently pursued her with his cheerless gaze. Strange was the only word she could find to describe Charles Treffort. He was very handsome in his royal guard's uniform, but she never saw him smile or speak lightly with anybody. His boring, unfathomable dark eyes made her profoundly uneasy.

Marguerite struggled to contain the tears of anger that began to overwhelm her as she read Isabelle's confession to her diary: "With every day that passes, I feel his silent power gaining over me more intensely, sometimes I think I am losing my own will altogether. Then again I feel an almost equally strong repulsion and I want to run far, far away from him, hide somewhere where he cannot find me if there could be such a place."

Several days after this entry, the tone of the diary changed:

"I was out riding all day with Charles Treffort. Never have I known a more thoughtful, more well-intentioned, serious man. Never have I been more wrong about a person. He was almost cheerful and a few times he even smiled. If I could make him laugh, I would count myself happy indeed. We rode hard until the horses needed a rest. When I observed the way he handled the horses, with such gentle authority, I was reminded of what the horse master at the castle always said to the children hanging around the stables. He insisted one can tell much about the character of a person by the way he treats animals, especially dogs and horses. If this is true then Charles Treffort must be a most forceful and kind man indeed.

We rested by a well in an open sheep meadow. So deeply were we engaged in conversation, I hardly noticed the sun going down until I became aware of its glowing red hues spread across the western sky by the reflection in his eyes. It was simply incredible how much we had to talk about. I am most pleased about his attitude concerning the current religious conflict. He firmly believes, he says, that no interference from outside should be tolerated—I guess he was referring to the machinations of the King of Spain—and he saw no reason why the French people could not live together peacefully, no matter what form of worship they chose."

Isabelle was impressed with the great knowledge he seemed to have on almost any subject and the authority with which he spoke about a great variety of things, whether it was philosophy or history, art or music, or even natural phenomena like the earth and the stars—he seemed to have studied everything. He took her on an imaginary journey, introduced her to the people and places he had seen with such vividness, she thought she was there with him, in a faraway realm, at the far corners of the world, a place to which she followed him only too willingly.

Three days later, she was ready to leave the security of Nérac for the great unknown: "All I know is I cannot live apart from Charles Treffort. I need to be near him to breathe, without him I am sure to wither like a flower without water or sunshine. When the Queen Mother pressed me for an answer, I knew what it had to be. I said yes, a thousand times yes, without hesitating one moment. Since Charles commands the Queen's armed escort, we shall always be near each other."

Despite her exuberance, there seemed to have been moments when she doubted the wisdom of her decision. A little further on she wrote still under the same date: "Sometimes I am still a little frightened of him, especially when he gets jealous which seems rather frequent. Although he has not proposed marriage—we never even talk about love and sometimes I wonder why he never tries to kiss me—the sight of another man near me, no matter who he is, prince or servant, inevitably sets off a furious storm that seems hardly warranted. This happened not only once, but several times within a few days. It is as if he wants to hurt me with his accusations of treachery and faithlessness. After a while he becomes very contrite, he weeps and begs my forgiveness. Such conduct is all very new to me. But, as I had occasion to observe during the past few weeks, sudden, often violent fits seem quite common among the members of the royal court."

Isabelle did not return to her diary for a week. Then with the elegiac tone of youth, the last entry before her departure: "Tomorrow it will be good-bye to good old Nérac and only God knows when and if I shall see it again. It will be goodbye to my good aunt Jeanne d'Albret and that rascal Henri, the Prince of Béarn and King of Navarre. I shall miss them all especially my little cousin, Princess Catherine. But I know now that it is my destiny to go wherever Charles Treffort leads."

The court had departed from Nérac three days before, but the slow progress of the behemoth lumbering through the countryside permitted her to catch up with them even before Maraude. Despite the shortness of their separation, Isabelle described Charles as very distressed about having to depart without her. Whether or not he feared she might change her mind and abandon her plans of joining the court, she could not tell for sure, but at the moment when they were bidding adieu to each other, he made her swear that she would be his as long as she lived, and they sealed the pact with a passionate kiss.

"Somehow I have the feeling that tomorrow I shall be only a three-day journey away from the real beginning of my life," she concluded. But Charles had not made his intentions clear, a fact which, although peculiar, she tried to discount as unimportant—the time was just not right, the circumstances not proper, he would no doubt correct this shortcoming soon.

Jeanne d'Albret adamantly refused to let her travel unescorted. Considering the hazards of the brigand-infested highways, this was understandable, but it annoyed Isabelle nevertheless that her aunt assigned a whole detachment of armed soldiers commanded by, of all people, the Count de Montauban. Sure, he was one of the most handsome and charming young men around and had let it be known that he was taken with her—at one time she even had a brief fancy for him—but he was a country boy and could hardly compare to the urbane, elegant figure of Charles Treffort. She waved farewell to her loved ones, bravely suppressing her tears, but as the towers of Nérac began to recede, their size diminishing by degrees, she wrote, her former existence already began to wane.

Marguerite put down the yellowing pages and rested her eyes. A sigh of exasperation escaped from her lips that her mother should have been in love with the hated Duke! How could she have been so foolish? It was difficult for her to think of the girl whose youthful gush of sentiments flowed from these pages as her mother. But she was only fifteen then, of impressionable age, and innocent in the ways of the world. It was quite remarkable how well this young girl perceived the darker side of this man's character despite the fascination he held for her.

Midnight had long passed. A low flame in the fireplace struggled against extinction, while the chill in the air made her wrap the fur blanket tighter around her shoulders. But Marguerite was unable to think of sleep. There was no turning back from this journey into her mother's short life and its tragic end.

When she picked up the pages again, she was surprised to find a gap of about three months between the next entry and the previous one. The date was the 15th of December 1565 and the place was again Nérac. Isabelle had left the royal party and had returned to the court of her aunt. Tears welled up in Marguerite's eyes as she formed the words of the lament that rose from the page: "Oh, I would I was dead! How can I ever again bear to face the sunlight? Darkness will be my lot henceforth!"

What could that monster have done to the trusting, innocent young girl? There was no doubt in Marguerite's mind that only the most heinous offense could have cast Isabelle into such utter dejectedness.

After this brief outcry, Isabelle did not pick up the pen again until early January 1566. Her tone was noticeably calmer, at first even factual and detached: "A severe winter frost has settled over our region. The fever that held me in a half-conscious state since my return to Nérac has subsided. Only the devoted care of the good Queen of Navarre brought me back to life. I don't know whether this is a curse or a blessing, but somehow I feel that I should be grateful to be alive. But my soul is as barren as the winter landscape outside my window. Out there, barely a sign of life is visible safe for swarms of noisy crows that touch down on the fields overlaid with a shroud of gleaming white. In the sky, a cheerless, leaden canopy of impenetrable clouds blots out the sun's rays. It probably is better this way. Everything is heavy, disconsolate, and barren, a perfect mirror of my soul.

But I am selfish and ungrateful to dwell on my anguish. I still have the love of my aunt and cousins. And what would I do without the kindness and patience of the Count de Montauban? He has done so much to help me get through the worst. His sole concern seems to be my welfare. The ladies-in-waiting have told me, he called every day during my illness and inquired anxiously about my progress while a delirious fever held me enthralled and blurred all awareness of my surroundings."

Despite the florid prose style, Isabelle seemed to recover fairly quickly. For the entries for the month of January told of balls and masques, and she did not seem to tire of dancing all evening especially with the devoted and now ubiquitous Montauban. Nurtured by the easy-going charm of the Count and the growing intimacy between them, Isabelle wondered how she could ever have fancied herself in love with Charles Treffort. Only now did she realize that she should have heeded the warning signs, his mad obsession, his jealousy, his dark moods, the fear and uneasiness he had inspired in her.

Everything suddenly fell into place only a few weeks after she had joined the court. One day the Queen Mother greeted the entering Charles with unusual warmth and hailed the joyous occasion of the birth of an heir to the House of Evreux. Shame and rage overwhelmed her as she became aware of what everybody else knew that there already was a Countess de Treffort who, she was told departed from the court for Normandy only a few months before since it had become too strenuous for her condition to keep pace with the constant movement of the royal court.

"What right did this man have to tie me to him, to exact vows and promises none of which he ever reciprocated?" she wondered.

Looking back she could not help but be grateful for her aunt's judiciousness in ordering the Count de Montauban and his men to remain with her under all circumstances! Isabelle was sure that without Arnaud de Montauban's protection, she would surely have perished. With his help, she expurgated Charles Treffort from her mind and soul, he became but a fleeting episode, a passing fancy of no consequence.

The love between Isabelle and Arnaud was deepened by the devotion they shared for the Reformed Religion. Their happiness did not make them oblivious to the growing conflict between Huguenots and Catholics that engulfed the kingdom with growing menace. The idyllic isolation of Nérac did not shield them from the tales of Catholic atrocities and Huguenot reprisals messengers to the court reported almost daily.

Isabelle vented her indignation in the pages of her diary and often punctuated the descriptions with visions of doom.

"Oh, Peace! will you ever again spread your protecting wings over the Kingdom of France? Every day we hear of the innocent, of women and children, murdered for their faith, we hear of houses of worship desecrated and burned. How many of us must be sacrificed before peace will come and people will learn to live together? The Edict of Toleration is nothing but a sham! The King is powerless to control his men. Montluc is still killing every Huguenot he can find in every part of France. The stories of his excesses that reach us from Toulouse are too horrifying even to put into words."

Her happiness with Arnaud and her hopes for their future

were frequently clouded by premonitions of her death. She prayed that she may be worthy of the early Christian martyrs, who were tortured and slain by the pagan Romans: "Dear God, I am ready to face death for the glory of your true faith. I only beg you to give me the courage to embrace my fate with uprightness and dignity, and that I may face the sword of those who seek to destroy us unflinchingly for your eternal glory, so your will be done on earth."

The conflict between Huguenots and the Catholics forced Isabelle and Arnaud to change the date of their wedding several times. Their plans had to be postponed indefinitely when in September of the year of Our Lorde 1567 another full-scale war broke out and Arnaud joined the Huguenot forces.

Separated from the man she loved, Isabelle found solace with her diary: "Arnaud left this morning to join the forces of the Prince de Condé. I gather from what Arnaud has been telling me that the Huguenots are putting a mighty army into the field and are ready to march on Paris to press their demands. What these demands are I don't rightly know, but I presume they have something to do with gaining the King's support against the enemies of the Reform."

"News from the battlefield is arriving very slowly and what we get are bits and pieces that are sometimes disheartening and sometimes give us cause for rejoicing. We cling to every scrap of hope. It seems the Huguenot army, commanded by the Prince de Condé, has laid siege to the capital and they expect to breach the walls of the city by storm any day. My prayers are with my Huguenot brethren, but more than anything I fear for the life of my beloved Arnaud. Please God preserve him, place your protecting hand over him. My life would be worthless were he to die."

Her prayers did not seem to have been heard, not completely

at least. Arnaud was wounded in the battle at Saint-Denis, which had ended in disaster for the Huguenots. The messenger, who brought the news of the defeat and subsequent withdrawal of the Huguenot army from the surroundings of Paris, was subjected to long interrogations. But all he knew was that Arnaud was recovering from his wounds at Poitiers and planned to head south as soon as he was able.

With the first fall of snow in December 1567, Arnaud returned home, but their happiness continued to be clouded by the vacillating fortunes of the Huguenot struggle.

"What terrible fate," she wrote, "has decreed us the greatest happiness in a world where the most horrendous acts of atrocity have become commonplace?"

Her indignation was directed against Catholic outrages, but she was mortified by the acts of retaliation to which, she was sure, the Huguenots were driven.

The scourge of the Huguenots at this time was a man named Montluc. Isabelle described him repeatedly as a vicious monster. Marguerite later learned that he was a nobleman and military commander responsible for several sinister plots aimed at eradicating the Reformed Religion from the Kingdom of France. To this end, he did not shrink from conspiring with the archenemy of France, the King of Spain.

Isabelle did not know of the man's treasonous connections with a foreign power, but she was well aware of the cat and mouse game in which this Duke tried to engage the Queen of Navarre. Isabelle squealed with delight every time the Queen eluded him and his henchmen, as on the night when Queen Jeanne and her party crossed the Garonne River practically under his nose to link up with the Huguenot army at La Rochelle. This was in September of 1568, at the beginning of the third civil war.

"As long as butchers like Montluc are permitted to hold

sway there will be no peace," she wrote. "Almost daily we receive intelligence of the trail of horrors cut by his henchmen, whole populations slaughtered at Bordeaux, Toulouse, Auxerre. These are just some of the incidents of which we have gained knowledge, who knows how many innocent people have fallen victim to the monster's sword for their faith!"

Isabelle had a particular fondness for drawing parallels between the struggle of the Huguenots and the struggles of the Jewish people. One of her favorite analogies was drawn from the book of Esther: "Montluc, that present-day Haman, would destroy God's chosen people, but just as God foiled the plans of Haman and destroyed him, so will he, I doubt it not, destroy this scourge of his faithful."

Arnaud's wounds healed and he rejoined the Huguenot army leaving Isabelle once again to pine and pray for his safety for the entire year of 1568.

Spring 1569 and finally an opportunity for a reunion: "We are traveling to La Rochelle tomorrow! I know I should not feel so elated. The news from the battlefield is grim indeed, but my heart nevertheless beats with mad longing for the arms of my beloved Arnaud. This does not mean that I am not deeply saddened by the death of my uncle, the Prince de Condé, who was cut down on the battlefield in defense of the true faith."

The next entry was dated La Rochelle, the 27th of June in the year of Our Lord 1569: "The time we had together was all too brief. But the war goes on and we all have to make sacrifices. Arnaud looked very well although he was dispirited by our defeat at Jarnac and the death of the prince. The Huguenot army is now headed by two boys, the new Prince de Condé, who is seventeen, and the Prince de Béarn, who is just sixteen. Of course, the most excellent Admiral Coligny is the real leader of the troops and the Queen of Navarre has plunged into negotiations with several foreign powers to solicit help and money for the cause. She even pawned her priceless jewelry to secure a loan from the Queen of England. All to keep the army supplied and going."

A few days later: "Again we spent much time waiting for news from the battlefield. The Admiral has amassed a strong force at La Roche-l'Abeille, but the heavy rainfall of the last three days makes it uncertain whether the battle took place."

During the entire summer and into autumn of the year 1569, the Huguenots engaged the royal forces, losing some engagements and winning others. Isabelle kept a faithful record of every skirmish that conspired to keep Arnaud away from her. Finally in November, a sign of hope: "The royal government has sued for peace! We hardly dare to hope that this time peace will finally come. Too many disappointments in the past, too many terms of agreement broken faster than signed have made us cautious. The Queen of Navarre leads the negotiations for the Huguenots and she is not about to squander our advantage. No guarantee of freedom of worship, no peace! All the Huguenot blood shall not have been shed in vain!"

Marguerite's heart began to pound madly with ill foreboding as she read the next entry: "I recognized him right away, his haughty, imposing figure stood out among the delegates sent by the King to negotiate the peace. I watched him from the window as he alighted from his horse in the square below, the same guarded manner, his eyes darting quickly from side to side, always distrustful as if he expected an ambush. Charles Treffort has not changed since our last encounter when he tried to induce me to stay with the royal party under threats of bodily harm. Had it not been for Arnaud, he might have strangled me."

Treffort had learned of Isabelle's presence at La Rochelle. He had the audacity to inquire of the Queen about her. Although Jeanne d'Albret told him Isabelle had no desire to renew their acquaintance and warned him that his presence in the city was only tolerated as long as he acted in a manner befitting an emissary of the King of France, Isabelle feared his violent disposition.

Her fears were justified almost immediately. The villain gained entrance into her chambers by a ruse. As soon as he was in her presence, he fell on his knees and begged her to go away with him. When he realized that she was unmoved by his display, he changed his tactic and threatened force if she did not follow him voluntarily. She tried to call the guard, but he quickly seized her and placed his hand over her mouth. In the ensuing struggle, she became convinced that he would kill her. She desperately tried to free herself, but with little success. Fortunately, the noise brought Arnaud and several guards to the scene. Treffort had no choice but to let her go. She was sure that Arnaud was ready to kill the knave and was only dissuaded by her reasoning that the killing of a royal envoy would have dire consequences.

Treffort used the moment when Arnaud's attention was diverted to make his exit. His parting curse echoed in Isabelle's ears for a long time. Only Arnaud's assurance that she had nothing to fear from this deranged man made her discount Treffort's warning that he would rather see her dead than in the heretic's bed.

After this incident, Arnaud insisted that they must be married as soon as possible for Treffort would not dare make good his threat against the Countess de Montauban. The two obtained her aunt's permission to be married by Christmas. Since the war did not permit their return to the south, they made plans to be joined in holy matrimony in the citadel of La Rochelle.

Isabelle jubilantly proclaimed in her diary: "Could there be a more fitting place in all the world for a Huguenot wedding?"

Was it coincidence or fate? Her parents were married in the city where she was joined to the Marquis de Launay. Only theirs was a marriage of love, not reason of state.

Marguerite paused. Her eyes burned from the strain of reading through a net of tears, but she did not grant herself the luxury of rest.

The diary entries were getting shorter and less frequent now. Isabelle seemed too preoccupied with day-to-day matters, and probably with wedding preparations, to find time to entrust her thoughts to her diary. There were a few sparse details about the wedding which Marguerite studied eagerly although she had already learned from other sources that her parents' wedding had taken place on the 6th of March in the year of Our Lord 1570.

A few short paragraphs, mostly undated, expressed her anxiety over Arnaud's long absences from La Rochelle. Several brief comments followed about a proposal made by Catherine de Medici to Jeanne d'Albret for a union between the Prince of Béarn and her daughter, the King's sister, Princess Marguerite de Valois. Isabelle expressed her approval of such a prospect. The union between the future leader of the Huguenots and a Catholic princess would heal the divided kingdom. She did not share the Queen of Navarre's reservations, but then she was not a mother concerned about joining her son to a young woman whose reputation was not above reproach.

Isabelle remembered how touched she had been by the timid subservience of the princess during her visit to Nérac several years before. It is hard, she wrote, to believe rumors about an amorous liaison between the princess and the Duke de Guise, a married man and a fanatic enemy of the Huguenots.

The next longer passage dated from September 1571 and was written again at Nérac. Its contents held special interest for Marguerite: "How wonderful it is to be home again, to see the familiar landscape, lovelier than any place on earth, the familiar faces and customs, even though this means a greater distance from Arnaud. But in my present condition, everybody thought it better that I should return to Nérac to await confinement. What a delight it will be to present the House of Montauban with an heir! To think that I had already despaired of ever conceiving a child. All those nights I spent alone at La Rochelle, kept awake by fears of barrenness! Arnaud was my only solace, he never doubted that we would have many children, but I wanted so much to give him an heir immediately.

Now when I lie awake at night, the new life growing inside me fills me with unspeakable bliss. I only wish Arnaud were here, I wish he could place his hands on my rounded belly to feel the kicks that are getting stronger by the day. Would he be surprised to see how big I have gotten? I am sure he wouldn't mind."

Then another pause of several weeks until 14th February 1572: "We have a girl! I know Arnaud will not be disappointed, the next one will be a boy. She is only ten days old and already the most beautiful girl in the world. This is not only a mother's pride speaking, the servants say so too. On Sunday she was baptized and given the name of her grandmother, Marguerite. This is also the name of Marguerite de Navarre, the mother of Jeanne d'Albret, the woman whom the poets called 'the Marguerite of all Marguerites.' One day I shall read her poems and writings to my daughter, the way my dear adopted mother, Jeanne d'Albret, filled so many memorable hours of my youth with her mother's beautiful thoughts."

The diary continued with a brief report about the progress

of the marriage negotiations between the Queen of Navarre and the Queen Mother. Each side tried to extract the most favorable conditions. Isabelle was preoccupied with the joys of motherhood and only wished and prayed most fervently for a successful conclusion of the negotiations so Arnaud would soon return home. All her hopes for the future rested on the union between Henri de Navarre and Marguerite de Valois. The prophecy of peace sounded its most wonderful chant in her ears.

Again Marguerite's eyes overflowed when she read the words: Our longing for peace is so great, we have chosen as the emblem of our union the gentle butterfly—two yellow butterflies separated by the red crossbar of the House of Bourbon. Arnaud chose the inscription from the Book of Psalms. It expresses the essence of our faith:

It is better to trust in the Lord than to trust in man.

It is better to trust in the Lord than to trust in princes.

Our enemies compassed me about like bees.

But the Lord extinguished them like a fire of thorns.

Hark the rejoicing and triumph in the tent of the righteous!

The Lord is our light and salvation,

For in times of trouble he shelters us in his sanctuary.

Then one more entry, made at Montauban in May 1572, before the diary ended abruptly: "The wedding plans are progressing well. It is almost certain that the Prince of Béarn will marry the Valois princess. So much hope attaches to this prospect. It almost seems like a miracle, but if anybody can bring about such a miracle, it is the Queen of Navarre, my dear aunt Jeanne d'Albret. We are traveling north within the week, first to La Rochelle and then, who knows, maybe on to Paris. It may be months before we return and I could not bear to be separated from my little girl for such a long time. I want so much for Arnaud to see her. This way he will hold his daughter in his arms that much sooner. I cannot help but feel that we are on the threshold of a new era of peace."

Marguerite searched in vain for Isabelle's expression of grief over the sudden death of Jeanne d'Albret before the wedding. Then she remembered that this was, of course, the diary she had left behind at Montauban. The Queen died suddenly and inexplicably while Isabelle was journeying north, she may even have been with her in her last hour. Did she suspect foul play as Princess Catherine did, without proof alas? If Isabelle kept a record of her journey, it perished with her.

"Like a fire of thorns," Marguerite murmured.

She did not remember when she fell asleep by the smoldering fire, the yellowing pages in her lap. She was still numb with drowsiness when Noël burst into the room. He was full of excitement as she had rarely seen him. Three riders were ascending the hill to the castle.

Hardly prepared to receive visitors at such an early hour, she quickly locked the diary in the box of inlaid wood and summoned her chambermaid for assistance in a quick freshening up of her toilet and smoothing of her disorderly hair. Who on earth could this be?

The unannounced visitors approaching looked like soldiers, Noël said. Could it be the Marquis? More likely they were mere passers-by looking for hospitality.

Noël preceded her to the rampart from where they observed the approaching horsemen. She strained her eyes for a clue to their identity or intention, whether friendly or hostile before she would give the signal to raise the gate.

The riders had now reached the point where the terrain took a sudden steep climb before reaching the plateau on which the castle was situated. Three men came into clear view as they reached the level ground. Marguerite's heart began to beat faster—it couldn't be. Yet, there was no mistaking, she would recognize the outline of the man riding in front, though slumped over from apparent exhaustion, anywhere in the world.

CHAPTER 15

In early November of the year 1594, the young Duke de Guise and the Count de Treffort-Salignac appeared at the royal court in Paris with an offering of peace. They were graciously received by His Majesty, King Henri IV of France, and the act of conciliation was consummated in a ceremony attended with the symbols and pomp of the ancient rite of homage. The two noblemen knelt before their King and swore an oath of fealty. The pact of mutual support was duly sealed by His Majesty with a warm embrace of his new vassals as had been the custom of liege lords since time immemorial.

Opposition to Henri's claim to the throne had by this time almost completely dissolved. Only a few scattered pockets of resistance from more obstinate members of the Guise clan and some fanatical monks remained. The Duke de Mayenne still operated with a dwindling force in the north but was rarely heard from since the time he stole away from Paris hours before Henri walked through the Montmartre Gate. A more serious threat was the Duke de Mercoeur, yet another brother of the slain Duke Henri, who did his best to keep the flame of rebellion alive in the remote province of Brittany.

The greatest hindrance to peace and unity in the kingdom however came from unprincipled local barons, who driven by greed exploited the peasantry for personal gain in defiance of the royal authority. The most dangerous of these was the Duke d'Epernon, one-time court favorite of the late King Henri III. He ruled the southern province of Provence in a high-handed manner as if it was an independent realm. Cries of help from the peasants chafing under his reign of terror reached the King in Paris almost daily. The pleas were not received with lack of compassion, but the good King, beloved benefactor of his people, was still preoccupied with solidifying his rule and had therefore been unable to intervene in this far-off corner of his realm.

No sooner had the Count de Treffort-Salignac and the Duke de Guise been received into the good graces of His Majesty than they were charged with the mission to rout the scoundrel d'Epernon from his fortification and subdue him to the royal will. Philippe accepted the King's charge with deep gratitude. He mobilized his troops with a verve he had not displayed in years. His old comrades-in-arms were elated to see in him the spark of action rekindled as they lunged south in a reckless, breakneck race, ahead even of the Duke de Guise.

The handful of loyal retainers who had been at his side during the vicissitudes of the past years knew his ardor sprang not only from a desire to prove himself a dependable servant of the King. An even greater spur was no doubt a desire to even the score with the man who had been responsible for his captivity at Blois, which had marked the beginning of his misfortunes. The opportunity to avenge the injustice done by the perfidious late King Henri III and his court favorite was like oil poured on smoldering embers.

With the heedless daring of one who had nothing to lose, who no longer had any illusions and expected nothing more from life, and is, therefore, impervious even to the threat of death, Philippe rode at the head of his men in a relentless rout of the renegade d'Epernon, hounding him from stronghold to stronghold. Only the ultimate triumph of capturing the hated enemy eluded him time and again. Every time the royal forces breached the walls of a fortress where he was believed to be hiding, they found the devil had already contrived his escape.

Early in December, the armies of the Duke de Guise and the Count de Treffort, displaying the insignia and the fleur-de-lys of the Royal House of France, caught d'Epernon's troops in a pincer maneuver on the heights of Luberon in the upper Provence hill country and utterly demolished them. D'Epernon himself, who never rode into battle but preferred to stay in the rear, retreated to his last stronghold in an area surrounded by mountainous terrain, too treacherous to traverse on horseback. The approaching winter season made it unlikely that a successful campaign could be launched before the spring.

The armies became locked in a stalemate, which they could not hope to break by siege alone. D'Epernon still had access to supply routes over mountain passes. The royal forces were in great need of supplies and materiel. The only consolation the King's emissaries had was that they had succeeded in placing the larger part of Provence under royal jurisdiction and the peasantry had been freed from d'Epernon's tyranny.

Such was the situation when a message arrived from the Duchess d'Evreux for her son the Count de Treffort with an urgent plea for his return home if he wanted to see his father alive once again. With the Duke de Guise governing the province and no chance for action until the thaw in spring, Philippe took his leave with the promise to return in due time. Commanding his troops during his absence was the Count de Chillon, the same young man whose courage of conviction he once had envied during a rain-drenched night on the plain of Arques in Normandy and whose loyal devotion to his King had never diminished.

The exploits of the army, dispatched to Provence with orders from the King to free the local inhabitants from the tyranny of the Duke d'Epernon, formed the topic of the dinner conversation in the grand hall at Montauban on New Year's day 1595, the day the three surprise guests arrived at the manor house. In truth, the conversation resembled more a monologue of wondrous tales delivered by that most eloquent of storytellers, Gaspard, the Gascon.

On this night, however, not even his talent could lighten the discomfort that hung like a cloud over hostess and guests. When he ended his story, an awkward silence ensued. The low-burning candles shed a dim light that only intensified the somber mood around the table. Neither Marguerite nor Philippe spoke a word.

Noël had resumed his pouting after his initial excitement about the visitors had been dashed. Marguerite had hoped that he would somehow be drawn instinctively to Philippe, that he would recognize him as a special person without having to explain just then that the gentleman was his father. Unfortunately, this did not happen. His behavior toward the Count was outright hostile and the boy asked permission to leave the table even before the meal was ended. Marguerite granted his wish almost with relief since it removed at least one source of tension that stirred her heart into a furor.

Gilles carried the child from the room, the others remained riveted to their seats, not daring to move nor knowing what to say. Philippe and Mathieu sat pensively brooding, even Gaspard was at a loss for words.

Finally, Marguerite turned to Mathieu asking him if he had news from Bonneval. As if there was nothing in this world that concerned her more, she probed into who had married whom, who had fallen ill, and who had departed this world. She seemed determined to draw out of him every last bit of village gossip. Mathieu did not have much to report, but she clung to any scrap of information, discussing it to death as if her life depended on it.

From time to time, she glanced at Philippe from the corner of her eyes. Had she been free to follow her impulse, she would have rushed to bury herself in his arms. Instead, she had tendered her hand at arm's length, the way she would have greeted any traveler.

In the afternoon, they had taken a walk along her favorite path where the vineyards slope toward the river. Shivering in the cold, they stomped through the thin layer of snow on the ground. Words did not come readily to their lips. They walked on lost in thought, not daring to look up or getting too close.

Finally, she asked in a whisper: "Why did you come?"

"That you should ask such a question is a sad testimony of how far we have grown apart." Bitter laughter throttled his words.

She saw tears in his eyes. How she yearned to kiss them away! But she stood motionless.

"What has become of us, Philippe?" she finally asked.

"I don't know what has become of you—I never changed, my love for you never changed. Until today I carried a faint flame of hope in my heart, a foolish hope as I can see now, that we somehow could still have a future together."

"But you forget I am another man's wife, Philippe!"

"Yes, a man whose amorous adventures are legend in all of France, who is, as everybody knows, more devoted to his mistress than to his wife."

She could hardly refute this fact. He was remarkably well informed about her situation. Suddenly he made a forward motion and emphatically seized her around the waist, pressing her trembling body against his. His passionate eloquence was sweet and alluring: "If I cannot have you for a wife, I want to be your lover. Nobody would disturb our happiness, least of all the Marquis, I assure you. He probably would think you foolish not to take a lover."

How tempted she was! How inclined she was to let herself be seduced by his argument he will never know. But her body stiffened and she pulled away.

"It cannot be," she whispered. "Not now, at least. Not while I am carrying his child."

Judging from the dumbfound look her announcement brought to his face, he had never thought of that possibility.

"Please, Philippe," she pleaded, "if you hate me, my life will not be worth living. Believe me, I didn't plan it this way. I had no choice, you know that, don't you? Please don't take away the only thing that has sustained me during the last few months— the certainty that we still have our love. I know how painful all this is for you, but it is no less painful for me."

He had pulled her slowly toward him again, muffling her last words by pressing her head against his chest. All she could think was if he kissed her, she would be lost. Reason had nothing to do with what they felt at the moment when their lips found each other when they clung to each other with desperate need. Forbidden hopes and dreams revived against their better judgment. How could a love as deep and abiding be contained forever!

Then she remembered the life that was growing inside her. She remembered La Rochelle, the sacred obligation to her mother's memory, the hopes of all those people who had come to her wedding—the Huguenot cause.

Gently, but firmly, she had disengaged herself from his embrace. She had tried to explain, but her words had died in the chill of the wintry air, incapable of breaching the chasm that opened between them. Only in the torture chamber of the inquisition had she felt as helpless as she did when she watched his bewilderment change to disgust. Then, without a word, he had turned away.

She had called after him. Only once did he reply, strident and cutting, the soldier's voice she first heard when he commanded Thierry to let go of her. His men and horses needed rest before moving on to Normandy, therefore they would have to indulge her hospitality until morning.

Marguerite's attention was abruptly brought back to the dinner table when Mathieu impulsively reached across and pulled her arm. The subject had turned to an unhappy love story Mathieu had heard on his last visit to Bonneval. For a moment he fell into the easy familiarity of those afternoons of long ago, in another existence, when they had huddled together like conspirators in the back of the inn or their secret meeting place by the brook.

The story was one of a girl they both had known from childhood, who had fallen in love with a lad from Saint-Villiers. As she knew, the inhabitants of Saint-Villiers and Bonneval had been engaged in a bitter feud for as long as anybody could remember and probably since long before then for reasons nobody, not even the oldest villagers, could recall. The girl's father was so outraged at the daughter's transgression, he locked her in a dark cellar, where she remained for months, and since no other suitor could be found, he forced her to marry the village idiot, just to make it impossible for her ever to be united with her lover. When Mathieu saw her in the village church, her misery had so ravaged her mind and body she had aged by twenty years, her gait had become that of a woman approaching decrepitude.

"That's what love can do to you," Mathieu punctuated his story.

"Some love stories have happy endings."

All eyes turned toward Philippe. Asked to explain, he continued with a note of bitterness.

"You are all familiar with the circumstances of the Baroness Louise de Montreuil and her lover, Raphael Floris, a man of great learning and excellent human qualities—his only failing is his bourgeois origin. This is, of course, in and of itself no shortcoming, only as far as our world is concerned where human beings are classified and separated into what I would regard as quite arbitrary categories."

It was somewhat unusual that the captain should speak thus with his men present, especially since it was not very likely that they knew the couple, but he was addressing himself to Marguerite without wanting it to appear that way.

"As you know the conventions of our world order frown on intermarriage between the estates. These conventions made it impossible for the two lovers to be joined in holy matrimony. Their children had to bear the stigma of illegitimacy. Now, thanks to the intercession of our good King Henri," Philippe was unable to suppress a certain sarcasm, "our lovers are the Baron and Baroness de Fleury."

"That is wonderful news!" Marguerite expressed her unconcealed delight. "I am so happy for both of them! So, all they had to do was petition the King and gracious as his Majesty is . . ."

"Sandrine! Don't be so naive!" Philippe broke into her rhapsodizing with uncharacteristic rudeness. "His graciousness was goaded by very practical considerations, he benefited quite handsomely from the deal. Yes, that's what it was, a business deal as far as the King was concerned. It is becoming a frequent practice nowadays for wealthy bourgeois gentlemen to buy their way into the nobility. I am very happy for our dear friends, don't get me wrong, and I wish them all the best in the world, but for the King, it was a profitable bargain.

Far be it from me to presume to criticize his Majesty's motives, on the contrary, I think the whole affair reveals the astuteness of a great leader. As you are aware, the war depleted the royal coffers long ago, the royal court and government are in chronic need of money. And who has money, large sums of money nowadays? Why, the bourgeoisie, of course—the merchants, the manufacturers! It just so happens that the elder Floris is one of the richest merchants in Antwerp—the man has accumulated a fantastic fortune through trade connections in the New World and a variety of manufacturing enterprises, money lending, investments, what have you. His wealth doubles with the rising and setting of the sun. His only son, instead of following in his father's business, prefers to spend his time studying books and making love to a noble woman. What is he to do with the wealth? He can't take it with him. So why not buy his son a nice noble title and a seat in the Parlement of Arras—five hundred thousand gold crowns is hardly too much to pay for a son's happiness. And since the elder Monsieur Floris, like most of his countrymen, holds a grudge against the King of Spain, he doesn't mind lending a helping hand to the King of France in the bargain. Soon there will be a whole new type of aristocracy, people who will enter the estate through personal merit and with money. I don't hold this against my friend Raphael. On the contrary, I welcome him with open arms. But as for the King being all magnanimity, he is a very shrewd, calculating statesman, as he should be, and he knows to seize his advantage."

Philippe raised his wine cup: "To the happiness of our friends Louise and Raphael, and to the health of the King!"

"I must congratulate Madame on a superb vintage!" He emptied his cup in one gulp and set it down with a thump. "A home-grown variety no doubt? We, Normans, who are raised on hard cider, still know to appreciate a good drop of wine. Some of your wines on occasion even find their way into our humble country inns."

Marguerite just nodded. She well understood his allusion to the Norman inn at Saint Martin-Le-Beau where they had found hospitality one Easter Sunday evening so long, long ago. She refused the bait and would not be drawn into an exchange that could only serve to prolong the agony of this meal. Mathieu and Gaspard finally took their leave with the excuse that the horses needed tending.

Lethargic tiredness overcame her. She just wished to be alone, but Philippe would not go away. Recounting the story of Louise and Raphael had roused him from his brooding and he now seemed determined to talk.

"Please forgive the insensitivity I displayed this afternoon," he began softly, the sweetness of his tone alarmed her more than anything.

"I only wanted to make you understand how crushing was and still is, the realization that there is no hope. Until today I still had dreams, I made plans, now this has been taken away as well. Believe me, I don't blame you—who is to blame I don't know, maybe fate. It just has been our misfortune, yours and mine, that our lives were caught up in a sequence of events neither of us could control. Maybe all we can do now is submit to that fate, unjust and cruel as it seems. Who knows some higher purpose may be served."

She did not answer. They rose and started for the door.

"Look at my sister Catherine and Robert," he suddenly held her back. "Theirs is a love as abiding as it is without hope of fulfillment, yet neither demurs. We must find the strength to follow their example. Look, our solace will be our memories of the time we had together and our son. Catherine and Robert don't even have that."

She had started to move toward him while he was speaking and she leaned her head against his chest as his words flowed over her.

"Please forgive me for seeming so ungrateful," he continued. "I should have thought of the sacrifice you had to make. Of course, I understand that it is your duty to produce an heir for the House of Launay."

She felt the softness of his lips against her ear. A pleasing dizziness filled her head. She inhaled his breath which made her feel as if she imbibed a heavy, sweet wine. Then she felt his arms enfolding her trembling body, rocking her gently while he kissed away the tears that streamed down her face.

"Sandrine! Sandrine! You will always be my Sandrine, nothing can change that." He held her for a long time, consoling her, the way he had held her on that night of their first encounter in the cellar of the inn at Bonneval.

"Must you leave already in the morning?" she asked. "The roads are all but impassible. For our son's sake, I beg you to stay. A few days would give the two of you time to get to know each other, maybe you could even get close. You noticed the look of suspicion in his eyes. I hope you don't take his conduct toward you too much to heart. He is a very distant and often difficult child, distrustful—he only really trusts Gilles and the twin nursemaids from Picardie. I try to be patient, but every time I am confident a barrier between us has been removed, he withdraws again, holds himself aloof. He is still cross with me because of his illegitimate birth. Somehow I think, or better I hope—at this point I am clutching at straws—that knowing his real father may ease his mind, make him less sullen."

"Believe me, there is nothing I would rather do than stay here with you and the boy." He took her hands into his. "But the Duke's health is deteriorating. I received an urgent message from the Duchess that he is not expected to live. I am afraid it may already be too late."

Abruptly, almost violently she freed herself from his embrace. The Duke! She hadn't thought about the Duke all day. Philippe and his father were so different, she had allowed herself to forget that the man she loved was the hated Duke's son, flesh of his flesh, blood of his blood.

"So the Duke d'Evreux is still standing between us!" she shrieked. "I should have known that in the end, your filial obligations will always take precedence. Forgive me, you can hardly expect me to mourn this man's passing."

"You are very unreasonable, Sandrine!" he protested sharply. He planted himself in front of her forcing her to face him.

"Will you please listen to me! I came here with the intent of asking you to accompany me to Evreux—this is our last chance to confront my father—at least on his deathbed he will not withhold the truth."

"The truth about what?" she asked.

"The truth about his conduct toward you. We must not let him take the reason why he banished you from Evreux to his grave."

"Oh, Philippe! You know so little about this man who is your father. What difference does it make why he did what he did, nothing can change the consequences. Let me show you something. His motive will become quite obvious when you see what I have to show you."

She took the lamp from the table and led the way across the corridor to the library. She halted in front of the fireplace and held up the light against the picture above it. Philippe almost did not trust his eyes. There, glowing in the dark, was the living likeness of Marguerite, his Sandrine.

"Who is this woman?" he whispered with awed intimation.

"It is Princess Isabelle de France, Countess de Montauban," she replied. "This is the woman the Duke saw in the courtyard at Château d'Evreux. But he knew she was dead. That is why he was so terrified. He thought he was seeing a ghost. Maybe he thought she had come back to bring him to justice."

"Justice for what?" Philippe was still trying to sort out the bits and pieces bombarding him. "He knew your mother then?"

"Not only knew her, tormented her, and I have good reason to believe that he was responsible for my parent's murder," she said coldly.

"But you said your parents died in the great massacre—so many Huguenots were killed on that day," he protested.

"It does not matter who delivered the deadly blow, the fact is that the Duke d'Evreux wanted them both dead and that he was there."

"Forgive me if I seem to doubt you, but this is a very serious accusation. I must ask you to explain how you arrived at this conclusion. Do you have definite proof?"

"For the sake of our love, I wish it were not true, but unfortunately there can be no doubt. Yes, I do have proof. It may cause you great pain, but you should know the whole story. It is getting very late now. I think it may be well for you to delay your departure at least for one day. You will find the diary of Isabelle de France of greatest interest."

On the morrow, Philippe closeted himself with Isabelle's diary. So absorbed was he, he desired neither drink nor food. When he finally emerged, he was shaken but strengthened more than ever in his resolve to reach Normandy before his father was to breathe his last. He handed the yellowing parchment back to Marguerite.

"Madame," he said stiffly, "please prepare for the journey to Normandy, we have no time to lose."

His tone permitted no objections. Her meek attempt at protesting the wisdom of such a journey given the seasonal hazards were discounted—any delay, he feared, would increase the possibility that the Duke would take his secret to his grave.

CHAPTER 16

In late January 1595, a small band of weary travelers arrived at Château d'Evreux in Normandy. They had set out on their arduous journey from Languedoc, had made it through impassible roads, through ice and snow and biting winds, had evaded bands of brigands, and had suffered hunger and lack of sleep. The hardships, intensified by a heavy foreboding of what lay at the end of their journey, had drained the health and energy of even the hardiest among them.

The itinerary led over narrow-winding mountain passes and wind-swept plains. At times the party advanced only a few leagues each day, hampered in their progress by a broken wheel or simply the need of rest for humans and beasts.

More than once the carriages became mired in mud or deep

snow. Several horses collapsed and expired by the roadside and fresh ones were often hard to find. Gilles, who oversaw the horses, pleaded for mercy, but Philippe permitted no slackening. He drove everybody and himself like a man possessed. Only those who knew his heart knew what abject fear pushed him on, fear of having to live the rest of his life under an oppressive weight of unanswered questions.

Several times they were waylaid by bands of brigands. Fortunately, Marguerite had insisted on being escorted by Captain de Bucheron and a detachment from the Montauban town guard as far as the border of Normandy.

Marguerite herself was indisposed most of the way. The constant jostling and swaying of the chariot, although it was laid out in deep piles of velvet upholstery and equipped with excellent Hungarian springs, caused her to spend the journey in a more miserable condition than she had ever been when traveling about in the primitive caravan of the Oranto Brothers' acting company.

The prospect of returning to the place where she had been subjected to the most degrading humiliation, of coming face to face with the author of her misfortune, plunged her into a state of utmost anguish. She even prayed most fervently that they may find him dead and buried. Over and over she relived the encounter with the Duke in the courtyard of Chateau d'Evreux on that rain-driven October day, saw his face turn ashen the moment he laid eyes on her. It was all so senseless then, but so clear now. She saw little purpose in a confrontation with the Duke. Only for the sake of Philippe's peace of mind did she go along with his wish.

At first, she had resisted the idea of Noël riding in the servants' carriage, but then she was almost glad that he preferred the company of his twin nursemaids who invented countless ways of keeping him entertained during the endless days on the road. Marguerite rode alone, neither the luxurious appointment of the carriage nor the piles of wool blankets and furs enveloping her body against the winter's frost could warm the desolate landscape of her solitude.

When at long last the massive towers and fortified walls of Chateau d'Evreux came into view, their attention was arrested by a somber, intermittent knell. Philippe, alarmed for he recognized the din of the spire of the castle chapel, spurred his horse into a gallop ahead of the rest of the party. To have come this far and find it was too late, was too cruel a possibility to contemplate.

The knell turned out to be not for a person who had died, but for one lying on his death bed. The Duke d'Evreux had not yet joined his ancestors, but he was breathing his last and was expected to expire during the night. The Duchess, his faithful wife of thirty-three years, and his daughter, the Abbess Catherine, knelt at his bedside in silent prayer.

A row of flickering candles at the head of the bed shed a ghostly light over the dying man's pallid face. The rest of the room lay in almost complete darkness and Philippe had to strain his eyes to make out the other persons present. As his eyes became accustomed to the dark, he recognized the outline of his old friend Robert de la Croix, stood at the foot of the bed, dressed in a black cassock and gently swinging a vessel of incense back and forth to the rhythm of a muffled chant. The old Baron de Montreuil, the Duke's faithful ally and comrade-in-arms, was there and so was his daughter Louise, now the Baroness de Fleury.

Philippe recognized most of the servants. Several of the women he had known since childhood wept softly in the background. His attention was attracted by the bent figure of an old man by the window. The man's lips moved in fervent prayer and he was wringing his hands as if he wanted to wrest one last concession from the Almighty. The image of a strange nocturnal encounter by the well in the rear courtyard of the castle flashed before Philippe's eyes. There was no doubt, this man was François, the Duke's attendant, who, he had been told, had retired to his native village long ago. Somehow Philippe had assumed that François had passed away. How neglectful of me, he thought, never to have inquired about him. He made a mental note that he must confront him before he would disappear again.

Philippe kissed his mother and his sister, and after assuring himself that his father was still breathing, he led Marguerite by the hand close to the bed. All eyes turned to Philippe who tried to rouse his father from his stupor. But the Duke lay stiff and unconscious, only his staggered, arduous breathing indicated he was still clinging to life. He gave no sign of awareness of the presence of his son or anybody else in the room.

Marguerite hesitated, uncertain what to do. Her uneasiness about attending the deathbed of the man she hated most in the world intensified. The scene brutal encounter in the courtyard, the crazed, pitiless gaze came back to her once again. She felt no pity, only disdain. The lifeless human shell, his head propped up by a stack of pillows, a grotesque ghost with drooping jaw and hollow, empty eyes, evoked nothing but disgust. She prepared to go when a horrifying scream arrested her step.

The scream continued, a hoarse staccato sound, at first indistinct, then clearer. There was no doubt, the Duke, suddenly sitting erect, his eyes lucid and fixed on Marguerite, called out her mother's name: "Isabelle! Isabelle!" His voice sounded more horrifying with each repetition.

He held out his arms toward her. Against her will, she drew

closer to the foot of the bed. The tears in his eyes stirred her to pity. She strained to make out his words. She realized that he took her to be Isabelle. His speech suddenly became clear for everybody to hear.

"I knew you would come back. All this time, all these terrible, long, long years of loneliness, I had only one thought: one day you would return to me. You must believe me, I never wanted any harm to come to you, never wanted to hurt you—I would rather hurt myself. It was all a terrible mistake, a misunderstanding. If you just hadn't run off with that heretic. Everything would have been straightened out between us, we had our love, but he had to come between us."

"You forget that I am a heretic too," Marguerite heard herself say.

"That is no great matter, with time I could have made you see the truth, but the heretic had to take you away from me."

"He did not take me away from you, it was you who betrayed me, you who lied to me. I trusted you, I believed your promise that we would always be together, when you knew you had no right to make such a promise, you had no right to bind me to you."

With a sudden burst of strength, he shouted: "You were mine, you swore to be mine forever. He had no right!"

"Is that why you killed him?" Hushed silence spread over those present, only a soft weeping sound could be heard from where Catherine was holding the Duchess.

"Yes, he had to die. He had defiled my honor!"

The irrationality of this statement suddenly made clear to everyone what should have been obvious for years, the Duke was mad—his fanaticism, his blood-thirsty religiosity, the cruelty and self-righteousness, all were signs of festering insanity.

Merciless, like the presiding judges at the trial at Chartres,

Marguerite launched her accusations: "So when the opportunity presented itself on that Sunday, the 24th of August in the year of Our Lord 1572, on the eve of the Feast of Saint Bartholomew, you went to the chamber of the Count and Countess de Montauban in the Louvre and you bludgeoned them both to death!"

"No, no," the Duke protested. "I never laid hands on you, only him. He had to die, don't you understand! It felt so good to plunge my blade deep into his chest, and then his bowls, then his organs of defilement, again and again. The warm smell of his blood spurting forth was so intoxicating, I could not get enough. I had to make sure he was dead, dead. But I made one fatal mistake, I lost sight of you, my love, and when I turned to find you, you were already gone, covered with blood, the mercenaries had butchered you almost beyond recognition. I picked you up, tried to breathe life into you, to no avail. Then there was the wailing of an infant, the offshoot of your defilement, and the sobbing of the nurse who had witnessed everything. It was clear, they both had to die. It was all I could think of. But then the nurse fled through a door in the wall. My loyal François followed and carried out my wish. You see, don't you, I could not permit the progeny of the accursed heretic to live. The entire seed had to be eradicated, crushed, so that there would never again be another Montauban—the entire race of the Montaubans had to be wiped off the face of the earth."

Unrepentant, naked hatred spewed forth against an innocent man and his family, even after twenty-three years. The Duke's self-righteous justification of a heinous crime even on his deathbed made every human soul in the room shudder with horror. Marguerite retreated before the trembling bony hand reaching for her.

"Don't you understand, my love?" he whimpered, confused,

uncomprehending. "Tell me you understand that I had no choice. Please don't forsake me now, don't let me die all alone without your forgiveness!"

Marguerite still heard him calling for Isabelle when the door closed behind her. She hurried along the maze of corridors, disoriented and unable to find her way. She paused in the berth of a window niche. She was panting, her chest heaved uncontrollably. Then a gush of gall issued from her in a violent eruption, wave upon wave, years of resentment poured forth in a cataclysmic upheaval, a stream of bitterness washed over the marble floor. Darkness enveloped her as she collapsed unconscious in Philippe's arms.

CHAPTER 17

arguerite awoke from a dream in which she was floating on a lake of warm, sticky fluid. With a jolt, she became aware that she was lying naked in a pool of blood. Peering through her half-open eyelids, she perceived two Carmelite nuns hovering over her. Then she felt lifted, turned over, and washed to the accompaniment of the incessant spinning-wheel hum of prayer. She had no recollection of who had removed her heavy garments. A shiver went through her, the thin linen gown the sisters slipped on her provided little protection. Her body felt light and airy, almost as if she was levitating.

Again a lapse of consciousness. The next thing she was aware of was that she was sinking into a mountain of fresh, soft feather pillows enveloping her in the pleasing sensation of tension easing from her mind and body. She breathed in deeply the smell of fresh linen. Only one desire held her: to lose herself in its soft comfort.

Suddenly, she sat up with a start. She felt for her abdomen—it was empty, void, a hollow shell. A cry of terrifying anguish rent the air. The sisters rushed to apply cold compresses to calm her flailing with admonitions that she must submit to God's will who for whatever reason did not mean this child to live.

When she regained consciousness, she found her hands and feet tied to the bedposts. Next to the bed sat the Duchess d'Evreux, her head bowed in prayer. Marguerite's astonished stare made the woman lift her face toward her. Their eyes met in a long, pained glance.

The Duchess finally broke the silence. She patted Marguerite's hand reassuringly as she confirmed the loss of the child. The long journey under such inclement conditions and the emotional turmoil of the encounter with the Duke had been too much for the fetus, the Duchess explained. Her efforts at maintaining a scientific detachment only thinly masked her own deeply disturbed emotional state. But despite the bizarre revelations of the last few hours, she seemed solely concerned about Marguerite's welfare.

How similar was her expression to the one she had seen on Philippe's face on the day she first looked into his eyes in the barnyard at Bonneval? Just then it occurred to her that he resembled so much more his mother than his father.

"I am so sorry," Marguerite addressed her. "Will you ever be able to forgive me for being the source of so much pain?"

"There is nothing to forgive, my child," the Duchess replied. "You are not the cause of pain. It is I who must ask your forgiveness for not having done anything to prevent the tragic death of your parents."

"But what could you have done? It was such a terrible time, what could one woman have done about this wedding of blood? You mustn't blame yourself for something that was totally beyond your power."

"Please hear me out!" the Duchess insisted. "I have never revealed to anybody the deep feeling of guilt that has been tearing at my soul all these years since that terrible day."

The Duchess motioned to the Abbess, who had remained in the background busying herself with some ministrations, to join them.

"You too, dear daughter, must finally learn the truth. As you know, my relationship with the Duke has always been a distant one. Words were never wasted between us. I never knew the reason for his great hatred for the Count de Montauban. But I was present at the fateful wedding of Henri de Navarre and Marguerite de Valois—I saw, even before it happened, the wedding wine turn into blood. When the orgy of death on Saint Bartholomew's Day was raging in almost every part of the Louvre, I knew of the Duke, my husband, and his men and their rampage of terror and destruction, but I remained silent, hidden in the background. Fear for my life prevented me from venturing out of the safety of my chambers when I might have sounded a warning to the victims. Neither the Duke nor I ever spoke about the terrible events—it was as if it never happened. We went on with our lives, reared our children, as if nothing had ever happened at that wedding, as if the thousands of people who died had never been slaughtered, or at least as if their deaths did not concern us. I guess there was always the rationale that they were heretics and had to die so the Apostolic Faith would be preserved.

The memory of that horrendous day has been alive in me for

twenty-three years. Not a day has gone by since when I did not see before me the archers, the mercenaries advancing through the corridors of the Louvre, breaking down doors, penetrating chambers, searching closets wherever they suspected their hapless victims to be hiding. Never have I forgotten the terrible screams of the dying. Every night, for twenty-three years, their unheeded pleas for mercy have echoed in my dreams.

I was a witness but I did not testify. I saw Princess Marguerite de Valois, the new bride, in a violent fit of hysteria because a man who was fleeing the archers had sought refuge in her chamber and was butchered by his pursuers while crouching on her bed. I saw the bridegroom, the King of Navarre, now our King Henri IV of France, then a mere lad of eighteen, and his cousin, the Prince de Condé, go to Mass at the point of a lance, and I saw both held prisoner at the Louvre. I saw all these things and more. I saw King Charles IX, who only a few days before had been the friend of the Huguenot Admiral de Coligny, permit the man he called father to be murdered by the henchmen of the Guise clan."

The Duchess's voice broke. Then she burst out: "The Guises have been the curse of this land for so long, three decades of suffering, of killing, and destruction have been brought on us to serve their ambitions."

Both Catherine and Marguerite understood that by lashing out at the Guises, the Duchess was lashing out at her husband, the Guise's most faithful ally and accomplice. The placid exterior had fallen from the Duchess's face, with unaccustomed vehemence she rebelled at long last against the tyranny of a marriage that had stifled her for all too long.

Filled with a sudden need to unburden herself, she spoke to the two younger women of the orphaned child bride—her mother died in child birth, her father was killed in the first

Huguenot War—who at fourteen had been bartered off to Charles Treffort in payment of a debt her father had owed the then Duke d'Evreux. Never, in thirty years, had Beatrice spoken of the ruthlessness with which Treffort took possession of his prize, his lovemaking without love, a nightly violation of her body until he no longer had any interest. He isolated her at the castle in Normandy, forbidding her ever to contact or even speak of her relatives in her native Poitou. Her children were never allowed to hear of the Fontenays, the Launays, the Mornays, and so on, a clan of proud aristocrats, most of them adherents of the Reformed Religion. To the Duke they were mortal enemies.

"I am only telling you all this," the Duchess said to Marguerite, "not to seek your pity, but to make you understand that Philippe is not only a Treffort, he has far more of the qualities of the Fontenays than I thought possible since he has never known any of his mother's kin. No Treffort has ever loved with a love that is Philippe's. Believe me, he too has been a victim of his father's tyranny. Now I am most pleased to see that the Duke's control over Philippe's upbringing did not turn him into an exact image of him—no, he did not succeed in suppressing the caring, compassionate qualities in him. Philippe does not deserve to be punished for his father's shortcomings and crimes."

The Duchess had spoken the last words softly, almost inaudibly and yet with firm emphasis, with her eyes diverted toward the ornament above the bed where Marguerite was resting. Slowly she had lowered her gaze and fix it fully on Marguerite.

"I wanted everything to be different," Marguerite said, searching for words to express the inexpressible. "How often have I asked myself what cruel fate could have conspired to keep two people apart who love with as great a love as ours? Why should it be that the fulfillment of the love we hold for each other has been made impossible! Maybe we have to learn to submit to God's will, maybe there is a purpose in all of this. I don't know. Even the most genuine, the most passionate love cannot set us free from the fetters of the forces that lie beyond our control."

Her eyes wandered to the Abbess, who was quietly listening to the exchange.

"How can we ever learn to live quietly when the yearning for the one we love erodes our sanity? Sister Catherine, do you have the answer to how to still the burning desire, how to live through the lonely nights of longing?"

"I am afraid, I am not the one you should be asking such questions," the Abbess replied with a slight tremor in her voice. "Dear Countess, you have already answered yourself. Only submission to the will of God, faith and trust in the wisdom of his ways will sustain us in moments of greatest trial."

"And our good friend, the Count de la Croix?" Marguerite pressed on. "Does he too find solace in such thoughts?"

Catherine's face turned from glowing red to ashen.

"I cannot speak for the Reverend Abbé, but I believe he has found fulfillment in the service to Our Lord, Jesus Christ."

"I beg your forgiveness, Reverend Mother, if I have been too intrusive and caused old wounds to open. Only my great affection for you and my genuine desire for your happiness made me forget the proper decorum."

"No, no," the Abbess protested. "You should always speak freely, dear Countess. I should hope our friendship can withstand the suspension of what is considered proper decorum. From the beginning of our friendship, it was your spontaneity, that particular openness and charm, that made you so dear to me during your stay at the convent of Sainte Hélène's. I am glad to see that all you had to endure in the years since has not erased these qualities."

"I am immensely grateful for your indulgence and affection, but things have changed since then. I can never return to that time at Sainte Hélène's. I am hardly the same person. but the time I was allowed to stay under your roof lives in my memory as the happiest time in my life. Although I should certainly hope that nothing can destroy the friendship we formed then. You must realize, dear Sister Catherine, that I am now a Huguenot. I can only hope that this will never cause a rift between us."

Before Catherine could answer, a lady-in-waiting approached the Duchess with a message from the physician attending the Duke. The Duke's condition was worsening and the ladies' presence was requested at the dying man's bedside for the performance of the holy sacrament of extreme unction—the Count de Treffort, they were told, was already with his father. The ladies excused themselves and Marguerite sank into an exhausted sleep.

When the women entered the chamber of death, they found Philippe holding a somber vigil. They gathered around him, silently giving to understand how well they knew what he was going through, that his heart, like theirs, was devoid of all feeling for the helpless man who in his prime had dominated their existence. They knew that it was not grief or guilt that motivated him to perform this last rite of filial duty, only the family name and honor were still of importance.

While he sat by his father's bedside, waiting for the inevitable to happen, Philippe's thoughts and prayers were with Sandrine. He now realized that she had suffered more than anybody from the volatile nature of the dying man. He could not help but wonder what their lives would have been like had the massacre of Saint Bartholomew's never happened. Chances are their paths would have crossed at some point at the royal court. Would they have fallen in love had they met under such circumstances?

Of what use were such thoughts now? The only thing that matter now was that she should recover her health and strength for the return journey to Montauban. In his innermost being, he could not suppress a certain sense of satisfaction that the child she had conceived in another union was lost, although he wished she could have been spared the pain.

He was grateful for his mother's and sister's reassurance that she would recover and only needed time to rest and heal. But what then? he thought. What would the future be like? There still was no future for them together. She would go back to Montauban and he to his war in Provence.

Suddenly his eyes came to rest on the corpse in front of him. There was the source of all his misery. What good was hating him now? Had he not better exercise Christian charity and pray for the unrepentant man's soul? Yet how could he pray for the soul of one who had caused so much suffering, who had ruthlessly, selfishly destroyed so many lives? Philippe thought of the woman in the diary whose life had been cut short because of this man's obsession, who had to die because one man decreed that she did not deserve to be happy with another man. He searched his father's waxen face. The familiar features had been wiped away, he hardly knew him. What demon possessed this man that he was capable of an obsession in which love and hatred were so closely akin that all distinction was effaced?

Could his obsessive love of Sandrine be compared to his father's obsession for Isabelle? Was it possible that he was like him? No! there was a decisive difference. He was certain that he would never wish her dead, even if she should love another man. Nothing was more sacred to him than Sandrine's life. He would give his own life for hers.

Everything within him rebelled against accepting the fact that a man thus obsessed could be the same man who gave him life. He wondered how a man came to be possessed of such an evil nature. It suddenly struck him that his father had never spoken of his own father or his grandfather. He had no idea what kind of men they had been, nor what relationship he had with his father? He probably would never find an answer. All he could do was make a new beginning.

The thoughts kept spinning in his head in a confused whirl. He had to talk to someone or he would lose his mind. It was then that he became aware that he was not alone. All along there was the quiet presence of his old friend Robert ready to dispense sustenance and solace.

The Abbé Robert had ministered to the Duke since his return home, broken in body and spirit, from the Bastille. Philippe had hardly thought of his friend since he had entered a world so distant from his. A crisp spring day on a hillside overlooking Bonneval came to Philippe's mind. It was there that he had first felt the growing distance between them and yet in times of need Robert had always been at his side.

It was Robert who now made him realize that no peace was to come to his father's soul unless he entreated God to be merciful. With Robert's support, he found the strength to beg God's forgiveness for his father's transgressions so that his soul may be saved from eternal damnation, even though his son could not find forgiveness in his heart.

Nobody was ever to know whether the Duke d'Evreux, before lapsing into a state of unconsciousness from which he never returned, had been aware that the woman to whom he had confessed the murder of the Count de Montauban was not Isabelle come back to life but her daughter whom he had condemned to death twice, as an infant at the Louvre and later as a young woman in the courtyard of Chateau d'Evreux.

It did not matter whether he knew or not, Marguerite tried to explain to Philippe as she was preparing for her departure resisting Philippe's entreaties to wait until after the funeral when he would be free to escort her.

"I cannot stay a minute longer in the house of the murderer of my parents," Marguerite insisted although she was still too weak from the ordeal.

"It is my house now," Philippe declared. "Will you shun my house forever?"

"I haven't thought about that. Let's say as long as he is still here I cannot be under the same roof. Please try to understand. You saw it yourself, he died unrepentant and unreconciled, no word of remorse came over his lips. Till the end, he insisted that he had a right to murder my father and his offspring!"

"But doesn't that show you that he was not in his right mind? He was insane and probably so for many years."

"How can you still defend him? Whether he was insane or not makes no difference to his victims—they are dead just the same. I understand your filial obligations. You have yours and I have mine. I cannot be a party to this man's funeral—seeing him laid to rest with all honors due to his position and status is more than I can bear. I cannot pray that God may have mercy on his soul—I know it is not Christian, but I cannot help wanting him condemned to the eternal fires of hell."

Philippe knew her too well not to realize that their discussion had reached a point where her stubbornness made any attempt at reasoning useless.

"Nobody is asking you to participate in the funeral rites. Only wait until I have discharged certain obligations toward my family. Wasn't it you who reminded me only recently that the duty to family must take precedence over personal desires?"

"I am not standing in your way, so please don't stand in mine. I cannot remain within these walls for a minute longer than necessary." Marguerite continued to pack her belongings, frantically ordering the servants around. She did not want a confrontation with Philippe. Quite to the contrary, but she could not bring herself to say a conciliatory word. The longer they spoke, the wider the gulf grew between them.

"Stop being so self-indulgent!" His voice trembled with anger, sounding echoes from a faraway Easter Sunday in a meadow by the Seine when she had so infuriated him with a self-righteous sermon on the evils of war that he felt she was turning him unwittingly into another Thierry. Back then their altercation dissolved in rapturous lovemaking. Now nothing was left but mutual recrimination.

The futile baiting between them might have gone on for some time had not at this moment something happened that turned their attention in an altogether different direction. Both let out a sigh of relief as the door opened and ushered in a man who was obviously in the decrepitude of his years, his hair a disorderly white, his gait encumbered by gout.

As soon as he caught sight of Marguerite, he advanced toward her and sank on his knees, ardently clutching the seam of her robe.

"Thank God for granting me this moment of beholding with mine own eyes my princess alive. Now I can at long last die in peace."

Before Marguerite could inquiry who the man was, Philippe declared: "François, what is the meaning of this display?"

For the man was none other than the Duke's valet, the same who had bewildered Philippe with cryptic advice on a moonlit night in the outer courtyard, had then disappeared and had been presumed dead, only to reappear at the Duke's deathbed and now made such an inexplicable, dramatic display of emotion.

"My Lord, I beg your indulgence, but I can explain everything. I am reaching the end of my life. Before I meet my maker, I must unburden myself of a memory that has haunted me for more than two decades."

Turning to Marguerite with the urgency of one who had little time left, he began his tale directly: "I was present on that accursed day when Your Ladyship's parents were felled by the blades of the murderers, right before my very eyes . . ."

"Why are you confessing this now?" Philippe interrupted him sharply. "Why not twenty-three years ago, or ten years ago, or on the night you spoke to me in riddles by the well in the outer courtyard? All you did then was leave me confounded with vague references and veiled warnings."

"My Lord, I was not free to speak then, loyalty to my master required my lips to remain sealed."

"A fine loyalty! Making yourself the accomplice to a crime!"

"Please, Philippe let the man speak! What good is all that anger now?"

"Your Ladyship must believe me, not one day has gone by since that fateful day," François continued, "not a single day when I did not wonder what had become of the little princess whose life I tried to save. Albeit there was so little hope that she should have survived. The soldiers were everywhere then, and I had every reason to believe that neither her nursemaid nor she had been spared."

"Isn't this a real heart-breaking story!" Philippe proclaimed impatiently. "All of a sudden we have an orgy of confessions when they no longer do any good."

"But a miracle has happened!" François declared ignoring his young master's sarcasm. "My Princess is indeed here before me. There can be no doubt that she is the same, nobody else could bear such likeness to the unhappy Princess Isabelle. I tried to warn her, you know when I saw her falling in love with my master, but what good would it have done?"

"For one, you might have saved a lot of people much grief and sorrow. You might have prevented the ruin and destruction of the lives of innocent people, you worm," Philippe exploded, infuriated by the man's attempt to justify himself. François burst into tears and buried his face in the seam of Marguerite's robe.

"My dear man, you must calm yourself," Marguerite made the old man rise from the floor and guided him to a seat. "Then I want you to tell me all you saw on that fateful Saint Bartholomew's Day of twenty-three years ago, unburden yourself of all that has plagued your conscience for so long."

The old man thanked her profusely and assured her that she was in every sense of the word a true daughter of Princess Isabelle, who was the kindest and most charming young woman he had the privilege of knowing in this world.

"You were present during her last moments?" Marguerite prompted him.

"Unfortunately, the Countess had already left this world when I came into the room. The mercenaries had killed her while, I must say it, my master, the Duke, took care of the Count de Montauban. I know he did not want her dead, he was too fond of her. It was the time—but, I guess, that matters little in the end. At first, I did not even recognize her. There was so much blood, the soldiers, they were like wild beasts. Then I saw Mathilde de Bécour—I remembered her because she was the same woman who had been attending Isabelle when she traveled with the royal court—well this same woman was clutching the child to her breast. It was whimpering without realizing what was going on, of course—how could it, it was much too small, only a few months old. His Lordship, the Duke, turned to where the whimpering came from. He waded through the puddles of blood toward the woman and child and just then the nursemaid pushed open a hidden door in the wall behind her and disappeared through it. His Lordship raged. 'Get the child! Don't let them get away!' I happened to be closest to the door still ajar and so I was able to block the soldiers from advancing. The Duke called them back, satisfied that I would carry out his command."

François was so overcome with reliving the memory, he breathed heavily. Marguerite feared he might expire right then and there.

She rose to pour some wine. She tilted the cup toward his lips and held his fragile back upright as if ministering to someone wounded in battle. The wine had remarkable restorative powers and holding on to Marguerite's hand, François continued.

"I caught up with them in the dark tunnel. She let out a scream, but I begged her not to fret, I assured her that I wanted to help, that I would never harm the child. Neither of us was familiar with the maze of secret passageways under the Louvre. We wandered around for what seemed hours until we finally came upon an opening that led into the street. It was almost nightfall by then, but the streets were still filled with the horrible screams of those who were being hunted down like animals and mercilessly run through. We waited until it was completely dark, then we made our way to the house of a young woman who had been kind enough to grant me her favors whenever we stayed in the capital. She did not have any customers that evening, the soldiers having spent their energies in the orgy of killing. She was a kind soul despite her sinful way of living and did not hesitate to take in the nursemaid and the child, promising to do whatever she could, although she could not promise much under the circumstances. I left them there and hurried back to my master, fearing that he might get suspicious about my long absence. That was the last time I saw Your Ladyship."

"What was the name of that kind Samaritan? Is she still alive? She kept her promise and helped the nursemaid and the child escape from the city, as my presence here testifies. If she is alive, she must be rewarded."

"I am afraid, she has since been carried off by the effects of the accursed Spanish disease. Several years after the massacre, I found her emaciated and near death, only a shadow of her former lusty self. The first question I asked her was what had become of the woman and the child I had left with her. She told me that her protector, that's what she called her pimp, had smuggled them out of the city through the Louvre Gate as he had done for so many other victims. She said she heard that many of those who escaped were caught and butchered in the countryside."

"Who was her protector?" Marguerite pressed him, filled with a sudden premonition.

"I don't know his name. She told me he was the most powerful man in the underworld of Paris, not even the police dared challenge the authority of the king of beggars and thieves of the court of miracles at Saint-Honoré. It only goes to show that even a criminal can have a good heart."

The old man had barely finished when Marguerite jumped up: "Did you hear that Philippe? This means the man who saved my life can be none other than Arsène Rigoud!"

She covered the old man's face with a shower of kisses and found no end in proclaiming: "Thank you! Thank you! This is such wonderful news! How can I ever thank you enough?"

She flung open the door and rushed out into the hallway calling: "Gilles! Gilles, get the horses ready! We are going to Paris!"

CHAPTER 18

On a windswept day in February of the year of Our Lord 1595, the earthly remains of the Duke d'Evreux were laid to rest in the family chapel alongside an illustrious line of forebears, an ancestral chain stretching back in time for centuries. Few of the mourners shed tears at the Duke's bier. The power and prestige of the House of d'Evreux brought out the flower of Norman nobility, of greater and of lesser order. Dignitaries of the Church, the Papal Prelate, and even an envoy from the King of Spain—the latter's presence went unacknowledged by the new Duke and he departed prematurely in a huff—came to pay tribute to the departed defender of the faith and to bring comfort to the bereaved.

Never was the world to know the sense of relief, the weight that was lifted at long last, the Duke's parting brought to those close to him. The new Duke d'Evreux greeted the mourners with the dignity befitting the occasion and his position as heir to the family fortune and title. Only he knew the meaning of the tears shed by his mother, the Duchess, who leaned on his arm while the funeral procession moved slowly, to the throbbing incantation of Dies Irae, from the castle to the vault that was to receive the body. Her tears were tears of regret for the passage of her own life, wasted and unfulfilled, sacrificed to the demands of a world in which personal happiness counted for little.

If mother and son, pained by a life under the cudgel of the Duke's will, now could not find it in their hearts to pray for the deceased, the daughter knelt beside the coffin immersed in fervent prayer that God may save his soul from eternal damnation. The Abbess, who had long ago escaped her father's tyranny by placing herself under the authority of the Holy Order of the Carmelites, she alone was able to forgive.

While Philippe performed the duties, odious and stale, but incumbent upon the heir, his thoughts were far away on the road to Paris where Marguerite had gone to meet another man. He was never quite sure what the nature of her relationship with Arsène Rigoud was and although he wanted to believe her that it was entirely chaste, he could not help but be consumed with jealousy about her unconcealed fondness for this criminal. Of what use were her assurances that her love for him was everything to her if there were important areas in her life from which he was excluded?

How could he go on with an existence that was nothing but empty pretense? he thought as he mechanically pressed the hands of mourners and well-wishers passing in line before him. What did these people know about him? Never would these shallow fobs understand his obsession with the ironic twist of fate that had deprived him of all reason for living.

He felt an urgent need to get away, to leave these surroundings of painful reminders behind him. He yearned to return to the campaign against d'Epernon in Provence. More than once before had the field of battle served him well in forgetting, for the moment at least, his misery. Now he might even find the longed-for death.

He was about to give himself over to dark brooding when his spirit was brightened by the sight of the Baron and Baroness de Fleury among the mourners. The friends embraced and after an exchange of the customary courtesies appropriate to the occasion, Louise broached the very subject that was the cause of his distress.

"I don't see the Countess de Montauban," she said. "I hope she is well. I was so sorry I was called away when she had just fallen ill. It was a comfort to know that she was under the excellent care of your dear sister and her nuns."

"Judging from your demeanor, Philippe," she continued, "something terrible must have befallen you besides the death of His Lordship, your father. I think it would be good if you unburdened yourself of whatever it is that oppresses your mind and spirit."

"Is it not cause enough to oppress the mind and spirit, as you put it so delicately my dear Baroness, she is the wife of another man?" Philippe burst forth.

"But surely you must realize that this marriage is a marriage of mere political convenience. Marguerite's heart belongs to no one but you, I am certain of it."

"I wish I could be that certain," Philippe grumbled.

"The Marquis's scandalous parading of his mistress is the talk of the entire court."

"No, no, it is not the Marquis, although she seems to entertain some strange notion of loyalty to him for the sake of the Huguenot cause or something like that. No, I wish it were the Marquis she is so fond of."

"Philippe, you cannot seriously think that she has another lover!" Indignation rang in Louise's voice. "You cannot believe that in all seriousness!"

"I wish I could be certain. Maybe you too would have doubts had you witnessed the alacrity with which she ran off to Paris to see this Arsène Rigoud. I don't understand her fondness with this thug."

"Fondness is one thing, love is another," Louise strained to explain to the distressed friend, pushing from her mind the thought that maybe Marguerite's lowly upbringing had left its mark after all.

"Did you say she went to see Arsène Rigoud?" Raphael interjected.

"Yes, when she heard from my father's old servant, who was present at the great massacre and was the last to see the infant and her nursemaid alive, that he had heard it said later the two had been smuggled out of the city with the help of the king of beggars and thieves, she immediately presumed that this man could be none other than Arsène Rigoud. She burst into such happiness that nothing in this world could prevent her from departing for Paris on the spot."

"You must stop torturing yourself." Louise took his arm and led him out on the terrace. "From all you have said, it is quite clear that what she feels for the beggar king is gratitude, friendship. How can you even think that she could love a man of such provenance."

"You forget she was not reared with our class prejudices. You should only see the way they seem to understand each through the subtlest of winks."

"But all this is not important anymore! Arsène Rigoud may no longer be alive." The two turned startled toward Raphael who was following behind.

"If she went to the court at Saint Honoré, her life could be in danger. For several months now, a bloody war has been raging in the underworld of Paris. While such ranklings are nothing new, open warfare seems to have broken out between the courts of Saint-Honoré and Saint-Marcel. I heard that several months ago Arsène Rigoud captured and executed a certain Jéhan Vignerie of Saint Marcel. Turmoil has been raging ever since. Rumors have it that Arsène Rigoud was captured and executed for his part and that the thugs from Saint-Marcel now rule the underworld on the right bank of the river as well as on the left. The new king is said to be a shadowy figure who directs operations from behind a screen of obscurity. He takes great care not to become the target of reprisals. These are, of course, all unconfirmed rumors, but if there is any truth to them, any friend of Arsène Rigoud's will not fare well."

While Raphael was relating the news, Philippe recovered his old mettle and presence of mind. Gone was the melancholy that had immobilized him. His son's life may be at stake as well! He lost no time in drawing the obvious conclusions and quickly decided what needed to be done. He summoned Gaspard and Mathieu and this very night, joined by Raphael, the old comrades scampered in a merciless race toward the capital.

The clanking of the closing gates resounded with ominous foreboding. The sound conjured up images of past captivities and, for a moment, fear of being trapped once again gripped Marguerite's heart. But the gates she heard falling shut behind her were, she reassured herself, the gates of the city of Paris closing for the nightly curfew. Was she not in the company of Gilles?

They had reached the city gates just in time. In the morning they would pass through the gate again free and unimpeded. No more prisons, no more sieges, all that was behind them. All she longed for was a brief reunion with Arsène. Then she would return to the inn at Saint-Cloud where she had left her son and the servants. Nothing would stop them from returning to their home in the south, to a tranquil if not happy existence. She swore to herself that she would never again return to this region of the kingdom where too many painful memories stood in the way of the healing of old wounds.

Her fears were allayed by a sense of joyous anticipation. She realized how much she had missed Arsène. And if he would not come out of his cave in this city, then she had to come to him. For the first time, she came to him, not as a supplicant, but because she wanted to thank him. That he should have saved her life as far as back as her infancy and under considerable risk to himself, just fit the image she had of him, of the bandit with the heart of gold, the benefactor of the poor and the oppressed. The other side of his character, the ruthless brutality with which he ruled over his territory and the fact that he did not shrink from murder to preserve his position, she rationalized away as necessary for survival in a brutal, violent world. Besides, it was of no concern to her. In her eyes, Arsène could do no wrong.

She took a considerable risk in entering this city where she had gained great notoriety and was almost as familiar as the Duchess de Montpensier. It would certainly be unwise to have her presence come to the attention of the royal court. Neither the King nor the Marquis de Launay would understand why she, in the guise of a gypsy—she had borrowed a pair of trousers, shirt, and short cape from Gilles' wardrobe and tucked her hair under a broad-rimmed felt hat and topped by a hood—should be roaming the lower-class quarters on route to a rendez-vous with the king of the underworld. Though the King of France had always viewed her escapades as the charming eccentricities of one not reared the right way, this time he may not be as favorably disposed of them. Then she also ran the risk of coming to the attention of certain friars who were still bent on capturing the witch of Chartres.

The pair passed through the shadow of the Louvre and without stopping began their descent into the murky, yet familiar, realm of narrow twisted alleys that was the belly of Paris. Marguerite was relieved to find only a sparse number of people loitering in the streets. The bitter chill of the March Saints kept them indoors. It was just the same to her. She pulled the hood over her face to shield it against the raw, moist wind. As they approached the court of miracles at Saint Honoré, she noticed immediately the gate had come unhinged again and was twisting slowly in the wind, the eerie screeching was reminiscent of a death knell. She fought against a vague sense of ill-foreboding. The court lay deserted, desolate almost, just as she had first found it during the siege, she thought, not at all teeming with life as only the year before.

"It must be the weather that keeps them inside," she whispered to her companion pulling the cape tighter to ward off the chill.

"Are you sure it is safe to go in there?" Gilles whispered. "It may be better for you to wait out here while I go and reconnoiter the area."

"Don't be silly. Arsène is probably at dinner just now. I must say I am mighty hungry. Come on, let's go, what should there be to fear!"

When they reached the middle of the courtyard, a gang of thugs, appearing out of nowhere, blocked their path. It was difficult to tell how many there were or whether their demeanor was friendly or hostile, since the glare of the torch held to their faces, blinded their sight.

"What is your business in this court?" The voice, whose owner's face remained indistinguishable behind the flickering torch, had the flat intonation of the Paris canaille.

"We are friends of the king of beggars and thieves, and wish to be taken to him." Marguerite tried to speak in a low voice so as not to reveal that she was a woman. The deception seems to have worked. For when someone inquired from inside the tenement what was going on, the same man answered that two gypsy fellows who claim to be friends of the king of beggars and thieves demanded to be admitted into the presence of his majesty.

"I didn't know the king had any friends. Tie them up and bring them in! We shall see whether they are speaking the truth."

The remark struck Marguerite as very odd. The dissolute tone of the man was not at all in keeping with the deference with which she had heard the men speak of Arsène. Suddenly it struck her like lightning. Something was wrong here, but it was already too late.

The thugs pushed them both inside, through the familiar heavy, wood-carved door and down the flight of stairs to the cellar where she knew was Arsène's "throne-room."

"Your majesty, we found these two gypsies snooping around the courtyard," the spokesman with the Parisian patois announced while the others pushed them inside the vaulted room, cluttered, as before, with furnishings.

"They claim to be friends of the king of beggars and thieves. I say they are spies."

The outline of the dark figure standing with his back to them in the far corner of the room was immediately familiar to Marguerite. But it was not Arsène who was two heads taller than this man. Even before he turned around and approached the middle of the room where they were standing, she knew she had walked straight into the hands of Hervé Hachette.

Unable to pull the hat deeper over her face since her hands were tied in the back, she lowered her head to evade his probing eyes.

"I say they are common thieves. What do you say, let's string them up," one of the thugs suggested.

"Maybe they are, maybe they are not. I shall decide what they are." Hachette's throat still emitted a croaking sound interspersed with high-pitched wheezing.

"Gypsies, eh? Well, we'll see. I've had enough of gypsies for a lifetime."

He started to pace in front of them, dragging his pain-ridden, wasted body, only his eyes were keenly alert. For about five minutes, he observed them intently without a word. Only a derisive smile in the corner of his mouth betrayed how much he savored the power he held over the captives. His ability to create an atmosphere of almost unbearable tension was what gave him the deepest satisfaction. Slowly and deliberately, he lowered his gaze on Marguerite, the bloodhound's nose had picked up a familiar scent. With a sudden, abrupt movement of the hand, he flung away her head covering causing her shiny blond curls to fall over her shoulders.

"Welcome, Madame! What a privilege to welcome the Queen of Sheba to these humble surroundings!" His voice rose to a shrill triumphant pitch. "But, of course, how could I forget, Madame is no stranger to this court."

He circled her as he had done at the police prefecture during their first encounter. He came to a halt behind her and ran his gnarled fingers slowly through her hair.

"I knew sooner or later you would come," he murmured.

"All I had to do was wait. I have learned to be patient, that is all it takes, patience."

"Where is Arsène Rigoud?" she finally managed to say.

"Oh, yes, of course, Madame came to see the king of beggars and thieves. I am not so vain to presume that she came to see me, old Hervé Hachette. Madame, the king of beggars and thieves is standing before you. Arsène Rigoud is no more—he is finished, over and done with."

With the last words, he described a telling gesture across his throat accompanied by a grating sound. Arsène dead? She could not believe it. Hachette must be bluffing. But all the evidence indicated that he may be speaking the truth.

"I am afraid it is true, poor Arsène is resting peacefully at the Cemetery of the Innocents, a place I am closely acquainted with, as Madame well knows. But I am forgetting my manners. We have so much to talk about, we should do it in a more comfortable pose."

He turned to the thugs and ordered them to untie her hands.

"Lock the gypsy up in the dungeon—we shall deal with him later." Then with an elegant gesture, he turned to Marguerite bidding her be seated in one of Arsène's luxurious, upholstered chairs. She cast a desperate glance at Gilles as they led him away. Then she was all alone with the man she dreaded most in the world.

"Now, it's only us, little queen. This is the night I have been dreaming of for so many years." He rubbed his hands together, gloating in anticipation.

"We shall have dinner together, you must be hungry, and if Madame is reasonable this night can be a night of unlimited possibilities for both of us. You must admit we both have made quite a career since that day when you came to me begging for the lives of those renegade gypsies. I should have had them shot right away then, riff-raff like that is hardly fitting company for a queen. Now I am the king of beggars and thieves and you shall be my queen. We shall reign together and live happily ever after."

Marguerite sat quietly, her body stiff and rigid, not for one moment did she take her eyes off this knave. Under different circumstances, she might have pitied this pathetic creature who was still spinning unattainable fantasies. But she knew she could never relax her vigilance for he was a dangerous man, whose delusions could not be taken lightly. The most effective tactic would be to pretend to go along with his fantasies, to turn his vanity and susceptibility to flattery against him. Nothing made him more vindictive and unpredictable than outright rejection.

"Congratulations, my dear Monsieur Hachette," she said, never knowing how she mustered such a cheerful, social tone. "You have executed a brilliant coup—to usurp the place of a man as powerful as Arsène Rigoud is no small feat. You must tell me how you did it."

This was all the encouragement he needed.

"You must call me Hervé," he replied, his chest heaving with elation. "You are right, it was no small feat and I must admit without the determination of my good friends from Saint-Marcel, you have met some of them, it would have been well-nigh impossible to dethrone the mighty Arsène Rigoud."

Hachette's speech was interrupted by the entry of a pitiful, grotesque creature, cursed with more deformities than Marguerite had ever seen in one human being. The man placed a platter piled with assorted meats and vegetables and a pitcher of wine on a table near her. Marguerite's interest was aroused but she could not fully understand the words they exchanged. Hachette thanked him profusely, cordially almost.

"I am sorry I did not introduce you," Hachette turned to her after the man had disappeared behind a screen where she knew was a door leading to what used to be Arsène's private quarters.

"This was Samson, my right-hand man, there is no man more loyal and devoted to me in this world. You might remember him, he was the gravedigger at the Cemetery of the Innocents. He saved my life after Your Ladyship left me there to die. Very callous on her part. But all that is now in the past. Madame shall see I am a very forgiving man."

"But let's eat and drink!" The pallor of his face disappeared under a flush of animation as he sat opposite her at the table. To oblige him, she sipped the wine and forced down a few bites of the boiled mutton while her mind searched desperately for a way out of her calamity.

"As I was saying, Arsène Rigoud made a fatal mistake when he killed Jéhan Vignerie, the king of the court of miracles of Saint-Marcel," he continued in a light conversational tone. "After that, the boys of Saint-Marcel had only one goal—to get even with Arsène Rigoud. All they needed was someone to lead them, someone who hated Rigoud as much or more than they did."

He took a deep gulp from the wine, smacking his lips as he slowly savored its bouquet.

"On the day when all of Paris celebrated Madame's remarkable victory—I am sorry I did not have the opportunity to congratulate her—well anyway, nobody paid much attention to Hervé Hachette. Most people probably thought, if they thought at all, that he had gone back to the cemetery to give up the ghost. Am I not right? But my friends from Saint-Marcel, who had followed the proceedings as avidly as everybody else in town, knew where to find their leader. Believe me, it was not easy to rout Arsène Rigoud. When he was finally captured, there was nothing I could do to save his life. My friends insisted on an eye for an eye. It was then only natural that I should be elected king of the court of Saint Honoré. Only one thing was missing to make my life complete. I waited patiently. I knew that one day Madame would return to this place. I knew she was nothing but the whore of a common criminal. But I forgive her, now she will take her place at my side as my queen."

Marguerite sat motionless, her face blank and without expression, not daring to give herself over to her grief for the lost friend.

"I must warn you, my husband, the Marquis de Launay, will kill you if something happens to me." Her attempt to intimidate him with threats of reprisal from a powerful nobleman elicited derisive laughter.

"How naive you still are! Death cannot frighten one who has already been there and has nothing to lose. Besides, I don't believe the Marquis knows of your whereabouts. Would he approve of his wife slipping into Paris in gypsy clothes for a secret tryst with a common criminal? No, it's just you and me. No matter how you look at it, the cards are all stacked in my favor. There is no way out."

"What do you want from me?" she called out, barely holding back the tears of frustration. "Why don't you leave me in peace? What have I ever done to you that you hate me like this?"

"First of all, I don't hate you, I never hated you. Would I make you my queen if I hated you?" Hachette now felt in total control. Sensing that he was finally on the verge of breaking her, he could let go just a bit and show himself to be human after all.

"Madame doesn't seem to remember what she did to me. It was probably not important enough. I have never forgotten, not for one moment have I forgotten your words that you would rather go to Asylum than let me touch you. Isn't that exactly what you said when I made a generous offer to save you from a miserable existence? You see, it is not nice to make a man feel as if he was more repulsive than the lowest creature on earth, that he is no more than vermin. I believe Madame even used that very word."

Marguerite remained silent. There was nothing she could say to a man as obsessed as Hachette. She could have told him that he was abusing his office to gain control over her, that he was trying to exploit her situation for his base ends. She could have told him that she has a right to choose or refuse a lover as she pleases. What good would it do? This man's twisted mind was hardly open to reason. The determination then formed in her mind that she would kill Hervé Hachette if he tried to force himself on her.

From the corner of her eyes, she scanned the room. There were plenty of heavy objects. She eyed, in particular, a wrought-iron candleholder that was heavy enough to crush his skull. Hadn't she been in situations like this before? Nobody, she swore to herself, as she had done on the night of her wedding to Etienne and again when she faced the monk at Saint Victor, nobody would ever violate her. Either she or the attacker would die.

To her surprise, satisfying his sexual appetite was not on Hachette's mind just then. He seemed to have a greater need to talk, to pour out his heart to her. She had been so preoccupied with devising a strategy to fend off the anticipated attack, she had hardly paid attention to the flow of words gushing forth from one who had long been deprived of human company.

Something in his disjointed babbling about misery and disease, abandonment and hunger, aroused her curiosity. Hervé Hachette was relating the story of his childhood, a childhood of poverty and misery in the streets of Paris. He spoke of a sickly child, cursed with rickets and abandoned by his father and relatives after his mother had been carried off by the plague. He had to learn to survive by his wits since he lacked physical strength.

He was not looking for pity, he assured her, only justice. One day while begging for alms, a gang of street urchins assaulted him, took his earnings, and left him in the gutter bleeding severely. He was taken to an orphanage run by the Society of Jesus. They saved his life but he never felt any gratitude toward the Jesuits, for the discipline at the orphanage was worse than a living hell.

He received a well-rounded education though, albeit accompanied by almost constant severe beatings, long hours in dark isolation, for his was a mind superior to that of his teachers. He grasped the nuances of the meaning of the ancient texts they studied with greater lucidity than anybody and most of all— capital sin of capital sins—he had a tendency to challenge the validity of any proposition with the most penetrating questions. The Jesuit fathers were soon convinced that a mind such as his was too dangerous to be left to develop freely and when he had grown into a young man of fifteen they tried to coerce him into taking the vows of obedience. He pretended to go along but secretly he attended more lectures on jurisprudence at the Sorbonne than on theology. Eventually, he was found out and was thrown out and left on his own resources, which were next to nothing.

For several years he existed on the brink of starvation and in ill-health but kept himself afloat through private tutoring. Bit by bit he scraped together the money so he could present himself for the examinations.

"You see, Countess," he said with a good measure of self-approval, "my whole life has been a struggle against odds, against injustice, and ill-treatment. In the end, I have always prevailed."

"I am very moved by your story," she replied. "But yours is not a unique fate in a world full of injustice and cruelty. I don't see how this gives you the right to inflict cruelty and injustice on others you happen to have in your power."

"Ah, I don't need your pity!" He shrieked incensed, lifting himself from his chair. "What I want is admiration for what I have accomplished. You women are all the same. Pity, that's the only emotion you are capable of."

He had talked himself into such a fury, he started to pick up some of the objects that cluttered the room and smashed them against the wall while he paced back and forth. Several times he came threateningly close to where Marguerite was seated. An insane spark lurked in his eyes. She had to stall for time—something might happen, maybe Gilles will free himself and get help.

She concluded that the only thing she could do was choose her words more carefully so as not to arouse his anger. She had to encourage him to talk more about his life since that was the topic dearest to him.

"Tell me about the woman who is so much like me," she said. It was not too difficult to feign interest since she was genuinely curious to hear about the woman who had so hurt his pride, had so inflamed him with a burning hatred for all women, that total power over the opposite sex had become his all-consuming obsession.

"Oh, that was so long ago, I hardly remember her at all." He stopped his raging and dropped into a chair panting.

"But she still seems to be on your mind whenever you are in the company of a woman."

"Of course, she is on my mind! How could I ever forget? She betrayed me, laughed me in the face, derided me. Vermin from the gutter, she called me. And that after I had proposed marriage to her. I wasn't good enough. Then she went and married that fop."

"Who was she? She must have been very beautiful that you loved her so much."

"Yes, she was very beautiful and at one time she was very kind to me. She was the daughter of a city advocate to whom I had become apprenticed as a law clerk. He was a kindly gentleman, a widower who lived alone with his daughter. He took me into his house, like a son I was received. For the first time in my life, I had a home. I took my meals at the family table. She served me as she would any member of the household. Her whole behavior seemed to justify my boldest hopes that the devotion and affection I held for her was pleasing to her and that she too shared these feelings. We never spoke about it, but words are not necessary where such warmth and harmony exists. How was I to know that she was meeting the other one on the sly? Then one day—I was so certain of her favor—I told her that I wanted to ask her father for her hand in marriage. Never will I forget the scene, her expression of outrage is forever singed into my memory. She called me preposterous, imputed to me all manner of ill intent like buying my way into respectable bourgeois society in hopes of taking over her father's law practice and property. There I stood, unable to respond to the abuse, my soul bleeding as if it had been impaled on a hundred swords."

He had raised himself out of the chair. He slowly approached his captive whose heart was pounding.

"I left and she married the other," he continued with an ominous whisper. "But I will share a secret with you, because you of all women, remind me most of her in deceptiveness and beauty. It will be our secret onto the grave. I did get even, I got my revenge—nobody noticed, a few more bodies didn't matter on the day of the great massacre on Saint Bartholomew's Day. I killed her myself and the daughters she had born the fop. Only the fop I could never get because he enjoyed the protection of none other than Arsène Rigoud. But now nothing will stop me from finally wreaking my revenge on him too. I know where he is and he cannot escape the wrath of the new king of beggars and thieves, the most powerful man in all of Paris. And you Madame, will help me lure him into my trap. For he trusts you, I know that."

His voice was hoarse with fever. He was devoid of remorse. He erected his frail figure in front of her, casting a menacing shadow over her by the dimming light of the candles, his face had become a contorted, pained grimace.

"You are the devil incarnate!" The horrified whisper died on her lips.

"The hour is getting close to midnight. You must get ready now, my dear, for the celebration of the mass." He rang a bell. Two women, who had no doubt made their living through the sale of their bodies in better days, accompanied by two armed thugs entered almost immediately.

"Prepare the Countess for the mass and bring her to the chapel at the strike of midnight. If she resists, the usual treatment will do. I must spend some time in meditation. We shall be together again within the hour, my queen." He blew a kiss in her direction, waving both arms with a gallant smile while the women tied her hands and led her away.

At the time when the exchange between Hervé Hachette and Countess Marguerite was taking place at the court of Saint-Honoré, four horsemen raced toward the city of Paris from the approach to the Louvre Gate in a thunderous cloud of dust. Philippe de Treffort-Salignac and his companions had no intention of letting the late hour keep them from reaching their goal. Albeit, when they arrived, they not only found the gate shut, as they had expected, but the gatekeeper proved incorruptible and no manner of pleading or cajoling, or offer of a generous bribe, was able to make him budge.

"Whatever happened to corrupt gatekeepers?" Philippe despaired.

"Gaspard, Mathieu see if there is a suitable spot for scaling the wall."

"With that many soldiers on the ramparts, we'd better wait till morning," Gaspard replied.

"We don't have time until morning! There must be some loose stones in the walls for us to slip through."

Their attention was commanded by whistling from above. By the torchlight, they made out a guard leaning over the rampart, motioning them to come closer.

"Go to the gate at Saint-Denis and tell the gatekeeper there that his brother-in-law sent you, for a nice reward he will let you through."

In a mad dash, they raced along the ramparts north to Saint-Denis where they found the gatekeeper perfectly willing to admit them for a gold crown a piece. The horses had to be left at an inn nearby.

Whether the gatekeeper was getting greedy or the moment was not propitious was not clear, but when they returned to the gate, they were told they had to wait for the changing of the guard at midnight. They huddled in the shadow of the massive wall impatiently waiting for quiet to return to the ramparts. Raphael engaged the gatekeeper in conversation to find out if he had any useful information. Casually he inquired about rumors of a bloody feud in the Paris underworld. The gatekeeper confirmed that Arsène Rigoud had been executed by the rival gang of Saint-Marcel and that the new king of the Paris underworld was a corrupt cripple, a former police prosecutor named Hervé Hachette.

Marguerite did not remember falling asleep, but she was suddenly roused from what must have been a state of unconsciousness by an unpleasant, putrid stench. An admixture of sweet incense and decaying flesh was biting her nostrils. She had no recollection of how she came to be stretched out on what seemed to be a table, clad in no more than a very light gown, her body shivering from a damp chill in the air. From somewhere in the room came a mumbling sound of Latin phrases, as if someone was praying. She tried to raise herself, but she was unable to move, her limbs felt heavy and numb as if they were held down by an invisible weight.

Whatever the two women did, they certainly succeeded in putting her into a state of total helplessness. All she remembered was that she protested against being bathed and oiled, but her senses were already dulled and her will to resist greatly weakened. Hachette must have poisoned the wine or the food! Her fighting spirit revived, but to even raise her head required the utmost strain. Close to her, she perceived a man, cloaked in black, whom she recognized as Samson, the gravedigger. Pulled over his face was a black henchman's hood. He was engaged in swinging back and forth what resembled an incense vessel on a chain, only this one lacked the sweet fragrance of true incense and seemed to be the source of the putrid stench that permeated the air.

Suddenly, the sound of prayer ceased and the gravedigger put away the incense vessel. He approached the table on which she lay with two massive candleholders and placed them behind her. He lit the half-burnt, pitch-black candles and placed them on some kind of altar. She was trying to remember what Hachette had said about a midnight mass when she caught sight of her adversary.

Hachette was dressed in what at first glance looked like priestly ceremonial garments, on his head a bishop's miter, but all, including the miter, was in black. Behind him on the wall she spotted a cross hanging upside down—she now became aware of upside-down crosses on the walls all around, casting elongated shadows by the glow of the candles over Hachette whose figure was magnified to demonic proportions.

She had heard of black masses and devil worshippers, but she never believed that anybody could be so depraved to commit such blasphemy. She realized that once again her greatest mistake had been to underestimate the depth of Hervé Hachette's depravity. He finally seemed to have won out.

Cold sweat broke through her skin and the cold silver chalice he placed on her sparsely covered abdomen made her quiver like a leaf exposed to the whim of the wind. Hachette leaned over her. He reached into the chalice and took out a round waver. He held it up in the manner of a priest holding up the host during the performance of the miracle of changing the host into the body of Christ. Only this waver was black and its consecration by this high priest of Satan was accompanied by chants in a language familiar and yet so strange. The cadence was similar to the Latin liturgy of the Catholic mass, only backward in a grating, cacophony.

Marguerite tried not to think of what Hachette's ultimate goal might be and for what role she had been chosen in this satanic ritual. She watched him intently as he began to intone a disharmonious hymn in praise of the Evil One.

Marguerite began to pray. She prayed fervently that the Lord Jesus Christ, who died on the cross to redeem all the children of man, may preserve her and bar the evil spirit from entering her mind and body.

She was only vaguely aware of the sequence of events that

followed—the sharp pinch of Hachette etching her wrist, the disturbance at the door, the exchange between the intruders and the devil's priest, the knife raised to her throat.

As if from far away, she heard the rattling voice with the wheezing sound: "I forfeited my life long ago, remember I was already dead, but I have come back for the devil's bride." His terrible laughter, fraught with madness, rent the air.

When Philippe and his companions reached the outer yard, they were accosted by a group of thugs. As they prepared to fight their way in, the spokesmen of the group, to their surprise, made a sign of peace: "If you want to save the lady who came here this evening looking for Arsène Rigoud you must hurry. We are thieves, but we are also good Christians and hope for ultimate redemption and salvation—we have nothing to do with devil's worship. Come on, we'll lead you."

Philippe and his friends broke through the door of the devil's chapel as Hachette was collecting drops of blood from Marguerite's wrist in a silver chalice. Realizing that he could not fight this overwhelming force and that he could not continue the sacrifice in the prescribed manner, he raised the knife to her throat.

"You won't get out of this alive!" Philippe called out.

The threat was answered with derisive laughter. What did he, Hachette, have to fear from death? He had already been there, but his master, the Almighty Prince of Darkness, had given him a second chance so he could bring this unfinished business to a conclusion and return to the netherworld with the bride Satan had promised him. No vain threat was to keep him from being united with his queen in death.

Philippe quickly weighed the odds. He measured the distance between himself and the adversary and calculated how quickly he could reach the other side of the altar where Hachette was barricaded. He was preparing for a lightning dash when the explosive sound of a pistol shot reverberated in the vaulted room. Hachette stumbled backward, blood gushed from his head, with a moan he sank to the floor.

A man whose presence nobody had noticed stood over the dying man calling out in a voice raised to such loudness as if he wanted to make sure that he was heard in the world beyond: "Let it be known that it was I, Joseph Perron, who had the satisfaction of eradicating this evil from the face of the earth!"

Almost simultaneously, the men tended to the half-conscious woman. Philippe wrapped her in a cloak while Raphael bandaged the wound on her wrist to stop the flow of blood. Amid the turmoil, Philippe, at long last, held his beloved Sandrine in his arms, holding her as if he wanted to console her for all the evil in the world.

Gradually, Marguerite regained consciousness. Still nestled in Philippe's arms, her body almost fused with his, she looked around the room. They were all here, all the companions who had stood by her through her most difficult trials: Raphael, Mathieu, Gaspard, Gilles, and Joseph Perron—only Arsène Rigoud was gone.

With Philippe's aid, she walked around, embracing each with gratitude and affection. When she came to Joseph Perron, she found him quietly weeping.

"It was your wife and daughter he murdered on Saint Bartholomew's Day in 1572," she said softly. He nodded. She took his hands and pressed them emphatically, letting him know how much she felt his pain and sorrow.

"When I heard that it was Hachette who had usurped Arsène's position, I planted several spies here at the court who reported to me everything that was going on. A few hours ago, a message reached me that a noble lady, who said she was a friend of the king of beggars and thieves, had come to the court and had been taken captive by Hachette. I knew it had to be Your Ladyship. I quickly made my way over here. For years, I had been waiting for the opportunity to avenge the death of my loved ones, but though I knew, I had no proof it was Hachette. Arsène finally furnished evidence of Hachette's guilt, but before we could act, Arsène himself fell victim to this interminable gang warfare. Now I can gladly die with the satisfaction that this evil is no more. I know, God in his infinite understanding will forgive me, if I cannot forgive my enemy and pray for his soul."

"There is one at least who mourns his passing." Raphael pointed to the contorted figure of Samson holding Hachette's body and letting out faint whimpers like a dog who lost his master.

"As well he should," said Perron. "He is a most charitable soul. I wonder if he understands the depth of the evil nature of the man he served so selflessly."

Turning to Marguerite, he bowed gallantly: "I must take my leave of Your Ladyship. Even if we won't meet again in this life, my prayers shall always accompany you. I hope you and His Lordship, the Count de Treffort-Salignac will find every happiness and fulfillment—sometime, somewhere in this world."

With this, he turned and was gone.

Marguerite stared at the door through which he disappeared for a long moment. A sad emptiness filled her heart at the thought that she would never again see this quietly suffering man, whose life had intersected hers in moments of greatest distress. Maybe she was saddened also because at this moment she realized that there was nothing more for her to do here. The past had given up its secrets and had, at long last, released her. She was free to go, free to somehow find a way to face the future. Frightened by the vast emptiness of the unknown before her, she pulled the cloak closer around.

She did not know how long she stood there staring into blank space. Philippe's voice brought her back: "It is almost dawn, the gates of the city will open soon. It is time to go home."

He placed his arm around her and without a word led her away from the scene of terror and evil.

Epilogue

Annus mirabilis 1598! Year of peace! Peace had come to the Kingdom of France at long last. Thirty-six years of strife had come to an end. In every town, village, and hamlet the dawning of peace rang out from the church towers—peace at home and peace abroad. Annus mirabilis 1598! Nearly a decade after he had become heir to the throne, Henri de Bourbon, King of France and Navarre, was master in his own realm. All resistance had been wiped out, every last rebel was subdued.

Nowhere was the rejoicing greater than among the brethren of the Reformed Religion. For four years the Huguenots had watched the events in the kingdom with mounting apprehension. Uncertainty had marked their existence since their leader, Henri de Navarre, had embraced the Catholic religion. Not that they did not look upon their King with pride, not that they did not support their King against his enemies in words and deeds— quite to the contrary, countless brethren had given their lives in the struggle to secure Navarre's throne.

One of their greatest hopes for the restoration of Huguenot power, the Marquis de Launay, fell before Amiens in battle with the Spaniards only a few months before the conclusion of peace. His army had fought side by side with that of the Huguenots' great Catholic friend, the young Duke d'Evreux, a Marshall of France, royal councilor and champion of reconciliation between the faiths. Together, the Marquis de Launay and the Duke d'Evreux had driven the Spaniards from French soil. But, so the story was told, just after Amiens was liberated, Launay was struck down while he was giving chase to the enemy to the Flemish border.

The Brethren could find consolation only in the fact that the Marquis did not die without an heir. After years of disappointment, a wave of excitement went through the Huguenot community, when the Marquise de Launay finally gave birth to a son and heir, now two years old, saving the line of the Launay's from extinction. Of course, everybody knew that the Marquis was not a very attentive husband—he was too preoccupied with the war and his mistress—only the most uncharitable minds would blame the Marquise for the delay in the arrival of an heir. Whatever the circumstances, what mattered was that the line of succession was assured, that a new generation had come into being, the first generation in half a century that was to know what it means to live in peace and freedom.

Many felt a sense of guilt for having distrusted their King, for having worried about how far their former leader might go to placate the Catholic Church. Some had never lost faith in Henri de Navarre and their trust was now vindicated.

Yet, even the most trusting souls among the Huguenots could not suppress suspicions about the King's intentions when, early in April 1598, he led a huge army southwest from Paris, ostensibly to appease the last remaining Guise hold out of the Duke de Mercoeur in the province of Brittany. But instead of giving battle, once he was there, Henri concluded a marriage agreement for his three-year-old bastard son César and the Duke's five-year-old daughter.

This business concluded, what, so the Huguenots asked, would prevent Henri from making a sudden sweep southward into Poitou and a lunge at La Rochelle? It was, therefore, against all expectations, when Henri stopped in the town of Nantes. From there he issued a solemn proclamation that from now on freedom of conscience and worship would be guaranteed in the

Kingdom of France. Perpetual and irrevocable were the words he used. The edict was celebrated as a gift from God himself.

What the Brethren did not know was that immediately after he issued the edict and before he went on to Vervin to meet the representatives of the Spanish crown to work out a settlement of the century-old conflict between the French and Spanish monarchy, Henri, still the eternal romantic at heart, charged his advisor, Philippe de Treffort-Salignac, the young Duke d'Evreux, with a delicate mission that was to serve as a living symbol of the spirit of reconciliation.

The sweet land of France shone forth brilliantly in all its splendor in the month of May in the year of Our Lord 1598. As if nature was aware of the significance of this particular spring, of the rebirth of the kingdom and its people, it unfolded in all its glory, nourishing the hopes for an era of lasting peace.

Philippe's thoughts lingered on past seasons and their significance in his life as he traversed the changing terrain of the French countryside on a course due south, from the plain stretching from the rugged shores of Brittany, where he took leave of his King, through Poitou and Limousin and a gently rolling sea of emerald hills, rising toward the interior to slope again in ancient terraced vineyards toward the valley of the Garonne River.

Graceful rows of poplars, oaks, and maple trees, stretched before him, as far as his eye could discern, in a seamless band of white and pink. Fanning out from the road, meadows, hemmed by the glowing yellow of forsythia hedges and dotted with buttercups and marguerites, spread out a luscious carpet, evoking the memory of another auspicious spring so many, many years before.

A decade had passed since he had fallen in love with a barefoot peasant girl and their all too brief time of happiness together.

Many a spring had come and gone. The melancholy that had held his heart in thrall had, for a long time, made him oblivious to the beauty of nature. Only dimly had he experienced the changing of the seasons, year after year, only aware that the passage of time seemed to make the fulfillment of his love ever more remote.

Now in the spring of 1598, he felt reborn, invigorated, fresh juices of life rushed through his body. A miracle had happened after he had resigned himself to live out his days without hope. He traveled the familiar road with his loyal companions, Gaspard and Mathieu, in a steady but unhurried pace, drinking in the fragrant spring air with deliberate savor. He knew he would find his peasant girl who had blossomed into a beautiful lady at the end of the road. No need to hurry now.

That she loved him, and only him, of that he was certain. But she was still in mourning for her fallen husband. He had to give her time, not press her too quickly for promises and assurances. Maybe more even than she, did he mourn the Marquis's death. They had fought many campaigns together. He had come to like and respect the jovial "Viking" who undertook everything with such uncomplicated zest. No, he did not rejoice in his passing. He wished that she could have been freed some other way.

The dark thoughts did not linger long, not in the spring of 1598. From time to time, he felt for the parchment tucked away inside his doublet, close to his heart—a message from the King of France to his cousin Countess Marguerite de Montauban.

"My dear cousin, Princess Marguerite de France, Marquise de Launay and Countess de Montauban," Marguerite read half loud as she unfurled the parchment. Philippe's eyes followed her as she moved toward the window for better light. She had matured, yet looked almost ethereal. Her cheeks were hollow as from lack of sleep and insufficient nourishment, her black widow's garb intensified the pale transparency of her skin. Years of torment and anguish had left their mark. Still, her frailty only enhanced her haunting beauty. More than ever he wanted to hold and protect her although he knew that under that gaunt exterior sparked an indomitable, independent spirit.

"We, Henri de Bourbon, King of France and Navarre," she continued, "have decreed that henceforth religious strife shall no longer divide the loyal subjects of our Kingdom. Although we recognize the Catholic and Apostolic faith as the dominant religious expression in the Kingdom of France, the Brethren of the Reformed Religion shall be permitted henceforth to live undisturbed following their beliefs and worship God Almighty and His Son Jesus Christ in the way they see fit and shall be guaranteed royal protection in pursuit thereof, so that the Kingdom of France may henceforth enjoy peace and prosperity.

In testimony to the spirit of toleration and reconciliation among my dear subjects, Catholic and Huguenot, and to set an example, it is our will that my loyal servant, Philippe, Count de Treffort-Salignac, Duke d'Evreux, Commander of the Royal Army and Maréchal de France, and my dear cousin, Princess Marguerite de France, Marquise de Launay and Countess de Montauban, be joined together in holy matrimony. The place and manner of the ceremony shall be decided upon by the contracting parties."

Marguerite's hand holding the parchment fell to her side when she finished reading. Slowly she turned toward Philippe, her face glowing red.

"Here, dear Maréchal," she said, tending the parchment with a haughty air. "Go tell your master that I am tired of having him dispose of my life as he pleases. Tell him that I refuse henceforth to be a pawn in his game of raison d'état. He may do this to his sister, my lamentable cousin, Princess Catherine, and any number of poor, hapless souls he holds in his power. I, for one, am not bound by the conventions and traditions of the nobility. I am free at last and I shall do as I please. Nobody, but nobody shall take this hard-earned freedom away from me, and were it the King of France himself!"

"May I remind Madame that she received this freedom through the grace and magnanimity of His Majesty. But if this is Madame's answer, she will have to tell the King herself." Philippe's tone was sharp and impersonal. "As for myself, I have no intention of returning to the royal court soon. With the war finally over, I shall have the leisure to follow the dictates of my heart and retire to my country estate in Normandy. There are so many books I want to read and subjects I want to study. I might even take up farming. Oh, how I look forward to a peaceful existence! I shall no longer serve as a messenger between Madame and her royal cousin."

"Madame, farewell, may you enjoy your freedom as I shall enjoy mine." He bowed deeply, waving his hat in front of him in the manner of a Spanish caballero, and turned toward the door.

"You could at least have had the decency to propose yourself, instead of hiding behind a royal decree," she shouted louder than was necessary since he had moved only a few steps away and his exit was anything but swift.

"But you never gave me a chance," he replied turning a stern look at her. "Are you sure you want to share your precious freedom with a lowly wretch like me, Sandrine?"

She flew toward him. Seizing his head with both hands and shaking it wildly with a reprimanding laugh.

"Of course I do! It's all I ever wanted, with all my heart and soul."

www.ingramcontent.com/pod-product-compliance
Lightning Source LLC
Chambersburg PA
CBHW021239200726
48288CB00014B/23